The Fires of July

**THEIRS WAS THE WEALTH OF TRADITION,
THE BURDEN OF LOYALTY TO KING AND CROWN,
AND THE CHALLENGE OF A RAW, NEW LAND . . .**

ELIZABETH MANNING—indomitable matriarch. The family secrets were her sacred trust, silence was her greatest weapon until, too late, she realized the terrible power of her deception.

ANDREW MANNING—her grandson. Bronzed, rugged, master of the land and of his own fate, he would defy his family's tradition to pursue a great dream—and the woman he loved beyond all law and reason.

LAUREL BOGGS—a gentle beauty. She dreamed of rising above poverty on the wings of a great love, only to discover that she was forever bound to her bitter heritage.

GWYNNE TEMPLETON—dazzling, impetuous. Raised with grace and breeding, she vowed to wait her whole life for her beloved—a man who had sworn his heart to another.

NATHANIEL DANCER—a rebel born of a restless spirit deep in the wilderness. He knew first his mother's love, but would later claim the passionate devotion of a father who might not be his own.

THEIR PASSIONS BLAZED IN . . .

The Fires of July

Also by Sharon Salvato

BITTER EDEN

The Fires of July

SHARON SALVATO

A DELL TRADE PAPERBACK

A DELL TRADE PAPERBACK
Published by
Dell Publishing Co., Inc.
1 Dag Hammarskjold Plaza
New York, New York 10017

Dell ® TM 681510, Dell Publishing Co., Inc.

Printed in the United States of America

First printing—April 1983

Library of Congress Cataloging in Publication Data

Salvato, Sharon Anne.
The fires of July.

I. Title.
PS3569.A46233F57   1983   813'.54   82-19947
ISBN 0-440-52680-9

# Prologue

The Manning plantation was nestled deep and hidden among the hills of South Carolina. Gracefully it stretched out along the Wateree River, beautiful and inviting to all who passed and to all who were welcomed into its hospitality as they wearily journeyed from Charles Town to Camden.

Manning was a vast expanse of untamed red hills densely covered with long-leaf pine. The house had been built a half-mile back from the river road, which was no more than a narrow cart path. To the unobservant only the unruly vitality of the wilderness showed, but to Joseph Manning the existence of any manmade path was a declaration of the planters' presence, an accomplishment he cherished with great pride.

Joseph could remember his first sight of this land, then untutored to the ways of the white planter. It had been a tangle of wild forest growth. Awesome pines stretched skyward, making the man painfully aware of his smallness and the magnitude of the challenge he accepted in daring to call this his home. Yellow blossoms and wild peach and plum peeked out from the green tangle, enticing the man into a paradise that could be as deadly as it was welcoming, hiding as it did the beleaguered red man who stood to lose it as his home, the alligator and the panther and the bear and deer, who would never survive the onslaught of his civilized world. The land had swelled, bewitching before Joseph's eyes, its rolling hills small sisters of the mountains that lay farther inland, and then dipping downward, letting the curving, corkscrewing Wateree seep from its banks and cover the rich green lushness of the soil with the dark watery seductiveness of the swamp.

Sharon Salvato

Both fear and awe had struck in Joseph's heart on that first visit to his Upcountry land. It was his legacy, his birthright, given to him as the youngest son of Walter Manning. His older brother John had been given the developed and profitable Lowland rice plantation just outside Charles Town and civilization. And he, Joseph, by quirk of birth order, had been given what was left: four thousand acres of wild, primitive land in the red hills of the Carolina Upcountry.

Joseph had returned to Charles Town, collected his two young sons, his wife and thirty slaves that had also been part of his inheritance, and had come back to place his mark as master on this land. As if in announcement of his determination, he had built the curving road leading to his house wider than the river-road cart path. Carefully and in so even a line that none could ever doubt that they had been planted by the hand and design of man, Joseph lined his carriage road with crepe myrtle. Late at night in those early days, the carriage road gave him solace that someone would one day know a man had worked here even if Joseph and his family didn't survive the rigors of their new home. He continued the practice. What Joseph built at Manning he built for the generations that were yet to come, never feeling secure that he would himself be alive to tell of the early days.

Joseph and his two sons worked alongside of and just as hard as the slaves. There had been only a log house then, not much more than a lean-to, and his sons had barely been old enough to handle the axes, saws and other tools needed to clear the wild, tangled forest. They had become tough battling the land and defending themselves against the displaced Indians. They had become patient and determined as they struggled to force from the earth crops with which to feed themselves over the winter months. And they had learned cunning and courage stalking game in the forest. It had taken him years, and his sons had grown to young men as his land cleared, but it had been cleared, and Manning had risen from the naked earth a brick at a time until today it stood a proud and regal Georgian mansion overlooking the river from its prominence atop the gently rounded hill.

By 1767, there was no longer doubt that Joseph Manning had succeeded in conquering the land, but what the land had done to Joseph and his family was still very much a question.

Part One

Andrew

1

The indigo field grayed out in the shimmering brilliance of noonday. Andrew Manning, his coarse blue cotton shirt sweat-stained, straightened from his work. His eyes wandered over the expanse of indigo plants, then came to rest on the comforting green darkness of the woods at the rear of the field, only to return again to the sky. He couldn't keep his eyes from the sky that was so blue it pressed down upon him, seeming to enter and stir him like a wind of restlessness he couldn't contain. Remembering, and then piqued by, his father's words, he tore his gaze away from the vivid blueness and picked up his hoe once again. He took a few desultory strokes at the dry, packed red clay earth, then once more placed the hoe upright, leaning his weight against it, his mind restless again, his eyes seeking the depths of the fathomless blue.

Perhaps he was as his father said, a young man enthralled by the impatient demands of youthful impetuosity. He discarded the idea as he had the previous night when his father had said it. He didn't like the notion of being like all young men. He enjoyed what he thought to be his own individuality and felt mild resentment that his father of all people should assume that he was no different, no more thoughtful or original, than dozens of other young men of his station and acquaintance. Anger and loss moved within him as he questioned briefly when and how he and his father had separated in their thinking.

Andrew looked up again in puzzlement, unable to see so great a difference between his father's time and his own. It was true that he had no memories of England as his father had, and he had never

seen a king or been to court, but there were so many other, more
vital events that they shared, Andrew couldn't see why his father's
insistence on being an English subject was so important. England
was far away, but the harassment by the outlaw bands that plagued
South Carolina was close at hand. And the formation of the Regulators to fight those outlaws for the Upcountryman was right at
hand. He didn't understand his father's continued faith in and
insistent dependence on the Assembly in Charles Town and the
royal governor to solve the outlaw problem. Charles Town and
the royal governor had already demonstrated their indifference
to the Upcountry. His father's continued loyalty to the royal government seemed misplaced to Andrew. It seemed to him that the
outlaw raids were very similar to the Indian raids of his father's
time, and he couldn't understand why his father had unquestion-
ingly defended the Upcountry against the Indians and now said that
the outlaws were a problem for the Charles Town Assembly and the
courts. He was sure he could make a good argument for himself
against his father's criticism, if only he weren't so vulnerable on the
point of his restlessness.

It was true. To himself, Andrew admitted that within him something was forming, burning away with a pleasant heat that drove
him to action. But he felt vulnerable to his father's criticisms,
because he was as yet unable to define what this newly forming
sense of justice and injustice was. It seemed to have so many
sources—so many things were wrong just waiting to be righted—
and Andrew wanted to be at the center of the change he was sure
would come.

He smiled at the audacity of his thoughts. He wanted to be an
influential part of his own history. He reached down impulsively
and grabbed a handful of the red earth. He felt a tremendous sense
of possession. It was his earth. He wanted a say in what mark the
future would make on it.

He glanced up at the sun to see the time, then, realizing he had
over an hour before he needed to head back to the house, he picked
up the hoe again and began to work, as if by muscle and sweat he
could make the time pass more quickly. The hoe cut into the clay
soil, and Andrew's mind churned with a thousand questions.

***

Joseph Manning sat at his desk in his study, staring out at the softening afternoon colors. His gaze moved from the window to the room. He took in the richly appointed bookshelves; the paintings from England that graced his walls; the sculptures, three of them, each on its own pedestal. Joseph was proud of those statues; they bespoke wealth and culture and reminded him of a past that he discovered he missed more the older he got. Their presence reminded him of his grandfather's home in Sussex and gave him the sense of still leading a way of life he knew was over. With all his possessions intact and accounted for mentally, he was feeling satisfied for the moment. His thoughts turned to his plans for his sons and their future. He glanced over at Arthur, his oldest son, who was sharing his study this afternoon, and he felt a sudden, warm flow of reassurance. Arthur was a proper colonial Englishman. He was at home in any company and could discuss politics and English policy with the best of them, Joseph thought happily. Then just as suddenly he began to scowl as he thought of Andrew. "Where is Drew?" he asked more harshly than he had intended.

Arthur looked up from his writing. "Where he always is."

Joseph slammed his ledger shut. "Milo! Milo!" As the black butler walked soft-footed across the room, Joseph barked out, "Send Polly after Mr. Andrew. You tell her I said he was to come to the house immediately." He turned to Arthur. "If he's late for your mother's do this evening, I swear by all that's holy, I'll disown him."

Arthur stared at his father in amusement for a moment. He had forgotten the inner workings of his family while he was in England being educated as a proper oldest son should be. Now that he was home once again, the life seemed cruder and rougher than he had remembered. Arthur decided without judging his father that he preferred the easier life and the relative quiet of England to his home. He sighed and smiled indulgently. "How many times have you disowned Drew since I've been home, Papa? Ten, twelve times?"

"I'll do it this time, by all that's holy, I will! It's bad enough he's leaving tomorrow for Charles Town and will be gone for who knows how long when we have guests in the house, but I will not tolerate him unsettling your mother as well."

Arthur laughed lightly. "Mother never gets as upset with Drew as you do, Papa. I'm sure she will take his trip to Charles Town without dismay. Someone has to take the cattle and produce into Charles Town."

"An overseer could do it—ours, Robinson's or any number of others."

"An overseer could see to our indigo, too," Arthur said firmly. "But we wouldn't have the crop we do now."

Joseph fixed his frowning gaze on Arthur. "Many other men turn out fine indigo crops."

"But none is superior to Drew's. We owe the fine reputation of Manning indigo to my little brother. Lord, Papa, half the time the agents don't even look at it—if Drew raised it, the indigo is marked superior grade sight unseen."

Finally Joseph's face relaxed. "He's a damned headstrong boy. I'll have to curb him one way or another. He's too caught up in the doings of these backcountrymen."

Arthur's laughter rippled through the room. "With all due respect, Papa, I'd advise you to give it up. Drew is more than half backwoodsman, and nothing on this earth is going to change him, I'll wager." With a pretense of returning his attention to the paper he'd been writing, Arthur added, "Not even Joanna."

Joseph immediately began to frown and moved uncomfortably in his chair as if it had suddenly become too small for him. "I suppose when he goes to Charles Town he'll visit her looking like a wild renegade from the hills. By damn!" Joseph burst out, getting up from his chair. "I don't know what I am to do with that boy! Will Templeton writes me near every month fretting about the marriage arrangement, and well he might. Drew won't commit himself to a date for that wedding. Every time the subject comes up he has some excuse as to why it can't be now."

"He doesn't want to marry her," Arthur said.

"He does want to! I gave my solemn word to Will Templeton that Joanna and Drew would marry."

"Drew has made it very clear that he does not care for Joanna."

"What has caring for her to do with it?" Joseph asked, bewildered. "Joanna is the perfect wife for him. He'll never want for anything with her behind him. Riverlea will be a showplace, and Drew's future in politics is nearly assured with a woman like Joanna. I gave my word! He's honor bound!"

Arthur put his hands up. "I agree with you. I'm not the son to convince; it is Drew. He doesn't want to be Joanna's husband."

"He'll marry her!" Joseph said through clenched teeth.

Arthur sat back, his face as set as his father's, his hands folded across his stomach. "Drew is an indigo man, Papa. Your word can't change that."

"He knows as much about rice planting as Will Templeton ever knew!"

"But he's an indigo man, and he loves the Upcountry," Arthur insisted.

Joseph looked at him. It was difficult to argue with the truth. But there were two truths. "Drew doesn't have an indigo plantation. Manning goes to you, and he won't be living in the Upcountry. His life waits for him in Riverlea and the Lowlands. It was settled long ago."

2

On the morning of October 7, 1767, Andrew Manning and several other planters from the Upcountry region near the Wateree River brought a wagon train of corn, tobacco, deerskins, indigo and cattle into Charles Town for shipment to England or sale to the colonial markets. They were tough, disreputable-looking men by Lowland standards, dirty and dust-smeared from two and a half weeks on a long, tortuous journey. They traveled by Indian trail because no roads had been built in the Upcountry. They cleared land every time they stopped for the night and posted sentries to guard themselves and their goods. The territory above the fall line was sparsely populated, and the wagon trains traveled expecting attack from outlaws, renegades, fugitives from other colonies and Indians. There was no protection for them except what they could provide for themselves. They had little time or energy left for such niceties as the baths, white ruffled shirts and perfumed wigs affected by the Lowland city dwellers.

Upcountry wagon trains, a common sight in Charles Town, still managed to warrant glances from women, who unconsciously straightened their postures, smoothed their skirts or conversely clasped the hands of small children, pulling them into the protective folds of their gowns, and hurried impressionable young girls into the safety of shop doors out of the sight of the Upcountry wildmen. Not unaware of the confused reactions an Upcountryman aroused, Andrew Manning sat taller in his saddle, already feeling some of the bone-bending weariness of the trip dissipate. His chestnut-brown hair glinted with red highlights in the strong morning sun. His

hunting shirt, fringed and drawn in at the waist with a broad, decorated belt, glowed a rich animal gold. A tomahawk, shot bag and
powder horn secured to the belt drew additional uneasy stares from
bystanders, reminders of the savagery of Upcountry life and perhaps of this man, too. His face was tanned a deep bronze, making
his teeth look startlingly white as he grinned impudently, returning
the side-eyed glances, deliberately fostering greater misgivings in
the hearts of the timid and greater fantasies in those of the bold.

Near the merchants' warehouses, the wagon train began to
break up, groups of planters separating themselves and their goods
from the main body of the train to take their produce to the houses
of their chosen agents. Andrew shouted orders for his men to
unload the Manning plantation indigo, cattle and produce at Benjamin Smith's establishment. Ned Hart, the Mannings' hired man,
took charge of penning the cattle. Drew watched Ned for a moment
and smiled. Ned Hart had been the first man his father had hired
when he had come to the Upcountry. Ned had been with Drew all
the years he had been growing up, almost a second father, and
always a friend. When Ned's gray head disappeared, Andrew rode
to the front of Smith's office, dismounted and stood stretching by
the horses for a moment, his mind far more willing to consider a
cold drink in Dillon's Tavern with some of the men than to tackle
the business at hand. Resignedly he glanced down at his bespat-
tered clothing and began slapping his hat against his hunting shirt
and breeches. Billowing clouds of red dust ballooned up around him
and settled down onto his clothing once more. Shrugging, he
decided there was little he could do to improve his appearance, and
he probably smelled a whole lot worse than he looked. Smiling, he
entered Banjamin Smith's office.

"Drew!" Smith said heartily, bounding out from behind his desk
before Andrew had closed the door. "Good to see you! We've been
expecting your train to arrive for days. You didn't have any serious
trouble, I hope."

"We're here alive and whole."

"Thank God," Smith said, a broad smile on his face. "Of course,
we always fear hearing of a raid, and—"

"No raids," Drew said quickly. "We lost a wagon down a ravine. It
was one of Jed Blake's. With Minnie sitting back home already

counting every copper he stood to make, we couldn't move on until he'd found space on the other wagons to load every kernel of corn he could salvage. We were losing so much time, Basil Robinson's man finally said he'd pay Jed the difference so we could move on."

Benjamin laughed. "That Minnie is quite a woman. Jed tells me she's got her eye on a big piece of land."

"It's Nathan Parker's land she wants. He's been looking at land up near mine—thinks he'd like to try a hand at tobacco planting, too. I'd like to have him there."

Smith cocked his head to one side, smiling at the young man across the desk from him. "What does Joseph think about your land?"

Andrew laughed silently. "Nothing very favorable. He's had a lot to say about my headstrong, impetuous, foolhardy, youthful follies."

"More likely his main objection is its nearness to Cherokee lands."

Andrew shrugged. "He's mentioned that."

"You might want to listen to him. The Cherokee War was only six years back . . . a lot of people remember it like it was yesterday, and for good reason. A lot of good people were killed and maimed, and more than that were ruined by it."

Andrew felt the involuntary reaction of his stomach as he remembered seeing the remains of a massacred family and the horror of a living scalped man. He remembered the daughter of a neighboring planter . . . but memories like that were many, one more horrible than the other. They were the stuff of nightmares and belonged to the past. He started to say as much to Benjamin Smith, then remembered Ned telling him that a goodly number of the outlaws had been victims of the Cherokee War and now used the same torturing tactics as had been used on them. Quietly and without looking at Smith, Andrew said, "That can't be allowed to keep us from going on."

Benjamin Smith sighed and looked warmly at the young face opposite him, wondering if what he read there was the wisdom of truth or the folly of it. "Perhaps you're right, Drew. Your father and I are old men, and we see differently than you do. But we're not fools, and our years have taught us lessons you can learn only with time."

"I know, sir, and I try to learn from my father, but I feel my father has changed in recent years. The Wateree was once as uncivilized as the territory where my plantation is now. He built Manning there when there had been nothing before but forest and Indians. And now he says it is unwise for me to do the same."

"His future was in the Upcountry. Yours is down here with us, isn't it? It doesn't seem likely that Joanna is going to take easily to a life in the wilderness. Nor do I see how you plan to run Riverlea down here and a tobacco plantation near a hundred miles inland."

Drew looked at him uncomfortably. If it were anyone else, he would have walked away from the conversation, but Benjamin Smith had known his father since they had both been boys. He'd have to be careful what he said, for most likely it would get back to his father, perhaps even in the return mail the men would take with them to the Upcountry.

"Are your plans changing, Drew?" Smith persisted. "There's talk that the Templeton-Manning match won't take place." He paused for a moment, then, seeing nothing discernible on Andrew's face, added, "Tyrus Kincaid's been asking about the wedding. He'd be more than happy to hear you had decided to turn tail."

Andrew's eyes glittered at the mention of Tyrus Kincaid's name; then he quickly realized what Benjamin Smith was doing. He smiled and said, "I didn't know there was a race for Joanna's hand, sir."

"There's always a race for a woman like Joanna—especially when a plantation the likes of Riverlea is attached to a lovely hand."

"Well, you can tell Tyrus there has been no change in my plans or in my father's," Drew said. Then he smiled, adding flippantly, "The plantation is just insurance for the future. If your Lowland Liberty Boys succeed in taking ol' mother England to task for picking on the northern colonies, my tobacco farm in the hills may be the safest place to be."

Benjamin scowled, pulled papers from his desk and wrote the preliminary order figures. "Let's get to business. I don't want my day ruined with talk of Christopher Gadsen and his radical nit-wits. Him and Sam Adams ought to be locked up together. One day some of these rabble-rousers are going to awaken to the fact that we are Englishmen and as such part of an empire, but not the focal point of it. Now, you do understand, Drew, that I'll have to have your indigo graded, but I'm writing it up as top grade. I'm correct in that, aren't I?"

Andrew nodded and watched Benjamin Smith's hand move across the business forms in an orderly scrawl. Bemused, he thought that he had never considered himself an Englishman. His great-grandfather was an Englishman. His great-grandfather had lived in England, but he, Andrew, was a Carolinian. He wondered what Benjamin and his father would think if he told them his thoughts on that. They would probably label him a radical nitwit along with Christopher Gadsen.

Business completed and no more to be accomplished until the Manning indigo was officially graded, Andrew stepped out of the office into the sandy, sun-drenched street. He leaned against the building, letting the hot wood press warmth through him, easing the taut, tired muscles of his back. Slowly he released the concerns of the trip and business and turned his mind toward the contemplation of the leisurely pleasures Charles Town offered.

He glanced up as Ned Hart shouted his name. Andrew squinted into the blaze of light bouncing off the white sand and buildings. Ned ran awkwardly toward him, his Indian boots sending up sprays of sand. Panting, his sweating face stained with rivulets of red trail dust, the older man grabbed Andrew's shoulder, supporting himself as he struggled to catch his breath. "You heard the news?" he gasped.

Andrew pushed away from the building and began walking slowly down the street. Ned followed him to the center of the road. "Better catch your breath, Ned. What's the news? It must be something to get you all riled up. I didn't know you still had it in you."

Ned ignored him, his face twisted in disappointment and anger. "The bloody bastard's tryin' to stop us. He don't seem to have a grain o' common sense in 'im. He's askin' for a war, is what he's doin'."

"Who's trying to stop us? From doing what? Did you have trouble at the pens with the cattle?"

"Montagu!" Ned shouted at him. "Damn his eyes . . . our royal governor issued one of his fuckin' proclamations to stop the Regulators. First the damned fool convicts six outlaws and turns around and pardons five and sets 'em loose again; now he's declarin' the business of the Regulators illegal."

Drew looked at him in bafflement. "He wouldn't do that. What are you talking about, Ned?"

"I'm talkin' about goin' to jail! You deef?" Ned shouted.

"What about Govey Black? And Winslow Driggers? What about the gangs . . . are they included in the proclamation, too?"

"Not a word. Not a damned word. The outlaws do as they bloody well please while we go to jail for stoppin' the bloody murderers."

Andrew stared at him disbelievingly. "Someone's been telling you wrong, Ned. That can't be right. Not even the Assembly is this damned blind to what goes on in the Upcountry. They know the outlaw raids have to be stopped somehow—by someone. They may not want to part with their money for roads and troops and such, but they don't want to ruin the Upcountry. They need us . . . our people won't stand for this . . . they'll have a war before accepting this."

"That's what I said! Half the men who come in with us have already headed for home. They ain't wastin' no time gettin' back to spread the news. Even Jed Blake left, said Minnie could wait."

"It'll mean a war," Andrew said in a barely audible voice.

"You're damned right, and I aim to be in the front of it. I'm a peaceful man, you know that, Drew, but this is one fight that's been a long time in comin'. I got a real hankerin' to tease the britches of a few of these overstuffed Lowlanders with some buckshot." He slapped the shot bag hanging from his belt.

Andrew walked a few steps and stopped. "I don't believe it. Some fool is spreading rumors to cause trouble—or you heard wrong." He began to walk away swiftly, not wanting to hear more.

"Find out for yourself. Ask your Lowland cousins!" Ned shouted after him. "Ask the bloodsuckin' Assembly. Ask 'em!"

Asking the Lowland Mannings the truth of the matter was exactly what Andrew had in mind. However, long before he reached his grandmother's house on Legare Street, he had heard news of Governor Montagu's proclamation from four other people. He went to the stables behind the Mannings' Charles Town house, turned his horse over to the groom, then stood angry and indecisive, staring up at the neat two-story brick double house. Music drifted across the courtyard from the open windows. It was probably his cousin Bethany playing for his grandmother and Aunt Eugenia and Lord knew how many other tea-sipping ladies. He thought briefly of storming in the front door and confronting his cousins Leo, Robert and George. He smiled, taking perverse pleasure in imagining the shocked fuss and flutter of skirts he'd cause among his aunt and grandmother's guests.

He began to walk down the drive to the street. He didn't give a damn about his aunt Eugenia, but he did care about his outspoken grandmother. The irony of it was that his grandmother would most likely side with him on the political issue while blistering him with her tongue for the breach of etiquette. Yet it was that supercilious, artificial sense of propriety that hindered the progress of the Upcountrymen in gaining recognition in the Assembly. The Lowlanders were so immersed in their own concerns, he thought, freely admitting that he unjustly lumped these concerns in his mind as soirées, balls and society that tried successfully to emulate London, that they could no longer see that part of South Carolina that he loved. Lowlanders didn't seem able to see the incongruity of Charles Town becoming a little London while the Upcountrymen lived in a raw, primitive state. He stopped again several yards from the house. He knew he should go inside, greet his relatives, bathe and change from the clothing that identified him, to all who cared to look, as an Upcountryman. And if what Ned had told him was true in total and the mood of Governor Montagu as adamant as everyone thought, he could be arrested, for most people knew he was a Regulator. Torn, Andrew debated with himself whether to fight the hypocrisy of the proclamation by the Lowlanders' methods of prescribed dignity and pomp and law or by boldly stating by his actions and dress who and what he was.

His father would call him a fool for even contemplating flaunting himself as an Upcountryman at this particular time, and his brother Arthur would laugh at his childish display. Angered anew, Andrew began to walk away from the house, his stride longer, his pace faster. He no longer looked back at the house or thought of his father's likely ire or his brother's sophisticated amusement. He headed toward Mazyk's land.

Long before he came within sight of the pasture, Andrew could see in his mind's eye the big live oak that stood there. The Liberty Tree, so named by Sam Adams's Southern apostle Christopher Gadsen, Charles Town's famed and loquacious radical. There, under the moss-hung branches of the Liberty Tree, Gadsen gathered his band of followers, the Liberty Boys, mostly artisans and tradesmen, and preached his doctrines of freedom and the rights of man. Guided by the principles of John Locke and Samuel Adams, Gadsen inexorably moved his followers along the path that would lead Americans to the belief that as long as any man, king or parliament could dictate colonial policy without the people's consent, they were not free, nor were they possessed of their God-given rights.

Andrew walked into the pasture. A burst of applause punctuated with loud, shrill huzzahs and shouts filled the air. An irregularly shaped man, a figure of bulbous protuberances and bandy legs, raised his hands over his head, quieting the crowd. In a hoarse, over-used voice he rasped his final broadside, "In '65 we showed 'em! We said we wouldn't tolerate the Stamp Act, and we didn't! They repealed it. Why? Because we stood firm. We ran their Stamp agents off! We shouted for all the world to hear that Liberty was dead! And England listened. Mother England listened! She'll listen again! We must not weaken in our fight for representation, and we shall not!"

The men shouted their approval, then moved aside as another of their number took his position beneath the tree and began to speak. "Two years ago this month many of us gathered at the pealing of St. Michael's bell to hear the reading of the Stamp Act. We flew our flags at half mast. We mourned the injustice done, the mortal blow to liberty. We made our own stamps of crossbones and skull and used those. We declared on another of our own stamps, 'Unite or die!' Those words are as true today as they were two years ago. The Stamp Act is gone—we won our victory over that—but we have not won the respect of the Parliament. We have not been given the proper rights or respect of Englishmen. Parliament still treats us as if we were pawns to be moved at will. The Stamp Act was re-placed with the Declaratory Act. As if we were naughty children, Parliament took for itself the authority to declare our Assembly res-olutions, votes, orders and proceedings null and void. Every year we have been pressed with new duties, taxes and obligations from Par-liament. We now have the Townshend Acts, and we shall protest and fight them as we have all other unjust English demands. But other acts and taxes and duties will come to replace this one, and still the respect we require will not be forthcoming. We must never give up or take our eye from the problems this lack of respect by the English Parliament brings upon us.

"Until we are seen as the Englishmen we are, with all the rights of Englishmen, we shall have to suffer the corruption of men like Vice Admiralty Judge Leigh. When His Majesty's magistrates engage in double-dealing and dishonest practices, we cannot hope to find justice. When the ships of our merchants can be seized without just cause, where do we turn? To whom do we plead our case when we are denied the strength of making our own law? Where are our constitution-guaranteed rights of free Englishmen? Who is to protect us? Those in Parliament who close off our lands to our own settlers in order to give them as political boons to British absentee landlords? Shall we always be prey to British speculators? When do we come to the realization that this land is ours? *Ours!* When do we ask the real question? Are we Englishmen? I say no! No! We are Americans! We know and love this land as no man sitting across an ocean can ever know it. Ours are the voices that must be heard. American voices. And if there is no one to hear us, then we must shout and raise such a din to the heavens that there shall be no one left who shall not hear us! We are Americans and this land is ours!"

The crowd roared their approval, and the man stepped down into a throng of hands reaching out to shake his or just to touch him. The din was so loud it made Andrew's ears ring. He waited for as long as he could stand it, then shouted over the continuing clamor, "May I speak?"

"Anyone may be heard here," a man said, shoving aside a wall of men to allow Andrew to pass.

"Let the backwoodsman through," Tyrus Kincaid shouted, and to make certain Andrew knew whose voice his was, he slapped him on the back.

Andrew felt an instant, hot shard of anger slice through his chest and annoyingly reach his face, making him blush as though he were a schoolboy thrilled by the attention he got. He wheeled away from Ty's groping hand and walked with greater force to the tree.

"Are you with us, man?" a voice called out.

Adjusting his position, Andrew stood near but not directly under the Liberty Tree. He felt strange and perhaps a little disloyal. He didn't know if he was with these men. He wasn't sure that these weren't the very people he looked upon as his enemy. For a moment he stood still, his mouth set, his eyes scanning the perspiring, excited faces of the men gathered there. Then he said quietly and firmly, "I am with you in principle. I love this land as do my fellow Upcountrymen. We believe in liberty and in justice. We hunger for it. What Upcountryman has not raised the cry that all South Carolinians are free men with the rights guaranteed to them by the constitution of England, and by the inalienable rights that all men have as God's children? What Upcountryman has not raised his voice in an effort to be heard? But who has been there to hear? The English Parliament? The Charles Town Assembly?

"You cry in protest that an English magistrate has stolen the ships of Henry Laurens. I cry in protest to you that my neighbor's lands, his property, his womenfolk have been stolen from him by rampaging outlaws. You cry out that the English Parliament usurps your right to representation. I raise my voice to tell you the whole Upcountry has but one representative in the Assembly. In principle I raise my voice to blend with yours. It is wrong, and we should fight with all our beings against injustice and arbitrary power!"

The crowd's response was confused and sporadic. Clapping could be heard here and there. A shout of support was heard, then as a whole the crowd shouted its approval.

As the sound began to die down, a voice Andrew recognized could be heard. "Come to the point, Manning!" Tyrus Kincaid yelled.

Some booed him, and others applauded. Andrew waited for the noise to subside, his eyes sparkling with suppressed anger.

"Now I raise my voice against yours . . ."

"Go home, woodsman! We don't want your kind around here!" Tyrus hooted.

Andrew glared at Tyrus, then continued. ". . . and I cry to be heard above your self-congratulatory din, for you Lowlanders are as arbitrary with your power as England is with hers."

The noise of the crowd swelled with disapproval.

"You deny your own Upcountrymen the basic needs for survival. We have no roads. We have no courts. We haven't schools for our children. We haven't protection from the outlaws and the Indians and the runaways that prey on us. You use us as a buffer to protect yourselves, but you offer nothing to us. When we attempt to protect ourselves, your Assembly calls us outlaws! Yes, I say your Assembly, because it certainly isn't ours. We are Carolinians, but we have no representation. We are Carolinians, but we enjoy no privilege.

"You look down your noses at our backwoods garb and our untutored speech and manners, yet it is because of Lowland indifference that we have no Bibles, no preachers to instruct us, no schools or churches in which we can learn. You give the Upcountryman nothing and ask all of us—our money for taxes, our blood in the protection of the colony, our sweat in the fields to feed your thriving markets.

"You care about the colonies up north. Do you care about your own fellow South Carolinians? Do you give—" Andrew sidestepped and ducked the very ripe persimmon that whizzed past his ear. "Do you . . ." he began again, and was drowned out by twenty or thirty loud, very angry voices.

Breaking up into smaller groups, members of the gathered crowd began to argue among themselves. Their voices were loud and truculent, not given to listening or speaking reason. Andrew glanced to the side just in time to see Tyrus Kincaid hurtling toward him. Drew held his ground until the last possible moment, then sidestepped, delivering a glancing blow to the side of Kincaid's bull neck.

Andrew, now enjoying the melee he had caused, began to speak again in a loud, raucous voice punctuated with laughter.

At the back of the milling mob, Andrew's three Lowland cousins fought their way toward the beleaguered, laughing orator. They elbowed their way through clutches of angry, fighting men, dodging fists, insults and missiles hurled by the more irate of the Liberty Boys.

"Drew! Shut your mouth before Kincaid and his friends fill it with knuckles!" Leo, the tallest of the Manning cousins and closest to Andrew, shouted as he raised a well-aimed elbow into a threshing man's windpipe. Long and as thin as string, Leo battled his way to his cousin's side. He took a playful poke at Andrew's midsection and received a hard punch on the jaw. "Son of a bitch, Drew, you don't know how to quit when you're ahead," Leo roared and came at Drew head down.

"You're damned right I don't know when to quit." Andrew met Leo's charge, both of them grappling for a death-dealing hold on the other.

Robert, Leo's oldest brother, grabbed Leo, trying to pull the two combatants apart. Andrew took advantage of the moment, pummeling Leo's ribs.

George, the third brother, entered the fracas, leaping onto Andrew's back and pounding him about the neck and shoulders. "Who in the hell do you think you are, Drew Manning? What gives you the right to tell us what we should do?"

Andrew spun around, swinging George into his brother. Blood spurted from Rob's nose as George's head cracked against his. Leo dived at Andrew's knees, bringing him down. The two men wrestled, kicking and punching each other. Leo, momentarily on top, yelled for his brothers, who quickly came to his aid. Rob held Andrew's arms, while George sat placidly and weightily across his legs. Leo straddled Andrew, grinning triumphantly into his cousin's angry face.

"Get your bony butt off me, Leo!"

"Not on your life, you mean-tempered bastard. As soon as we saw that nag of yours in the stable, we knew you were around causing trouble somewhere."

"Shut up. I do what needs to be done."

"Listen to him," hooted George. "He does what needs to be done. Noble words, oh noble one!"

Leo began to laugh. "My God, if you don't look a mess for a noble one. You gonna come quietly with us, Drew? Or are you going to make us drag you to Dillon's?"

"I'm not going anywhere with you quietly or otherwise!" Andrew said, struggling against the combined weight of the three men, then falling back panting. "One of you—just one of you let go of me, and I'll take the others of you. Damn it! Get off me!"

"No," Leo said placidly. "I like being the fellow on top for a change."

"You may be enjoying this little spectacle, Leo, but I'm not. My nose hurts like hell, and the whole incident of the Mannings fighting like common trash under the Liberty Tree is probably being whispered into Grandma's ear right now. I don't know about you, but I'm more afraid of her than I am of our battling cousin. I say we go home and mend fences as quickly as we can," Rob said, blood still dripping from his nose.

George leaned from around Leo and handed a handkerchief to

his brother, who snarled, "What am I supposed to do for an extra hand?" Then he looked at Drew. "Come on, Drew, stay still long enough for me to stop this nose bleed." Tentatively he released one of Andrew's hands and received an awkward, glancing blow to his already-swollen nose.

Caught off guard, Leo toppled off Andrew's heaving body, and all four of them were raining blows on each other, not completely sure whom they were hitting. Around them the rest of the gathered men were engaging in their own verbal and physical battles and occasionally getting entangled in the Mannings' private fight. Bodies tumbled and were shoved aside, pummeled and kicked. Exhausted, the four Mannings staggered at one another again and again until they were all lying on the ground, their chests heaving, their arms at their sides like pillars of lead. "I don't give a damn who's a narrow-minded hypocrite," Leo moaned. "I'm too tired to care. You want to call me that, Drew? You really want to call me that?"

"Yes, you son of a bitch!" Drew said in no more than a whisper.

"Then you may," Leo sighed agreeably. "I'm a narrow-minded hypocrite. And I'm thirsty. Let's go to Dillon's Tavern."

"I can't," George wailed. "That goddamned Drew broke all my ribs."

Rob and Leo got up, pulling George to his feet. The three of them, once more united, looked down at their cousin, sprawled on the ground. "You coming with us, Drew?"

He nodded his head and lifted his arm for Leo to pull him to his feet. Leo looked at him suspiciously, then put his hand out. Andrew steadily pulled himself to his feet, his brown eyes sparkling and holding Leo's gaze. "What's the matter, Leo, don't you trust me?"

"Not a bit," he said, a smile beginning.

Andrew took a couple of steps ahead of Leo, then waited for him to catch up. Hesitating just a fraction of a second, Andrew stuck his foot out. "You were right. I can't be trusted," he said, grinning down at Leo, spread-eagled facedown on the grass. Relenting, he went back and pulled Leo to his knees by his belt. "You buying? You're the tallest of the rich Lowland Mannings, so it stands to reason your pockets are the longest."

3

Elizabeth Manning's warm brown eyes sparkled as she turned from her reflection in the pier glass. Her seventy-odd years rested gracefully on her deceptively delicate-looking frame. She had had a pleasant and all-too-proper afternoon tea with her daughter-in-law Eugenia's friends. Bethany, her only granddaughter, had played the piano beautifully, and Elizabeth had been proud and happy with her family, but now she was preparing for the evening, which promised to be more entertaining if somewhat less proper. Practicing, she snapped her small ivory fan open, moving it subtly before her face, her eyes coquettish.

Pelagie, Elizabeth's personal maid and the only woman from whom Elizabeth kept no secrets, laughed, her large, dark face quivering with pleasure. "Lawd, Miz Lizzybeff, nobody got to tell me Mistah Drew in town. A body jes' got to look at you behavin' like a young girl an' they knows."

"Don't you start in on me, Pelagie. Eugenia reminds me quite enough that old ladies are supposed to wither up and sit quietly in a corner like dried flowers on a table. Of course, we are still permitted to look wise, but it is better if we keep that wisdom to ourselves and maintain silence."

Pelagie made a sour face, her jowls shaking harder than the rest of her head. "What ol' ladies we know gwine do dat?"

Elizabeth smirked wickedly, then said in a low voice, "My dear daughter-in-law Eugenia. She should make an admirably wise vase of dried flowers." She turned back to her mirror and poked critically at her no-longer-trim waistline. "Walter always said there was no reason a man shouldn't remain a man until he was dead, and I say that it follows that there is no reason a woman should not be a woman until she is dead. Life is too full of pleasure for any of us to retire from it before we are forced to. I see no reason I should not enjoy Drew. Drew enjoys me, and he is the only one of my grandsons who bears the slightest resemblance to Walter."

Pelagie sighed. "Mistah Waltah . . . Ah still misses him. Ain't nobody jes' like him. Seems like nuthin' much happen 'roun' heah since ol' Mastah pass ovah."

Elizabeth's fan snapped shut. "He did make things exciting, didn't he. Walter always liked to be in the thick of everything. I used to tease him that God couldn't run the world properly if Walter wasn't there to help." She walked to the window. "I think, Pelagie, that were he alive today he'd be right there with Christopher Gadsen and the Liberty Boys. Most likely he'd be telling Gadsen how to organize."

"Ah doan knows. They's sayin' mighty harsh things about the king. Ol' Mastah think pretty highly o' de king."

"Bosh! Walter would have loved the idea of crossing wits with the king of England. He always did think he was smarter than any king. I think he would have been particularly interested in the idea of American independence, Pelagie. I remember many times Walter talking about a mistake the king had made. He said that the king had allowed the wrong kind of people to colonize here for them to remain loyal to England. Most of the people who live here fled some form of injustice, and some of the others, like us, were given a great deal of land—we're little kings in our own little kingdoms. At least that's what Walter said, and he felt that we were not good colonists because of it. I wish he were here now when so many of the things he predicted seem to be happening. Well, now it's up to Drew to figure it all out, and I'm sure that . . . " Elizabeth drew in her breath then began to laugh softly. "Come, Pelagie, look out the window."

Pelagie stood beside her mistress, looking down into the courtyard. Drew, Leo, George and Robert moved stealthily across the expanse, close to the house, making their way to the servants' entrance in the hopes of being cleaned up and fairly respectable looking by dinnertime. "Lawd, Lawd, they looks like they been fightin' the whole o' Chas't'n. What you s'pose those boys been up to?"

"I'm sure I wouldn't dare guess. Eugenia will be furious, and I want to know what they have been doing. Pelagie, send Peter to town to find out what Drew has done today."

"Them others lookin' like they been up to no good, too."

Elizabeth let out a delighted peal of laughter, "Yes, they do, don't they. But tell Peter to ask about Drew. Whatever happened, I'm sure the others weren't the cause of it."

"Yassum, I do dat right now. You gwine see iffen you kin soothe Miz Eugenia down?"

"I'll do nothing of the sort. I intend to show off tonight with all the mysterious information that Peter will get for me. My family never understands how I know what is going on before they do, and I thoroughly enjoy it. Eugenia can soothe herself." Elizabeth quickly checked the powdering of her hair and began her own toilette, too impatient to wait for Pelagie to return from sending Peter on his errand.

After she had dressed for dinner and was satisfied that she looked quite beautiful, Elizabeth paced her sitting room in a welter of impatience waiting for Peter to return with his report of the day's activities.

When Peter finally arrived, Elizabeth sat down and listened attentively as the wide-eyed black man told of the trouble in Mazyk's land. Sending him back to his normal duties, Elizabeth walked to the door of the room and paused, looking back at Pelagie. "Be sure to peek in on the doings tonight, Pelagie. I'm sure you will enjoy it as much as I will. I think, to help matters along, I shall go down now and have a small discussion with the musicians."

Elizabeth went downstairs, checked on the seating at the table and gave last-minute instructions to the serving girls and the musicians. She then told Peter to be certain that the family members were shown to Elizabeth's private drawing room before they joined their guests.

Smiling to herself, Elizabeth went to her drawing room satisfied that she had arranged matters so the family discussion would be accomplished behind closed doors and their guests would never know there was so much as a seam in the united front the Mannings displayed to the world. Of course, keeping that seamless front would prove difficult if the boys continued to battle each other in public. That, she decided, was something she would speak to all of them about. When they fought they should all stand together and fight someone else.

By the time the first of her family came down, Elizabeth was sitting composed in her favorite chair, sipping a glass of sherry. "Good evening, John," she said sweetly as her eldest son walked into the room. "I suppose you have already learned that Drew is with us for a while."

He kissed his mother's offered cheek. "Eugenia has informed me. Our meeting in your drawing room while our guests sit twiddling their thumbs wouldn't have anything to do with Drew's arrival, would it, Mother?"

"You know perfectly well it has," she said tartly. "I felt we had better do our family disputing privately."

"I doubt there will be a dispute, Mother."

"Do you, John?"

John poured himself a glass of whiskey, then turned and smiled at her. "Yes, I do. You approve of his ruffian ways, so there is little any of the rest of us can say."

"Ahh," breathed Elizabeth. "Eugenia has cast me in the role of matriarchal tyrant this evening, has she! Well, I suppose I shouldn't disappoint her. I have a great deal to say." Elizabeth frowned at him. "Some of what I think is for your ears, John. I would feel vastly relieved if I knew for certain that you did not agree with your wife in the manner your sons are being raised. It isn't that I have any objection to proper manners, as you well know. I certainly boxed your ears often enough for misbehavior. But there is another side to living, too. One does not always exist in a ballroom or a drawing room. People who live too long in cities tend to forget that there are times when all of us must call upon our more natural responses to protect ourselves."

"My two-fisted mother," he mused. "How can you sit here with the fragile air of a gardenia, I ask myself, and speak of young men beating themselves into bruised pulp with such enthusiastic gusto?"

"Because, dear John, between the man and the woman, the man is far more the tender of the two, but we both love living with the delusion that he is not. Like all delusions, this one needs nurturing. The pomp and circumstance must be maintained, and his most readily available and harmless means of demonstrating his masculine invincibility is to beat another man to a pulp, or at least to threaten to."

"My word, Mother . . . is that what you think?"

Elizabeth gave him a twinkling smile. "No, dear, it is what I *know*, and so do you, but you have not yet gained the age or the courage to admit it." She snapped open her fan, spread it across the lower part of her face and flirted outrageously with him.

Helpless to do otherwise, John burst out in loud laughter. "Will you dance the first set with me tonight, Mother?"

"Perhaps . . . if Eugenia doesn't lay claim to you or one of my bruised grandsons lay claim to me."

"*Any* of your grandsons, or Drew?"

If he intended to make Elizabeth feel badly for her obvious favoritism, he failed, for she cocked her head to one side and said, "Most likely it will be Drew. He is the only one of the boys with sense enough to ask for a dance. Your sons will do as their mother thinks proper and will sit by my side for the prescribed fifteen minutes, talking dutifully." She looked closely at her son for a moment, then said, "And, John, they will be talking to an old lady—not a person. Drew, you see, knows the person, Elizabeth Manning. Your sons merely have an old grandmother."

John found that he was listening intently to her. His mother never ceased to amaze him. He often felt he didn't understand what he was hearing, although she was perfectly clear. She so often spoke of things that he hadn't thought about. He wondered, somewhat sadly, if he, too, had only had a mother when he might have had a charming and good friend named Elizabeth Manning. He felt a sudden loss, and it showed on his face.

Elizabeth laughed and tapped his forearm gently with her fan. "Don't begin to fret, John, you'll ruin your whole evening, and Eugenia, dear single-minded creature that she is, will assume you disapprove of the boys' behavior, too." Then, birdlike, she peered up into his face and added, "You don't, do you?"

"No!" John said quickly, shaking his head for emphasis. "Oh, no, of course not . . . perfectly acceptable young-man behavior . . . have to let off steam every now and then."

"That's what I thought," Elizabeth said smugly, then, placing her hand through John's offered arm, she let him lead her to the sofa, where he joined her in awaiting the rest of the family. "Andrew's visit will be much more fun now that you have decided to assist me in convincing your wife that a scuffle or two is not the equivalent of dissipation."

John laughed heartily. "Mother, you are hopelessly female, and I shall bow to your greater wisdom and help you. However, my influence stretches only to Eugenia. What shall you do when we all go to the Templetons' later this month?"

"Oh, I need do nothing there. I already have my abettor within the castle walls. And," she added, "my own candidate for Andrew's wife."

John frowned. "That is a state of affairs I think you should leave strictly alone. What the situation needs is clarification, not more muddling."

"We'll see."

"I'm sure we shall," John said distractedly, his attention on the young man walking across the room toward them. Andrew's brown eyes were very much like his grandmother's and danced with the same merriment. As he neared Elizabeth, he smiled, his teeth startlingly white in his sun-darkened face. His chestnut hair was unpowdered and cut unstylishly short. To John's mind it was sloppy. His thick hair curled about his ears and over the collar of his brown velvet suit. John glanced quickly at his own three sons, trailing into the room with their mother. Neat. All with hair powdered and a proper pigtail at the nape of the neck held in place by a black satin ribbon. Gentlemen. Leo was tall and gangly and could stand to put some meat on his bones, John thought. A man was, at least in part, judged successful by his girth. Leo was somewhat lacking in this. George, on the other hand, was quite substantial. Stocky and no more than five and a half feet tall, George was sandy-haired under the powder, plain and pleasant. Robert, slightly taller than George, was also a substantially built young man. His features were regular, his nose perhaps a bit too long for beauty but aristocratic-looking. Robert always gave the impression of being serious, and John looked upon him with a great deal of approval. No one would ever suspect Robert of frivolity.

Last of all Bethany came into the room. John went over to his daughter, smiling broadly. Bethany was a petite, lovely young girl with sparkling eyes and her own easy smile. Just being around her soothed John. She stood on tiptoe and kissed his cheek. Together they joined the others, and John once again looked carefully at his nephew. He confirmed his original impression. Despite some very hard truths in what his mother had to say, he still believed that on the whole his sons were what Mannings should be. For his money, Andrew looked and acted like some poor backwoodsman, unprepared to participate in finer society, certainly not as a Manning.

Elizabeth viewed him otherwise. His waistcoat of pale copper satin heightened the rich warmth of his natural coloring and made even more noticeable the quick, broad smiles that he flashed so readily and that did not stop at his mouth but carried on to light up his eyes to warm her. Walter had told her that one of the ways she could know if she could really trust a man was to look for what shone from within. Andrew was a man to be trusted, and for Elizabeth, more than anything else, that made him a Manning. She offered him her cheek to kiss. Andrew kissed her, then slipped his arms around her.

"It's good to see you, Grandma," he said softly. "I've missed you."

Elizabeth hugged him tightly.

Eugenia looked away, embarrassed and offended by such a display of animal passion. Her eyes sought John, her ally against the Upcountry Mannings. It had never sat well with her that Andrew had been designated the husband-to-be of Joanna Templeton. Fiercely loyal to her husband and family, Eugenia saw only that Joseph, the youngest son, seemed always to be a step ahead of his older brother and to reap the benefits of the family tie. Any one of her own sons was for more suitable to be master of Riverlea than Andrew, and yet none of them had ever been considered. As usual, John and his family had been overlooked. She had mentioned as much to Elizabeth. Elizabeth had replied tartly that Eugenia's sons should fight Andrew for Joanna's hand if one of them wanted it. Offended, Eugenia had turned for help to John. Now she moved closer to him and said in a low voice, "I know we must make allowances for Joseph and his family, living in the wild as they do, but I do think this animal display is more than can be stood, John."

John patted her hand. "Be easy, 'Genia, he won't be here for long. Mama is simply enjoying herself."

"If her enjoyment continues, our children will end up with nothing. Your sons and daughter will go abegging."

"Mama isn't taken in by anything, dear. One has only to have eyes to see which of these young men are superior and of true Manning stock."

Eugenia gave him an acidic look. "Do any of your sons have a marriage arranged, a dowry set or a plantation to run in the future?"

"Robert will inherit our plantation," John said.

"And George and Leo—what have you planned for them?"

John stirred uncomfortably. "This is not the time for a discussion of our family fortunes."

"No, indeed it is not! Particularly not when I've been speaking to these young men and reminding them of their obligations to stand together as Mannings and not be seen publicly battling with each other," Elizabeth said with a smile.

Eugenia put her hand to her throat. "You have told them to *fight* as Mannings—in public?"

"Only when the occasion calls for such activity, Eugenia," Elizabeth replied.

"John! John, did you hear that? Surely you're not going to stand for such advice being given your sons."

"Well, I—"

"Eugenia, this afternoon there was an altercation in which all the men were involved. But instead of standing as one against strangers, they spent most of their time fighting each other. That will not be tolerated in the Manning family." Elizabeth snapped her fan shut to end the discussion, then said, "I am hungry. It is time we joined our guests and had dinner."

"What altercation? Rob? Why haven't I been told what has happened?" Eugenia asked, looking from one member of her family to another.

"I'm sure your sons will be pleased to tell you of their adventures," Elizabeth said, rising from her chair.

"May I?" Andrew asked, hastening toward her and offering his arm.

Elizabeth's eyes fastened on John, then she looked pointedly at her other three grandsons, all of whom were talking frantically to their mother and paying no attention to her or moving to the dinner guests. "I could ask for no finer escort, Drew," she said, then added in a low tone meant only for his ears and John's, "And I'd most likely be left with none if you weren't here."

"My cousins aren't treating you right?" Drew asked, his eyebrows raised. "They're fools. I'll have to speak to them about the art of enjoying beautiful ladies. They don't know what they are missing."

Elizabeth laughed. "You'd do better hog-tying their mother."

Andrew's loud guffaw enlarged in the quiet, staid hallway. Eugenia turned quickly, her hand once more at her throat, her eyes wide with shock. "My word!" she breathed. "You have me so frightened now, the slightest noise sets me on edge. I thought something dire had happened."

Andrew smiled at her. "It may have," he said, and left her to wondering what, if anything, he meant.

She turned to John, clinging to his arm. "I must excuse myself, John. I'm sorry . . . it's my nerves . . . I can't stand such . . . such disorder."

As the Mannings entered the parlor to join their guests, John excused himself, asking Elizabeth to make his excuses. "I shall be as quick as I can, Mother, but Eugenia must lie down. She feels quite poorly. It's been too much for her."

"Oh, Eugenia, what a pity it is to be so delicate. You'll miss all the dancing later. Don't be long, John dear; we'll wait for you." Elizabeth turned toward the parlor, her face bright with a smile, her step brisk as she greeted the several people waiting there.

The Mannings avoided any more discussion of the day's events that evening and managed to have a successful, lively dinner party, but they all knew that the subject matter of Andrew's speech beneath the Liberty Tree would not be avoided for long. Each of them recognized that Andrew had unwittingly opened a topic that concerned them all and that they most likely would not agree upon. The ideas of rights, liberties and justice were real and practical concerns in these days, and Elizabeth was determined that the feeling each of them harbored privately be brought out in the open. She was certain that was what Walter would have advised, in the hope of avoiding a rift among them later.

***

Three days later Elizabeth was once more sitting at the foot of her dining-room table, looking at her family and trying to read the tempers of each of them. "I'd like to hear more about that speech you gave in Mazyk's pasture the other day, Drew."

Leo, Robert, George and Drew all stopped eating and exchanged glances. "You know about the speech, too?" George blurted out.

"Of course I do," Elizabeth snapped. "Did you think I'd heard about the fight and not the cause of it?"

"What kind of speech?" John asked. "Surely you're not one of the Liberty Boys?"

"No, Uncle John, I am not with Christopher Gadsen," Drew said, then looked at his grandmother. "It wasn't much of a speech— more passion than sense, Grandma. Governor Montagu had just issued his proclamation about the Regulators, and I had just come into town with the wagon train. I don't think the Lowlanders have any true understanding of conditions in the Upcountry, and I'm afraid I was in the frame of mind to announce my feelings to the world on that day."

"And so you did, and caused a riot," Elizabeth added.

"Now, just a minute," Rob said, forgetting that his mouth was full of food. "I don't think this is something to make light of, Grandma. Drew sees only what he wishes to see, and when the Assembly doesn't give him what he wants for his precious Upcountry, he says we don't understand or care. The Assembly has innumerable items on its agenda to be considered. Too many, in fact; and everyone wants his own interest considered. There is no reason that the Upcountry should have special consideration or that normal delays in legislation give the Regulators the right to take matters into their own hands. There is no justification for the Regulators. They're just an excuse for a lawless band of rowdies to run rampant."

"That's right, Drew!" Leo said. "You've got to admit at least to that. When the militia went to the aid of the Upcountry, there wasn't a man to be raised to serve."

"Charles Skinner tried to raise the militia around Camden—your area, Drew. That was right after last Christmas. If the Upcountry-men are so interested in stopping the outlaws, why weren't they coming out to serve in the militia? Why gather in an outlaw band of their own?" George asked.

"George! Leo! Rob! Hush with your nonstop questions and comments. Let Drew have a say," Elizabeth said.

"There's nothing to say," Leo insisted. "Those are the facts. Tom Moon and the Black brothers were yours for the catching, but no, not a man would join Skinner in riding after the gang. And then you say there is no help for the Upcountryman."

"With all your fact gathering, Leo, did you happen upon any of the details of Moon's activities?"

"He's a robber. Everybody knows that."

Drew laughed softly. "It sounds innocuous, doesn't it?"

"Well, it certainly isn't innocuous," George said. "But neither is it as dire as you Upcountrymen make it out to be, I'm sure."

"I wonder what reply you would get if you were to ask Charles Kitchen his opinion of the outlaws."

"Kitchen? Who is Charles Kitchen?" Rob asked. "Should I be recognizing his name? Have we met him?"

"I'm sure you haven't. He probably wouldn't interest you and would only disturb your complacency."

"Oh, bosh and twiddle," Elizabeth snapped. "I am tired of all this cryptic sparring, Drew. Say right out what you are hinting at."

"Perhaps another time, Grandma. It isn't the kind of thing one talks about in front of ladies."

"Since when have Manning ladies become so delicate they can't hear what is important to their menfolk? If your mother can live in the Upcountry, I am certain I am strong enough to hear about it. I will not be treated like a piece of porcelain! Why, your grandfather and I lived through things that could curl your toenails, my boy. Speak your mind!"

Drew smiled at her and nodded. He turned back to his cousins. "Charles Kitchen was one of the men attacked and robbed last summer by the outlaws. They took what valuables he had, and not satisfied with that, they beat him, burned him with red-hot pokers and gouged out one of his eyes. He was left to die, and the band went on to Gabriel Brown's place."

"Oh my God," Leo said. "But surely that is an exception. After all, you are free to pick and choose the worst story you have heard about and relate it to us as if it were commonplace."

"It is commonplace. Gabriel Brown received no kinder treatment than Kitchen did. He was burned, beaten and bruised nearly to death . . . he still hasn't fully recovered. Torture with hot irons is one of the Black brothers' favorite forms of entertainment. Whether a man resists or gives them what they want in the way of goods matters not at all. If the Black brothers strike, there will be torture."

"But still—to form a vigilante group such as the Regulators. I mean, there is no law or restraint upon them, either. It is an extreme and uncivilized method of dealing with what is essentially a problem for the courts. Once these outlaws are captured, what becomes of them?"

"Most of them are hanged," Drew said flatly.

"That's barbaric!" John sputtered.

"What would you suggest we do, Uncle John?"

"What any decent man would do. Place your petition before the Assembly. Make use of your legal representation and take legal and civilized steps to curtail these outlaws."

"Our petitions have been presented and ignored innumerable times. How many petitions should we present? How many months—years—should we wait for response?" Drew asked and, receiving no reply, went on. "Two representatives for the entire Upcountry is hardly going to gain priority for our problems. We have done everything but beg the Assembly to respond to our needs. But we all know nothing will be done unless the Lowland is threatened. Once the problem is in your own backyard and it is your wife threatened, and your plantation, then something will be done.

"Safe as you are, you can sit here and talk politely about questions for the legislature, but men like Kitchen and Brown and Dennis Hayes are talking about all their possessions, their health and their very survival. The outlaws ravaged Hayes's ten-year-old daughter while he was helpless to do anything to save her. Think of that when you tell us to be patient, Uncle John. Think of how civilized you'd be if it were Aunt Eugenia or Bethany threatened thusly." Drew looked at his family, his eyes resting momentarily on each of them. He folded his napkin and laid it on the table. "I apologize, Grandma. There was no need for you to hear all of that. I should have used more restraint."

Elizabeth took a deep breath. "I will admit I haven't enjoyed a word of it, Drew, but I need to hear it. We all do. I am ashamed that I haven't been more aware of what you and your family suffer." She looked at her son. "John, now that we have all been made aware of the situation in the Upcountry, I'll expect you to be talking to your friends and business acquaintances and making them aware as we now are. Stir them to action. I'll expect the same from my grandsons."

"Mother . . ." John began.

"John, we'll not be fainthearted in this matter. We are concerned here with the well-being of your brother and his family. We are all Mannings, and we shall look after our own. Now, enough has been said. Shall we retire to the parlor? Perhaps Bethany will be good enough to play some music for us. I believe it is time for a respite from this."

4

Andrew stayed on at his grandmother's, putting off his departure a day at a time at her request.

"If you are sincere in your desire to have the Upcountry's grievances taken care of by the Assembly, you'll stay right here and fight where the most good can be accomplished without bloodshed," Elizabeth said. Softening slightly, she got up and stood beside his chair with her hand on his shoulder. She looked down at the letter from home in his hand. "I know it is difficult for you to be here feeling as though you are doing nothing while the Regulators are in the field."

"On Sunday, while the villagers were listening to Reverend Woodmason preach, their homes were robbed." Andrew folded the letter and returned it to its envelope. "At least they aren't sitting around doing nothing. They took to their horses and chased them fifteen miles up Twenty-five Mile Creek. One of the outlaws was wounded, but the others carried him off. The property and many of the horses were recovered, though. That's something."

"I know it is difficult for you, Drew, but you must take my word that you can do more good here talking about the need of the Upcountry and moving the Assembly to action. Any one of several men can take your place on the Regulator campaigns, but you can be of value both here and at home."

Drew looked up at her, taking her hand. "Grandma, it is only your word and the fact that I have faith in your wisdom that has kept me here this long. But if something doesn't happen soon, I am going back home."

"That is reasonable, Drew, but I am happy to know that you are also a man of mental action as well as physical. A month or so of your time is not a great deal, when so much heartache and bloodshed could be avoided if the Assembly can be moved."

Elizabeth swept from the room, her mind already on the afternoon's tea. She was not one to give advice and then stand by idly while others worked. Elizabeth had her own campaign going. While she sent her men after the men of the Assembly and community, Elizabeth worked with the women. Her Legare Street house was filled with prominent ladies every afternoon for tea and a little political conversation. Aside from feeling that she was helping Drew and her son's family, Elizabeth was amazed at the change in the general feeling of the women who came into her home. Just a few years ago she would never have heard a critical word about the king or Parliament. During these afternoon teas she seldom went without hearing something about taxes, freedom, rights, justice or liberty.

Elizabeth checked with Cook about last-minute arrangements, then went to her morning room smiling to herself. "Pelagie, there is no question I feel more alive when Drew is here than at any other time."

Pelagie fluffed and arranged the cushions on Elizabeth's favorite chaise longue, then helped her mistress onto it for her morning rest. "This ol' house sure has been hummin' ever since he got here, an' that's a fac'."

"It isn't just the house, Pelagie," Elizabeth said. "We tend to get lazy in our thinking and allow important issues and movements to go past us as if they were merely daily matters. When Drew is here, I think of a broader view. My eyes see beyond the boundaries of my home, and I begin to think of nations and power." She giggled suddenly. "Most likely what I think are seditious and treasonous things."

"Ah hopes not! Ah shore doesn't want none o' them king's men comin' heah fo' us."

Elizabeth sat up straight. "That is exactly the kind of thing I mean. Before Drew came, we would never have considered the idea that a king's man would dare question us. Yet Drew's being here has not made us think anything different of ourselves. What he has done is to make us aware that the colonies are not in England's eyes what they are in ours. Perhaps they never were, and we simply let that knowledge slip past us with yesterday's laundry."

"You bes' take yo' nap, Miz Lizzybeff, or you gwine be too tired to talk them ladies' ears off later."

"Why, Pelagie! That is positively insolent."

"Yassum, tha's a fac'."

"Don't forget to awaken me in an hour if I should fall asleep."

Elizabeth kept up her endless efforts, and her enthusiasm grew with each passing day. She expected and got a daily report from all her Manning men on their conversations and the progress they were making in arousing sympathy for the Upcountry plight. Though he appreciated his grandmother's efforts, Andrew was becoming more and more convinced that little would be accomplished. Charles Town was not yet ready to be bothered with outlaw raids that did not directly touch them. Neither were they prepared to give greater representation to the Upcountry in the Assembly, for every seat given would have to be taken from a Lowland area, as the size of the Assembly was limited by English decree. No one was going to give up willingly what power he had. The Upcountryman would have to defend himself as he had always done in the past.

Andrew had remained at his grandmother's house for a month when November came in bright and crisp. As the weather cooled, the activity in the Upcountry and in Charles Town heated up. Lieutenant-Governor William Bull, a colonial himself, recognized the volatility of the situation and wrote to Reverend Charles Woodmason, asking him to use his influence to persuade the Upcountrymen to present their grievances in writing to the Assembly.

On November 5, 1767, Governor Montagu, not nearly so aware or concerned, sent a message to the Assembly asking for legislation suppressing "those licentious Spirits," the Regulators.

The Mannings gathered around their dinner table that night, heatedly discussing the new turn of events.

"We must remember," Elizabeth said, "the Assembly has not acted. To their credit—and perhaps ours as well, I hope—the Assembly have asked for further information."

"But what will the Upcountrymen do?" George asked. "What do you think, Drew? The Regulators aren't known for their patience."

"I don't know," he said simply and truthfully. "After the proclamation back in October there was some pretty heated talk about marching on Charles Town, . . . but I just don't know."

"I fear we should be prepared for anything to happen," John said wearily. "Lieutenant-Governor Bull has been extremely concerned of late and corresponding regularly with Reverend Woodmason. It seems he has heard of this march on Charles Town and takes it quite seriously. Bull seems to think it is possible this situation could burgeon into a full-fledged rebellion against the Charles Town authority."

"Oh, my dear word!" Eugenia breathed. "Might there be fighting . . . here? We are no longer safe?"

"Must you take on so, Eugenia," Elizabeth said. "How likely is it that the Regulators would actually take it upon themselves to make the Lowland their enemy, Drew?"

"Very, Grandma. In effect, you are our enemy. It is merely a matter of declaration."

"I can understand none of this! Why must people be constantly mucking up what we have?" Eugenia said. "Why is it necessary for these . . . these backwoods people to come here and threaten us? Why isn't something done about it?"

Andrew smiled at her. "Something is being done, Aunt Eugenia. Governor Montagu wants us jailed for our licentiousness."

"Bravo! The sooner the better. You people have no right to come here with your demands, wanting us to give to you what we worked for ourselves. Act like true Englishmen and you'll be treated like true Englishmen."

"I am an American," Drew said.

"That doesn't change the fact that you are an English subject, Drew," John said.

Drew looked at his uncle for a moment, then agreed. "I suppose it doesn't."

"You suppose?" John asked. "Perhaps you'd better do some thinking on that, Drew. I have involved myself in your current concerns with the Upcountry primarily because Mother wishes us to stand as one, but I'll have no part directly or indirectly with the rebellious meanderings of the Liberty Boys. If you are leaning in that direction, I think it only fair that you state your position honorably so that others of us may state ours."

"My interest is in the Upcountry, Uncle John, nowhere else."

The dinner ended in silence, each of the Mannings thinking of his or her own feelings and misgivings. They spent an unusually quiet evening, and when Drew arose the following morning he was surprised to see his cousins already in the dining room eating breakfast.

"You're all up bright and early," he said as he entered and took his own seat.

George laughed. "We've heard the talk, too, and will be front and center when the Assembly meets today."

"As a matter of fact, we were hoping to get there before you and be able to gloat that we had better seats."

Rob offered Drew the serving tray piled high with eggs, ham, kippers, dry toast and marmalade. They ate quickly and left for Meeting Street and the Assembly.

The four Manning cousins remained outside the Meeting Hall not knowing whether to expect four thousand Upcountrymen to come marching into Charles Town or not.

"What will you do if they come, Drew?" Rob asked. "They'll be your neighbors and friends."

"I am going to join them, Rob. I'm sorry, I know that will cause you and Uncle John some discomfort, but I belong with them."

Leo and George exchanged glances. "You know we wish you wouldn't, so there is little point in arguing about it," Leo said.

"Maybe they won't come at all," George said. "I don't see or hear anything out of the ordinary, and surely we'd hear something of four thousand men."

"They'll be here," Drew said. "Maybe not four thousand of them, but the Regulators will be here."

The Mannings waited for nearly half an hour longer before they saw Benjamin Hart, John Scott, Moses Kirkland and Thomas Woodward stride into the building, their faces serious, their backs squared and straight, intent on enlightening the Assembly.

Andrew and his cousins followed the Regulator leaders into the building and hurried to a good vantage point.

The Remonstrance, which had been written with the aid of Reverend Charles Woodmason and signed by over four thousand Upcountry planters, was read before the Assembly.

"Though we contribute to the support of government, we do not share the benefits enjoyed by our fellow provincials. We are practically denied trial by our peers, as few persons north of the Santee are on the jury list. Forty-four members of the Commons are elected south and six north of the Santee. It is the number of *free men*, not *black slaves*, that constitutes the strength and riches of a state."

Drew looked over at his cousins, smiling. "That was beautifully put—and just what I told you, remember?"

"And debatable," Leo said under his breath.

Drew began to answer, but his attention was drawn once more to the speaker as he launched into the reasons the backcountry felt it had never been properly divided into parishes and thereby never gained representation.

". . . we conceive to be due to the selfish interest of those in and near Charles Town, who seek to have everything center from there. To our absence was largely due the voting sixty thousand pounds for an exchange for the merchants and a ballroom for the ladies of Charles Town, while nearly sixty thousand back settlers have not a minister or a church, as if we were not worth the thought or deemed as savages and not Christians! As loyal subjects and true lovers of our country we beg leave to sum up what we conceive necessary to afford us our equal rights as British subjects."

The Remonstrance went on citing the improvements the Upcountrymen felt it was their right to have, and as it was suggested that the money designated for a statue honoring William Pitt be used to provide Bibles for the people, loud hoots of derision broke out in the Assembly.

The afternoon ended without decision and the Upcountrymen and the Lowlander still at odds.

Andrew and his cousins left with the other men, and for the most part the group headed for the tavern. They spent the rest of the afternoon talking about the events of the day and speculating what tomorrow would bring. There was good-hearted frivolity in their bantering about serious matters, for which they could thank their grandmother. On their way home they walked past the state house. There was posted a message: "Inscription for the statue of Mr. Pitt:

What love to their adopted sons
Is by our fathers shown?
We ask to taste the Bread of Life,
And, lo, they give a stone!"

"Wait until news of this goes 'round!" Drew said, laughing.

"It's not funny!" Leo said. "I don't even think Grandma is going to see the humor in this. Mr. Pitt is a great friend of the colonies . . . they have no call to put something like this on the state house!"

The following day the Assembly demanded the arrest of the deputy Regulators and the burning of their petition. Debate raged in the Assembly between those who were most irate about the actions of the Regulators and those most worried that the Upcountry problems would not be solved and worse troubles were to come. Finally the reminder came that were it not for the intervention of Lieutenant-Governor Bull, four thousand representing fifty thousand settlers in the Upcountry would have been at the door.

The deputies were finally persuaded to apologize for some of their more heated remarks, and the Assembly made promises that action would be taken. John Rutledge was given the task of codifying the laws, and six new parishes were promised. Jury reform was promised, and a number of schools with free tuition were offered provided a college be created in Charles Town.

The Upcountrymen returned home with a few stories to tell of their adventures in Charles Town and promises that only time would determine to be realities.

Andrew stayed at his grandmother's the rest of that week. He spent a good deal of time with his cousins in Dillon's Tavern, agitating and generally causing trouble among the young men. Drew made many new friends, a few friendly enemies and some real ones. When he argued he argued heatedly, not giving way to any man no matter how logical his opinion. If it was not in the interest of the Upcountry, as Drew saw it, the man was wrong.

Drew debated sometimes eloquently about the essence of liberty. Was it a quality of an Englishman's birthright, or was it God's gift to any man? He, for the first time, felt the power of his own words. And in the process, he acquired a black eye and bruised knuckles. The jubilance ended abruptly.

George, Leo and Rob, prompted by their grandmother's insistence and the camaraderie that had grown among them, had sided with Andrew's view of justice as it should be dealt out to the Upcountry. True to the blood that ran in their veins, a dedicated Manning was a Manning with enthusiasm and zest that went well beyond the boundaries of reason or prudence.

"We should be riding with the Regulators, not condemning them!" George, completely converted, declared loudly for all the patrons of Dillon's Tavern to hear, one of whom took offense.

"What the hell do you know about it?" a coarse, slightly drunk voice said.

"Who are you?" George asked.

"Will Rather, for all that matters."

"I'm George Manning," George said, smiling.

"I don't give a damn what you say your name is. In my book it is *Fool*. If you knew anything near what you spout out of that ignorant mouth of yours, you'd be saying those Regulators gotta be stopped right now. They already have a notion that they're the law!"

"And who is the law, if they are not?" George asked, his chin jutted out, his smile gone.

"We are! The law is right here in Charles Town. It's in England. It's in London. And do you know why? I'll tell you why. 'Cause that's where it belongs, and don't you forget it. No one . . . *no one* has the right to do as he pleases here. We live by law!"

"All but the *outlaws!*" Rob said, giggling because of the ale he had downed in one draft as a result of Andrew's dare.

"That's my point, fool!" Will Rather said. "The Regulators are outlaws."

"Like hell they are!" Leo shouted. "They are the only law up there."

"They're outlaws!"

"Take that back!"

Will laughed grandly. "I'll never take back the truth!"

George leaped from his chair and grabbed Will by the shirt front. "You'll take that back!"

Will stood up. George staggered back unsteadily. "I'll settle with you, if that's your wish. We'll be gentlemen, however, and not brawl in the tavern." Will waved his hand, indicating all of Dillon's. "Where shall we meet and when?"

"Now!" screeched George, regaining his feet. "In the field out back."

"George, for heaven's sake, shut up! You can't shoot!" Rob whispered.

"You'll be my second?" Will called to a man on the other side of the room, and received a slow nod in confirmation.

"Drew?" George asked, not as sure of himself as he had been a moment before.

"Drew, talk him out of this," Leo pleaded. "He can't shoot worth squat!"

"He'll get his head blown off!" Rob said.

"Why don't you be *my* second, George?" Drew said, moving closer to Will.

"I've got no quarrel with you. It's loudmouth here I want to shut up."

"All of your quarrels are with me, Will," Drew said pleasantly. "Not only do I agree with every word George said, I *am* one of those despicable Regulators. Here's your chance to prove your point and rid the world of one of the enemy."

"Pistols," Will Rather said quietly.

"Pistols," Drew repeated.

George, Leo and Rob followed Drew out of the tavern and around back, deep into the dark field behind.

"Let's call this off. You can't see a thing, Drew," Rob said.

"We'll light torches," Drew said.

"This is all my fault," George moaned.

"Let's back out of it."

"Rob's right, Drew. This is stupid. What do we care about Will Rather anyway? I don't even know him. I don't think he's from Charles Town at all," Leo said.

"He isn't," Drew said. "I heard him say he's from Virginia."

"Then what's he matter? Who gives a damn what he thinks?"

"I do."

The small procession of Mannings and Will Rather and his second walked unsteadily out to the field behind the tavern. Rob and Leo gathered reeds and materials to make torches, then ran to catch up with the others, the torches high above their heads.

"Jesus, Rob, we've really done it this time. Suppose Drew gets hurt? Suppose something worse happens? What will we do?"

"Blaspheming isn't going to help! Nothing bad is going to happen," Rob said tensely. "Drew can take care of himself."

"But he can't see! It's pitch black out here!"

"Damn it, Leo, stop saying things like that. If he can't see, neither can Will."

"I think I'm going to be sick."

"Leo!" Rob growled, then added in a lower voice, "We'll stand by Will and throw light on him. That way Drew can see, but maybe Will won't be able to see so well."

"What if Drew misses? Maybe he'll hit one of us."

"For God's sake, Leo! Shut up! You're makin' me so jumpy I can't think. George is the idiot that got us into this. Make him hold the torch."

When they all caught up with one another, Will and Drew were discussing the distance from which they would shoot and, to Rob's dismay, the positioning of the torches. One would be at each end, lighting both men.

"If he wanted a torch, he should have brought one," George said sullenly.

"We're wasting time, George," Drew said curtly and walked to the area he and Will had agreed upon as the dueling range.

Resignedly George positioned himself at the point Will would end up after he had walked his twenty paces. Leo stationed himself at Drew's end.

"Rob, take George's place. He's my second; he can't be down there."

"I'll take George's place," Leo said.

"Look, will you just leave things as they are! Let's get on with this," Drew snapped, and stepped into position with Will.

Drew and Will stood back to back. George and Will's second began counting, then hurriedly ran to stand beside the respective torch bearers in case they should be called upon.

Drew and Will walked steadily to a called count away from each other. At the sound of twenty they turned, took aim, and the darkness shattered with an orange burst as the pistols fired. The torch lights quivered, their bearers unable to concentrate the small, weak circles of light. Tight puffs of smoke clung tenaciously in the air and then slowly began to shred. Drew moved slowly from the darkness into the range of Leo's wavering torch.

"Drew!" Leo cried, his voice breaking into a high shrill. "Drew, are you all right? Were you hit?"

"Will's hit!" his second called from the darkness.

Leo ran with the torch over to where Will lay on the ground. He relit the fallen torch. "Where's he hit?"

"I don't know. I can't tell. Help me—we've got to get him home." The man looked up at Leo. "Do you have a carriage, by chance?"

"Is he alive?" George asked as he ran up to them.

"We only have the horses we rode. Is he too bad off to put him on his mount?" Leo asked.

"I don't know," the man said shrilly. "I can't get him to come round, and I can't see a bloody thing. Can't you hold that still?"

"Is he alive?" George asked with greater fright in his voice.

"I don't know!" the man shouted.

The five men carried Will back to the tavern. Experienced in such matters, the barkeep assured them Will was very much alive and not so badly hurt as his silent, pale appearance would indicate. Shaken and unsure what they should do, Leo asked, "Do you think he'll be all right? How do you know? Should we take him home . . . or somewhere?"

"Leave him to me," the barkeep said gruffly. "Soon's I get this shot out of his shoulder, he'll mend." Rolling up his sleeves, the barkeep reached for his knife, placed it over the candle flame and turned his attention to Will.

Leo groaned, covering up his mouth. "Drew, I can't watch."

"Get him out of here! All of you, be gone and let me do what is needed," the barkeep barked, waving his knife at them. "Out with you! And don't forget to come here and get him tomorrow! I'll tend him, but I won't keep him for you—and there'll be a charge!"

They went out into the street and stood there, still not feeling right leaving Will Rather behind.

"It doesn't seem right to shoot a man and then leave without doing something," Rob said.

George shuddered. "If it hadn't been for Drew stepping in, that would be me lying there. Drew, I thank you . . . I wouldn't have known what to do. He would have shot me as I stood . . ."

Drew put his arm around his cousin. George took a deep breath but continued his nervous chatter. "I'm no good at that sort of thing. I don't know why I challenged him. Why do I do such stupid things? I would have stood there and let him shoot me, Drew. I would have! You saved my life. Oh, I thank you . . . I—"

"You would have been fine," Drew said, but his mind was more on Will Rather than on what his cousin was saying.

"No, no, I wouldn't have. Ask Rob; he'll tell you. Rob, tell him. He saved my life."

"Let's go home," Rob said. "We can't do anything here tonight. We'll come see to Rather first thing tomorrow. Perhaps then we can help in some way . . . ." he let his voice trail off.

"I think we'd be very smart to get out of Charles Town as fast as we can," Leo said.

"What—" Drew began.

"It'll mean little to you, but when Mama hears about this, Rob and George and I are going to hear about it for years to come. We'd be smart to be sure she wasn't around to hear anything for a time."

"I wouldn't mind a bit if Daddy wasn't here either," George said. "But where'll we go? We can't just tell Mama to leave town. Where can we get her to go?"

Leo pressed his lips together, his eyes on Drew. "Well, in a manner of speaking, Drew got us into this mess, so I think he should be the one to get us out. We don't have many options. No good ones, but there is Riverlea. There is nothing to stop Drew from having a sudden yearning for Joanna. He could be anxious to see her—too anxious to wait until next week as planned. We could all go to Riverlea."

"Just to set things straight, Leo, this wasn't my fight. I didn't get you into a damned thing. I stepped in to help George out. So while you're spreading blame, you might consider that."

"It's your shot being dug out of Will Rather's shoulder, Drew. And it was an argument about the Regulators that began the whole altercation. Those are the facts. Like George said, he wouldn't have fired a shot had he been fending for himself."

"I would have been dead!" shrilled George.

"Maybe. Most likely not. Rather may not have fired, either. In any case, it wasn't you, it was Drew who shot, and all this talk is getting us nowhere. What are you going to do, Drew? Will you tell Grandma you want to leave for Riverlea right away?"

"I don't know why I should," Drew said angrily. "You're a damned prick, Leo, and if you had a backbone of your own, you would have been the one to take your brother's place in that duel."

"Will you?"

"Yes, I will," Drew said and walked to his horse. He rode off, leaving them behind.

The following day Drew told his grandmother that he wanted to go to Riverlea sooner than planned. Elizabeth's eyes narrowed. "My, this is sudden—and unusual."

"Yes, I know, but . . ." he looked away from her. "It's been a long time since I've seen Joanna."

"And you are just a wilting flower waiting for her tender hand to revive you," Elizabeth said sweetly, a staid little smile plastered on her face. "All right, now you have given me your planned speech, shall we get to the truth? What happened? What deviltry have you boys gotten into that requires a hasty departure from Charles Town?"

Drew looked at her, then remembered his promise to his cousins. "Everything is fine, Grandma. I'm just eager to see Joanna."

Elizabeth snorted. "In a pig's eye you are! You've never in your life been eager to see Joanna. Now, Drew Manning, I have reached the end of my patience. I'll have the whole story from you, and no more avoidance of the truth, and no bending of it."

Drew told her of the previous night's misadventure. "And is Will Rather on the mend?" she asked, when he had concluded his story.

"Yes, I have checked on him. As of this morning he is lucid, free of fever and complaining about a mighty sore shoulder." Drew laughed suddenly. "He's well enough to curse me in two languages and threaten me to a rematch as well."

"He'll do. In that case, I had better find Pelagie and begin the packing. There is much to be done, and it galls me, Drew, to have to do all this under the guise of your longing to see Joanna."

"No more than it does me, Grandma."

"I can imagine. But Eugenia must be kept in the dark about this, I agree, so we shall do what we must. Pelagie and I can keep her busy enough to curtail her gossiping. If we are careful, it is likely she'll not hear a word about it for some time, and perhaps the furor will be lessened."

An hour later, Elizabeth had the house turned into a hive of activity. Servants ran up the main staircase carrying trunks to be filled with ladies' gowns and more slowly down with trunks bulging with finery. The carriages and wagons were systematically packed and loaded to move the entire Manning family to the country for an undetermined length of time. Visits to Riverlea usually lasted a week for Drew and nearer to a month for his cousins and grandmother.

On the morning of the sixteenth of November, John, Eugenia, Elizabeth, Leo, Bethany, George, Robert, Pelagie and an assortment of other servants got into the carriages and began the procession down the drive from Elizabeth's house. As he was accustomed to doing, Andrew rode on horseback, as though protecting the small train of Manning carriages from the same dangers he guarded his wagon trains from on their long journey from the Upcountry. Tirelessly he rode ahead of the entourage, then returned to warn of rough spots in the roads, of oncoming wagons or merely to peek into his grandmother's carriage to point out to her the sights of pettiaugers, heavily laden flatboats making their way upstream. Periodically he would ride by the servant wagons and stir them to song.

Elizabeth hadn't enjoyed a trip so much as this one since the last time Drew had come to Charles Town, and before that it had been her husband who had taken time to point out the small wonders along the way. Walter, too, had enjoyed the sweet sound of singing voices. The sound of them now stirred pleasant, almost-lost memories in Elizabeth. She leaned her head comfortably against the carriage back and mused over the oddity that some men seemed to know instinctively how to enjoy life and allow others to enjoy with them, while others, no matter how extensive the reminders or opportunities, never learned. She sighed contentedly, feeling well cared for and well loved.

She was almost sorry to see the stone-pillared entrance to Riverlea loom up before them. The Riverlea dogs came racing out to meet the newcomers. Dalmatians vied with gold and red setters to reach the carriages first. At the gate a black man, the welcomer, stood waiting to offer the hospitality of Riverlea, the Templeton home. Elizabeth looked out of her carriage at her grandson, the beautiful black and white dogs, the golden and red setters, and the graceful white pillared plantation house showing through the thick green of the trees at the end of the road, and tried to imagine Andrew as master of Riverlea. As she had so many times before, she failed, and wondered why. He was certainly capable. Andrew could make trees grow from stone. Riverlea wasn't stone; it had rich, fertile rice lands. She wanted only happiness and success for him, and Riverlea and Joanna Templeton seemed to offer all that and more. Most men would give anything they had for a chance to walk in Andrew's shoes. Yet she couldn't feel in her heart that this was right for him, nor did she believe that it would ever take place.

5

Ruth Templeton hurried down the broad front steps of Riverlea to embrace Elizabeth. "What a surprise! We hadn't a hope of seeing you before next week. When your message came saying you'd be here early, I couldn't have been happier!"

"I hope we aren't here at a bad time for you. I didn't leave you enough time to refuse us," Elizabeth said, returning her cousin's kiss.

Ruth laughed and took Elizabeth's arm as they walked slowly toward the house. "Oh, you know us, Elizabeth, we've never got things done as they should be. It's a perfect time. William is late with harvest, as usual—no, worse than usual. The rains will ruin the whole crop if he doesn't hurry. He'll be in ecstasy when he learns that Andrew has actually arrived. He's been a bear all month, sure he'll lose his crop. When he read your message, it was the first time he'd been fit to be around. If you recall, Drew was here at harvest two years ago, and we never had such a good harvest—before or since. Andrew has such a way with the men, and he knows his crops. William doesn't really, you know. It was his brother who had the expertise, and when he died, Riverlea suffered. William tries, but he doesn't have the knack that Edgar had and Drew has."

"Drew does have a fine hand, doesn't he," Elizabeth mused, and wondered if this trip was as wise a move as she had first thought. Ruth's next words increased her doubt.

"Elizabeth, I don't mind telling you, I'll be pleased when he and Joanna set a date for their marriage. No one is more eager than I to have William free of the responsibility of this plantation. Sometimes I feel that we are held captive here and I long to visit England,

and I haven't seen my sister in Philadelphia in years." She turned quickly to give Elizabeth another hug. "Listen to me chattering away like a magpie, and you standing out here in the bright sun. You can see how starved for company I am."

"Where are the girls?" Elizabeth asked.

"Oh, they're on their way. Primping, you know." With another smile Ruth turned her attention to Eugenia and her family, talking rapidly and saying much the same as she had to Elizabeth, with suitable variations to please Eugenia. "Oh, my! All these young men to help with the harvest! We'll just have to have a festival to celebrate. Oh, we'll have such fun!"

Ruth was a small, compact woman of enormous energy. She seemed to be everywhere at once, ordering the servants about the unloading of the carriages, instructing the houseboys as to which bedroom belonged to whom, talking nonstop to her cousins and exclaiming over and over how happy she was to have company. "Where are those girls of mine? Honestly, Eugenia, you don't know how fortunate you are to have boys. Don't you find that Bethany is more trouble than the other three put together, and always the last to be ready for anything? Joanna! Meg! Gwynne!"

Eugenia winced at the way Ruth called for her daughters. Untroubled, Ruth shouted again and louder when the girls did not appear immediately.

In the next moment two young women came through the front door. Meg, the taller of the two, dressed in a pink dress covered with tiny rosettes, walked directly to Elizabeth, curtsying and properly kissing the older woman on the cheeks. The other girl looked like a much younger and prettier version of her mother. Her dark hair curled around her face, accentuating her dark blue eyes and creamy complexion. She was dressed in a vivid green dress that accentuated her tiny waist and full bosom. Ignoring the clutch of women, she turned her complete attention on Drew. "You're finally here!" she cried and flung herself into his arms.

Drew, smiling broadly, embraced her. He caught her to him closely and spun her around. Gwynne Templeton let her feet fly out behind her, clinging to him and laughing with abandoned joy. "I've missed you! Why do you leave such great amounts of time between visits? Don't you like us?"

Andrew laughed. "I love you all, Gwynne, you know that. You just like to hear me say it over and over."

"I do, I do, I do!" Gwynne said happily. "Say it again! And tell me you missed me—just me."

"I missed you," he said, smiling down at her.

She cocked her head to one side, her eyes twinkling. "How much?"

Drew looked at her for a moment, wondering when the playful talk between himself and Gwynne had made such a subtle shift and if that shift was intended or even noticed by her. He looked into her eyes and found that he could no longer think of her as Joanna's younger sister.

"Come now, Drew, it isn't polite to leave a lady's question unanswered. How much did you miss me?" she repeated.

Behind them, her eyes scanning the scene, Joanna Templeton walked sedately and slowly down the wide front steps of Riverlea. Two of the dalmatians, her particular favorites, came to her side and walked with her.

Gwynne watched Andrew's eyes change and followed the direction of his gaze. "Oh, the queen has made her appearance," she murmured, then added, "You'd better be prepared to make decisions this time, Drew. People are beginning to talk and ask questions, and Joanna is hopping mad."

"Talking about what?" Drew asked. He moved away from Gwynne slightly, his eyes on Joanna as she moved gracefully toward them. She was slender and well shaped. He thought she looked as if she had just stepped out of a painting. She was someone's impression of what an English lady should look like. Her hair was soft brown, her tight, stylish curls having just been done. The crown of her head was covered modestly with a silk calash. Her face was nearly a perfect oval, with skin so smooth and fair it didn't seem real. Nothing about Joanna seemed quite real to Andrew. As she walked toward him, her hazel eyes studying him, he moved farther from Gwynne until a foot of space divided them. He looked over at Gwynne and realized she had been talking to him, answering the question he had asked her.

Annoyance showed in her eyes, but she went on talking as if he had been paying attention the whole time. ". . . now that she is twenty years old, even Mama is getting concerned that in the end you'll never marry Joanna." She looked up at him, a penetrating, curious look in her eyes. "It isn't at all in character with you, Drew, so it's hard not to doubt."

"What isn't in character?" he asked distractedly.

"Marriage to Joanna. Such a marriage, such a match as you and Joanna are, seems at odds with everything else about you."

He glanced sharply at her then. "You and I both know the marriage was arranged a long time ago. And I'll do what must be done to maintain my family's honor. I hope you don't think that out of character for me."

She pursed her lips and made a humming sound. "I don't know. I believe the intention, but it is yet to be seen if you can or will carry through. A life you don't choose for yourself—or even like—can be a very long and tedious life. But my parents would be happy. They're both eager for you to take over Riverlea . . . before Papa's ineptitude makes it a losing plantation."

"Oh, no!" Drew groaned.

Gwynne's dark eyes sparkled. "Why, Andrew, is that groan for Riverlea or yourself?"

"Gwynne, be quiet! Joanna will hear you."

"Wouldn't that be a pity. Why are you dishonest with her? You aren't with anyone else."

"Hush! Hello, Joanna," he said, and realized how guilty and stilted he sounded. Gwynne's perceptiveness disturbed him. He wasn't sure why he behaved and talked differently around Joanna. He simply didn't know how to be himself with her. Her sense of superiority overwhelmed him, yet he was committed to her by honorable agreement and could not betray his family. He walked a middle line as best he could with her. At least that way her seeming distaste for the way he lived in the Upcountry didn't become an open contention.

Joanna smiled tolerantly, a veil of reserve clouding her beautiful eyes. "How was your trip, Drew? Pleasant, I hope." She took his arm, stepping between him and her sister. "I believe Mama was looking for you, Gwynne. She would like some help arranging the bedrooms and luggage."

Gwynne looked mutinous. The expression on Joanna's face

didn't change. Her voice was calm and well modulated. "Run along now. Andrew is my concern."

Gwynne vanished into the house like magic, and Drew soon found himself in the cool, muted interior of Riverlea. Joanna had a way about her, he admitted. She had the ability to make anyone or anything seem petty and insignificant compared to what she was saying or doing. Without a look or a gesture or raising of her voice, she had dismissed her sister. And Drew knew that when she had satisfied herself with him, he too, would be dismissed.

Joanna called for cool drinks and a light repast. "I'm sure all of you must be hungry after such a long trip," she said, smiling first at Drew, then including Leo and Robert as they came into the drawing room and sat down. Other of the Mannings were entering the room. Joanna waited patiently, greeting each as he or she entered, and then gave the correct number of guests to the hovering servant. "It's good to see you again. I am eager to hear the news from Charles Town. Except for the kind people who pass by and occasionally stop long enough for a chat, we hear so little. And the newspapers are not nearly so informative as talking to someone. Do tell me, Cousin Eugenia, what has been playing at the Dock Street Theater. I have been longing to see a good performance, but Papa won't hear of leaving until the crop is in."

Drew sat back in his chair, watching and listening to the lively conversation among his cousins and gradually realizing he cared little about what was being said. After they had eaten and talked for a time, Ruth gently but firmly maneuvered the Charles Town Mannings from the room, leaving Drew and Joanna alone.

After an awkward silence Joanna took a deep breath and folded her hands on her lap. "How are your mother and father, Drew?"

"They're well, thank you, Joanna. Mother sends her love to you."

Joanna paused, then said, "I'm glad to hear they are well. We've been hearing stories of terrible goings-on in the Upcountry. We hear from you so infrequently, we weren't sure if you and your family were affected or not—nor did we know whether to believe all or any of what we heard."

"You can believe what you heard. If anything, I imagine you heard a prettied-up version of what has been taking place." He felt angry with her. How quick she was to lay guilt on him for all the things he neglected to do. He didn't write to her. He never had and didn't anticipate starting now. His voice grew more curt. "As to my family, we have been fortunate so far. Aside from the thievery of cattle and a couple of horses, Manning has been left untouched. But then we keep a guard round the clock—a heavily armed guard."

Joanna shuddered. "What a hideous way to live!"

Drew's anger rose another notch. "It's hardly by choice. We wouldn't be living that way at all if the Assembly would . . ." She wasn't listening; her silence was merely polite. He stopped talking mid-sentence and was rewarded with a weak smile from her. As she reached out to touch his hand sympathetically, he had an irrational urge to pull away. He felt uncouth around her and wanted to do uncouth things.

She looked at him with large eyes, her smile confidential. "Would you do me a service, Drew? I hate to ask, but since you will soon be master of Riverlea perhaps I can be forgiven for putting you to work. Would you supervise the sleeping arrangements of the men— George and Rob and Leo, I mean? There is always such confusion in their quarters. I'm sure you could manage far better than my parents."

Before he had a chance to answer, she had risen from her chair and offered him her arm. They walked together to the hallway and parted in silence, him to the task of seeing to sleeping arrangements and she to whatever it was she wished to do. He felt conveniently disposed of and it enraged him. Gwynne accused him of being less than honest with Joanna, but he had no idea how to be honest with her. There was no sharing between them, no common ground upon which they could meet. Joanna's life was a busy social whirl. As long as he did not deter her, she didn't care what he did or who he was. A husband was a social necessity. As long as he would serve that function for her, that was enough.

He walked around the dining room feeling the emptiness of it all. It bothered him greatly that he should feel as he did. Whenever he was at Riverlea he found himself withdrawn and avoiding people, a switch from his normal tendency. He couldn't understand why he was so different around Joanna. He puzzled this as he stood looking out the window at the beautifully manicured front lawn of Riverlea. It was lushly green and impeccably kept, yet Drew found it strangely irritating. Thinking of the lawn and questioning his own feelings of dissatisfaction, he decided he disliked intensely the perfection of Riverlea—and of Joanna. He also decided there must be something drastically wrong with him.

Joanna was beautiful and she was wealthy. Why was it so important that they connect on an emotional level? For two years now he had been putting off the wedding, hoping somehow his feelings would be resolved. First it had been postponed so that he could complete his education, then he claimed to need experience before he dared take over a plantation. Was he going to come up with another excuse this time? Restless, he got up and walked out onto the wide veranda.

Riverlea was beautiful. Only a fool wouldn't appreciate it. Only a fool wouldn't be champing at the bit to lay hands on this plantation. He stared out across the lawns, his eyes on the fields hazy in the distance.

"Are you making plans for the future or plans to avoid it?"

"Gwynne," Andrew said, a deep affection in his voice. "Has your mother never told you more bees can be caught with honey than vinegar?"

"But Drew darling, honey is so sticky and messy."

Drew looked at her but said nothing. Gwynne's dark hair shone in the sunlight. Her almond-shape eyes were deep blue and sparkling with life. She was sixteen and the youngest of the Templeton daughters. And the most difficult to manage. How often he had heard his cousin Ruth shake her head in amusement but also with real concern over what would become of Gwynne. Beautiful as she was, she would be a difficult daughter to marry off. She was irrepressible and headstrong. Her tongue could be as sharp and devastating as a barbed thicket. Over all she was too intelligent and too independent to be appealing. Drew had heard many young men claim to want to bed her but none who wanted to marry her. Gwynne represented too much of a burden. She was a woman who would demand too much personal involvement of her husband.

Gwynne studied the thoughtful look on Drew's face and knew he was thinking about her. "What are you thinking?" she asked.

He kept his eyes steadily on her and smiled. "That you are probably very much like Grandma was when she was young."

"Were you really thinking that?"

He nodded. "In a roundabout way, yes."

"Everyone else says I'm like Mama."

"You are, in a different way. I didn't mean your appearance, I meant the kind of person you are."

Gwynne looked off into the distance. "I wish—I wish I could lead a life like Cousin Elizabeth led. She and Cousin Walter were happy. You can see it—even now when she speaks of him, the happiness is still there."

"Theirs was not an easy life," Drew said mildly.

"It was a happy life," Gwynne insisted. "I'm not sure an easy life can be happy. It seems as though hard lives are those that hold the greatest reward. Perhaps it is because people have to try harder, or maybe they learn to value each other more because they are all they have. And once they learn that, nothing can ever take it from them."

"Who told you all that?"

"No one told me. I know love is supposed to be a debilitating thing in a marriage, but I don't believe it for a minute. I may not be very old, but I've seen quite a few things, and I've seen hard lives and easy ones, and easy ones don't make people happy. Cousin Eugenia has had an easy life and she's not happy. I've never seen her look as Cousin Elizabeth does. Joanna has had an easy life and she is never happy."

"You have an easy life," Drew said.

Gwynne, silent, looked at him for a moment, then her blue eyes filled with tears and her face crumpled. She turned and said before she ran into the house, "And I'm not happy!"

6

Andrew was thankful when early the next morning William Templeton had him rousted out of bed to go to the fields. Anything was better than a repeat of yesterday, and work in the rice paddies even sounded enticing. Perhaps he could make up there what he was unable to give the rest of the family. Somehow he had hurt Gwynne, and with Joanna he was at an impasse. He had no idea how they would manage once they were married. Joanna bored him, and he, by his very nature, offended her. He thought now, as he had so many other times, that Arthur would be so much better a choice for her. He thought of Leo and Robert; even George would be better suited to Joanna than he.

Fate was a strange mistress, he decided. He could never be what Joanna wanted and, he thought, worst of all, he didn't really care. He admired her beauty and her poise as one might admire a work of art, but he didn't care about her.

Gwynne had made him understand that, and he wasn't sure he thanked her for it. Yesterday evening, just before the family had gone upstairs to dress for dinner, Joanna had touched the fringe of his Upcountry tunic. She smiled at him, her eyes steady on his. "When in Rome, Drew—I do so love seeing you at your elegant best."

Drew had said nothing, but Gwynne, who had been standing a few feet away, was seething. "Why do you let her treat you like a naughty child? Why do you tolerate it? I don't understand you, Drew. I don't! You seem so strong and capable, except when it comes to my sister. You let her walk all over you. She makes a fool of you. Why do you allow it?"

"What she says makes no difference," Drew had said.

Gwynne put her hands on her hips, her blue eyes flashed angrily. "It should make a difference! The words and thoughts of one's loved one are supposed to make a difference. Does that mean you don't love Joanna, Drew? Will she ever make a difference to you?"

She had stood waiting for an answer until he had lowered his head, muttering almost unintelligibly that it was none of her concern. He had been embarrassed and ashamed then, but she hadn't finished with him yet.

"Why aren't you man enough to tell my parents you don't want to marry her? Does Riverlea mean that much to you? Will you sacrifice yourself and my sister—and perhaps others—just to gain control of this plantation?"

He had gotten angry then. "It isn't that simple, little girl. It is much—"

"Little girl! You're either blind or stupid, Drew Manning. I haven't been a little girl for a long time. And I have the courage to say what I think. I don't hide behind things like family duty, and I don't adhere to promises that someone else made for me unless I want to. Where's your backbone? All my life I've admired you and looked up to you. Was I wrong, Drew? Can anyone look up to you?" She had turned sharply and walked up the stairs. She hadn't spoken to him the rest of the evening, and he hadn't been able to look her straight in the eye. He had a feeling that this trip to Riverlea wasn't going to be one of his more memorable ones, unless he could redeem himself by helping William with the rice.

William Templeton was a red-faced, bluff man filled with a sense of duty and an abiding awareness of his own temporality. Generally he was a pleasureless man. Drew often thought William felt that pleasure was somehow tinged with evil. Despite this he was good-natured and good-hearted for the most part, and Andrew liked him. He also felt sorry for William. No matter how hard he tried or how long he worked at it, William would never be a planter. He simply did not have a feel for the crops or the soil that nurtured them. William's ineptitude added to Andrew's reluctance to tell him that he did not want to marry Joanna or to be master of Riverlea. It seemed that whatever William attempted or planned went awry. In Andrew, William thought he'd acquire the son that had been denied him in his marriage.

"Rice day Thursday," William said in his booming voice. "I'm an old fool, and that's a fact. Anyone who thinks workdays like these are the best days of the year has got to be a fool, wouldn't you say, Drew?"

"Then there are two of us riding out this morning who are fools, sir."

"You feel the same as I," William said with satisfaction. "I always knew it. I may not be the best planter, but I know men. Birds of a feather recognize each other, or something like that. I knew you for a planter when you were just a little tad. Told your father then that you'd be the man to take over my estate if Ruth never gave me a son. That's how the marriage agreement came about."

Andrew looked out across the fields, Gwynne's words pricking his mind, making him feel guilty. He could see the rise and fall of black backs as the men moved through the fields with their small reap hooks, and with each wave of rhythmic motion he said to himself, I should tell him now, I should tell him now.

"Amos has them all hard at work," William said, jolting him back to attention. "He's the best driver I've ever had. Tell the truth, without Amos, I don't think we'd make a shilling here. Amos is the heart of Riverlea. Remember that, Drew. A good driver is hard to come by. Treat 'em good and make sure they're always in good health. Best investment you'll ever make and worth every copper spent. Now Amos there is a rare one among the rare ones. I made him patroon of my pettiauger as well. I've never yet had a crop wet when it reached the market—not, that is, since Amos came to me. And you know how late I always am getting my crops out."

"I remember you telling me about him last year," Drew said.

William gave one of his rare laughs. "And I'll tell you about him the next year and the year after that, no doubt. When I have an enthusiasm about someone, I tell the stories until my whole family is despairing of ever again hearing news from me."

"Has he started a family?"

"Not yet," William said, his voice again warming up with interest. "I hadn't found the mate for him. For a man like Amos, it had to be an equally superior woman. Richard Murdis tells me he has just the woman I'm looking for. He's sending her to me—ought to be in Charles Town on the next packet from Barbados." William leaned over and grasped Drew's arm. "Had to pay the devil's price for her. She'd better be all he says."

"What was that?"

"He made me promise to send the second man-child Amos and Orelia bring forth. Don't like that kind of price. Somehow it doesn't seem right. Maybe the old goat will die before I have to pay off, or maybe the cub will be sickly and I can pay him some other way."

"Why did you agree to it if you don't want to pay in that manner?"

"Too much drink and too little sense," Williams said, then spurred his horse, cantering the last hundred yards to the field where Amos had the men reaping the rice.

The rich field looked like a golden lake. The heavy heads of the rice stalks bent and swayed in the gentle breeze. Nearer in, where the men were working, Andrew almost hated to see the golden shafts fall to the knife.

The rice fields were laid out in sections. The fields that had been flooded earlier were now drained, and the laborers moved methodically with reaping hooks, cutting down the rice. The long, golden heads were carefully laid on the stubble to dry.

The sun beat down on their backs, and Andrew soon found himself shirtless as were the slaves. He worked in the cuts alongside the Negroes, claiming to William he needed the knowledge he'd gain. The truth was that Drew would never be the kind of planter William was. He'd always be at the side of his men, working with them, knowing firsthand their job. He'd always be his own best laborer. William rode the perimeter on horseback, talking, encouraging, suggesting, imagining he was part of the work but touching the soil only in his imagination. He rode up beside Drew. "I love this. You'd think, feeling as I do, I'd have a better hand at it," he said, looking at the sky. "There's nothing on earth like knowing you've got your hands in God's soil and are reaping a harvest. If I'd allow it, Ruth would be here, too. Good woman, Ruth is. That's something you ought to note, Drew. You can tell more about a girl by looking at the mother than you can from anything the girl will tell you."

Evasively Drew said, "I see Cousin Ruth as she must have been every time I'm with Gwynne. Meg, too."

"But not Joanna," William said.

"Uh—not so much as the others, sir," Drew said, and quickly picked up the reap hook.

"I'm not a fool, boy; you needn't try to hide the truth from me. She's my daughter. I know every contrary habit she has. And I know Joanna tends to seem a bit cool, but it's all a pretense—the mark of a modest woman! Mark my words, that girl has never yet been awakened to the ways of a man. By heaven, it's innocence you're seeing. Once you marry her and bed her, we'll see some big changes, I'll wager." For the second time that day William Templeton laughed. "You'll teach my cool little Joanna a thing or two. Be a joy to see her cheeks pink and her eyes alight in that special way. There's nothing so beautiful as a breeding woman. I'm hungering for grandchildren, Drew."

Drew started to answer him, then stopped. After a long pause he said, "I don't know what to say to you, sir. I know what you want and are hoping for, but I don't think I could change Joanna if I spent the rest of my life trying."

"That doesn't mean . . . ." William's face turned red. "I have your father's honor-bound word on the marriage agreement."

"I don't mean anything, sir, except that I don't think I could change Joanna. I would never abuse my father's honor."

Mollified but wary, William went back to his overseeing. But he didn't miss that the cutting course that Drew followed took Drew farther away from him, ending the possibility of more talk unless he rode through uncut rice to Drew. William watched Drew and admitted silently that he and Joanna were a mismatch. But Joanna was his daughter, and she'd need a strong man. And Drew would make an excellent husband for her and a reliable master of Riverlea.

The men stayed in the field until it was too dark to work. The plantation routine shifted to accommodate the harvesting. Andrew and William ate a nourishing meal and shortly went to bed. The normal socializing was gone from Riverlea and would remain absent until the rice was on its way to market.

Andrew and William were awake and on their way to breakfast before the sun rose the following morning. The house was quiet and sleeping, all but the men and the servants who made sure they were well fed and ready for the day. In the muted sunrise Andrew and William rode across the lawns to the rice fields.

One of the Negroes finished the small amount of cutting that had been left from the previous day. The rest of the men, under Amos's direction, began to collect the rice and tie it into sheaves. Drew watched for several minutes as the Negroes speedily tied the sheaves together, using a wisp of the rice itself to accomplish the tie. He was not so dextrous as they, but he determined that by the end of the day he would be. He moved along the rows, his back bobbing up and down to the rhythm of the songs the blacks sang and the tempo of their movements. Amos came near him on his regular patrol of the fields.

"Bettah res', suh," Amos said.

"No thanks, Amos, I'm not tired yet."

"You res' now, suh," Amos said with more authority. "Ah doan means to be disrespec'ful suh, but Ah says you res' or you woan be wuth nuthin' near the en' o' the day."

Drew grinned at him and stopped working. "You're right, Amos. And so is Mr. Templeton. You're a rare man and a good driver."

Amos's face broke into a wide smile. "Ah thanks ya, suh." Straightening his already ramrod back and squaring his massive shoulders, Amos walked on, watching the men, selecting those he wanted to rest, placing others in the line and prodding those who moved too slowly. He patiently instructed the inexperienced workers and the young ones who were harvesting for the first time. Sheaving rice was an art, and Amos was a tireless teacher.

At the end of the long day the rice was all cut and bound, waiting for the following morning to be put into the small cocks to dry.

On Monday the rice was loaded onto the flatboats, commonly called pettiaugers. The pettiaugers came in a variety of shapes, sizes and styles ranging from twenty feet to eighty feet long and from ten to twelve feet wide. They were guided by poles and steered by one large oar at the stern of the boat. Occasionally the pettiaugers were equipped with sails, but William Templeton had only his slaves to man the poles and his trusted Amos to guide them through the changing channels of the river. Amos's keen eyes and his knowledge of the river led them past the shoals and snags that were part of every trip to market and the time during which the rice was in the greatest danger of being ruined. The rice had to be loaded properly and kept dry, and the trip had to be made before the seasonal rains caught them. With Riverlea rice that was a touchy situation, for William Templeton seldom had his crop harvested as it should be in October.

Drew looked at the sky, which had begun to look threatening, and then at Amos.

"If dey's any way we kin do it, we'll get there bone dry. Onliest thing kin stop us is if God doan wan' us to git there."

William walked up to his patroon before the man boarded the pettiauger. He took Amos's hand and shook it warmly. "Godspeed to you, Amos."

Amos smiled, his teeth showing strikingly white. "We get this rice to market without a drop o' moisture touch it, Mastah. Doan you worries. Amos tek care o' Ribberlea rice."

Those of them who stayed behind were rewarded for their hard work with a festival to precede the three days of horseracing and the tournament the Templetons would host. All work on Riverlea came to a halt for the day. The white members of the plantation became onlookers as the Negroes sang and danced and participated in games and feasted on cooking that came straight from Ruth Templeton's kitchen.

It was no surprise to Andrew to see his grandmother behind one of the long tables of food Ruth had had set up to serve the black workers. As always Elizabeth was smiling and talking to anyone who came up to her. Beside her was Gwynne. As though the sight of her reminded him that he was looking at the wrong woman, he looked around the yard for Joanna. He didn't see her but caught sight of George carrying a tray of food to one of the tables.

"George, have you seen Joanna?" he asked.

"A lot more than you have, Cousin. She's inside with Bethany and Rob. I left them mid-duet."

"Thank you—I'd better go find her," Drew said, his feeling of guilt already muted and his enthusiasm lacking.

George laughed. "You're hopeless. I don't know why she still wants to marry you."

"Perhaps she doesn't," he said flippantly and headed toward the house at a run, realizing halfway across the expanse of lawn that his efforts would bring him into the house heated and probably sweaty. He slowed to a walk.

Joanna stood beside the piano, her brow slightly furrowed as she concentrated on teaching Bethany an intricate arpeggio. Rob stood to the side, watching her with unabashed admiration.

Drew remained at the far end of the room, looking at them. Joanna is lovely, he thought. She wore a chintz cotton gown with a rich lavender skirt that she and Elizabeth had designed and made. Her hair was swept atop her head with two rolls at each side. Her cap was of lace. Again he thought she looked like a painting, not a hair out of place or a wrinkle to be found in her attire. He decided then that one of the things he would do when they were married was to have her captured on canvas. Joanna Templeton would be painted as he thought she ought to be. He daydreamed for a moment, thinking about the artists with whose work he was familiar. This was a decision not to be hurried.

"Why, Drew, when did you come in? I thought perhaps Daddy would keep you busy with plantation work the whole time you are here."

"Ahh, my cousin, the stranger," Rob said.

Andrew immediately felt awkward. "I know . . . I've been neglectful of . . ."

"Aren't you always?" Rob said.

Joanna moved around the piano. "Nonsense," she said sharply. "I was not criticizing. We are both mature and know what life on a plantation demands. I expected nothing more. This is as it should be."

"Leo said Drew works more than he should. More than a master should," Bethany said. "He says that a gentleman owner should never be seen working in the fields with his laborers."

"Leo knows nothing about a plantation," Joanna said icily, then added, "But he does have a point, albeit a mild one. You do tend to overdo, Drew. No one expects you to strip down and become a slave yourself. Once we are married, I'll see to it that you're dressed properly and know exactly what to do and what not."

"Bethany and Rob, would you excuse us, please? Joanna, I'd like to walk with you in the gardens," Drew said.

Joanna laughed lightly, allowing her hand to touch his sleeve. She bit her lower lip, looking at him for a moment. "How sweet you are to think of it, but I can't possibly, Drew. The sun is still high. My skin is delicate—it would injure me." She laughed and looked at Bethany. "He knows so little about women. I find it terribly naive and charming, don't you?" Then she looked at Drew from the corner of her eye, adding coyly, "But you'll learn. I'll teach you."

"My grandmother is out in the hot sun. She seems to be faring well. Your own mother seems to be all right and so does your sister Gwynne . . . and Meg, too, just went out."

"But I am by far the fairest of the family. You certainly can't expect me to do something merely because my mother or my sisters do," she said with a trace of anger showing in her voice. It was just enough to warn Drew that now was the time to make amends.

Drew stood stubbornly, his jaw set, his brown eyes flashing anger signals, too. Rob cleared his throat. Both Joanna and Drew looked at him as though he were a stranger, an intruder.

"Bethany, I believe we promised Mama we'd visit her in her sitting room, didn't we? Will you excuse us, Joanna, Drew?" Rob bowed slightly, grabbed Bethany's hand and hurried out of the room.

Joanna and Drew stared at each other for a moment; then Drew gave an imperceptible shrug. "Perhaps you are too fair to be in the sun. I wouldn't know about such things."

"No, you don't," Joanna said in a milder but patronizing tone. "A wise man knows to keep quiet when he is ignorant on a subject."

"And only petty people make an issue of another's ignorance," Drew snapped back before he realized what he had said. He looked stricken. "I didn't mean that. You know I didn't. I was angry. Please accept my apology."

Joanna sat down, her back straight.

"All right, perhaps if we change the subject entirely," Drew said.

"To what?" Joanna said.

"Well, us . . . When I was in Charles Town this time, I heard Christopher Gadsen speak. He is a most eloquent man. I think many of the things he says at least bear thought, although he still remains somewhat extreme in my view."

Joanna, still piqued, refused to look at him. "He is *very* extreme, a radical at best and perhaps a revolutionary. He is dangerous—a rabble rouser. Men like him should be hanged for the traitors they are. He's an ingrate without the slightest comprehension of or appreciation for the king. We won't speak of him. I won't have it in my house."

"Suppose I was to tell you that I admire the man?"

"Haven't you already?"

Drew's shoulders slumped as he walked to the window. "Is there nothing we can talk about, Joanna?" he asked tiredly.

"There doesn't seem to be, does there? I saw a production of *The Oracle* at the Dock Street Theater when Daddy took us there last. We even got to meet some of the performers. Have you been to the theater lately, Drew?"

He didn't answer. She glanced up to see him staring out the window. "Drew?" He still didn't answer. Joanna's hands clenched in her lap. She repeated loudly, "Drew, have you been to the theater lately?"

"No!" he said, quickly snapping back to attention. "Are you sure you won't come for a walk with me?"

"You are just itching to be out of doors, aren't you? Not for one moment can you remain in a parlor and act like a gentleman!"

"I think I'll go back to the festival. I wish you'd change your mind and come with me, if only for a short time. There is a cloud cover now . . . your skin should be safe."

"You are an utterly crude, thoughtless boor!" she stormed.

Andrew walked toward her. "Yes, I am. You might give it some thought, Joanna, because I won't change after we're married any more than you will."

"You would if I wanted you to!"

"I don't want to, Joanna."

Her mouth set tight. "*I* want you to!"

7

Andrew left Joanna standing in the parlor, glaring after him as he went outside to join the others as they watched the blacks at their holiday games, but he couldn't regain the spirit of it. Uncustomarily Drew Manning found himself outside the activities, unable to bring himself to be part of the merrymaking.

His cousins stood in clusters together, laughing and enjoying themselves. His grandmother animatedly pressed second helpings of food on the Negroes. She waved at him, indicating he should join her, but he didn't. Even Elizabeth couldn't stir him from the dulled and confused feeling of anger Joanna had left him with.

Elizabeth kept watching Drew from the corner of her eye. Finally unable to stand it any longer, she left her post at the long table and went after him as he began to walk across the lawn toward the barren fields.

"Drew," she called, and had to repeat it twice before he heard her.

Drew walked back to her, took her arm and began walking again slowly. "You're not afraid of the sun on your skin, are you, Grandma?" he asked.

Elizabeth looked at him in puzzlement for a moment. "Well, it certainly does it no good. If I had good sense I'd be carrying a parasol, and when I was younger, I imagine I would have been concerned about the sun."

He looked away and nodded.

"Surely that isn't what you and Joanna argued about this time."

"What makes you think we argued? Everything is as it was with Joanna and me."

Elizabeth laughed. "Oh, Drew, what am I to do with you? You don't even know to whom you should be loyal and to whom you owe no loyalty."

Drew sighed. "Grandma, if you don't mind, I'd rather not hear about any more of my failings. I seem to have more of them than I dreamed possible."

"I apologize, dear. I should have known from the look of you that Joanna had been critical. May I give you my opinion on this once more though?"

"Of course, but I can't promise to be a good listener."

"You might be surprised, for what I want to say is that I believe you are not ready to commit yourself to Joanna. I don't pretend to understand what is holding you back, but I feel there is something which is probably important to you. But the Templetons are eager to have this wedding."

"I can't marry her right now, Grandma."

"I know that, Drew, and I think you should leave—immediately. Go back home, think it over alone without others pressing you for answers."

"They expect me to stay for at least another week . . . I'd be very rude."

Elizabeth squeezed his arm and smiled. "No ruder than you're being now, and I'm sure you can concoct an important-sounding reason for the necessity of your hasty departure. If need be we can arrange to have a letter delivered to you, calling you home."

"I'd like to go home and do as you say."

"Then do it. Tell Ruth and William you are leaving at first light tomorrow."

They turned back to the house. At the veranda Elizabeth turned and hugged her favorite grandson. "God be with you, Drew, and keep you safe." She hurriedly left him and went into the house.

Drew went in search of William and Ruth. Both of them were disappointed and upset but accepted to a point the fact that it was necessary for him to be with the Regulators in the Upcountry. They did manage, however, to obtain a promise from him that he would stay three more days and participate in the tournament.

"If you leave before that, Drew, it will cause so much disagreeable talk," Ruth said. "Joanna will undoubtedly be the queen, and everyone knows that if you enter the horserace, you'll win. It is as if you are handing her to any man who wins the race. Oh, Drew, you and Joanna must make definite plans. We simply cannot have things continuing as they are now." Ruth put her hands to her face, then down at her sides. "There, I've said it. I apologize, William, I know it isn't my place, but . . . I just couldn't keep still any longer."

"Well, Drew?" William said.

"I'll stay for the tournament," he said, then moved uncomfortably from foot to foot. "I have nothing to say about our plans. I know how awkward it is, but I don't know what to do about it."

"Set a date," William said bluntly.

Drew's face turned crimson, and his voice was thick in his throat. "I can't do that, sir . . . not yet."

The tournament was set for the following day. That evening Riverlea began filling with friends who came to William Templeton's tournament every year. The stables were the most active part of the plantation, for the tournament was a favorite place to show off a man's best horses.

Committed to his promise and determined to make the best of it, Drew joined the men at the stables. He had to admit he wouldn't have liked missing this. Excitement was rampant as each man touted his horse. Money was held and wagers made in amounts that made Drew shudder. He walked to the stall that housed Prince William, the best horse William Templeton had ever raised, and the horse Drew would ride in the race. He edged his way through the milling group of men to stand by the horse. He let Prince William nuzzle him and find a sweet tucked in his pocket, then quickly looked around guiltily, because William Templeton did not approve of such things.

"I think I'll tell Daddy," a voice said from behind him.

Drew jumped and spun around to face Gwynne's smiling, impish face. "Lord, you frightened me," he said, and wiped his hand across his brow.

"That's because you have such a guilty conscience. He's beautiful, isn't he?" she said, touching the horse's velvety nose. Prince William was nearly black, with highlights of chestnut showing in his silky coat. "I know you'll win. Prince will do anything you ask of him."

Drew looked down at her bemused. "How would you know?

Don't tell me Cousin William allows you to ride him. This horse will never see a sidesaddle in all his days."

"Of course not!" Gwynne said, insulted. "But that doesn't mean I haven't ridden him." She smiled up at him. "Daddy doesn't know everything I do. And I could tell you a thing or two about this horse that would be helpful to you."

"Such as?"

"Such as that he'll ignore a horse coming up on him from the inside but will run harder if one comes from the outside."

"How would you know that?" Drew asked, and tucked the information away for use in the race.

Gwynne laughed but said nothing.

"One of the grooms told you."

"Would you like to find out how I know?" she asked, looking at him sideways.

Andrew couldn't help but laugh. "That's why I asked you. Are you going to tell me?"

"No, but I will. Meet me here tonight after the others have gone to bed if you really want to know." She turned and walked away from him.

"Gwynne!"

"That's all I have to say," she said merrily, and disappeared among the people standing near an Arabian John Stollen had brought and claimed could beat anything on four legs.

Drew stood by Prince William, looking after her, knowing she wouldn't really be at the stables later and enchanted by the prospect that she might be.

It was nearly midnight before Riverlea quieted down and Drew could leave the bachelors' quarters to which he and his cousins had been relegated with the influx of new guests. Riverlea glistened in the pale light of the moon. He was surprised to find that he was excited as he walked to the stables and knew that if she wasn't there he was going to feel disappointed and alone. Of all his cousins, Gwynne was the only one he truly missed when he was away. He had fun with her. She was full of life and talk and not in the least afraid of a little deviltry or the consequences that might come.

He walked into the dimly lit stables and saw and heard no one. Slowly he walked the length of the well-kept, sparkling white line of stalls. Near the tack room sat a contented and intent groom. Squatting, his back braced against the tack room wall, the young black boy's complete attention was on a basket of chicken and corn bread, delicate petit-fours and some fancy-looking things Drew assumed were the shrimp he'd had at dinner.

"Got a friend in the kitchen?" Drew asked as he stopped in front of the boy.

The boy broke into a huge grin and scrambled to his feet. "Ah sure does. She gwine mek me fat an' happy. Miz Gwynne waitin' fo' you right ovah theah," he said, pointing deeper into the stable.

Drew looked and saw nothing but an unlit cavern. Then he heard a giggle and walked toward the sound.

"What are you doing here in the dark?" he asked.

She took his arm and moved toward Prince William's stall. "I wanted to see you come in without your seeing me."

"Why? You're the one who said we should meet here."

"I wanted to see if you thought I'd really be here. And you didn't, did you, Drew. Tell the truth. You thought I wasn't here."

"I'm here . . . but I don't see any reason that you should be. You don't have to come to the stable to tell me how you know so much about Prince."

"That's true, so there must be some other reason."

He stopped and pulled away from her. "You're not pulling another of your pranks on Joanna? Gwynne, if you are, I'm leaving right now. I'm already in enough trouble with your sister and your parents."

"No, I'm not," she said coldly.

"Then what?"

"A ride. You and me, on Prince and his favorite lady."

"Now? It's the middle of the night. You can't take that horse out now, before a race, and in the dark. Your daddy'd hang us. I think he has half of Riverlea bet on Prince."

"Daddy always goes overboard. But you wanted to know how I knew so much about Prince—this is how. I ride him quite often at night, and on the track. Kofi usually provides me with competition, but since you're here and haven't really ridden Prince that often, I thought I'd give you some competition tonight." She looked at the stunned expression on his face. He said nothing. "But if you're afraid of displeasing my daddy, or worried about a woman racing and perhaps bea—"

"Now, wait a minute . . ." Drew said, and before he could finish, Gwynne was laughing happily and opening Prince's stall.

The horse knew what was coming and whinnied to her as he pranced, saddled and ready, from the stall.

"I'll get Gray Lady. She hasn't the stamina of Prince, but in three quarters of a mile, she can give him a good run, and if I can get her on the inside, she can beat him. It'll be good practice for you."

Drew shook his head and watched her as she hurried down the row to Gray Lady's stall. It was only then that he realized she wasn't wearing skirts. He felt his face flush as he stared, unable to take his eyes off her. She was wearing men's riding breeches that fit skin-tight across a well rounded, firm little rump. Her waist was nipped in and banded by a wide black belt. As she turned, he saw that under her jacket was a man's shirt buttoned only to the top of her cleavage. He had never seen a woman dressed like this. Embarrassed, he looked away from her, his eyes seeking the pitch blackness of the hayloft above. Then, quickly, as though he had no control, he looked at his cousin again and felt stirring within him something that left him without thought of the midnight race or the race to come in the tournament.

Gwynne released Gray Lady's reins and walked up to Drew, so close her breasts touched his chest, and her upraised mouth was but inches from his. Drew stood still, barely breathing. She raised herself on her toes and kissed him, her lips lingering at the side of his mouth. Drew put his hands around her waist. Before he had time to think of Joanna or any of the other reasons he shouldn't be with Gwynne, his mouth was on hers and they were locked together tightly. Gwynne's lips were sweet and full against his.

She put her arms around his neck, then slowly moved them across his shoulders and down his arms, moving slightly away from him. She was standing firmly, on her own and away from him, before he realized what he had been doing. Her eyes were wide with surprise and a warmth that made him want to take her in his arms again. He stood looking at her on the verge of embarrassment, yet his desire still rode high. Neither of them spoke or moved. The moment of stillness and indecision held long enough for thoughts of Joanna to intrude upon both of them.

Gwynne moved slightly, her body swaying back and forth in con-
flict. Her cheeks were highly colored. Her voice was husky and weak
when she finally spoke awkwardly. "We'd better take the horses to
the track . . . we can't . . ."

Drew stepped up to her, taking her by the shoulders. He pressed
her against him. "I'm sorry, Gwynne. I shouldn't have touched
you."

Her face was buried in his shirt front. "I don't want you to be
sorry. I just didn't expect . . . I didn't think . . . Drew, why did you
kiss me that way?"

Drew's body stiffened, and he released her. His laugh was tense.
"I have no answer for that, Gwynne. Only a humble apology, and
my word that it'll never happen again or be mentioned between us
or anyone else."

Gwynne kept her head down. Her blue eyes watered, and she
squeezed them shut before he could see. She wanted to ask him
more, press him for answers she knew were there and was afraid he
would never realize unless he spoke them aloud, but she couldn't.
She stood very still for a moment, regaining her composure, then
she turned from him, took Gray Lady's reins and led the horse from
the stables.

Drew followed her, his own eyes showing a sadness that matched
hers. He felt a sense of loss and a hungry emptiness but attributed it
to shame and the price of yet another of his failings. If he married
Joanna, Gwynne would be his sister-in-law, and what he had done
tonight was unforgivable, something he would have to remember
and regret every time he saw her. Yet the sweetness of her mouth,
the clean, flower scent of her lingered and haunted.

She knew as much about her father's horses as she claimed, and
he learned much about Prince William. Tomorrow when he ran his
preliminary heat, he had no doubt that if he won, it would be due to
Gwynne's teaching him how to handle the horse and showing him
Prince's particular whims.

The Templeton household awakened the following morning to
trumpet blasts signaling the opening of the tournament. Drew
joined the family, escorting Joanna and making himself obvious as
her fiancé. He greeted friends and neighbors of the Templetons,
smiled until his cheeks ached and listened guiltily to the sly, often

shy hints the women made and the thinly veiled comments of the men regarding the approaching wedding. Gwynne stood with her family as well, avoiding contact with Drew's eyes, looking pale and unhappy.

Drew remained with the Templetons until the first game was announced and then excused himself, saying that he wanted to participate. Joanna looked at him with raised eyebrows, knowing as well as he did that he'd participate in anything, even bob for apples with the children, if it would release him from the constant questions about the wedding.

By late afternoon Drew had climbed ropes with his cousins in hearty competition, run obstacle courses and was tired, hot and feeling worse than he had earlier. He kept avoiding Joanna, and there was no doubt that Gwynne, too, was unhappy with him. The Templeton elders' looks were turning from mild annoyance over delay to real consternation. He was nearly certain that the only thing restraining William Templeton from giving him a thorough talking to was the horserace still to be run.

More from a sense of duty than any feeling for her, Drew made one more attempt to establish some warmth and understanding between himself and Joanna. He could barely stand the idea of running the race to claim her as his queen when he didn't like being in the same room with her. He wasn't sure it was possible, but he had to try. Even as children he and Joanna had never been natural friends. She was too finicky, too cautious, too prepared to please others, too aware of what others thought. She lacked the deviltry and independence that Drew throve on. And she disapproved of him. Instead of making him wish to do better by her, it drove him to extremes of rebellion and distaste.

After the obstacle race he went into the bachelors' quarters to freshen up, then remained near the house waiting for Joanna to seek out the coolness of the interior. Even with her broad parasol, he knew she would not remain in the sun with the others for long. He sat on a bench near a trio of magnolia and tried to quell the urge to walk over to Joanna and her parents right in the midst of the festivities and tell them he'd never be master of Riverlea or Joanna's husband. His fantasies grew quite elaborate as he began to embellish them. Often he had thought that his discomfort with her was enough to justify doing exactly what he was dreaming of. But that had been a long time ago. Joseph Manning had thought it highly amusing that his fourteen-year-old son was thinking about the characteristics Joanna would have as a wife and was impressed that a boy of that age could or would think so far ahead. Accordingly he began to talk to Andrew about his responsibility to the family, to his nation and to himself to be a success.

Joseph had instilled in the twenty-two-year-old Andrew a sense of duty and of destiny. Andrew still could not put it all into words, nor did he understand many of the things he sensed, but he felt them and could identify those things important to him by the feel. Joanna was not one of the people who fit into the pattern his thought-feeling gave to him. No matter how hard he tried, she remained alien to him. But still the sense of duty kept him from cutting the arrangement off entirely. The price he'd have to pay for abandoning the proposed marriage came in the form of his family's disgrace, the castigation that polite society would level at him and his father for such a breach and the deep humiliation he would render to Joanna herself. He couldn't do it, except in daydreams.

He stood up as soon as he saw Joanna enter the house. He ran across the space between the two buildings and walked briskly to the morning room, where he knew he'd find her.

He knocked at the open door and entered before she had a moment to grant him permission. She smiled tightly at him. "Your action has made the knock superfluous, Andrew."

"Were you going to refuse me entrance?"

"No, but—"

"Then there was no call to wait for you to say what I already knew you were going to say. Now that we have that clarified, come for a walk with me."

She gave him a look of incredulity. "I have just come in, Andrew."

"There are things you and I need to discuss."

She sighed, frowning at him. "I can see I'll be hard pressed to accomplish anything of value after we're married."

"Accomplish?" he repeated sarcastically.

She fixed him with an icy stare. "Yes, accomplish. I am an excellent hostess, and contrary to your narrow view of the world, it is not merely a matter of smiling prettily and sipping tea."

"Yes, I understand that," he said with no patience and less understanding. "But there are important matters, and there will always be another tea and another party." He paced in front of her, his hands gesturing uselessly. "It would be different if something were accomplished.

"Are you suggesting—"

"I'm suggesting that all this time and energy be spent in something more useful—something that could have meaning beyond the moment—something for our future."

She laughed softly, tiredly. "What might that be? Shall I blister my hands learning to wield a hoe? Had you one iota of the understanding you pride yourself with, you'd know that in the hands of an astute woman, all secrets private, political, discreet and indiscreet come forth through judicious entertaining. A hoe in my hand will get you nothing that you'd not do better hiring a thick-skulled buck to perform."

"You're an obstinant b-b . . ."

"Bitch? Is that the word you're groping for?"

"I wasn't groping for anything, Joanna," he said, running his hand through his hair. He walked away from her, trying to regain his composure. She wouldn't defeat him that easily. "I came in here, Joanna," he said with deliberate calm, "to talk with you. I'll be leaving as soon as the tournament is over. I didn't want to leave you like this—I thought it would be well to reach—to try to reach an amicable . . ." He threw up his hands. "We'll be in public, Joanna. People know we're to be married, and we can't even talk privately."

She shook her head, her own agitation quieter now. "Why don't you just tell Daddy you won't marry me? You could do that."

"Why don't you tell him? You feel the same way. You don't want to marry me—we're both honoring a contract made when we were too young to know anything about it."

"That isn't true! That's your truth, but only partly mine. I would marry you tomorrow—today if we could."

Andrew looked at her wide-eyed. "Why? Joanna, I know you don't like the way of me—you don't love me. Whenever we talk, all you can think of is how you will change me. Why do you now say you want to marry me?"

Joanna laughed, and this time he could hear the unmistakable bitterness clearly. "Because before I was old enough to understand anything of marriage, or womanhood, or the desire to achieve something on my own, my father sold me to your father to become your mate. Now it is likely that you are the only man I could ever marry."

"There are dozens of men—men I know—who would give their right arms to court you."

She looked at him for a moment, then looked down at her hands on her lap. "And then perhaps I could pick one of them—provided he met my Daddy's approval, and was able to run Riverlea and be called the head of the Templeton household—the Riverlea manor lord. Tell me, Andrew, do you really think any of my imaginary suitors would be any better than you, or would they be more suited to me than you are?"

Drew was shocked, and for the first time he felt some of Joanna's inner pain, which she so carefully kept wrapped and locked away from others. He touched her arm gently, feelings of protectiveness rising in him. "You must feel as though you are being sold or traded for the benefit of Riverlea," he said.

She smiled then. "If I am being traded or sold, then you are being bought. At least we have that in common." She looked up at him, their eyes meeting. "It is something, isn't it, Drew?"

"It's not enough, Joanna. I'm grateful for your telling me. We've never before managed to talk like this, but it isn't enough to carry us through the years. It doesn't change how we feel or who we are. I am a—a planter—no, I'm a farmer, and whatever else may be with us, you don't—can't—love the things in life that I do."

Joanna looked at him steadily and coldly. "You're wrong, Andrew. What you are won't interfere with our marriage at all. I don't really care what you do or what you love—or who, as long as appearances are kept up. That, more than anything we might have in common, will become our strength in this marriage. We can meet the expectations of my family, which I suppose will be one or two children, preferably a male, and then you are free to do whatever you wish—and so am I."

"You'd live like that? You would settle for . . . so little?"

"It would be enough. It would have to be. It's all I have. I don't . . . I don't want to become the Templeton spinster. I couldn't stand that. I'd hate being poor old Aunt Joanna to the whole family, living alone in my provided suite of rooms, seeing all the sly smiles, the looks that are meant to be behind one's back but are always seen, the pity, the talk, the endless talk of how you wouldn't marry me. They would all speculate about what was so wrong with me that even Riverlea wasn't bait enough to force Andrew Manning to take Joanna Templeton to wife. I'd take my own life before I'd let that happen to me, Andrew. I won't be left behind. I won't be destroyed. I'd leave you behind first to answer the question why I'd prefer death to being your wife."

Andrew put his head in his hands. "I had no idea how miserable you are."

"Let's not get maudlin. I am not miserable, and you have no cause for concern in marrying me. You have nothing to lose. You'll gain Riverlea. I come with a large dowry—more than you deserve. And you'll have most of the freedom you now have. I ask only that appearances be kept up."

"Is that what you think of me?"

"What does it matter what I think of you? Would you care?"

Andrew shook his head and sat in silence for a long time. "I don't know what we should do, Joanna."

She picked up some embroidery and began to work. "We'll do what we are expected to do." She looked straight at him. "I shall begin to talk of our coming marriage and shall begin preparation for it." She offered her cheek. He hesitated for a moment, then kissed her and walked out the door.

The following day Drew raced Prince William and won. When he walked to the stand to claim his queen, he felt a sense of protectiveness he had never before felt about Joanna. The pomp of the ending ceremony of the tournament fostered his glowing thoughts. Instead of the cool, self-sufficient woman that Joanna appeared to be waiting for him on her tournament queen's chair, Andrew claimed a young woman caught in an arranged marriage which she was determined to make work. She had courage and a deep sense of family duty, and she was devoted to his success as master of Riverlea.

That afternoon, with congratulations buzzing in his ears and merrymaking keeping his mind occupied, he could even imagine himself as master of Riverlea. Joanna, too, seemed to loosen up with all the attention centered on them. She danced all evening with him, not complaining of fatigue or duty. She was beautiful in her virginal white gown. Her smile was offered to all the neighboring planters. She carried on pleasant conversation with their wives and daughters and kept an alert eye on the household as well. The punch bowl was never empty, nor was there ever an empty platter on the collation table. Joanna was a superb hostess, and Drew got a healthy supply of compliments regarding her. Riverlea would be his, and so would Joanna. Now, he asked himself, wasn't that enough for any man?

8

Andrew arrived home in time to find the countryside astir with tales of the latest outlaw raids. Even Manning was filled with talk of the rampage of the outlaws through the Camden-Wateree area. One of the Negro guards who watched the plantation at night was sporting a heavily bandaged arm and telling of the horrible band that had swooped out of the darkness with guns blazing, intent on entering Manning property.

Andrew sat down with his parents and brother for the noon meal and heard the remainder of the tale of heroism. Joseph was beaming with pride for his guard. "Not a sign of panic. Why, you would have thought the man had been in battles all his life the way he stood there calm as a pickle, sending out the warning to others and fighting off the mob until help came."

"It's a cucumber, dear," Georgina Manning said.

"Other than the injured man, no other harm was done?" Andrew asked.

Arthur smiled at him. "At the risk of making you feel unmissed, we did very well. Not another man injured, not a scrap of property taken, and the fields were left undamaged."

"But we did miss you, Drew, terribly," his mother said. "You will be staying home now, won't you?"

"Yes, and I will need to be talking with you and Daddy. I have had a long talk with Joanna and some highly pointed hints from her parents. Soon I am going to have to make plans, and I'd like some advice."

"I can hardly believe that is my brother talking. Did you fall off your horse and hit your head on the way home, Drew?"

Drew looked at Arthur and laughed. "I might have. I feel as though something has hit me. I've received more advice this trip of conflicting views than I knew was possible. Grandma thinks I ought to tell Joanna we'll never marry."

"My mother said that?" Joseph shouted.

"It sounds exactly like something she would say, dear," Georgina said sweetly.

Joseph stared at her angrily. "This is one matter Mama should remain silent about. This involves family honor!"

As the Manning family readied themselves to engage in a long and heated discussion, Milo, a tall, dignified butler, came into the room.

"Mistah Hart to see Mistah Drew. He says it's impo't'nt, suh."

Ned Hart stood, hat in hand, in the entry hall. He smiled when Drew came through the dining room door. "It's good to have you home, Drew. You've been missed."

Drew shook his hand. "It's good to be back. What brings you here at this time of day, Ned?"

"Well, you know I wouldn't be here if it weren't important. I suppose you've heard about the raids?"

"Yes, Arthur and my father told me. How bad were they?"

"Bad enough that we're riding to clear out them damn towns, Drew. I come here to ask if you're gonna be with us. I gotta tell you it's gonna be a hard ride."

"I'll be with you. You go on ahead. Tell the others I'll be there."

Andrew made his apologies to his family and listened patiently to Georgina's complaints, then went to meet Ned and the other Regulators.

Andrew and Ned met with a group of twenty other men in Camden, or Pinetree Hill, as so many still called Camden. After a gathering designed to stir up the wrath of the Regulators in which a bottle was passed just enough to promote a feeling of camaraderie, the men set off into the tangle of the Carolina hills in search of the outlaw settlements. This outbreak of violence, thievery and woman-stealing had come about as had so many others. When the population of the outlaw communities thinned out, they resorted to abduction. Girls of respectable families were stolen or forcibly made to take up with the outlaws. The Upcountrymen knew from painful experience that if the girls were not brought back quickly, there was often no way to reclaim them. Many of the Regulators knew the pain of losing daughters, sisters or wives to the outlaws.

This time the Regulators were certain to do something about it. They all stood together, pledging to each other that they'd follow the outlaws until justice was done and their homes were safe.

"Even if we travel every byroad in Carolina!"

"Ninety-Six, and Orangeburg and Cheraw!"

"Saluda! Savannah!"

"No more of our women doin' outlaw work!"

"Time's a wastin'."

Andrew, Ned and the others mounted and put their horses through some fancy maneuvers in the spirit of their crusade. The horses cut sharply as the men reacted to the excitement of the beginning of the search they knew would soon become frustrating and tedious and then dangerous, when and if they encountered the outlaws. Every opportunity for bravado and a lifting of spirits would be taken, at least at the beginning.

The countryside that Andrew loved so became boringly the same as he rode mile after mile, hour after hour, seeing nothing of import, always feeling tensed for action though none was to be had. As the hours passed, the pace of the riders slackened, and it became increasingly difficult to remain alert to the possibility of attack from the cover of bush and tree.

Andrew finally gave up the battle for attention and submerged himself in his own thoughts, trusting that one of the other men would sound the alarm if something untoward was seen. When the cry to halt came, it startled Andrew so badly he jumped for his musket and readied it without thought. Several other men followed suit, while others laughed, understanding what had happened and glad it hadn't been them caught dreaming.

Embarrassed and chastised by a curt word from their commander, Andrew paid closer attention. They had come upon a trail the bandits had left. Andrew noted every bent twig and kept himself constantly alert.

The trail was confusing, for much of the destruction had been done in the summer, though two plantations farther along looked like more recent crimes. There seemed to be no pattern to the outlaw path; maliciousness for its own sake seemed to be the rule. Robert Buzzard's house looked deserted and empty as the men rode up to it, hoping for a place to stay the night and feed their horses and themselves. Buzzard had encountered the outlaws and asked for passes, a method by which he thought he could protect his property. The Black brothers, the Moon brothers and the Tyrells massed around him. One of them said, "Here is our pass!" pulling out his gun and shooting Buzzard in the neck and chest. The gang had ridden away then, and the Buzzards thought they were safe. The gang returned a few days later to clear the house of furniture, the stable of horses, the barn of livestock and the yard of anything usable they could haul back to their own settlement.

From Buzzard's house the gang had gone to the Wilson house. They robbed and bound Wilson and burned him with lightwood sticks and red-hot pokers, laughing gleefully at the horror they created. After the gang had satisfied its need for sadistic entertainment, they robbed Wilson of all he owned and left him, confident that no one could or would stop them.

With each stop Andrew's outrage grew, and he found himself fighting the same feelings of viciousness within himself that he detested in the outlaws. "I can't help it, Ned," he said that night in front of the campfire. "I don't just want to catch up with them, I want to tear them apart. I want to gouge out Tom Moon's eye and stare at the bloody socket just as he did with Charles Kitchen." Andrew still recoiled at the memory of the sight of Kitchen's empty socket. "Did you see that, Ned? My God, did you see what they did to that man? I was giving a fine sermon to my grandma and my cousins when I was in Charles Town about how they didn't properly appreciate how serious crime was in the Upcountry. I was describing the horrors, and . . . I didn't know what I was talking about. That was before I saw Kitchen."

"You seen others with lost eyes."

"But not like that! I know how that happened. When he took that patch off his eye I thought I was going to be sick. Didn't you see it?"

Ned, considerably older than Andrew, leaned forward and poked the fire thoughtfully, taking his time with a reply. "I seen," he said slowly, "and I seen worse'n that. So will you before we get back home again. What you're feelin' now, Drew, is fear. Y'want to be worse'n them 'cause it looks like the only way to win."

"Isn't it?"

"Yep, it is, but it's a different feelin'. You'll learn to do what's got to be done and feel no more about it."

"I never will," Andrew said, shaking his head sadly and staring into the fire. "I feel it—all over me—and I hate them, Ned. I can't help it. I hate them and I want to hurt them. I want to see the same thing in them that I saw in Charles Kitchen. I want to see pain. I could never be like you're saying I will be. I could never learn not to care."

Ned looked at him for a time, thinking about the young Andrew he had watched grow up ever since Joseph Manning had brought his two boys to clear the land and build Manning. He had seen Andrew grow from a redheaded, freckle-face boy who was as much Indian by nature as he was full of vinegar and vitality. Ned loved Andrew as a man can only love a son, and now he watched the young boy as a man, a troubled man. Ned could feel the nebulous olio of thought and feeling churning in Andrew, and he wondered how it would come out. Aloud he said, "Well, mebbe you're right. Some folks always feel too hard an' cain't do nothin' about it. Mebbe you are one of those. Hope not, though. Feelin' like that can cause a man a lot o' sorrow in one life."

Andrew's eyes remained fixed on the fire, the shooting yellow flames entrancing him. "I am," he said in a barely audible whisper.

"Well," Ned said with finality, "we'll find out tomorrow or the next day. We're bound to catch up with those thievin' bastards sometime soon. You'll know what your insides are made out of then. Good night, Drew. Best get some rest."

The following day the Regulators nearly stumbled into the outlaw settlement. One moment they were deep in the forest and the next they had come upon a clearing cluttered with shacks and one or two more substantial houses. Cattle pens and livestock fences ran haphazardly in the area and on the outskirts of it. There was a sense of moldering filth and disorganization about it. The Regulators had no chance to plan an attack. From one of them came a war cry, and Andrew, without thinking, found himself opening his mouth wide. From deep within him came a cry of rage that rang clear in the dawn. He dug his heels into his horse's sides and wheeled the animal toward the center of the sleeping settlement.

From the leaning, decaying shacks women and children tumbled out into the open, then ran for the cover of the underbrush. Andrew, his concentration on the cabins and the men who still remained secreted in their confines, ignored the women in the beginning. Ned and several other of the men built a bonfire and began making rush torches. Others emptied the pens of their cattle, pigs and other livestock, rounding up the animals to take back to Camden and their rightful owners. Andrew and half a dozen other men continued their wild and noisy encirclement of the settlement, occasionally shooting guns to keep the men at bay inside the huts and to keep the women from returning.

"Ho, Drew!" Ned called out, raising his arm high, offering Drew a flaming torch. "Go to it, lad! Watch fer them women!"

With another war cry, his face flushed with excitement, Drew rode back past Ned, the torch flame leaping and smoking wildly above his head. In a graceful movement he turned the horse, zigzagging along the path around the huts. He held the torch high until he noticed movement in one of the huts. With a wild whoop he reined the horse in, forcing the animal to rear, front paws ripping at the air. He hurled the torch against the canvased front window. He then circled the hut, coming around the side as two of the outlaws, scruffy, thin men, ran from the shelter. His pistol ready, Andrew smiled and shouted at the men. As they turned, his pistol released a small burst of flame. The lead man clutched at his collarbone, moaning and staggering with pain and the exaggeration that fear lent it. Bartholomew Cole rode up beside Andrew. "Goin' to end him, Drew?"

Drew stared hard at the man, trying to see if in that thin face he could see the anguish he had seen in Wilson's face, or Kitchen's. He saw nothing but fear and hate. "No. Hang him with the others."

Bart glanced at Drew, withdrawing somewhat but with new respect in his eye. "That's a hard road, Drew. You sure? You could make it nice and quick right now."

"I'm sure. The other one, too." Drew reloaded his pistol as he spoke, then deliberately aimed at the man standing fearfully near his felled companion. He looked pleadingly at Drew. "You ain't gonna shoot me! I ain't armed! I ain't done nuthin' to you!"

Drew aimed the pistol and shot, hitting the man in his hip.

The man rolled on the ground, screaming and cursing Drew. Andrew sat astride his horse, looking at the man writhing on the ground. He felt no satisfaction, just anger, revulsion and an emptiness that made his stomach ache.

By the end of the afternoon the Regulators had cleared the settlement. The shacks were smoldering heaps of ash and smoking, charred wood. The two buildings that could have been called houses were still blazing. Children scampered through the bush, peering out at what had been their homes. Amid the sounds of men shouting orders and horses' hooves pawing at hard-packed ground came the cries of young children searching for their mothers or watching and howling in fear as the men they had known as fathers were bound and dragged to the hanging tree.

Five outlaws lay at the foot of the tree the Regulators had chosen. Two had been shot, but the others were very alert and spewing their hatred forth with foul language, taunting their captors with invective.

Andrew stood back from the main body of the group, holding as still as he could because the taunts coming from the beaten outlaws were raising an anger in him that threatened to break loose if he moved at all. His eyes were hard on the bound men, and he found himself envisioning more than were there. He wanted so badly the others who had managed to flee that he could almost convince himself they were there. Two men gathered and uncoiled the hangman's rope, affixing it to the tree limb. As Ned had mentioned, most of the men went about the business of hanging the outlaws with near-indifference. It was an unpleasant task they had to do, and they did it with the same sense of unemotional practicality with which they butchered livestock in hog-killing season.

Though his fascination with revenge and the need to make the guilty suffer had abated somewhat, Andrew still could not look at the hanging of the five outlaws with the same calm that the others were able to achieve. He still felt within him the stirring of a hot-blooded passion that made his skin tingle with cold. Every part of him was reacting to the emotion of the moment, and he could no longer tell where the pleasure separated from revulsion. He knew only that no matter how often he experienced a time such as this, he would not view it with indifference.

The Regulators camped in the ruined outlaw settlement that evening. The grisly reminders of the morning still hung from the limb of the hanging tree. Andrew couldn't keep his eyes from staring at the dead men. Andrew, Bart Cole and John Haynes sat up late by the campfire, drinking coffee, talking and thinking. In part they were too keyed up to sleep, but as always they were hoping and keeping watch for some of the women who had been taken in raids by the outlaws to return to camp so they could be taken back home. "We don't have all that much livestock to take back. We could take a goodly number of women back with no trouble."

Andrew mused at the turn of the conversation. "We sound as though the women are livestock, too." The others looked at him, and he ended in a self-conscious chuckle.

"Some are," John Haynes said. "Especially them that's been with these critters for a while. Why, you wouldn't believe some of the things these women will do. They're worse'n the men when they've been turned bad. Steal anythin', they will. You can't trust 'em, not even in the bed. Why, they's as like to lay with a man to git up with the dawn, shoot him in the head an' make off with his purse an' horse an' come right back to her outlaw man."

Bart listened with open mouth. "I've heard stories like that before. Why do they come back to these jackals? What kind of man is an outlaw? Why do you suppose women stay loyal to 'em?"

"Think mebbe they got somethin' special 'bout them that we ain't?" John Haynes said and then burst into a raucous cackle. "Le's shuck 'em dead ones down an' see."

Andrew glanced at him, then immediately away. With his eyes he indicated where he was looking. Slowly Ned shifted his position so that he, too, could see the area that Drew was watching.

"If my woman ever got took, I wouldn't have her back," Bart Cole said.

John laughed loudly. "You ain't got no woman. Ain't one been born yet kin stan' the smell o' that bear grease you favor."

Angrily Bart said, "T'ain't true! They's lots o' women hankerin' after me. I jes' ain't gotten 'roun' to makin' my choice."

John hooted, pushing at Bart, then quickly got to his feet with Bart, bull-like, clambering to his feet in pursuit. Both men shouted, startled, as a shot crackled in the darkness. Ned and Drew were already on their feet and running for the bush.

The men plunged into the dark tangle of growth, converging on the spot where each of them thought they had seen movement. Drew's arms closed around a body in the darkness. He found himself roughly tumbling about in the dark bushes, his hands frantically grasping for the claws that raked his face and neck. Hair was in his mouth and tangled in his fingers. Briefly his mind registered that it was a woman with whom he was fighting, but the thought fled and he concentrated on subduing the kicking, scratching female before she did him harm. He was panting when he finally had her pinned on the ground and relatively quiet.

Ned patted him on the back. "That big, husky girl give you a battle, boy?"

"Don't laugh. She's not finished by a long shot. She's just waiting for the chance to leap up and get at me again."

"She likes you," Ned said, and went about tying the girl's hands behind her. He looked over at Drew and laughed. "You look a damn sight."

Andrew got up from the ground and touched his face gingerly. His cheek was scored where her fingernails had raked down his face. His skin was sticky and wet. He spit blood out of his mouth and patted gently at the tear in his lip. "She's a real handful. Watch out for her, Ned; I don't think a rope will hold her. We shoulda put her in a bag or something. I know one thing—I'm never going after one of their women again unless I do have something to throw over her. She sure doesn't fight like a man."

"And that's a fact," Ned said with a chuckle.

They dragged her closer to the fire, and because she refused to bear her own weight, Ned let her drop to the ground near the fire. Bart and John and several other Regulators who had been awakened by the commotion came to see the woman.

She was young, probably no more than fifteen or sixteen. Her long black hair was a matted, tangled mass surrounding her head and her tiny, angular face. Her mouth was drawn in a hard, thin line, as angry-looking as her eyes.

"What's your name, girl?" Ned asked.

She spat at him and tried to kick high enough to reach his crotch. Ned jumped back to a chorus of laughter from John and Bart. "Damn little bitch!"

Bart Cole stepped forward, pushing Ned aside. "You don't know how to talk to her, Ned." He slapped the girl hard across the face.

Her head snapped back and she lay still, with her face against the earth.

"Now let's see what she has to say." Bart grabbed her by the hair, lifting her partially off the ground. "What's your name?"

The girl glared at him but remained silent.

Bart slapped her again and again, her head snapping back and forth, until one of the other men realized she had been trying to say her name.

"Hold it, Bart, she's tryin' to say something!" Peter Dobbs said.

"Then let her say it fast," Bart raised his arm again.

Andrew grabbed hold of his arm, pulling Bart off balance. Firmly he asked the girl, "What's your name?"

"Melanie."

"Melanie what?"

"Just Melanie," she said defiantly.

Bart pushed forward again. "Let me ask her. I tol' you you don't know her language. I do!" He stood looking at Drew with his arm drawn back.

"Williams!" the girl screamed. "Melanie Williams!"

"Jeez-zuz!" John Haynes breathed. "I knew a Melanie Williams— Rob Williams's sister. She's been gone for over a year. You her?"

"No!" she said and burst into tears.

"It *is* her!" John said. "What are we gonna do?"

"Take her home," Andrew said.

"Like that? Look at her . . . she'd kill us if she could. She's one of them now." John looked at Melanie, then turned away, a look of disgust on his face. "What'll I tell Rob? What'll I do?"

Peter Dobbs cleared his throat and said diffidently, "We could just forget we ever saw her . . . turn her loose to find her way back to the pack of them. She'll find her man."

"Just turn her loose in the forest?" Drew asked. "We can't do that. It isn't right. John, you just said she's a decent girl from a good family."

"Oh, Christ, Drew, look at her."

Melanie had stopped crying and was now moving provocatively on the ground in front of them. "She's . . . she's nothin' but one o' their whores."

Drew looked at the girl and looked away immediately, not able to bring himself to watch her. She was making herself a living contradiction of what he was trying to say. He kept his eyes on John. "No matter what has happened to her, she's a Williams. What about her family? Shouldn't they have something to say about what is done with her?"

John's eyes were level with Drew's. "Would your father be pleased to have her back if she were your sister? Would you want her—like she is? Could you ever trust her again? Do you really think the Williamses would thank you for bringing her back to them? At least now they can mourn the loss of a lovely girl who was their daughter. They still have their memories of what she was, and their pride. This girl isn't Melanie Williams anymore. This bitch is one of Govey Black's whores."

Drew looked down at her and hopelessly asked her, "Are you?"

She shrieked with pathetic laughter. "What kind of fool are you? What do I look like?"

"Looks don't always tell the story." Drew persisted, not quite knowing why he did.

She covered her ears with her hands. "I am Melanie! Melanie! Melanie!" She kept repeating her name, crying harder and then softer as the wailing turned into a quiet, rhythmic sobbing.

Andrew turned away from the group standing around the girl and walked to the edge of the clearing. He looked into the cool darkness. Soon Ned came to stand beside him. "Nights like this are what make this business troublesome for a man. We learnt to expect innocence in our women, and when it ain't there, we don't know what to do."

"Must we throw the woman away? She didn't choose to go with the outlaws," Drew said.

"She's choosin' right now."

For some time after that the two of them stood in silence, looking up at the star-studded night. Finally Ned said gently, "Come to the fire. Sleep."

During the night Melanie disappeared, her ropes cut by some well-meaning Regulator.

The Regulators remained on their search for the outlaw settlements another two weeks. They returned home tired and disgusted by what they had seen, felt and done in the past fortnight. They had completely destroyed another of the communities but had been thwarted in the attempt at a third. They brought home with them thirteen horses, ten cows and a supply of assorted livestock including pigs, goats and sheep. Several wagons had been commandeered and loaded with furnishings that they knew had been stolen. Silver urns and candlesticks were thrown in haphazardly with ornate hand-carved mirrors and delicate chairs and bedsteads.

Andrew rode with the Regulators into Camden and deposited the goods at the house of the justice of the peace. The men, now used to being with one another, stood around in clusters, not quite knowing how to part. Bart came up to Drew, placing his arm on Drew's shoulder. "There's a grave cleaning next Saturday, I hear. I'm going to go. What about you? You be there, Drew? John?"

The raid on the outlaw settlements had left all the younger men with a feeling of need for each other. Not hardened as the older men were and not comfortable with their feelings of vengeance and the sickening that came when they found what they sought left them wanting the security of those who had had the same experience. They were more than happy to hear any excuse offered that would allow them to meet again without having to admit outwardly that they needed each other. Several of them said immediately that they would be at the grave cleaning. Drew was one of them. After the plans to meet were made, he suddenly found he no longer needed to linger in Camden. He was free to go home.

9

Joseph Manning was feeling patriarchal the evening of Andrew's return. It had been a long time since he had had his whole family together, and though he considered it unmanly to admit it, he worried when his sons were away from home. Nothing was certain in the Upcountry. He had spent many restless nights while Andrew was on his way to Charles Town with Manning indigo, and several more while he rode with the Regulators. But now he was home, and safe. The trip to Charles Town had been a success. Manning's future was assured for the following year. The Regulators had accomplished their task, and the neighborhood, while not free from danger, now had a little insurance. The outlaws knew there would be retaliation from this sector. Perhaps they would stay away.

Smugly Joseph patted his belly and thought of his blessings. Yes, he thought complacently, he was well satisfied with his family this evening and mighty happy to have Drew back home. It was a strange thing how a man could be aggravated almost to despair by one of his offspring, but let the boy be gone for a time and all that was forgotten in the joy of having him back. There was no question Drew was a handful, but he was Joseph's son and he loved him fiercely.

Joseph sat back comfortably, sated from the dinner he had just consumed, one hand still on his stomach, the other cradling a cup of tea. Benevolently he looked over his table, his eyes resting momentarily on his wife of twenty-eight years, Georgina. She looked remarkably young and fresh for all those years she had spent with him, raising their two sons and hewing Manning plantation from the wilderness. His eyes moved on to his older son. The satisfaction in his brown eyes deepened. His hair powdered and held neatly in place with a black satin ribbon, Arthur leaned engagingly toward his dinner companion, Adela Robinson, the daughter of a neighbor and Joseph's good friend, Basil Robinson. His uncut velvet suit fit well across his broad shoulders, accentuating his lean, hard body. Across from him the other two Robinson daughters divided their conversation and attention between Arthur and Andrew. Joseph chuckled silently, remembering many happy whispered conversations between himself and Georgina in the night in their bed, when the rest of the household was sleeping, about the charm and appeal of their two sons. How often they had speculated what kind of wife this girl or that would make for one or the other of their sons. The speculation over Arthur had some validity, for as the oldest son he would remain at Manning and carry on the next generation. But Joseph had the security of knowing that his younger son was already set for life with a young girl who would make him a fine wife and bring with her a substantial dowry and one of the finest Lowland plantations.

Joseph's gaze had just traveled on to Basil Robinson, tonight's dinner guest, when Georgina, with a meaningful look directed at him, brought his attention back to the conversation. As he floundered, trying to pick up the thread of the talk, she said gracefully, "We ladies shall excuse ourselves now, Joseph. I can see you men have weightier matters on your mind than we have interest for. But mind you, don't be too long about it. You're not to be forgiven this evening. The Kimbles and the Fishers will be arriving soon . . . and so will Micah Frobish—with his fiddle."

Joseph nudged Basil. "It's the dancing they don't want to miss. It has nothing to do with our company."

"Indeed we do not want to miss the dancing," Georgina said firmly. "See that you resolve your political gossiping with dispatch or you shall find your male sanctum invaded with fiddlers and dancing ladies."

Joseph laughed jovially and promised the gentlemanly talk would be held to a minimum. Amid such bantering and laughter, the ladies retired to the parlor, the gentlemen to the study attended by Milo, the Mannings' black butler.

Joseph had not had an opportunity to talk at any length with Andrew since his return from Charles Town. Both Joseph and Basil turned to Andrew, asking him first about the Regulators' venture and about his trip to Charles Town. Andrew was in no way prepared to talk about his ride with the Regulators, so he told them the bare facts of the happy results of the search and the return of farmers' property. The men waited for a moment for him to go on, and when he didn't, Joseph asked him about the proclamation issued by Governor Montagu. He knew his son well enough to know that Andrew would not talk about a subject he did not wish to talk about.

Milo moved easily among the men, serving brandy and passing Joseph's Delft humidor.

"I imagine he ignored the validity of our requests to the Assembly," Basil Robinson said without letting Andrew answer. He poked in the humidor, his thick fingers closing over one of the cigars. "We'll not receive a flea's notice from them, no matter what their promises. They still have their minds on the Stamp Act."

"The Stamp Act is a thing of the past," Joseph said. "Never did warrant the fuss it stirred up, in my opinion. George Saxby and Caleb Lloyd pledged officially not to enforce the act. When the king's own stamp officials refuse to enforce the law, can't call it much of a law. It should have come and gone damn near unnoticed."

Andrew laughed. "Our cousins wouldn't agree with you. From what Leo tells me, Charles Town was in quite a huff over it and thought it important. He and George and Rob were in town watching the doings of the crowd when the *Planter's Adventure* anchored at Fort Johnson."

Joseph's heavy dark eyebrows lowered. "What were John's boys doing down there with all the riffraff? I'll have to write to him. He most likely doesn't know what the young scamps are up to." He looked up suddenly, his eyes boring into Andrew. "What were you up to in Charles Town? You've never taken sides with that anarchistic rabble down there, have you?"

Andrew looked uncomfortable for a moment, then shrugged. "If I were, I wouldn't be likely to tell you, especially with you breathing fire at me. Anyway, I don't think you'd really want to know if I were."

"Now, listen here, young man, I will not have you—"

Arthur intervened before his father could work himself up into a snit over Andrew's breach of etiquette. "Shall we forego the family quarrel and hear from Drew what did take place in Charles Town? I hear there was quite a bit of apprehension for a time after the proclamation was issued." Arthur paused, then in a lower, calmer voice said, "Tell us how you came to hear of Montagu's act, and what you know of it."

"As you know, the Regulators sent a remonstrance to the Assembly, and for a time there was the possibility of a march on Charles Town in response to the proclamation. But what actually caused the discord this time began when the term of the Court of General Sessions managed only six convictions of outlaw gang members, and of those, five were pardoned by Montagu."

"A lot of good the courts do us. Any fool can see that it isn't worth the time and expense it costs to haul them into Charles Town if the court is going to turn them loose as fast as they're caught," Basil said gruffly.

"They had John Ryan, Ephraim Jones, Sol Rivers, Anthony Distoe and James Ray all convicted, sentenced and set to be hanged, and danged if Governor Montagu didn't decide it would be a good time to show the people what a benevolent man he was going to be as governor. He frees them and we get them again, and they're on the loose to do as they want. One noteworthy light to this is that it shows clearly who Governor Montagu thinks are 'the people.' Obviously he was not thinking of the Upcountrymen when he freed the outlaws to impress the people." Arthur reached for another cigar. "Go on, Drew, sorry I interrupted."

"You were doing quite well, brother," Drew said. "And I agree with you—a major part of our problem is that we aren't considered political entities at all. When the government talks of people, it refers to the Lowlanders and their interests. I think that is one of the main reasons—beyond our safety—that the Regulators are necessary. I know you don't like the idea of a vigilante group, Daddy, but something must be done. You surely agree with that, don't you?"

"Of course, something must be done, but I still think it must come through legislation, not by taking the law into our own hands. That's too dangerous and smacks too highly of anarchism. We can't have everybody who has a grievance making his own law and enforcing it in his own way. There's no order in that, and there must be order."

"Legislation!" Basil snorted. "Joseph, I agree with you that there must be order, but it isn't going to come through legislation this time. What legislation are we going to get through the Assembly with only two representatives for the entire Upcountry? Why, by God, Joseph, we are the greater part of South Carolina, and we have only two elected men to plead our cause, and half or better of our people can't even get to the voting places."

"That will change in time," Joseph said.

"I don't doubt that, but will we still be here to enjoy the change when it comes? Are you so wealthy that you can afford to be robbed at every turn? Think of it, Joseph. Have you so many sons that losing one every now and then to the outlaw bands means nothing to you? It's a damned lucky thing for you that you have no daughters. I wonder how complacent you'd be if you were worried about them being taken by some of those men."

"Now, Basil, I know how you feel, but cool heads must rule. We can't be letting our personal concerns override our sense of—"

"Like hell we can't!" Basil shouted. "What the devil are we settling here for if not personal concerns? Why have any government at all, or order, or anything else if not for the concern and preservation of a man's family. You're a cold fish, Joseph. Drew, what did Montagu say in that proclamation?"

"Not a great deal, really. It was short and to the point. He noted that our activities were illegal and accused us of committing riots and disturbances, then ordered that we disperse."

"And what did he say about the outlaws?"

"According to Montagu, we are the outlaws," Drew said.

"See! Hear that, Joseph? We are the outlaws! We are! Damn me, if that doesn't make up my mind for me. I've been sitting on the fence too long. Drew, I'm going with you the next time the Regulators gather. You stop by the house for me, you hear? I'm comin' with you from now on."

"I hope everyone doesn't react with the same vehemence you have," Arthur said, "or we could have a real crisis on our hands."

"It seems to me that we already have one," Drew replied. "I don't know how much worse things have to get before the Upcountry-men show some unity. Perhaps you don't like the Regulators or the idea of burning outlaw towns, but I don't hear either you or Daddy coming up with an alternative. All I am hearing is disparagement of what is being done, while the Regulators' efforts are what keeps us and this plantation safe."

"I think the armed guard we keep on constant patrol around Manning has something to do with our safety," Arthur said.

"And why should we have to live with an armed guard patrolling our property day and night?" Drew shot back.

Joseph pulled out his pocket watch. "We won't settle this tonight. For now, whether we like it or not, the Regulators have taken it upon themselves to be the guardians of the Upcountry, and I am sure the ladies are waiting impatiently. Which of those two crises do you think we should tend to?" He smiled at those in the room.

Slowly and reluctantly Basil let go of the anger he had come to feel during the discussion. He returned Joseph's smile and rose from his chair, dusting the front of his waistcoat free from the ash that had dropped from his cigar. "Good brandy, good smoke and good talk. I thank you, Joseph."

"As always, you are welcome, Basil. Now shall we, gentlemen?" Joseph said, opening the door and leading them across the hall into the parlor.

The rug in the parlor had been rolled back along the wall. At the front of the room Micah Frobish and two of his sons stood with fiddles in hand, waiting for the signal from Joseph for them to begin.

Drew waved at Micah, then went to talk with his oldest son, Jason.

"You comin' to the grave cleanin' tomorrow night, Drew?"

"Wouldn't miss it for anything. When did Reverend Fowler get back, or did he?"

"He's back. Came ridin' in just this afternoon." Jason laughed. "He's prayin' tonight. He said he saw a heap o' sin on his travels. I just bet he did. He tol' me that out of fifteen weddin's he did, twelve of them women had bellies so big they had to sit through the cere-mony an' one already had a boy child she carried to the weddin' with her. Well, we'll be able to show him a little sin of our own after the cleanin'."

"I could use a little old-fashioned Upcountry sin," Drew said. "I just came back from Charles Town. All they've got down there is snooty sin."

Jason drew his bow across the fiddle, producing a wailing, melancholy sound, his eyes on Drew in mock sympathy. Drew punched Jason's arm, making the violin squawk. "What's the matter, can't you play that thing? I'll see you tomorrow night. I'm getting the eye from my mother." He turned to leave and then turned back. "It's at the churchyard right near Reverend Fowler's house, isn't it?"

Jason nodded.

As the fiddles tuned up and then went right into a song, Drew approached Phillipa Robinson. He danced with her until Arthur tapped him on the shoulder and took his place. Glancing around the room, he spotted his mother and with a wink took her from Basil.

"Now I have the pleasure of dancing with the prettiest girl in the room."

"Andrew, you're incorrigible. It's no wonder you cause your father despair and your Aunt Eugenia to write me long letters with recommendations as to your upbringing."

"Aunt Eugenia did that? This trip?" He laughed lightly. "Hmm, I thought it would be Cousin Ruth writing to you, not Aunt Eugenia."

"I didn't say hers was the only letter I received. Our Lowland family has quite a lot to say about you, and I can't say much of it is complimentary."

"What was Aunt Eugenia's complaint? I already know Cousin Ruth's."

"Mainly that you led her sons astray, causing them to come home to her in a disheveled state and with broken noses and bruises, brawling like street urchins," she said.

"She exaggerates! There was only one bloody nose—Rob's—and he deserved it."

"Drew, you didn't!"

"I'm sure she wouldn't have cared if she hadn't been out of sorts to begin with. She's a very sour lady. I'll have to lie politely next time I'm there and tell her she's pretty, too."

His mother giggled wickedly. "She'd know you were lying. She has only to look at George. He is the image of her, only prettier."

Jeremy Fisher cut in, and Andrew went in search of Hope Robinson, then to the Fisher girls and Gloria Kimble, the Kimbles' only daughter. Jack Kimble, too, asked Drew if he was going to the grave cleaning the following night.

"Wouldn't miss it," Drew answered. "You going?"

"Yes, and I've already got the best girl in the . . ."

"Jack Kimble," his sister said tartly, "watch what you say! You and Drew are already the rudest men in creation."

"Then we have nothing to lose, little sister. I'll tell you about her later, Drew, when big ears isn't listening."

"He's awful," Gloria said, making a face. "I hate going anywhere when Jack is going to be there too."

Drew prudently said nothing but danced her as far away from her brother as he could manage.

The Mannings' guests left near midnight, with the whole family walking outside for the last-minute good-byes and confidences to be passed among themselves and their friends.

Tired and pleased, Georgina came back into the house. Looking around at the disarray of her parlor, she said happily, "We don't do this often enough, Joseph. I am not astute in the way of politics as you are, but I believe that the Upcountry must have society as well as protection and courts. We should see more of our neighbors, perhaps form a discussion group."

Joseph looked at his two sons and rolled his eyes. To Georgina, he said, "I agree, my dear. We should have sociables more often, and I shall contemplate the matter of a discussion group."

10

Georgina made a face of disapproval as Drew told her that he was going to the grave cleaning on Saturday evening, but it was harmless and both of them knew it. Georgina had not interfered in her son's decision making for two years now. She did not like the ease with which he seemed to fit in with and enjoy the Upcountry entertainments. For the most part, entertainment in the Upcountry was primitive and centered rather vaguely around what they called church. Otherwise it nearly always had some connection with their work or welfare.

Georgina didn't dwell long on her reasons for disapproval. There was nothing she could do to change the situation in the Upcountry, and about such matters she was very practical; far more so than Joseph. He envisioned two country gentlemen for sons, who happened to live in a wilderness. Georgina smiled. It was in Arthur's nature to be rather phlegmatic and traditional no matter what his surroundings, but not so with Andrew. He was going to become part of his surroundings and participate to the fullest. Georgina assumed that when he married Joanna and lived at Riverlea, the change in surroundings would take care of Andrew's current Upcountryman ways. His morals were something else. She wasn't sure the Upcountry view of right and wrong could be so easily erased, and when she worried at all, it was about this.

There was a tempo and a law up here that Georgina respected. She didn't try to keep her sons from it, for it was all around them. Loneliness, wide expanses of nothingness populated by dense trees and underbrush that seemed to have a special knowledge of its own, could change a man in his soul. The animals that roamed freely and predatorily, Indians who had still not accepted the onslaught of the white man's civilization, outlaws who roved and took what they pleased, and over all an unknown that thrived and beat and pulsated in the forests surrounding them could make a man restless. Knowing how tentative their hold was, the Upcountry people became different from others.

She kissed Andrew when he was ready to leave the house and held him with her until he grew impatient to be on his way, as he had done as a child. "Andrew, you will be cautious . . . and circumspect?"

"You will not have a wrong-side-of-the-blanket grandchild, Mama," he said, and hurried through the door in high spirits.

It had been a long time since he had felt the freedom of pursuit that the Upcountry socials offered. He nearly laughed aloud at a vision of Joanna being chased through the bushes after the work had been done and the picnic supper consumed. He sobered for a moment as a pang of loss shot through him. Once he was married to her, these carefree chases would be gone forever. He would most likely never again go to a grave cleaning or a Dumb supper or any of the dances or other things the Upcountry people did to lighten their days and nights. But all that was premature, he decided, and immediately felt better as he once more concentrated on the evening before him.

He arrived in time to see John Haynes, Bart Cole and Jason Frobish being coerced into setting up tables for the supper to be held later. He listened to the pretense of laziness from the young men, and their laughter made him feel good. This was going to be a good night, he thought, a very good night. Everyone was in the mood for it. Charity Bellows, tiny waisted and big busted, leaned against John as Andrew looked on. John nearly dropped the platter of thinly sliced pork meat one of the older women handed to him. His face turned a deep shade of red as he stammered an apology to the woman and tried to move away from Charity's warm, pressing body.

Off to the side Drew saw Bart Cole grab his sister Lisa by the arm, ferociously warning her to subdue her behavior. Lisa, dark-haired and impish, sniggered at him and continued unrepentantly dancing away from him as far as her captive arm would stretch. The angrier Bart got, the more devilish Lisa behaved, and the more she enjoyed it.

"Want some help, Bart?" Drew called. "Looks like you got more lady than you can handle."

"You stay away from her, Drew. My daddy's gonna skin us both if anything happens to her. She doesn't know what she's doin'." He pulled Lisa nearer to him, whispering frantically. "What you're doin' gives a man ideas he oughtn't to have, Lisa. Shit, girl, don't you know anythin'? Don't you know what kin come of a man an' a woman . . . you just stop it, you hear me, Lisa. I'm lookin' out for your own good."

"Hello, Lisa," Drew said more calmly.

"Hello there, Drew. It's good to see you. You're lookin' mighty fine," she said sweetly, batting her long eyelashes at him, then looking defiantly at her brother from the corner of her eye. "I'm surely happy you came tonight. You gonna escort me to the cleanin'? I already picked out a real nice spot over there." She pointed to a place some distance from the others, who had already begun working.

Drew was silent, wondering what he could say without offending Lisa or angering Bart, when she turned suddenly and stuck her tongue out at her brother.

"Lisa, I . . ." Drew began, trying to hold back his laughter.

"Oh, never mind! I don't want to go with any friend of Bart's anyway." She flounced away from them.

"That does it!" Bart exploded. "You see, Drew, she's nothin' but a baby, doesn't even know what she's about. I thank you for the thought that you wouldn't escort her. I appreciate it . . . I'd hate for her to be taken advantage of." Bart quickly shook Drew's hand, then ran off after his sister, shouting her name.

Drew shook his head, laughing silently at them. He was very glad he had no younger sister to look after. As he stood there, John Haynes came panting up beside him. "Watch out for that Charity! Lordy! I thought I had myself set for the night when she came up to me, but Lord-y! She's more'n I can handle. I allus thought it was the man to do the chasin', but I sure 'nuf feel like I already been caught, skinned an' readied fer roastin'."

At a call from Elijah Spelling, the unofficial coordinator of this grave cleaning, John and Andrew joined with the others near the food tables. With dash and aplomb Elijah raised his fiddle aloft. "Now, y'all, let's git to workin', an' if we make a hasty job of it, Micah an' me's gonna give you the bes' damn fiddle music you ever heard. Y'all do a good job fer the Lord, an' then we got that good praise raisin' music to come after! Y'hear me now?"

Choruses of yeas were heard from around the stacked wood that would be a bright bonfire when the sun went down. Elijah, pointing with his bow, began to pair off couples to work on the graves. "Now here I am atop the mountain," he sang out from his prominence on a tree stump. "Noah here to lead you all to the Ark two by two. Go, my little pairs of God's creatures, and do honor to those who come before you an' now are layin' quiet in the ground. Josie, you go there with Tom Wright. Tom, you mind you keep thinkin' on them who went before an' not so much on Josie." Elijah waited for the laughter to quiet. Everyone knew Tom and Josie were to be wed within the week, and neither could think of much but each other. "Tom Freewell, you take Polly with you. Laurel, go there with your brother Ben. Jasper Spikes, you . . ." He continued calling names until there were only a dozen or so left, whom he didn't know well enough to call and pair off in a way their parents would tolerate. Those remaining he brought close around him and paired off with his best judgment and a stern warning. "There'll be no tomfoolery back there on sacred ground. Y'all keep that in the fore of your thinkin'. That earth you'll be treadin' on is filled with the bones of them who come before us an' given us breath. They fought the Cherokee an' lived an' died earnin' the right to our respect. See you give it to 'em."

"We will, sir," Drew said solemnly along with the others.

Elijah stood quietly eyeing each of them, commanding their respect for a few minutes longer, then released them. "Git on, the sun's on the wane. Don't waste what's left o' the light, now. That ain't no way to do."

With trowel, spade and brush, the young people joined the older ones already working. They attacked the growth of scrub, grass and weed that obscured the markers, growing along the sides of the stones and trying to root in the crudely carved markings. Drew actually liked this part of a grave cleaning as well as he enjoyed the later frivolities. It was all too easy to be forgotten in the Upcountry. He somehow felt he was preserving part of his heritage and of himself as he straightened the crosses, uncovered stones and cleaned the markings back to their original legibility.

Andrew's partner suited him well. She seemed as intent on her duty as he was. They worked in silence for quite some time before Drew realized how young she was. She was not so intent on work as she was shy and inexperienced. He glanced at her, only to see her redden and turn from him. Her hair was long, straight and dark blond. It was beautiful hair, he thought, silky and clean. He then realized that Elijah had called her only Miranda, and he had no idea who she was. He waited until she was engrossed in removing thick, spongy moss from the lettering on a marker stone.

"What is your name?" he asked, careful not to look at her.

"Miranda Spelling," she said softly.

"Spelling?" he repeated. "Your father's . . ."

"Yes. He's my father."

Andrew moved to another grave, slightly farther away from her. "I see."

Miranda sighed. "That's the problem. Papa always leaves me till last, and my partner always 'sees' as soon as he learns my name."

Andrew smiled to himself, wondering what made that shrewd old man pick him to be Miranda's guardian, and then he wondered about Spelling's wife. Miranda seemed very young to him to have a father as old as Spelling appeared to be. "You're still very young," he said. "Your daddy is just looking out for you."

"I'm thirteen!" she said indignantly. "And I've been a woman for near a year. My mama was married at my age and near to birthing my big sister."

"Maybe they met at a grave cleaning," Andrew said, laughing.

Miranda blushed a fiery red.

"They did!" he said, and burst into a peal of loud laughter.

Miranda cringed away from him. Contritely he got up and came to her. "Miranda, I'm sorry. I was unforgivably rude. I'm honored that your father chose me to be your partner. I am, truly. Please, accept my apology."

"How could you want to be my partner? Everyone looks forward to the grave cleanings . . . to meet, and . . . and . . ."

"But I have. We're having a good time. At least we were until I opened my big mouth out of turn. I've met you, and later, well, later I'm sure to find you again."

"You will?" Miranda said, her face lighting up. "You're really going to come looking for me later?"

Andrew hesitated, realizing she had taken his words to mean more than he wished. Then he smiled and said, "Yes, I will. It's a promise."

As the sun began to set, the cleaners started to move toward the food tables. Several of the younger boys hurried to the bonfire, vying for the privilege of lighting it. They busily added the final touches, throwing dried stalks and small twigs, laughing and shouting with each other. One of the boys struck a flame and gingerly tossed it onto the pyre. Quickly a golden spiral of fire climbed up, pushing ahead of it a snakelike column of smoke.

Others finished making long-stemmed torches and placing them in the ground around the periphery of the meeting place. A warm, cozy feeling enveloped them as the workers ate and drank and exchanged news and gossip with neighbors they saw all too infrequently. Newcomers to the Upcountry were introduced to older settlers, and talents and needs were discovered, recipes for food and medicine were exchanged, patterns and ideas flowing as freely as did the food, drink and laughter.

As the sky turned black and the stars sparkled in clusters, the talk died down. The young children were taken home, and the thoughts of the young men and women turned to each other. Quick, shy glances that had been sent across the firelight were now ready to be acted upon. Elijah Spelling tapped Micah Frobish on the shoulder, and the two men left their wives' sides and walked to the tree stump, their fiddles in hand. The people were quiet, watching and listening for the fun to begin. Elijah and Micah and a newcomer tuned their fiddles. Another man Andrew didn't know but guessed to be part Indian according to his features tapped gently on a set of homemade drums.

Soon the tuning became music, and the older, married women led the way to the center of the clearing, dragging reluctant husbands shod in work boots behind them. Calico skirts swayed and flew out behind their owners as fast Upcountry dances warmed the blood and stirred the laughter and fun.

Andrew sat down, panting from the dance. Bart sprawled gracelessly at his side. "Them women can dance all night an' never stop. Why d'you s'pose it is that they can do all that but can't lift a hoe in the field without gettin' the vapors?" He lay back on the cool grass, his cheeks and face red, his hair damp with sweat. "You found you a girl you like yet?"

Andrew shook his head, then remembered his promise to Miranda. "I guess I have, in a way."

"What d'you mean, in a way?"

"I promised Elijah's daughter I'd meet up with her tonight, but I wouldn't dare touch her."

"How'dja get into that?"

Andrew shrugged. "I felt sorry for her, and she . . ."

"She asked you?"

"Well, sort of."

Bart laughed. "Boy, are you ever a sucker." He rolled over on his stomach, plucking a piece of grass and sticking it in his mouth. "But maybe not. If she asked you, I don't see why you shouldn't have a little fun out of it. She ain't so young she doesn't know. Just make damn sure her ol' man has his eyes occupied elsewhere. Fact is, this is soundin' pretty good to me. Come on, let's go scare up Miranda Spelling. I'll come with you—keep you safe and out of trouble. I kinda fancy that long blond hair o' hers. Looks kinda like cornsilk on a sunny day."

"That's what I need, a poet as a chaperon."

The two of them looked over the group of people near the campfire and saw no sign of Miranda. Bart nudged Drew in the ribs, his eyebrows raised. "Mebbe she's not so innocent as she led you to believe. She ain't around the fire, an' I don't see her nowhere in the dancin'. That leaves the dark an' them nice hidin' bushes, ol' frien'."

They walked to the edge of the clearing, the area where lovers and would-be lovers gravitated once the amenities had been satisfied and the evening was well under way. As they moved along, squinting in the darkness, they passed several couples entangled in embraces, heard the soft tones of whispered promises and ran across several of the younger boys peeping at their elder brothers and sisters.

Suddenly Bart pointed and whispered. "Look! Over there. There she is, Drew. Well, I'll be. Miranda Spelling is no innocent chil'. I just saw her peep from that bush and then duck out of sight. C'mon, she's playin' with us!"

Drew looked in the direction Bart had pointed, and soon, a few feet away, he saw her unmistakable blond hair flash in the moonlight as the girl raced to cover in a clump of pines. "She *is* playing," Drew said in amazement. "I'll be damned! Here I've been thinking what a pure little flower she is, and her papa's all for lookin' out for her. I'm ten kinds of a fool, Bart."

"Them's my thoughts too," Bart agreed.

"And it makes me damned mad. What do you say we have a little fun with Miss Miranda Spelling. Let's go get her; give her a bit of a scare."

Bart rubbed his hands. "She'll know better'n to tease next time. An' I could stan' a little fun anyhow. All the pretty ones got took up right off, an' what did I get? You."

"The night's not over yet."

The two of them ran at a slow trot, darting in and out of the bush and avoiding others. They kept their eyes trained on the darkness of the pine grove. As they neared the pines they separated, each moving silently.

Drew crept through the underbrush, his eyes now on the sheen of her hair. She was sitting at the base of one of the pines, her knees drawn up, her arms wrapped around herself. With a quick dash he ran from his cover and grabbed her by the shoulders, pulling her backward onto the ground. He pressed her down with the weight of his body and kissed her soundly. Her lips were soft and pliant. He was breathless as he said, "I thought you never met men in the woods," his mouth placing small kisses along the side of her face.

The girl remained still.

"What's the matter with you?" he asked, annoyed at her games again. As he moved away from her, she took advantage of the moment and twisted away from him, screaming.

He grabbed her and put his hand over her mouth. "What in the devil is wrong with you? You asked me to meet you!"

She began to kick him, her teeth biting hard into his hand. He pulled his hand back, hurt and surprised.

"Get away from me!" she screamed and hit him.

"Where are you?" Bart's voice called from the darkness. "I hear you but I can't find you."

Andrew laughed and nuzzled the fighting girl, ignoring her blows. He wanted to look deeply engaged when Bart finally popped his head through the bushes and located them. "Quiet down, Miranda. Nothing is going to happen to you," Drew whispered, and again clamped his hand over her mouth.

The girl struggled to free herself. "I'm not Miranda," she hissed. "Let me be, sir, or I'll call for help until I get it!"

Drew sat up straight, releasing her. Her voice was far too husky for Miranda's, and she had just said she was someone else. "Who . . . are you?"

She was already on her feet and running away from him. He scrambled to his feet and ran after her. "Wait! Wait! I won't touch you. I promise! Wait, please. Who are you?"

Bart caught up with Drew. "What did you do to her?"

"Nothing! That's not even Miranda. I don't know who she is, but she sure is mad!"

The girl ran toward the campfire and the other people with Drew and Bart following. She pushed her way through the dancers and disappeared. Bart and Drew followed but couldn't see her anywhere. He asked everyone he came upon if they had seen the girl run past. He followed every suggestion given as to her whereabouts, but he didn't see the girl again.

Bart had tagged along with him through most of his search. "Aw, Drew, give it up. We'll never find her, an' I'm sick o' lookin' for her."

"Just give it a little longer," Drew said.

"Not me. Miranda's over there by the fire. She's the one you were lookin' for in the first place. Let's go there and sit a spell. Look, they're roastin' sweets in the fire."

Drew looked wistfully at the dark walls of trees. "Nothing has gone right tonight." He slowly followed after Bart and joined Miranda at the bonfire.

"Drew, I didn't think you were going to join me at all. Why didn't you come when I called to you?"

"Uhh, sorry, Miranda. I didn't hear you. I was looking for someone. I guess my mind was on that."

"Oh, I'm glad," Miranda said with relief. "I thought perhaps you didn't even want to talk to me. I know I was very forward when we were cleaning the graves."

Drew immediately felt bad and sat down beside her. "Oh, not at all, Miranda. I am utterly charmed by you, and it was my plan to meet you this evening. Bart will vouch for that. I just didn't hear you."

"He's tellin' you God's truth," Bart added, his eyes soft on Miranda. He found he liked her shyness and the way she looked at him quickly, then away. "We were lookin' for you, too. We didn't see you, though, till just now."

Drew sat with them for some time. Slowly he began to realize that neither Bart nor Miranda was paying any attention to him. It had been some time since he had been included in their conversation. Soon after Bart and Miranda got up. "You'll excuse us, Drew?" she asked. "Bart and I are going to take a walk."

Andrew was left alone by the bonfire with a strange sense of abandonment. But it wasn't Bart or Miranda he missed, it was the girl, the girl he didn't know. He didn't know her name or what she really looked like. He didn't know if he'd ever find her again, or even if she lived in the area or was merely a guest of one of the other families. He couldn't think of any sane reason he should want to know these things or why the memory of the girl was lingering so strongly. He tried laughing at the absurdity of his feelings, but he didn't feel much like laughing.

Part Two

Laurel

11

Laurel Boggs hurriedly picked up the bedclothes from the hard-packed floor of the one-room cabin that was home to her mother and father, her seven brothers and sisters and herself. The youngest Boggs, Laurel's infant sister Pamela, cried fretfully in her cradle.

Mary, eleven years old and too sickly to join in the work or pleasures of the family, said, "She's hungry, Laurel."

Laurel reached into the cradle, fumbling through the coverings and retrieving a grimy sugar tit that she stuffed into Pamela's mouth. "Ma will be here soon enough," Laurel said and hastily completed what little straightening was possible in the overcrowded room.

Mary smiled appreciatively, her thin little face pale, her eyes dull. "It looks real nice when you do it up, Laurel."

Laurel affectionately patted her cheek. "Don't you worry none, Mary, there'll come a day when it's lookin' nice all the time. We'll have a big new room built on the back, and maybe even a separate room for the kitchen. It won't always be like it is now. God brought us to the biggest chunk of land any Boggs has ever seen, didn't He? We're just startin' out here, aren't we? Why, only the good Lord hisself knows how high the Boggs can rise. But I can promise you the Boggs will be among those who help themselves. You watch, Mary. It's comin'. We're on our way to a good life now."

Mary giggled softly. "I like it when you tell stories. You an' Ben, you're allus dreamin'."

"Dreamin', is it?! Not so! And it won't be long before I show you. We're not like the other low people hereabouts. We'll grow an' become . . . important. We'll be substantial folk. Like the Mannings. Yes, like the Mannings."

Mary considered that for a time, then said sadly, "Mama says the only way we're ever gonna be anythin' but low people is for you to marry us out of it. She say it don't matter who he is iffen he's young or old or nothin'. All that matters is he's gotta be rich, an' you git him fer us. Are you gonna do that, Laurel? I don't think I'd like bein' important people iffen that's the way we do it. I like your dreams best."

"They're not dreams, Mary. Dreams is only when you don't do anything about them. If you work toward 'em, then they're plans. I've got plans, and not a one of them is about marryin' some old geezer whose own mother wouldn't have him."

Mary laughed.

"That's better. When I marry, it'll be to someone wonderful, an' I think it has to be someone I love. Love a whole bunch."

"Mama says love is hogwash. Don't put nothin' on the table, an' fuddles the mind. Mama says a man or a woman in love ain't worth nothin', 'cause they cain't keep their minds on what's needin' to be done."

Laurel didn't know what love was. She had never felt it, never had it that she knew of, but she'd read about it, and somewhere inside her there was a part that knew it. It only took the finding. She said nothing to Mary but moved quickly, readying the cornmeal the family would have for their morning meal. Pamela cried softly in her cradle. Laurel went to the small child and placed the lost sugar tit into her mouth again. Pamela turned her small head away.

"Will she die, Laurel?" Mary asked in a whisper, afraid when she saw any sign of weakness to remind her of her own fragility. She had dreamed often of Pamela, and now she thought the two of them were somehow connected. As long as Pamela kept breathing and fighting for her small life, Mary, too, would be able to cling to hers.

Laurel was at Mary's side in an instant, knowing the feeling she had, for Mary was as close as she had ever come to knowing love. She tucked Mary's blankets in around her slender frame. "No, Mary, she won't die. We got through last winter, and there'll never be another as bad as that one was for us. I'll see to that, I promise you. We'll have food—every day, and even a little hard cash to buy what we need extra . . . maybe there'll even be enough money left to get some store-bought candles . . . and ribbons. You'd like having ribbons, wouldn't you? You could tie all that pretty brown hair up real nice."

Mary nodded gravely, then leaned forward, hugging her sister with desperately thin arms. "Oh, Laurel, why can't I be like you? I'd like so much to help you. I want to make plans and dreams, too. Laurel, ask God if I may. Please ask Him when you go to Reverend Fowler's today. I ask Him, but He doesn't hear me. You ask Him, please. Tell Him I want to help."

Laurel hugged her sister, promising she would ask God to make Mary strong. Laurel doubted very much that the Reverend Fowler could be of much help in soliciting God's aid. She had spent a good part of last night at the grave cleaning hiding from him. For a moment her mind wandered to fanciful thoughts of the young man who had found her and kissed her as she hid from Reverend Fowler in the pine copse. But it was only a moment, for Laurel had more important things on her mind, and she wasn't easily distracted. It was not the time for young men; it was the time to learn and to improve herself. If she couldn't maintain her resolve to better herself, then her dreams would remain dreams, and all she had told Mary would be a story, just as Mary thought it was.

Laurel shook her head, repeating *no* over to herself. It was all going to be as real as she promised it would be. For the time being that meant she put up with Reverend Fowler leering at her and talking at the same time about the sin and perversion rampant in the Upcountry. He made her think about a lot of things, but hardly ever did he make her think about God. But he knew his letters and numbers and had agreed to teach her in exchange for cleaning his cabin and tending his hogs.

She finished the mush, then went to the front door of the cabin. At Laurel's call the other Boggses stopped work and came toward the cabin. Laurel stood in the doorway and watched her family climb the hill from the outbuildings and the small field below. She loved them fiercely, but her visits to Reverend Fowler's cabin had opened her eyes to the way other people viewed them.

Of fifteen children, Mathilda and Harley Boggs had eight of them alive. Two of the living children were not right in the head and were unable to learn anything, not the simplest acts or speech. Mary and Pamela were sickly, and though Laurel would never allow the thought to consciously come to mind, she knew that neither of them was likely to reach her own present age of fifteen. Only Ben and Mandy and Little Harley and herself were robust.

To outsiders, and sometimes to herself, her family looked to be shiftless and uncaring. They appeared to be a backwoods family oblivious of the condition of their life and looking little beyond their next meal. Laurel resented it. She cared. With every fiber of her being she cared passionately.

The Boggses had originally come from England to Pennsylvania, where Harley had put every penny he had into a worthless trading post. With his usual penchant for trying to get more than he was willing to pay for, he had been cheated by a man shrewder than he. Laurel had been very young at the time, but she could still remember seeing her father stomping around their one-room house, laughing and shouting about how he had stolen the place from the man. And she remembered the fights and tears from her mother when they moved to the trading post, only to find it reclaimed by the forest. For months they saw no one. Not even the Indians bothered them or came to trade. The winter was cold and harsh. Harley had thought the seven- and eight-year-old boys old enough to help him search for roots, herbs and game to keep the family alive. But they hadn't been. Both Michael and James had come down with fever and died. And Laurel herself could remember what it felt like to be hungry, so hungry she dug in the cold earth till she could get a handful of soil to eat just so her stomach wouldn't hurt so.

They had moved to Virginia then, her father certain he would never again be bamboozled; from that time on, he said, he'd always be the bamboozler. They had escaped in the dead of night, warned by a friend that the justice of the peace was on his way to arrest Harley for selling land that didn't exist. Behind them was the grave of a sister. On the way to South Carolina two more of the children were lost in a raid—or traded to the Indians in exchange for the safety of the others, if Laurel was to be honest with herself. During that same time Mathilda had suffered a stillbirth, brought on, she said, by the fright of their night journey. All of them thought that no more could be suffered, that they had finally reached the nadir of their ability to withstand ill fortune and pain. But their first winter in South Carolina had been little better. They nearly starved. Jeremiah, the eldest of the Boggs children, was killed in a tree-felling accident as they tried to clear their first field. Mary lay sick, racked with fever and congestion all winter, and even now she wasn't fully recovered. Yet Mary had survived, and somehow Pamela had held onto her slim thread of life.

To Harley and Mathilda, the survival of the two children meant little. They didn't think about hope anymore, and they didn't believe in signs, especially not good ones. They had already become tired and old, no longer believing in a bright future and sometimes not wanting it, for it asked too much of them. Clawing and cheating to eke out whatever fortune they might find had become their accepted way of life.

Though Laurel despised what her parents had become, she laid no blame for their condition of poverty on them. With all of her heart she meant to return to her family some of the joy their journey through these vast, forest-darkened colonies had cost them. She would do it here in the Carolina hills, for she knew instinctively that this was home for her. The Wateree River that curled and corkscrewed down through the land, flowing past the Manning plantation, the lush greenery of the hills, the wild peach and plum that bloomed so profusely and fragrantly that they permeated the hills, had allowed her to promise a fruit cobbler for supper whenever she wished.

Laurel thought dreamily that it was here that she had really been born, not in Pennsylvania, where she had come squalling from her mother's womb. Reverend Fowler talked a lot about being reborn, but she didn't think he knew nearly as much about it as she did. It had happened to her. Right here. Not in the way Reverend Fowler meant it, of course; in a more real way than that. The Lord had given them this land, and He had said in the giving that it was a new beginning, to make of what they could.

She looked up suddenly at a shriek from her fourteen-year-old brother Willie as he yelped his incomprehensible sounds. She smiled broadly as Willie waved his arms, his ungainly body lumbering toward her.

"Come on, Willie!" Laurel cried, laughing and running the last few steps to take his hand and lead him to the house and the wash basin. She washed the grime from his hands and face and sat him at the table. Before the others had entered, Willie was eating, shoving food into his mouth with both hamlike hands.

One by one, Laurel washed the younger children and seated them at the table. Last she lifted Mary from her pallet and brought her, too. From the hearth she carefully brought Mary's plate, kept hot and safe from the grasping hands of the healthier and stronger Boggs. "Eat all of it. Remember, if you want something of Him, you must be willing to do your part," Laurel said sternly. She turned to her mother. "Mama, Pamela needs to be fed."

Mathilda shoved another chunk of corn mush into her mouth with a grimy hand. "I'll get to her straight off. My milk's not up, Laurel," she whined, then her eyes changed and she smiled at her daughter. "See what Harley brung me from town, Laurel? Ain't that purty?" She pulled a filagreed gold locket from inside the neck of her dress. "Won't be long till a man be bringin' you play-pretties like this, iffen you jes' learn to be a mite more encouragin'."

Harley laughed, punching Mathilda with his elbow. "Ain't never given her anythin' but the finest. Ain't been often, but allus been the best I could lay hands on, ain't that right, woman?"

Mathilda smiled. Laurel admired the locket, then repeated, "Mama, Pamela needs to be fed, she's been crying for a long while now, and she won't take the tit anymore." She picked the infant up from her cradle and brought her to Mathilda. "Please, Mama, she is so small. She can't wait any longer."

Reluctantly Mathilda accepted the child, and without looking at her, bared her breast and placed the baby's face to her. Pamela's small head bobbed around until she found the nipple and began sucking.

Laurel watched anxiously for a moment, wanting to help Pamela. When Pamela settled down and began sucking more peacefully, Laurel relaxed and looked warmly at the baby. Pamela's tiny head was mottled with blue veins that showed through her pale, thin skin. Her little face was pinched and wrinkled, but her large blue eyes were filled with intelligence and understanding, Laurel thought. She smiled at Pamela, believing the baby knew that well was meant her.

Mathilda looked up at her older daughter. "I cain't feed her no longer. She's gonna take to the cow's milk or get none. Y'hear? I'm doin' this jes' to shet you up."

"I know, Mama," Laurel said. "I'll try her on cow's milk again."

"Ain't no tryin' to it. I cain't feed her no more."

"I'll make sure she—"

"We ain't got no cow's milk to spare," Harley said. "We already usin' all we kin git an' wantin' fer more. Healthy ones git it first. We got to have workers here. Them fields ain't gonna plow themselfs."

"I'll get it!" Laurel snapped in irritation, then turned her back on her father.

Mary sought her eyes and found the reassurance of bright sparkling blue shining from Laurel's. Quickly the little girl looked down, a shy smile on her lips. She diligently ate her mush.

Laurel folded her apron over the back of Mary's chair, gently touching her sister's shoulder as she did so. She moved across the small room to stand before the broken piece of looking glass she had found on the trail coming south. She straightened her hair and tried to smooth the rough material of her well-worn shift.

Mathilda watched her daughter with jealousy and a deep sense of pride battling each other. Of all her children she sensed that it might be Laurel who was capable of climbing out of poverty. In her, Mathilda saw herself as she imagined she might have been if life had not been so stacked against her. "Laurel, you be careful, hear? Stay in the open on your way to the Reverend's. Iffen you see any of them good fer nothin's lurkin' aroun', you run an' hide, y'hear? I don't want you bein' wasted on them critters."

"I hear you, Mama. I'll be careful." She kissed her mother, then said cheerfully, "I'm off! I'll be sure to bring peaches home with me. We'll have a grand cobbler for supper tonight or my name isn't Laurel Boggs!" With a saucy flip of her short skirt, she ran out the open door. Her warm brown hair raised and lowered like a shining pennant in the breeze as she raced down the hill from her cabin.

12

Laurel's mind was barely on her duties at Reverend Fowler's cabin. She left earlier than she normally did and wondered guiltily if he'd notice that his cabin was not as spotlessly clean as she normally left it. For a moment she hesitated in the doorway, looking back into the room critically, evaluating each mote of dust that glistened in the sunlight. Before she was tempted to do anything else, she turned and shut the door firmly behind her.

She'd make it up to Reverend Fowler some other time. Today was her big day. She couldn't think of anything but going to Manning to seek work as a day girl. She was frightened and excited at the same time. She inwardly quailed at her audacity. She didn't even know if the Mannings hired day help, and no one she had asked knew either. They certainly didn't need to with all the slaves they had. As far as Laurel knew, Manning was the largest plantation and its owners had the most slaves of anyone in these parts. She caught her breath in doubt. Here she was, one of the low people, coming right to their front door, no back door, to ask to be hired.

She walked across Reverend Fowler's yard and headed for the Indian path that served for a road. Now that she was on her way, the idea of the step she was about to take seemed monumental. She thought of Mrs. Manning. Would she be the one to interview her? Or would it be Mr. Manning himself? The more she thought about what the rest of the morning might bring, the more frightened she became. She thought of her speech, her diction. She practiced what she would say over and over until the words began to run together, and she couldn't remember how to say anything properly. She was going to sound backwoodsy and uneducated.

She stopped walking and leaned her forehead against a tree, unable to take another step. She remembered her father saying, "Iffen they cain't git a whole lot more from you than they's given, they won't hire you, girl, don't you know nothin'?" He had laughed at her and added, "What kin you do that a good nigger cain't do a whole lot better?" The humiliation she would feel was unbearable even in imagination. She could already feel the hot, sickening bile of her shame rising.

Laurel stood hesitantly, not clear what she wanted. She wanted to be someone. But she didn't know how. There was no one to guide her. Even if she could find the courage to continue to Manning, she knew she could never follow Mathilda's advice. Honor to Mathilda was the same as getting what one wanted. Whatever means could accomplish the desired gains was good, no matter that it made Laurel's flesh crawl to think of bedding herself with Reverend Fowler or that it made her cringe with shame to think of enticing one of the Manning men in the hope that they would keep her in favors. To Mathilda Boggs, honor rested hidden in the succeeding; to Laurel, it lay in some unknown place she hadn't yet traveled but that she knew was deep within her.

It wasn't until her thoughts returned to Mary's small pinched face that Laurel found any hope at all. Mary would never realize that the fault was in Laurel and not in God. Laurel knew that Mary would place blame everywhere but with her. She'd never be able to admit that Laurel was as frightened, and sometimes as overwhelmed, by the world as she was. Even if it was a fairy tale, Mary would cling to the belief that Laurel was someone who could make dreams come true.

Laurel started to walk again. She managed only a dozen or more steps before she knelt on the ground, her stomach tight and filled with fear. She cried and talked to herself and the trees, the sky, all those living creatures with the patience to listen as none of the human creatures she knew would. When she finally got to her feet again, she was once more prepared to walk to Manning. She was not just going to ask for a day job, she was going to get one. Regardless of what her father said, Laurel knew she was worth more than most workers, and if she wasn't she'd learn to be.

She was hot and sticky by the time she came to the top of a gentle slope. She slowed down, letting a soft breeze cool her so she wouldn't look a mess when Mrs. Manning or the housekeeper interviewed her. At the top of the hill was the edge of a field. The men, black backs bent in the warm autumn sun, worked at a leisurely pace. Laurel let her eyes rest on the peaceful sight of slow work, so much easier than the hot, steamy labors of summer or the frantic, hurried rush of harvest. She looked from one end of the field to the other. Near the far side, in the direction she'd be going, she saw a white man, and next to him a water pail. Her eyes fixed on the speckled gourd that hung from the side of the pail. She felt an additional lift at seeing a white working with the blacks. It was a good sign that the Mannings at least occasionally hired outside help.

She moved steadily toward the man, assessing him. He had a nice look to him, she decided. There were no hard lines in his face that she could see, and he moved easily and well—no pains to make him disagreeable. The closer she came, the younger she realized he was. Without thinking she tucked stray damp strands of her hair under her cap and smoothed the apron of her dress as she walked.

"Good morning, sir!" she called cheerfully as she neared him. "Couldn't ask for a better day, could you?" She didn't wait for his reply. She pushed a stray hair under her cap again and went on. "I'm just on my way to Manning. I'm going to seek day work there. Seeing that you work for them, I thought perhaps you wouldn't mind telling me anything that might help me seeking employment for myself." She glanced at the water pail but said nothing.

He watched her for a moment. "Would you care for some water? It's a hot day."

"Thank you," she said, taking the gourd from him. "But I'd prefer if you'd tell—"

"Oh, I haven't forgotten your question." He stood feet apart, arms crossed over his chest, seeming to be delighted in watching her. The man broke into a broad grin. His eyes never left her. "Go ahead," he said. "Ask whatever you want about the Mannings, but I'll tell you from the outset, they are superior people. I'm sure you have nothing to worry about from any of them. You'll be hired on the spot."

Laurel choked as she let water drip from the gourd. She couldn't stop blushing, and the harder she tried, the worse it became. She knew him! With a rush, memories of the grave cleaning came back to her. Oh yes, she knew him! Her face was on fire and her eyes were watering. "Who are you?" she asked as aggressively as her choked voice would allow.

He smiled and came closer to her.

"Stay where you are! Keep your distance! I don't want to know who you are. I want nothing to do with the likes of you, and I'm not sure I'll have anything to do with the Mannings if they hire your such. Or maybe I'll just tell them a thing or two about their overseer they don't know!" Determined to have the last word, she turned on her heel and hurried across the field to the house.

Drew stood where he was, staring after her in bafflement. Then suddenly he threw down his hoe and began to run after her. "Wait! I remember you! Wait, please, I want to talk to you."

Laurel looked over her shoulder and shouted, "I don't want to talk to you—not ever!"

He caught up with her and walked beside her. "Wait, you don't understand. I thought you were someone else."

"Someone else! You probably maul every girl that comes within arm's reach."

"No, I don't," he said, genuinely hurt. She kept on walking, leaving him standing. He caught up with her again. "All right, I'm sorry. But please listen to me. I'm really not like that." He jumped in front of her. He put his hands behind his back and hopped back and forth, preventing her from going around him. "Look, no hands. I won't touch you, I promise, but please let me explain. I feel very badly about what happened, and I'd like to become acquainted with you on a better basis."

"I'll listen as long as you sound truthful, but mind you, it is only my curiosity and the fact that you won't allow me to pass that causes me to listen at all to what a cur like you would have to say."

He winced a bit. "I suppose I deserve that. Do I?" He waited to see if she'd soften a bit. When she didn't, he took a deep breath and began to explain. "I had made arrangements to meet a certain young lady, but I couldn't find her. Then I saw someone running away and peeping through the bushes. I thought it was she, playing hide and seek, but . . . it was you. It was your blond hair in the moonlight that threw me off. I thought . . ." He paused, looking at her hair. "Of course, now I see you don't have blond hair at all, but it seemed . . . I mean it looked blond that night. I know this isn't sounding truthful, but . . ."

Laurel's bright eyes began to sparkle with amusement. She stood still, waiting for him to stammer on, her foot tapping in impatience on the stubbly field.

"I'm not doing this very well, am I?" he asked and looked at her for an answer. She said nothing, and he added quickly, "But it's the truth! Every cockeyed word of it is true! I looked everywhere for you so that I could apologize that night, but I couldn't find you. Then I was afraid you didn't live around here and I'd never see you again. To apologize," he said awkwardly.

"Is that all you have to say?"

"Not quite. I'd like to introduce myself properly now and begin again with you. Would you . . . is that possible?"

"Meeting accidentally in a field is not a proper meeting," Laurel said, glorying in the idea that she could say such a thing to a man without him realizing that she was one of the low people and he needed no introduction to her.

"You're right," he said contritely. "I don't know why I make so many stupid mistakes with you. Would you please consider coming to the house, and I'll have my mother introduce us? That's certainly proper, and you'd have a chaperon, and I could put in a good word for you, and we—"

"Your mother works for the Mannings, too?"

"Uh, well, no, not exactly." Drew laughed lightly.

"What then?"

"My mother is the Mrs. Manning you're going to see. I'm Drew Manning." He watched her pale. "Are you all right? Let me help you."

"Don't touch me!"

"But you look as though you're about to faint."

"I'm fine. Oh, no, I'm not fine, I'm ruined. Why did you let me go on so? I thought you were . . . just someone . . . anyone." Tears welled in her eyes and began to overflow. "Working here meant so much to me, and you let me spoil it all without even knowing." As a sob burst from her, she ran back down the hill crying.

Slapping his leg in annoyance with himself, Drew ran after her. He caught her and turned her toward him by both shoulders. "Dry your tears. Nothing has been spoiled."

"Oh, yes it has!" she wailed.

"I'll escort you to the house and introduce you to my mother."

Laurel shook her head frantically. "Oh, no! I won't do that. I won't have her thinking that I'm the sort . . . that I'm one of your . . . I may have been a fool once today, but I'm not going to repeat it again."

Andrew felt a twinge of annoyance. "If that is what you feel, I wish you luck and good-bye. You might try seeking employment at the Robinsons'. They have a good-size place—and no sons. Should be just what you're looking for."

She blew her nose furiously and glared at him. "I was looking for work at Manning."

"And at the first difficulty, you gave up!" Andrew shot back. "We don't need that kind of help. A Manning stands up to difficulty. A Manning can be counted upon . . . knows what he believes in and never backs away from it!"

Laurel blinked in surprise. He was shouting, but she didn't think it was at her. What a puzzle this chestnut-haired man with his straight nose and his firm jaw had turned out to be. She liked him, and yet he had caused her nothing but trouble on the two occasions they had met. She began to laugh softly. "Which, in my case, shall you stand up for? Attacking me in the bushes or apologizing in the light of the sun?"

He stepped back from her, his lips tight, his eyes smiling. "I'll stand by my apology . . . but I had more fun the other night."

"Then I, too, apologize. Would you escort me to your mother, please?"

He put out his arm for her to take, and when she looked confused, he took her hand.

13

Laurel's feet barely touched the ground when she came through the door of the Boggses' cabin that evening. Her color was high and her eyes were sparkling.

"Meet the Mannings' new hired day girl," she said and twirled around, a sack swinging from her right hand.

Willie's huge hands batted at the sack. He laughed happily.

Laurel threw her arms around him and hugged him tight against her. "Oh, Willie, it's a good, good day! Do you feel it too? I have a special treat for you."

"A peach cobbler," Ben said in mock surprise.

"Ha! I said special," Laurel bantered back. "It is not *just* a peach cobbler. Mrs. Manning took one look at me and thought to herself, My, my, this is a fine girl from a fine family. I think I'll do something nice for her. I know they would enjoy some preserved cherries from my very own cellar to put in her cobbler. And she gave me some!" She triumphantly held aloft a small container of cherries. They had been a gift from Drew, not Mrs. Manning, but a white lie now and then didn't hurt.

"She gave you that! Are the Mannings gonna give you stuff to bring home every day?" Mandy asked, her eyes shining.

Laurel put her finger to her chin, pretending to think hard. "Well, I doubt that it will be every day that she gives me something special, but I wouldn't be too surprised if I came home with something every now and then."

"When do you think you'll start working and bringing things home?"

Laurel tweaked Mandy's nose. "I started working today, silly. And you, greedy little Mandy, shall have your treats soon enough. Now! No more talk. I must see to supper and our cobbler. It won't make itself. Mandy, take care of Willie."

Laurel went to Pamela's cradle and changed the baby's sodden napkin, then picked her up, cuddling her and singing softly to the infant. As she moved around the room rhythmically, her eyes were on Mary.

Mary sat on her pallet, her eyes shining with tears and love.

"You're very quiet," Laurel said. "You didn't ask me about my job."

"I can't talk very well," Mary said. "I keep wanting to cry, but I am happy, Laurel."

"All right. We won't talk now." Laurel leaned down and whispered in her sister's ear, "Tonight we'll go outside, and I'll tell you everything."

Mary nodded and smiled.

"Pamela needs to be fed. I think she is going to get stronger and stronger. She seems more eager to eat now, I think," Laurel said. "But, little sweet one, it must be cow's milk. You have worn your mama out." The baby blinked at her. Laurel laughed. "Ah, so serious. You'll like the cow's milk, Pammie. It is very good."

"Do you think I could feed her?" Mary asked. "She's not very heavy, and I could sit right here. I'd like to try."

"Yes, I think you could. Pammie would like that, too. She loves being held." Laurel placed the baby in Mary's arms.

Mary glowed, her eyes shining up at Laurel. "I'm doing it! Oh, Laurel, maybe it's already happening. Your prayer for me is already being answered and I'm stronger too. Look, Laurel, I'm helping!"

Laurel began singing in a loud, clear voice.

> "Oh how lovely is the evening, is the evening
> When to rest the bells are ringing, bells are ringing.
> Bim, bam, bim, bam, bim, bam."

Soon Mandy joined in the round, her voice sweet and high. She and Laurel repeated the song several times, then Ben's voice joined in, and finally Mary's.

When Mathilda and Harley came into the house they were greeted by the sounds of their children's voices in a rousing round that had begun to get confused and dissolve into laughter.

"Don't that sound nice, Harley?" Mathilda said and urged the children to start it up again. They began, and she clapped time.

It didn't take long before they were all laughing again and the round was lost. Mathilda came to the hearth to help Laurel prepare the yams and fatback they'd have for supper. Soon the Boggses' table was filled with steaming platters, and the sweet smell of cobbler permeated the room.

Laurel sat at the table, unable to stop smiling. This was the nicest evening she could ever remember spending at the supper table with her family. She had started out the day so full of fear, and then as if by magic, blessings had been heaped upon her.

She cleaned up the cabin after supper, practiced her reading and her writing, figured her numbers and bedded the younger children down. Harley was already snoring beside Mathilda on their pallet when she was finished with her work. It was very late, but she wasn't tired. She thought she might never be tired again. She looked carefully at Mary to see if she was still awake. Mary had her eyes closed but couldn't keep her lips from twitching in a repressed smile.

"Oh, you faker!" Laurel whispered and helped her sister to her feet. Cautiously, with Laurel supporting Mary, they went outside. They walked a short distance from the house and sat down on the stump of a tree that Ben had fashioned into a seat. Laurel threw a blanket around the two of them, and they huddled close together against the cool night air.

"Is Manning beautiful, Laurel?"

"Oh, Mary, I can't tell you how beautiful! When I come over the last hill on my way there, I can see plowed fields until my eye can see no more, and way off, almost hidden by the trees, is Manning House. It's so big, our house would fit into one room. The walls are hard plaster, and they have angels on the ceiling in the parlor! Can you imagine, Mary, looking up in your own parlor and seeing an angel on the ceiling! And on the walls there is paper of all colors and patterns, flowers and swirls and one that looks just like blossoms blowing in the wind."

"You are so lucky, Laurel," Mary breathed. "Tell me more. Tell me what was the best of everything you saw at Manning."

Laurel looked at her, then away, her eyes seeking the star-bright sky. She thought of running across the smooth green Manning lawns with Drew's warm, strong hand holding hers. She thought of falling to the ground, breathless, to cool off before she entered the house. It was almost as if she could see again his warm brown eyes looking at her, liking what he saw, telling her secrets of her feelings.

"Laurel?" Mary said tentatively. "Did I say something wrong?"

"Oh, no, Mary. You didn't do anything wrong. I was just thinking."

"About what? Why are you so quiet? Don't you want to talk about Manning anymore?"

Laurel laughed gently. "I love talking about it. I can't think of anything else—I have a head full of Manning—but you asked me what was the best of everything today, and I was remembering that best time."

"May I know what it is?"

Laurel's laughter bubbled up again, and she wrapped her arms around her knees. Her eyes sparkled as she looked at Mary, her face bright with an inner light Mary had never before seen in her sister. Laurel pressed her lips together for a second, then said quickly, "I met Drew Manning today." She kept looking at Mary, waiting for her to share the joy, then, unable to wait, she went on, "Well, really, I met him at the grave cleaning last Saturday night, but I didn't know who he was then, and he didn't know me. But he remembered me, Mary! He said he had looked everywhere for me."

Mary remained silent and confused. Finally she said, "Is he the papa?"

Laurel burst into laughter. "No! He's Mrs. Manning's son. He's not a whole lot older than I am, I don't think. You know what, Mary, I guess he's about as old as Jeremy would have been."

Mary's eyes instantly got a faraway look. "I miss Jeremy. It was better when he was alive. Why did the tree have to hit him? It could have fallen on—"

"I know. I think about that sometimes, too, but I don't want to talk about gloomy things tonight. Jeremy wouldn't."

"Does that mean you are in love with Drew Manning?" Mary asked.

"I don't know. They say that love is a foolish thing and that it makes a person stupid and thickheaded. But I don't feel that way. I feel . . . I don't know how to say it. When I run I run so fast I don't touch the ground, and when I look up the sun is brighter, and the color of the trees is so green it hurts my eyes, and there are no bad thoughts, and it seems that Drew is part of everything I see and think and feel."

"That must feel very strange," Mary said doubtfully. "Do you like it?"

Laurel nodded. She rested her head on her knees, a smile on her lips.

Mary was silent, too, thinking, trying to imagine what Drew was to Laurel, and her dream plans. The fairy tales that Laurel read to her all had a charming prince in them, but all the families she knew had rather grouchy papas and no princes at all. But maybe that wasn't so. She thought of Ben and decided her brother would make a fine prince for someone. Perhaps men only became grouchy after they were papas. She didn't like that, because she didn't want Ben ever to become like her father, and she didn't want Laurel's prince to be like her father, either. Mary was afraid of Harley, and she knew he didn't really like her.

Laurel fixed breakfast for the family the next morning in a welter of impatience. She wanted to hurry to Manning early, so she'd have time to linger at the fields and perhaps see Drew.

As soon as she got everyone to the table and settled, she raced from the house with a hasty good-bye and a quick kiss on Mathilda's cheek. She wanted Drew to see her looking her best, but she couldn't help herself—she ran down the Indian path, and her hair was flying out from her cap when she came across the final hill.

Drew was waiting for her at the top of the hill. He stood in the shade of the big live oak. Laurel's heart was pounding, and she couldn't catch her breath. He grinned broadly when he saw her. Without a thought of hiding her feelings from him, Laurel ran to him. After a time she began to think of what she had done and how it would appear to someone like Drew. How could he know that she had never done this sort of thing before. She looked up into his face, prepared for a look of knowing and perhaps even that awful look of lust she so often saw in Reverend Fowler's eyes.

He was smiling slightly; his eyes were deep brown and filled with warmth. There was no need to fear.

14

Georgina noticed that Drew had begun to spend more time around the house than usual. Her eye went immediately to Laurel. She sighed deeply, resigning herself to living through what Joseph assured her was just a young man's best way of sowing wild oats. Joseph had chuckled and said, "If you ask me, he's got damn good taste. My milkmaid had a bulbous nose and a big bottom." Georgina had airily turned her back on her husband for such coarse talk, but she had listened. She supposed it was a natural part of emerging manhood, a subject about which she was infinitely curious, although she didn't admit it. However, she was finding it difficult to turn her head and pretend she didn't care or that nothing was happening when it was her son and it was taking place under her own roof—or at least she supposed it was.

Georgina was in a quandary. She simply could not keep her mind off Laurel and Drew. There was something about the way they looked together that warmed her, captured her mind and imagination. She found herself dwelling in a most satisfying way on forbidden thoughts of what it would be like to be a woman of Laurel's station without an arranged marriage looming in her future, without a prescribed life laid down upon her future years. She wondered if love was the same outside marriage or if it was, as she suspected, quite different. It must be different, she concluded; otherwise no one would bother with it. They'd all wait until they were married. But what was it? What were the secrets? Many of her Charles Town friends had "arrangements," which they claimed were most satisfying. She had never had such an arrangement and probably never would. And now here was Andrew, her own son, with a mistress, a beautiful young girl, and Georgina found her thoughts single-minded and her penitential prayers long and repetitive.

Georgina took special care in training Laurel. Her curiosity about the girl was boundless, and her special attention pleased Andrew. To justify everything, however, she claimed that the special training was a part of her penance for her sinful thoughts. Actually the strongest pull for Georgina was that she liked Laurel and enjoyed her company.

There were few women with whom she could talk in the Upcountry. Though she and Joseph entertained often by Upcountry standards and always had a welcomer standing sentinel at the Manning gate to issue an invitation to passersby, travelers were too few and visits were far too short to establish friendships. Often she never again saw the people who stopped at Manning for a night's rest and food.

Laurel delighted in Georgina's attention. She was learning far more than she could ever have hoped. Even Mathilda had been impressed when Laurel had set the Boggses' table properly for supper. They hadn't had silver, and not even enough utensils to make a complete setting, but Laurel had used sticks to represent salad forks and dessert spoons and soup spoons. They had had a raucous but enjoyable time pretending with their imaginary silver. Laurel smiled as she remembered Mary's shining eyes and her whispered confidence late that night: "You'll live in a house that has all them pretty things one day, Laurel. I know you will."

"If I do, you will too," Laurel had whispered back.

Mary had curled up close to her and fallen asleep listening as Laurel told her of the grandeur housed in Manning. Laurel remembered staying awake long after Mary had closed her eyes, thinking about what real grandeur was. It was only through Georgina and her description of houses in Charles Town and Europe that Laurel knew that Manning was not truly grand as a place might be. The world was a strange, mysterious place. There were layers and layers to it. Just when a person thought she had hold of something, it was only to find out that there was yet another layer hidden beyond. Mary didn't know anything about the layer that held Manning, but Laurel did. Laurel didn't know anything about the layer that held villas in Italy or Spain or palaces in England, but Georgina did. What were they like? What lay beyond Georgina's castles, and who knew of those places? Was there an end to the wonders of earth? Was there a last step in the ways in which men went to make themselves comfortable and honored? Laurel felt a chill go through her. Those were forbidden thoughts. The world was the devil's domain, and it was he who held the secrets of its pleasures. But even fear of the devil couldn't keep Laurel from dreaming of all the delights Manning held for her. She never tired of handling the beautiful ornaments or of hearing what Georgina was willing to tell her. Fortunately Georgina was generous with her time and her thoughts. She was also generous with gifts. Georgina loathed waste and at the same time hated to be out of fashion, so Laurel frequently became the recipient of many of her castoff gowns.

"You'll have to remake this, of course," Georgina said the following day, and held up a green silk gown she had worn three seasons ago, when Joseph had taken her to Charles Town for a visit.

Laurel thanked her profusely, her hands caressing the beautiful, soft material. She folded it carefully and made it into a manageable bundle to carry home.

"Everyone close your eyes!" she said as she came through the door at home. "Come on, eyes closed, or I don't show you my surprise." She burst into a peal of laughter.

The boys made sounds of disappointment, and the girls caught their breath in a unison "Ahhh!"

"See all the material in the skirt," Laurel said and spread it wide. "We can easily get three dresses from that, and the trim for one or two others."

"Can we begin sewing tonight?" Mandy asked.

"We can begin now!" Laurel replied.

It was a wonderful time for the Boggses. The fall was mild, and late as they were, Harley and Ben were getting in a decent harvest from their plot of tilled land. No one would starve this winter. And Laurel had never known she could be as happy as she was these days. Her dream was beginning to seem too small for the bounty she was being given. She had never thought of being loved by a man like Drew Manning, and even now she knew it wasn't something she could count on.

Without meaning to be cruel or discouraging, Georgina had told Laurel about the Templetons and the arranged marriage to Joanna.

Her dreaming and wishing wouldn't change that. Though she and Drew might one day lie in the coolness of the soft grass and draw warmth from each other's arms, that wouldn't alter Laurel's background or make her a suitable wife for him.

She had thought for a long time before she had finally decided to lie with Drew for the first time. She had thought she would know only one man—her husband. Reverend Fowler and Reverend Woodmason both said it was wrong to know a man before marriage, and she had vowed she never would. She never had until she had met Drew, and there was no other way for them to be together. She didn't have a fine family name, or a plantation, or political connections or wealth, and she never would. All she had was herself, and that was only enough to permit her to lie with him, but not to be his wife. She decided she wanted him in any way she could have him.

After she finished her duties for the day, Laurel removed her apron and carefully placed it in the pantry, ready for the morning. She smoothed her hair and washed her face, then stepped out the back door into the still-bright sunlight of late afternoon. Her thoughts were left behind with her apron. Now was her time with Drew, and Joanna couldn't intrude, at least not yet. She ran to the field where Drew was working. She burst into a smile as he looked in her direction immediately. He always knew when she was near. The smile spread deep within her as she watched him look for his shirt, find it caught on a bush where he had thrown it and come running toward her, dressing as he came. His hair gleamed reddish in the bright golden sun.

She clasped her hands and held them tight. She could barely look at him, he so filled her with love. He made her feel like laughing and crying at the same time, just looking at him.

"I thought you'd never get here! Were you especially busy today?" he asked.

"No," she said with a laugh. "You're just especially impatient. Look at the sky—it is still very early."

He looked up at the sky. "Is it?" He watched her nod, then gave her a speculative look. "Do you think you could be a little late going home this evening?"

Laurel looked curiously at him. Then her eyes began to twinkle. "What have you in mind?"

"Remember the property I told you about . . . mine?" Again she nodded. "I'd like you to see it. I'd like you to be the first to see it . . . for us to make it ours."

Laurel's chest tightened. She couldn't breathe very well. "Ours?" she asked in a small voice.

"We will have to have a place of our own," he said and took her hand. "We'll have to hurry if we want to be back at a decent hour."

He hitched a small farm cart, and the two of them sat close together on the seat meant for one. At Drew's side was his rifle. He headed the horse up a winding, narrow trail.

They came to a line of live oak, and as his father had done before him at Manning, Drew had planted trees lining what would eventually be the carriage path to his house, with such detail that all would know the trees had been put there by a man.

Laurel was very quiet by his side. As he did so often, he was pulling her into a part of his life in which she felt she belonged and yet knew she could never be. Just as the Carolina hills had seemed to call themselves home for her when her family first arrived, this land that was Drew's did the same thing. He hadn't told her where he planned to build his house yet, but she knew where it would be. She could see it in her mind's eye; she could feel it. She looked down at her hands, no longer able to stand being so taunted by a perverse fate, and stayed that way so long he assumed she was bored.

He laughed self-consciously. "I forget not everyone likes to stare at open land. I don't suppose it is much of a treat when there is so much of it around."

She still didn't look at him but said softly, "I love being here, Drew. It's beautiful, and I can imagine what it will be like when your fields are cleared and you have your first tobacco growing."

"You can? You can really imagine that?" he asked, surprised, and turning fully toward her. She kept her head averted. He reached up, his hand under her chin, and turned her face to him. "Then why do you act as though I'm putting you through a trial of fire?"

"Because you are," she said simply. "I can only look, but I can't touch. I can visit, but it will never be home to me, and it feels like home." She angrily flicked a tear from her eye.

"But Laurel, I brought you here to see it because I'd like it to be your home—our home. I wanted you to see it and then tell me if you could live this far from civilization. It wouldn't be for long, I'm sure. More and more people are moving here every day, but for a time it would be lonely. Would you be afraid?"

"No, I'd never be afraid where you are. But Drew, it isn't possible. You and I can't live here."

"Why not?" he asked, his eyes troubled and puzzled. "If you aren't afraid of being so far from your neighbors, what is there to stop us?"

"Oh, Drew, I know you don't mean to be, but you are being very cruel. By this time next year you'll be married and living at River-lea."

"I didn't know you knew about Joanna."

"Your mother told me about her."

"I'm not going to marry Joanna—not this year, not any year. I haven't told anyone yet, but I've made up my mind. I want you to be my wife, Laurel."

Laurel began to cry, pressing her face against Drew's chest. "We can't! Your family would never stand for it."

"I know. That's why I wanted you to see this land before I asked you. We'd be on our own—starting with nothing—and it would be very hard for a while—maybe years."

"You'd do that for me?"

"With certainty. I've never felt better about anything I've decided," Drew said. "My grandma told me I'd know when I was heading in the right direction with my life. She said it would be a feeling I couldn't help but recognize. She's right. I feel good, and free, and as though the whole world is at my fingertips waiting for me to do what I will. We'll have a family as big as yours, Laurel, and all the children will be healthy, and we won't lose a one of them. See all those trees I planted? We'll have one son for each tree."

Laurel laughed as she looked at the long double line of trees. "And girls?"

"One for every flower you plant."

"You'd better build a big house."

"You'll marry me?"

"I'll marry you," she said with doubt in her voice. "But we'll see whether you will be able to marry me."

He threw his arms around her, kissing her forehead and working his way down her cheek to her mouth and then to her neck. He pulled away from her, his eyes caressing her. Without speaking he got down from the cart and lifted her into his arms. He carried her a short distance and stood looking around. He moved a few feet to the side and farther in. "Your bedroom, Mrs. Manning."

Laurel put her arms around his neck. Around them the forest stirred. Birds called as they settled for the evening. The sky began to turn golden. Laurel let her head go back, staring dreamily at him silhouetted against the brilliant color of day's end. Andrew gently lowered her to the ground, and his weight slowly pressed against her. Beneath her back she felt the still warmth of the grass. Atop her she felt the smooth softness of Andrew's flesh, his weight, his strength. She closed her eyes contentedly and let herself float free, reveling in the thoughts and smells and feelings of love and home until the demands of her body called her attention and she became lost in Andrew's kiss. Entwined with each other, they moved together. Andrew touched the smooth whiteness of her skin, his fingers lingering at her breast, then moving down across her ribs and abdomen. Laurel had never known what it meant to know that one was beautiful until Drew had touched her as he was doing now. She arched toward him, and her legs locked around him. The red sky turned to lavender, and with the cooling of the day, they lay in quiet passion, once more touching each other and feasting with eyes that could see only good in each other.

It was dark and quite late when Drew brought Laurel to her home. At her bidding, he reined the horse in a hundred yards from her cabin. "I will leave you here," she said.

His arm tightened around her waist as she tried to alight from the cart. "I am not letting you walk. I'll take you home and explain that there was a gala affair at Manning tonight, and it would not have been a success had you not been there. You see, the absolute truth, with just a modicum of misleading."

For a moment she was tempted to give in. She imagined herself walking into the small cabin with Drew at her side. All the eyes of her family would be wide with curiosity and admiration, and they would be on her and on Drew. She would so like to have Mary know what Drew looked like and how his voice sounded, so that when they spoke of him late at night, Mary would know the wonder of him as she did. "Drew, I want to go into the cabin alone."

He kissed her, his mouth lingering near hers. "But I don't want you to be alone—not now, not anytime ever again. I'll go with you."

Laurel straightened in her seat, pulling away from him. "No. I'll go alone. You don't know my family . . ."

"It's time I did."

"And I don't want you to!" she said over his statement.

"Laurel," he said, and let her name hang between them as a question for some time. "Why don't you want them to meet me? One day they must if we're to marry—or is it that you don't . . . that you aren't as sure you want to be my wife as you seem?"

"I want to be your wife. I shall be." She turned from him, not knowing how to tell him about Harley and Mathilda without being disloyal. "Please, let me go to the cabin alone. Stay here and watch for my safety if you must, but let me go alone tonight."

Drew did as she asked, but the uncomfortable question of why she wouldn't allow him to meet her family lingered. She didn't seem to be ashamed of them and talked of them with great affection. It didn't make sense to him. His way was always to confront his problems when the time for it came, but Laurel seemed to want to evade. He thought it odd and foreboding that on the same night he had asked her to become his wife, he also had his first doubt of her love. His thoughts went strangely to his cousin Gwynne and how she might have acted. He could imagine the defiance, the pride, the fervor with which Gwynne would have declared her triumph—and it was a triumph for Laurel. Drew knew that. Not many girls of her background would ever marry someone such as he.

He drove home slowly. Laurel was all he wanted in a woman—warm, beautiful, intelligent, attuned to the wilds. He was as sure of it as he had ever been of anything. She made Joanna pale to a shadow, insignificant, but he was uncomfortable in spite of his knowledge of Laurel. He was afraid she didn't believe it, and if Laurel didn't believe she could be his wife in all ways, then she could not be. One could reach far beyond one's abilities, but never beyond one's belief.

He hurried the horse. He'd make her believe. He had enough vision for both of them. He smiled and thought again of Gwynne. Perhaps he should ask his cousin to give his future wife lessons in true pride. Gwynne certainly had it.

It wasn't quite a week later that Laurel met him after work.

"I was hoping you'd come earlier today. There's a meeting tonight, and now we have no time."

"You've gotten word from Charles Town," she said, looking down.

"Yes, finally. The Assembly and the governor have given us funds for Rangers. We'll be authorized to do our job now. I want to be part of this, Laurel. I want to know, when we are safe in the Upcountry, that I've done my part."

Laurel looked away, unwilling to meet his eyes.

"I know you don't like to hear about the Regulators."

"I'm afraid for you. The Regulators have cut themselves so lonely a path—there is no one to help you or to turn to if things go wrong. It frightens me, Drew. How do you know that Governor Montagu won't change his mind tomorrow and send the militia after you? How can you trust him?"

"We have no choice but to trust him as long as he'll grant us his help."

She lowered her head and bit her lip. "I wish it were otherwise."

He smiled. "I'll be safe. You must learn to believe in us, Laurel." Gently he pulled her against him. His lips touched her hair. Laurel remained quiet, enjoying for the moment what he pressed her to make hers forever. He kissed her cheek; then his mouth moved toward hers. She kissed him hungrily, taking what she could, because no matter what he promised, she couldn't make herself believe that it wouldn't be taken from her.

Drew pulled away from her, breathless. "Do that again and I'll never get to the meeting."

She buried her face in his shirt. "I'm so afraid."

He soothed her. "Of what, love? Nothing will harm you, I'll see to that."

"It isn't that," she cried. "I don't know what is wrong with me. Everything is happening to me, and I can't believe it. You keep talking about how it will be when we are married, but Drew, I'm so afraid it will never happen. How can it? We're so different. I could never be like your mother . . . or Joanna, and I can't stand it when I think of all you'll give up to be with me. I'm afraid I can't live up to all this. My dream was so small, and this is so . . . so impossible."

He shook his head. "What puts these thoughts into your head?

Where do they come from, and how am I to dispel them? I give up nothing of value to be with you, Laurel, can't you understand that? And Joanna—Joanna is nothing compared to you. She's cold and hard . . . a—a hostess and no more. It's you I want, Laurel. Where you are is where I want to be."

It felt good being next to him, and she didn't want him to stop talking. His words were balm to her. She eagerly accepted his kisses, but she wanted more. She wanted a magic formula from him that would make her doubts and fears disappear.

Her voice was husky, her eyes half-closed in the contented pleasure of his embrace, but her words told what was inside her, "When I want to raise Mary's spirit I tell her that one day we'll be just like the Mannings. I tell her that because it is as high as she can imagine, but I know it isn't really so. We . . . we aren't the same."

Drew looked at her for a long time and remembered the ringing words of a man under the Liberty Tree. "We are all equal under the eyes of God, and here on this soil, this American soil where there are men of all colors and religions, it is meant that a great experiment take place. We shall live in harmony, with all men having the same opportunity, the same right to live and pursue his fortune and his happiness." He didn't remember the man's name—he had just been a man—but Drew remembered and believed in what he had said, not knowing how closely it would touch his own life. He continued to look at Laurel, his eyes caressing the soft curve of her cheek, his hands touching her thick brown hair. "You're wrong, Laurel," he said softly. "Nothing will stand between us and our being together. It is a new day and a new land, with no one and nothing against our marriage."

"Your father wouldn't agree."

Drew looked toward his house. "Perhaps the things of my father's day are gone. Perhaps my father's time has passed."

15

The night after the Regulators meeting Drew packed his bag for the ride to Camden the next day. He would be part of the Regulator Rangers in rounding up the outlaws, and then upon his return he'd go to Charles Town and Riverlea.

Georgina stood in the doorway the next morning, waiting for him. "Did you remember everything, Drew?" she asked with a mother's concern. "I am aware that I am nagging you, but will you be warm enough? And provisions, did you—"

Drew hugged her. "I have everything I need and more. I can't get another scrap of anything in my saddlebag, and yes, Mama, I will be warm enough . . . and well fed."

Georgina nodded. "Drew, be careful, please."

"I will. Good-bye, Mama." He took the reins from the waiting groom and mounted his horse quickly. With a backward glance at his mother, he turned and brought the horse to a slow canter down the long drive. As soon as he was sure she could no longer see him, he edged his way carefully through the hedge and across the field that would take him to the back of the house, where he knew Laurel would be waiting for him.

She was watching for him out the back window. As soon as she saw him she ran from the house. Her arms were outstretched, and there was no restraint or care that she might be seen or judged. "Oh, Drew, keep safe. I am so frightened. Don't let anything happen to you." She buried her face against him.

He raised her head, his hands stroking her forehead. He kissed each cheek, her eyelids, and then, slowly and warmly, her mouth. "Think of me while I'm gone—every day—every night."

"I'll pray," she said. "And think of you constantly. Not a moment will you be out of my thoughts. Come back safely, Drew. Don't let anything happen to you. Promise me you'll be careful."

"You know I'll be careful . . ."

"Promise me."

"I love you."

"But, Drew . . ."

"I love you." He placed his fingers on her lips keeping her from replying.

Tears sprang to Laurel's eyes.

"You are going to marry me?" he said, teasing.

Laurel nodded her head, trying to catch her breath. "It's just so difficult to believe it could really be so. I want you to tell me over and over again." She raised her mouth to his. "I wish you didn't have to go this time, Drew. I'll miss you so, and I won't have you here with me to tell me that we will be married and have children and a house and . . . and that we'll be together."

He stood with his arms around her for some time. "It will all happen just as we planned, Laurel. Don't doubt it." He squeezed her tight and held her pressed against him. "I must go now. You'll be all right while I'm gone. Should you need anything, go to my mother. Tell her I instructed you to come to her. She'll listen and help you in whatever way you might need."

He kissed her once more, then reluctantly went to his horse. Mounted, he still lingered, looking at her. She looked so alone and small. He didn't want to leave her. Thoughts flitted through his mind, bits of conversations heard among other Regulators, older, married men, now came back to him with new meaning. They worried when they left their homes. They wondered about the safety of their property, their wives and daughters. As he looked at Laurel standing outside his house, he realized that she wouldn't be within the safety of its guarded fences. Every day she would leave its protection and walk alone to her house. There was nothing he could do, no way he could protect her except to do what he was about.

The Rangers, established by Governor Montagu and the Assembly, formed at Camden. Each company consisted of a captain, a lieutenant and twenty-five privates. Many of the Rangers were taken from the ranks of the Regulators, and in effect the formation of the companies legalized the Regulators movement. Joseph Kirkland and Henry Hunter became the captains, and both men were Regulators.

Andrew's voice blended with the cheers of the other men as the news was told. "And we're to be paid!" Bart Cole said. "Fifteen pounds a month for doin' what we've been doin' all along for nothing."

"Could be you'd make lieutenant, Drew, good as you've done on our Regulator raids. They're givin' lieutenants eighteen pounds."

Drew laughed. "I think I'll stick with being a private. None of you fellows would obey an order I gave anyway. I don't want to be held responsible for your mistakes."

"You implyin' that we're headstrong?" Bart asked with mock belligerence.

"It's likely that I am," Drew shot back with a war cry that sent Bart's hands to his ears.

Soon after the meeting broke up, to be rejoined at Swift Creek near the Wateree River, about fifteen miles south of Camden. It gave Drew both a feeling of reassurance and of melancholy. He was closer to home, but in time he had taken another step in removing himself from Laurel.

The two captains brought their companies up before Charles Woodmason's pulpit, asking for his blessing on their mission. Reverend Woodmason, always a defender and supporter of the Regulators, once more proved his faith and his sympathy with a sermon that lasted well over an hour. The men tried to keep their attention from wandering lest Reverend Woodmason not realize their true gratitude. Drew became edgier with every word spoken, listening as he was with his newfound fears.

". . . I know that many among you have personally been injured by the rogues," Woodmason said in his clear voice. "Some in their wives, others in their sisters or daughters; by loss of horses, cattle, goods and effects." He went on to talk at length of the ravages of the outlaws, but Andrew could not stand to hear any more. He couldn't rid himself of the vision of Laurel as she had stood at the edge of the field when he rode off. There had been tears in her eyes, and he had wanted only to stay with her. Nothing ever seemed to be as it should be. Charles Town should have provided help for the Upcountry long ago. He should not be going out on this ride to clear away the outlaws; he should be at home, preparing to marry Laurel and start a family of his own.

Ned Hart stood to the side, watching Drew and listening to the sermon. He would not be riding with the Regulators this time, but his heart would be with them, and particularly with Drew. Sadly Ned noted the play of conflicting emotions crossing Drew's face, and from Harley Boggs's bragging he knew about Drew's interest in Laurel. He couldn't help himself; he felt fatherly toward Drew, for in this instance he knew that Joseph Manning was not going to be helpful. And he was just as sure that Drew would need a strong older man to lean on through this. Drew and Laurel were going to have a difficult time if they chose to be together, and Ned was already feeling great compassion for them. Laurel was a jewel in the midst of sterile rock, and Harley Boggs was just beginning to understand the value of his jewel. Andrew was too young, too idealistic, too privileged and too much in love to protect himself against the trouble a man like Harley Boggs could create.

As Reverend Woodmason ended his sermon and came down from the pulpit to talk with some of the men, others went to their horses, checking last-minute arrangements and seeing to provisions. Others milled about, talking and anxiously awaiting the call to be on their way. Ned walked up to Drew.

"Hello, Drew. Sorry I won't be with you men this ride."

"So am I, Ned. You sure you won't come?"

"I'm sure. Your daddy can do without one of us, but not both of us. An' I got my own farm to look after."

"I'll probably miss the first planting, won't I?"

Ned smiled as he watched still another facet of Drew's young life. pulling at him. He loved his fields and had a pride in his indigo that went well beyond the mere pride of a man for his crop. It was the land itself with Drew, that and his own identity with nature. Ned had seen that before, but not often and never in one so young. It usually took a man a lot of years of growing, ripening and hurting before he recognized that his roots were sunk deep in the soil he trod and started moving with it. "Don't worry about your fields. If you don't get back in time, I'll see that we do jes' like we would if you was there. I know your ways, don't I, boy? Taught you a few of them myself." Ned slapped him on the back and winked at him, waiting, then winked again until he got a return smile from Drew. "Now that we got that cleared away, good luck to you, Drew." They shook hands, then Ned placed his hand on Drew's shoulder, looking at him in silence for a moment. "Try'n remember what I tol' you las' time we was out, Drew. Y'can't get your heart tangled up in this. It's business, boy, a dirty business. You keep it that way or you're gonna feel the hurt of it."

At a command from his captain, Drew mounted his horse. "I will, Ned. I'll try."

But they both knew he couldn't.

Drew had been too young to participate in the Cherokee War. This was the first experience of a long campaign, relentlessly hounding the enemy mile after mile, that he'd ever had. By the end of the first day of hard riding, Drew was exhausted. He was accustomed to tough physical labor, but he had never ridden harder, longer or with greater tension than he had today with the Rangers.

The outlaw bands knew the Rangers were coming after them and had accordingly fled, leaving behind small groups of men to harass and skirmish with the Rangers. Every tree, every clump of shrubbery, every curve in the trail was a potential ambush, and yet every stranger met had to be judged friend or foe. Protecting the innocent wasn't as simple as it sounded, for the innocent could be as frightening when come upon unexpectedly as were the guilty.

Drew slept soundly that night, relying totally on the men who had been posted as guards for the camp. When he awoke the following morning it seemed that he hadn't slept at all. Only the smell of coffee brewing and thin-sliced pork cooking over the open campfire prompted him from his bedroll.

Breakfast was short and businesslike. The Rangers were riding again half an hour after Andrew awoke. The countryside began to take on a sameness. They rode into and out of woods, across wide expanses of marsh and grasslands. Slowly Drew began to recognize the likely spots from which the outlaws might attack and the escape routes they were most likely to take. As they rode through a deserted outlaw community, Drew noticed a stone wall butted up against the side of a hill and extending along a gentle rise until it reached the woods. He touched Bart Cole's arm, pointing with his musket at the thicket. With a nod Bart silently passed the word to

John Haynes and several others. Six of them moved with the main group of Rangers, then as they neared the wall, broke away, their voices raised in a piercing cry, their muskets ready. Drew's horse went up to the wall, then turned aside. He turned to take another run at the wall. Bart's musket fired, and from the dense cover of the thicket a heavily built man came from behind Bart, in his hand a long-bladed knife. Drew kicked his horse, giving the war cry to attract attention. Without time to steady himself and fire, Drew jumped the wall and rammed his horse into the man. His face distorted, John Haynes rode past Drew. "My turn!" he shouted, and deftly threw his hunting knife. The man shrieked and fell against a tree. Several yards deeper into the thicket the other Rangers fought with two more of the band.

"Half a dozen of them ran that way!" Will Platt shouted, pointing due east.

Drew and Bart crashed through the underbrush but saw nothing. For the next fifteen minutes they moved carefully around the area, guarding each other's back, poking in the thick bush and searching the craggy places at the base of the hill.

"Let's give it up," Bart said. "They're gone. Probably lookin' down at us from higher up there an' laughin' their fool heads off."

Drew agreed. "We'll get them soon enough. I think I'm beginning to understand what Ned is always talking about—this being a business. It's more like a boar hunt. You go out and you know you're not going to leave until you have a boar slung over the back of your saddle. Sometimes it gets to taking a long, long time, and you wonder if there's a boar left in creation for the catching. But you keep on tracking and sure enough, you go home with a boar. We're doing almost the same thing. After this expedition there won't be a one of these outlaws left."

Bart shook his head. "You are the doggonedest man for thinkin' so much. How you come up with them ideas? What do you care as long as we git 'em?" He slapped his horse on the rump and started back to the main square of the settlement. Two scruffy-looking men stood in the center of a ring of Rangers. Rob Willson, one of the Rangers, fastened a rope to the tallest tree in the square. Without emotion or ado the Rangers hanged the two outlaws, one for murder, the other for rape and horse thievery.

Drew looked around him and listened to the men talking and

joking, paying little or no attention to the two dying men. It gave him a strange feeling, for he realized that he too felt little for those convulsing men hanging at the ends of the ropes. He blinked and forced himself to look at the two figures. There was no blaze of emotion as there had been that first time. Perhaps this trip would, after all, teach him to look upon the business of war dispassionately. But as it had disturbed him that he could feel the galling hatred that made him want to destroy the outlaws as they destroyed, he found that dispassion brought him a different feeling, one that was equally uncomfortable. Was the feeling that these outlaw men were no more than vermin to be disposed of any better than hating?

During the first two months of the hunt the Rangers rounded up wagons of stolen property and hundreds of stolen horses and retrieved many stolen Negroes and young girls. Children were found wandering through the open fields and in the bush, lost or left behind by the escaping renegades. They took the children, the booty and the captured outlaws to the nearest justices of the peace, to be escorted back to owners, homes or courts. Over one hundred horses and thirty-five girls were returned to the Camden area. They also sent the news home that in over two months of fighting, not one Regulator had been killed.

The route they had taken was grueling, and it wasn't nearly over. Drew tried to write faithfully to his family and to Laurel. But he found there was little to be said. He let them know where he was and that he was safe, but most of his day was spent in an endless ride. Their replies seldom caught up with him, and he often felt as though he were talking to himself when he told them of his days. He felt a strong need to talk with someone, and the feeling grew the farther he rode from home. The times were changing, and he was changing. He didn't know how and began to long for a quiet place to rest and perhaps even to heal, for he knew there was something damaging in being able to kill dispassionately, never letting it touch his heart, viewing it as nothing but a duty to be performed. But he couldn't understand it, for he granted that Ned was right in that he couldn't be so involved that his feelings were always raw. A man couldn't survive that way, either.

He had ridden every square inch of South Carolina, he thought, and then the company headed for Bethabara, North Carolina. They arrived there on January 17 and rested for a time. Even though it felt good not to have to rise before the sun to ride endless trails, Drew was eager to be on his way again. The longer he was away from home, the lonelier he felt. He wasn't sure for whom he was lonely, but there remained with him a feeling of misgiving and displacement that he couldn't shake. He was impatient and irritable by the time they were once more hounding the outlaw band across the province to the hollow. Sixteen fugitives were hanged. As he stood with the others, he couldn't recall how many men he had seen hanged, nor could he recall what he had once felt about Govey Black just a few weeks ago. And now the man was here. And so was Drew. John Haynes and Rob Willson brought Black to the hanging tree. Drew looked at the man and was frightened. He couldn't even keep his attention on this hated outlaw. All he could feel was a tiredness in his back and legs. Something had happened to him, and he was afraid because he didn't know what it was. He kept staring at Govey Black, trying to bring back some sense of reality.

Govey Black was the son of one of Fredericksburg Township's early settlers. John Black had been a decent, hardworking man who had left his two sons George and Govey a sizable amount of land and a name to be proud of. Govey had had 331 acres, which he had sold for 250 pounds after the Cherokee War. George had also sold his land, and the two brothers had become outlaws. Some said the Cherokee War was to blame for much of the crime—that it had turned good men bad for all time. Others said the Black brothers were just bad naturally. Either way they had come to an end here at the hollow. George had been hanged awhile back, and now Govey stood in the midst of the Rangers, looking at the Carolina sky for the last time, and Drew Manning stood less than a stone's throw away and couldn't make himself care.

From North Carolina the Rangers rode to Augusta County, Virginia, where they recovered horses and Negroes stolen from plantations in South Carolina. They were far from home, but their mission was accomplished, and the riding from this point on would be taking them back home. On February 29, after riding and fighting across hundreds of miles covering three provinces, the Rangers arrived in Charles Town with recovered slaves and two horse thieves, Ebenezer Wells and Absalom Tilley. The thieves were turned over to the authorities, and at last Drew was free to go back to Manning.

16

While he was away, Laurel missed Drew terribly. She had never been in love before. In all her dreaming of what the world could hold for her if she was willing to work for it, she had never included a man she loved. It had seemed too much to ask with all the other things she wanted for herself and her family. She was unprepared for the wrenching loneliness she now felt when he wasn't with her.

She tried valiantly to put Drew out of her mind and concentrate on her work. In work alone it seemed that she was able to behave normally, and it helped to dispel her sense of loss. The crystal in Georgina's cupboard sparkled. There wasn't a floor in Manning that didn't have the fresh gleam of waxed and polished wood. But as soon as she went home in the evening, the emptiness within her returned. Laurel tried to be cheerful. She smiled a lot and talked whenever she could think of anything to say, but no one was fooled. All the Boggses knew something was amiss.

It didn't take Mathilda Boggs long to read the signs and come up with the correct answer to her daughter's peculiar behavior. She watched Laurel for several days before she said anything, and when she did speak it was at the dinner table with the whole family gathered round.

"Secrets is hard to keep," she said and went back to picking peas with her broken fingernails from her plate.

Harley grunted and continued eating. The children looked up curiously, but none said anything.

"Yeah," Mathilda said drawing the word out. "Secrets is mighty hard to keep, 'specially hard from them that know ye."

"What are you talkin' about, woman?" Harley said, throwing down his dinner knife. "How's a man to have a meal sit right in his belly with a magpie blatherin' at his side?"

"Ain't the blatherin' that's botherin' you, Harley, it's the wantin' to know. Curiosity is allus bad fer the stummick." Mathilda concentrated on her food for a time, watching her husband from the corner of her eye. He sat rigid in his chair, his nose turned down, his mouth in a thin line of annoyance.

"Woman," he shouted, pounding the table with a thick fist. "Iffen you don't want this hand hittin' on you, you'll shet up or speak what's on your mind now. I'm a hungry man, and I want my meal in peace."

Mathilda gave him a withering look. "Touch me agin, Harley, an' I tol' you what you'd be expectin' in return. In the dead o' night, mind you, when you're not aknowin' what I be up to."

Harley made a noise deep in his throat but quickly became interested in his food. Soon after he asked again, in a pleasant tone, what the secret was.

Mathilda smiled triumphantly. "Thought you'd be curious sooner or later. Summon' here's got her a big secret, an' it's poppin' out o' her like red bumps." She looked at Laurel, her gaze pointed and unwavering.

Mary shrank down in her seat, her food untouched on her plate.

Harley looked from his wife to his daughter. His shrewd little eyes were squinted tight. "What you keepin' to yerself, girl? You gettin' money you ain't been turnin' over to me? You tryin' to cheat your own family?"

"No, Papa!" Laurel said. "I don't know what Mama's talking about. I haven't kept anything from you! There's no secret!"

Mathilda laughed knowingly.

"Mama! What are you doing? The Mannings aren't paying me more than what I gave you." She looked warily at Harley, watching his suspicion and anger rise.

"Mebbe I'd best get my belt, girl." He laid his hand on the table, stretching out so that it was near Laurel. The thick fingers twitched, and a smile came to Harley's lips. "Think mebbe you want to tell me that secret before it gets to twitchin' so bad I jes' cain't keep it off'n my belt?"

"There is no secret, Papa. I don't know what Mama means," Laurel said in a small voice. She looked at Mathilda. "Mama, why are you making him think I've kept something from him? You know I give him all my pay."

"Whyn'cha tell us your secret, Laurel?" Mathilda said, cackling.

"What secret? There is no secret!" Tears sprang to Laurel's eyes. She looked again at Harley.

"Ain't there?" Mathilda asked, thoroughly enjoying herself.

"No!"

"Ha! Money ain't nothin' when you think of what you could get other ways, is it, Laurel?"

"Mama!"

"Ain't you been took down by that Drew Manning? Ain't that happened, Laurel? Think I cain't tell when a girl's no more a girl?"

Laurel blushed to the roots of her hair.

Several of her brothers and sisters giggled. Harley looked hard at Mathilda.

"Lookit her, Harley!" Mathilda said, laughing and pointing at her daughter. "Di'n't I tell you she had a secret. Jes' lookey there, iffen you want proof. They's jes' some things a woman kin tell by lookin' at another. I knowed, I sure did!"

"That the truth, girl?" Harley asked.

"Mama!" Laurel cried.

"You shet up, Harley." She turned back to Laurel. "Cain't you git it in your head, girl, we's on your side. Harley an' me think you done real fine. How bad's he a'wantin' you?"

Laurel wanted to shrivel up and vanish from the room. She couldn't remember ever having felt so ashamed or dirtied. No matter what she felt about Drew or had hoped might come true despite good sense telling her otherwise, she knew she couldn't let him become part of her family. Tonight Laurel thought it would be wonderful never to have to see her mother and father again, but she loved her brothers and sisters, and she knew she would feel differently about Harley and Mathilda later.

Laurel had never doubted that, given a chance, her family could rise to a higher level and be like other decent folk. Tonight she learned that despite her work and her hopes, her family wasn't going to change. They had been defeated too often; their dream was dead. Her stomach churned, and she felt sick deep inside. She knew now she couldn't help them ever.

Laurel sat outside until the moon was high, thinking and questioning herself endlessly. She stretched out on the cold, damp earth and sobbed. She didn't know how long she had been there before she felt Mary's hand on her back. Laurel rolled to her side.

"I'm sorry, Laurel," Mary said in a whisper.

"There's nothing you can do, Mary. I guess some things can't be, no matter how hard I wish or work."

Mary said nothing but shifted her weight.

"What is it, Mary?"

"Mama won't feed Pammie. She said you're a liar, an' she won't talk to no one an' won't do nothin' till you tell the truth, so Pammie is squalling in her crib, an' she smells real bad, Laurel."

A memory of Drew stabbed through her. She got up, brushed the soil from her skirt, wiped her eyes and walked with Mary back to the cabin and Pamela. "Don't worry, Mary. Pammie will be all right. You and me . . . we'll take care of her."

17

By the end of January, 1768, the outlaw activity had nearly come to an end. Everyone knew that the Rangers were succeeding in their task. The names of hanged outlaws were on everyone's lips. Stories that grew with each telling were passed from neighbor to neighbor about the Rangers' exploits and their battles with the desperadoes. The Coles had a social and invited nearly everyone they knew to show off the silver that the Rangers had returned to the family, and to announce the forthcoming marriage of their son Bart to Miranda Spelling. Georgina and Joseph attended and basked in the adulation Drew received, as did the others who had family riding with the Rangers.

Joseph enjoyed his son's sudden popularity. He found he liked being greeted by nearly everyone he saw and being asked about Drew. A hero's father was a good person to be. And he told all who would listen about Drew's part in the hanging of Govey Black.

Harley Boggs was doing a little bragging as well. He found that he liked the idea of having Drew Manning as a son-in-law, and even if it were never to happen, it didn't do his reputation any harm to let a few people think that it was going to. As he and Joseph often told of the same adventures, it sounded as though Harley knew Joseph as well as Drew, and a greater credibility was given to his claims.

Harley was a better practiced storyteller than Joseph was, and he embellished his tales at will. Drew began to sound like a one-man army riding through the countryside, his saber in his teeth, his pistols flaring at every man who had ever been on the wrong side of the law. Harley's audience was also different from Joseph's. The men to whom Harley told his stories in the daytime were to be found in the general store and were relatively harmless. Those to whom he told his tales in the night, however, were found in the taverns of Camden and along the back roads at places known only to and welcoming of men who easily slipped across the lines of legality. Their morals followed their need for money and the press of survival. Their inclinations were to take the easiest route to fortune, and their windfalls often came in the form of stolen property traded for information. Harley joyously and ignorantly informed them of the name and whereabouts of their enemy and his point of vulnerability.

As the days followed one another, Mathilda grew in her certainty that she had been right about Laurel and Drew. Mathilda set about to mend the damage she had done. Laurel was her most valuable possession and most likely the only means by which the Boggses would ever climb out of the poverty they lived with.

Late one afternoon Mathilda sat with Pammie in her lap while Laurel tidied up the cabin before dinner. "Miz Manning ain't never called her man from the fields, most like. Probably never sat with a sickly chil' clingin' to her, neither. Iffen she ain't got the milk, they'd bring her a wet nurse." Mathilda sat staring out the door for a time. "Don'chu wunner what it'd be like to have summun to do fer you?"

"Yes, Mama, I do wonder."

Mathilda laughed. "Folks like us never git beyond the wunnerin'. We allus is sittin' in the rocker with the sickly chil' aclingin'. Mebbe we got them chillern 'cause the Lord jes' wouldn't dare give 'em a sickly chil'. They's Mannings, after all."

Laurel put her hands in her hair and turned to her mother. "Oh, Mama, don't you ever want to be something more than what we are now? Can't you see there is no one who cares if you're lying in the road? Only those people who walk the road are worth noticing. Why can't we be among those who walk, Mama?"

"You think your mama ain't tried? You think I di'n't have the same big ideas you tellin' Mary 'bout now? Well, I'm tellin' you, I did, and here's where I got to."

"I don't understand, Mama. If you felt as I do now, how did you . . ."

" 'Cause I got myself took down one summer night by Harley. He could sweet-talk the honey from the bee, but he weren't worth a farthing. I had my sights set a whole lot higher than him."

"But you married Papa."

Mathilda snorted, her mouth twisted in a bitter smile. "I had a belly full of his chile. Ain't no high-born man wantin' a girl with a big belly full o' chile, 'specially when he know it ain't his'n. Purty don't count fer so much then."

"Oh, Mama, I'm so sorry for you. I didn't know."

"That's why I'm tellin' you—fer your own good. Iffen you got that Drew Manning apantin' after you, you git with chile an' do it quick as you kin. Mebbe he won't wed with you, but he be payin' somethin' fer that chile . . . or mebbe payin' jes' so's you'd leave hereabouts. Laurel, you'd be set fer a long time to come, an' later you'd marry up with a man . . . men like Harley don't mind so much iffen another's bedded you first, 'specially iffen you got a little hard money tucked away somewheres."

Laurel said nothing. Listlessly she reached out and touched Pamela's head. The baby's hand raised, and Laurel placed her finger in Pamela's grasp.

Mathilda leaned forward in the rocker. "I'm talkin' fer your good, cain't you see that, dotter?"

Laurel walked slowly to the door and looked out. She stood there for a long time, then said, "I'm going to see if I can find something to make a pie with for supper, Mama." She walked down the hill, past the field where her younger brother diligently removed rocks from the earth. She tried to imagine Mathilda young, and pretty. She wondered even more if there ever was a time when her mother had been like she herself was now.

One morning when Laurel went to Manning, Georgina handed her a letter from Drew. She read it and did so poorly in her work that day that Georgina sent her home early, thinking she was ill. Drew would be returning any day. He had said it would be about two weeks when he wrote the letter, and that had been ten days ago. He might come upon her unexpectedly at any time. She both longed for his return yet dreaded it. It seemed ever since her parents had sensed her feelings, her dreams had become tinged with fear and foreboding. For the first time she began to doubt that the future held infinite possibilities, and that she would ever escape her horribly deprived and oppressive background.

When Andrew arrived home he didn't even go into the house. He sent the groom to Amma, the black mammy who had taken care of him since birth, and had her ask Laurel to take a message to the stables.

He stood near the tackroom, out of sight, as she came in. Holding an envelope of Georgina's stationery in her hand, she looked for the groom, and seeing no one, she called, "Worthy? Is anybody here? Worthy, where are you?"

Drew stepped up behind her. "Worthy isn't here right now, miss. Could I be of service to you?"

Her breath caught in her throat. Then she cried his name and flung herself into his arms. "I've missed you so terribly."

He held her close against him, his hands moving slowly along her back. Her hair smelled like sunshine and violets. Then he stepped away from her, taking her hand. "Wait here for me. I have to go inside to say hello to my family, and I am going to tell them you are taking the day off with me, and we're going to our plantation."

"Drew, you can't do that! What will they think?"

"They can speculate all afternoon, because tonight I am going to tell them you and I are going to be married as soon as I return from Charles Town."

Laurel frowned. "Drew—not yet. Please don't tell them yet."

Drew laughed. "All right. But it must be soon—very soon." He ran toward the house.

Laurel stood at the door of the stable, watching him, her hands pressed against her burning cheeks. This wasn't at all what she had wanted. She couldn't keep seeing him; it could never work. Yet she was waiting for him to take her to his property, the not-yet-built plantation he called their home.

Drew returned to the stable and saddled two horses. He brought them out into the yard, then looked stricken at Laurel. "I'm sorry—I wasn't thinking and saddled both of these the same." He turned with her little mare to put a lady's saddle on the horse.

Laurel laughed and took the reins from him. "You forget who I am, Drew Manning. No one has ever given me a special saddle. I can ride with or without a saddle, but I cannot sit a lady's saddle. I'd fall off on my nose."

They both mounted, and Laurel dug her heels into the mare and bolted from the stable yard, with a surprised Drew hurrying to catch up. They raced across the fields and then slowed the horses to a walk. Soon they were racing again, the hot sun beating down on them. When they arrived they were both hot and tired. They took the horses to the stream and let them drink and graze. Laurel and Drew dropped to the ground and let the lush grass cool them. Laurel lay back, her arms above her head, her eyes on the vivid blue sky. "It doesn't seem real when I'm with you, Drew. I always feel as though I'm dreaming. The sun is always warm, the breezes blow just right, the sky is always blue, even when it's pouring down rain. I forget about the things that bother me when you aren't here . . . You know that isn't the way the world really is."

"As long as it is that way with us, does it matter that it isn't that way with other people?"

"I don't know. I think it should. I mean, the rest of the world is still there. One day or another it will catch up with us, won't it?"

"I imagine so," Drew said, then rolled onto his stomach, his arm encircling Laurel. "But it won't happen today. Today is ours. All of it." He unbuttoned her bodice, and she shrugged out of her dress. Drew kissed her, then rested his head on her chest. He lay there, content, feeling the softness of her skin, reveling in the feeling that she was his.

His troublesome world had been left behind as well. For now there was no Joanna, no outlaw problem or angry family to deal with. For now his day and his life were his, and he was where he wanted to be. Here, with her skin touching and blending with his, he was home.

It was late when Drew and Laurel returned, and he took her to the top of the hill near her home. As always, he stood and watched until she was safely inside, chafing at her insistence he not accompany her. He stood for a moment, allowing his anger to fade and be replaced by the excitement of his next move. He remounted his horse and pulled hers behind him. All the way back to Manning he thought about what he would say to his father. He would have to be firm. Joseph would be angry, and with cause, for the breaking of the marriage contract was a serious matter—but so were his own wishes, he reasoned.

He walked with brisk determination to the house. Milo met him at the door. "Your father is waiting for you in his library, Master Drew."

Drew looked at Milo, hoping for something more, but the tall black man's eyes moved away from him, his face impassive. Drew walked slowly toward the library, no longer so confident or filled with excited purpose. He took a deep breath and entered the room.

Joseph indicated for him to take a seat but said nothing. His face was set in hard, rigid lines. Drew shifted uncomfortably in his chair and cleared his throat. Joseph remained silent. He walked over to the table bar and poured a jigger of whiskey, which he downed in one swallow.

Drew watched him and wished he, too, could have the fortification of a glass of whiskey, but Joseph offered nothing, and it was understood that Drew would not serve himself. The silence in the room continued until Drew thought he could no longer stand it. Then finally Joseph spoke.

"Have you an explanation for your behavior today?"

Joseph had sheared away years from Drew. He did not feel himself his father's equal but the young child he had once been when brought to his father after he had been disobedient. He had visions of Joseph being aware of everything he had done and thought today. With effort he made himself remember that this was not possible. What exactly was Joseph referring to? He didn't know, so he took the relatively safe route. He needed more information. "None that would please you."

Joseph approached him, then stopped several feet away. "Drew, I have had as much of your impudent retorts and indifference to this family as I will tolerate. Your lack of decorum is a disgrace. You insulted your mother this afternoon. I admit amazement, in view of your actions, that you bothered to come to the house at all. I am not certain that it would not have been better had you not. To come in here and hastily greet your mother, who has worried about you the whole time you were gone, and then run out of here announcing that you were spending the day with one of the servants is inexcusable. Now you stand before me arrogantly claiming you can give no explanation that would please me! Damn it, son!"

"I spent the day with Laurel Boggs," Drew said softly.

"I know that! Surely there were women on the trail, and even if not, a man must have some restraint to his appetites. Surely you need not flaunt it before your mother."

Drew flushed with anger and embarrassment. "I—I didn't mean to flaunt anything. It is nothing of that sort. Laurel and I . . . I'm in love with Laurel, Papa. I'm going to . . ." He looked hesitantly at his father, then took a deep breath and went on. "I'm going to marry her."

Joseph's face reddened until it was dangerously purple. He was shaking with rage and unable to speak. His lips were compressed and deathly white against the violent red of his face and neck.

Drew tried to touch him, but Joseph slapped his hand away roughly.

"Papa, sit down, please . . . calm yourself . . . you don't look good. I'll explain everything to you. I've given this a great deal of thought."

"B-break a solemn contract, disgrace the Manning good name, humiliate your cousin and all our family to marry your mother's hired house girl! You have the audacity to say you'll explain!"

"I can't marry Joanna."

Joseph glared at him, his eyes filled with anger. "You speak to me with such ignorance and nauseating self-indulgence? Is this what I hear from the mouth of my own flesh and blood? I am raising a fool, to be led around by his loins, not a man!"

"I don't love Joanna," Drew said in nearly a whisper.

"That's as it should be! Love is not for men such as we! You talk to me of history and of new lands. Lust has its place, but not love. It only addles the brain and confuses. It ties a man to appetites that should never be awakened. It reduces a man to the call of demands made by a woman that cannot be answered. Only a boy or a fool would voice the thoughts you voice to me. Take your fill of the girl if you must, but open your eyes, Drew. Grow up and take your place in the world as you were meant to do. Joanna Templeton does not require your love. She requires a man, as do all true women. She has beauty, position, breeding and wealth. There are no better qualifications for a wife. And," he said, pointing a finger at Drew, "there is nothing about Joanna Templeton that you cannot live with."

"I'm not going to marry her," Drew said stubbornly.

Joseph stood before his son, his own face closed and obstinate.

"This is not a simple choice, Drew. A contract between myself and William Templeton has been made and honored before God on the faith and good name of this family. If you dishonor and break that marriage agreement, it is not merely Joanna you lose but this family as well."

"I don't believe Joanna will be unhappy as long as I manage to allow her a way to be the one who publicly refuses the marriage," Drew said.

"She most likely won't be," Joseph agreed. "She is intelligent. She had far less to gain from this marriage than you. Had you ever considered that? No, of course, you would not have. But you miss the point, Drew. Whether Joanna is satisfied being set free of the contract or not, the willful disregard of the solemn word of this family by your indulgence is an unforgivable offense, which shall not be overlooked. You shall no longer be a member of this family, or my son. I shall write you off as though you never existed."

Drew sat stunned, saying nothing.

"I suggest you take some time to consider this decision more carefully before you act upon it. Good night, Andrew." Joseph walked to his desk, sat down and began to read. Drew knew his father was as upset as he, but Joseph would not look at him or acknowledge his presence in any way.

Drew walked slowly from the library up the stairs to his room. He couldn't sleep that night. He dozed off to reawaken, acutely aware of his bedroom and his home. Everything fought against his believing that Joseph would actually disown him, but deep within himself he knew that it was true. The breaking of such a contract was as Joseph had said—grievous and not to be forgiven.

Tonight was a night during which he would have to say good-bye to his childhood and all that had been important to him if he carried out his plans. And if he did not carry out his plans, he would not have Laurel; at least not as his wife. He found it strange that the idea of not marrying her did not hurt him as much as did the idea that he would be severed from his family. It was a long and sobering night. It was not his love of Laurel that drove him to hold fast to his decision; it was something quite simple and inexplicable. He wasn't able to turn back. It was as if he had set his foot on a path and there was no way off it. In a sense, what he was thinking made Joseph correct. Love would not be the ultimate influence in his life. His own sense of destiny, even when it seemed destructive and painful, was his mistress. Suddenly he felt terribly alone and longed for Laurel. Even though he now knew she'd never hold the position in his life he had previously thought, she could comfort him. He did love her. He did want her.

Before first light he arose, dressed, went to the stables and left for Charles Town. Now that his father had been told, he had to tell his grandmother and the Templetons as quickly as possible. Doubtless Joseph would be writing William Templeton as soon as possible, offering to pay restitution. Drew cringed at the idea that his father would be humbling himself and trying to make some form of payment to William Templeton for his son's behavior. Slowly and agonizingly Drew began to comprehend the enormity of what he was doing, and still he felt compelled to progress on what was perhaps a self-destructive path. He packed only his backcountry clothes, leaving himself no means of concession to the ways of his family in Charles Town or at Riverlea. He would appear there as what he now was: a backcountry farmer without family or financing, only a step or two ahead of the Boggses.

It was a long, lonely trip that gave him far too much time to think and feel. He had not cried since he was a child, but he made no effort to hold back the tears that came so easily as he rode along. Memories of himself and his father haunted him, and he could barely think of his mother or what this would do to her. He had left without even saying good-bye, and he wasn't sure he'd see her again to talk with her.

Laurel arrived at Manning at her usual time for work. She was greeted in the pantry by Amma.

"Mastah say he see you in the liberry," she said coolly, her eyes sparkling with animosity and her head high in the air.

Laurel stood for some time before the library door before knocking.

"Come in," Joseph snapped.

She walked to his desk and stood silently before him.

"Your time here has occasioned a trying and tragic episode for this family," he said coldly. He took from his desk an envelope. "Your employment is herewith terminated. Though it is not necessary or customary, I am paying you for this month's labor out of respect for my wife. I shall not give you a letter of recommendation, you understand. In view of what has happened here, I would feel remiss in my duties to suggest that your services would be an addition to any household. However, again out of respect for my wife, I shall say nothing to discourage others from employing you. That is all, Laurel." He handed her the envelope and bent to the papers on his desk.

Laurel had said nothing the entire time. Now she turned and walked back through the library door, down the long hall to the kitchens, through the pantry and out of Manning. No one spoke to her, and she didn't see Georgina. She walked slowly across the yard and headed for the edge of the field, just as she had done previously to meet Drew when she was finished for the day. She sat down near the live oak tree and looked at the fields being plowed and prepared for the coming planting.

After a time she looked back at the brick house. It had been her dream such a short time ago. Through her employment here she had meant to better herself and bring her family to a style of living they hadn't been able to gain for themselves. Her eyes grew watery as she stared back at the house. It had all been a sham—a girl reaching above herself. She saw things more clearly now and admitted that her dream had been childish and doomed to fail, but she knew there had also been something clean and good about it, and that she was losing.

Still she wandered around the grounds of Manning, unable to make herself leave. She didn't know exactly how long Drew would be gone, but she wasn't going to tell her family that she was no longer working. She'd hand over a portion of her final month's wages to her father each week, as she always did, and hope something came up before her money ran out.

When she started for home it was already growing dark. Long evening shadows bobbed in front of her as she walked the first half of the way. She enjoyed them then, and in a way they kept her company. Then they began to gather, one running into the other until they formed a massive block of darkness that crept around her. The green woods that had been cool and welcoming turned inky dark and foreboding, not willing to give up the secrets of its inhabitants as she trespassed through it.

As she walked deeper into the woods the sounds of a busy day were cut off as if by some unseen hand. The thick silence closed in on her until she began to hear the quieter, stealthier sounds of the wood creatures. She shivered and wished she had thought to bring a shawl when she left the cabin this morning. Her heartbeat sped up and she jumped, then felt silly as she listened to the beats of a horse's hooves, loud and close at hand. She looked behind her, expecting to see a rider, but there was nothing but the closed-in darkness of the trees. She shivered again, then chided herself for an overactive imagination. All the thinking she had done today had made her spooky, and she was just feeling uncertain about what she and Drew were about to do. She walked a little faster, talking to herself, reassuring herself. She thought she heard shouting. Again she stopped, her hand at her throat, trying to quiet the wild beating of her heart and her short, quick breathing so she could hear more clearly. There was no shouting. There was no one anywhere around to be shouting. There were no houses, no cabins, no settlers; nothing but the trees, and somewhere just beyond in the darkness was the open field she would cross to take her to the top of the hill where Drew left her when he brought her home. There was nothing to frighten her, she told herself. It was only the night playing with her like a wicked child tormenting his mammy.

She looked up into the pitch darkness of the sky and was surprised to see it glowing rich purple on the horizon across the clearing. It made her think of sunrise, and for a moment that was what she thought it was. In the night there is no rising sun, just the tease of unkept promise, she said nastily to herself, liking the sound of a scolding biting into the silence. She walked on, putting her hand to her back. She had done nothing today but walk and sit and think, but she was very tired. Of late it seemed to her that she tired far more easily than she used to do. In fact, if she told the truth, she hadn't been feeling quite well of late. It was nothing specific, but a nagging feeling of something not quite right. Even Georgina had commented that she didn't seem to have the stamina that she had had when she had first come to work.

She looked at the horizon again. The teasing color was still there in the sky. She stopped for a moment, staring at the light and the color. She put her hand over her mouth and broke into a run. She raced madly across the open field. "Mary! Mama! Oh, no! Please don't let it be home!"

She fell as she ran down the hillside. Flames leaped high above the burning barn. As she rolled and bumped down the hill, the flames spun crazily above her to the side, then disappeared. She scrambled to her feet, tripping, then regaining her feet once again. She could hardly breathe, and her side hurt. The cabin looked so close, but she ran and ran and still it seemed far away to her.

18

The sky had just been turning colors when four men rode into view of the Boggs cabin. Harley and Ben were still in the fields. Harley was sprawled out on the ground, his head propped up on his rolled-up coat. Lazily he lifted a jug to his lips, made a sucking sound and rolled to his side. "Ain't we done enough fer one day?"

"Just about ready to go in, Pa," Ben said. He struggled, wedging a green tree pole under a rock in the field. Only the head of the rock showed, and Ben had dug a hole at its side. He now placed the pole under the rock and pressed his weight against the pole. The tree bent and sprang back. "Give me a hand, Pa, I'm not heavy enough to move this."

Harley yawned, took another drink from the jug and got to his feet. "Seems like it'd be there tomorrah, an' I'm tired tonight. Beats me why you an' Laurel are allus crowdin' each day with things that kin wait."

Ben laughed. "Iffen we allus waitin' fer tomorrah, we never are gonna have a field to plant come spring."

"Pity that'd be, now wouldn't it." Harley grumbled and stretched. "Hey now, lookit there." He pointed to the hill near their property. At the top of the hill four horsemen stood, watching Harley and Ben. "Who dya s'pose them are?"

"I don't know any of 'em," Ben said, his hand over his eyes against the sun. "They prob'ly jes' passin' an' restin' fer a spell. Help me with this boulder or we ain't never gonna get any supper, an' I'm fit to eat near anythin'. I sure do hope Laurel brung somethin' good home with her to eat."

Harley leaned against the pole, just hanging on it, while Ben nudged and moved around, trying to find the right leverage.

"Mebbe we ought to ask them fellers to help us," Harley said. "They sure is int'rested in what we're doin'." Harley kept looking at the four mounted men.

Suddenly the men spurred their horses and began to ride in a circle around the perimeter of the Boggses' property.

"Damn my eyes, Ben, lookit that. What them doin'?"

Ben watched the men make one circle of the property, then move slightly closer and again ride the inner perimeter. "Le's get in the house, Pa. I don't like them men, an' we ain't got a musket out here with us."

Harley and Ben dropped the green tree pole and ran for the house. Harley labored up the hill to his front door, with Ben several steps in front of him. The men came in closer, riding hard and shouting. Just as Harley reached the top of the hill and was about ten feet from his door, one of the riders cut his horse across the lawn and stopped, blocking Harley's path.

"Wheah you think you goin', ol' man?"

Harley stopped and straightened, his face pasty white and covered with perspiration. As he always did when he was in a tight spot, he looked ingratiatingly up at the man on horseback. "Why, me an' my son jes' come in from a day in the fiel's. Be mighty nice iffen you strangers would partake o' mah hospitality an' watah your horses over there. Be my guest."

The leader of the men turned in his saddle and smiled at his companions. "Friendly sort, ain't he. What you bet he jes' han's her over to us to save his own stinkin' skin." He turned back to Harley. "Weah goin' to partake o' your hospitality, ol' man, but it ain't goin' to be watah. You got a daughter, ain't you?"

Harley said nothing but stood playing with the soil with the toe of his boot.

"I ast you a question, ol' man!" The horseman brought his musket down and around, hitting Harley in the stomach. He waited for Harley to stop coughing and gagging. "Now, le's try agin. You got a daughter?"

"I got four daughters," Harley gasped. Then he looked wildly at the door to the cabin. "Ben! Where you at? Ain't no one gonna he'p me?"

Mathilda and the children huddled against the wall, peering through the crack in the door. "Lissen to him!" Mathilda hissed. "He gonna get us inter this or else."

"Mama, let me take Pamela and Mary out the window. If you'd jes' talk out the door a li'l an' keep them attendin' you, I kin get the girls away. Mandy, you follow when I get these out."

"What you think I am!" Mathilda hissed. "Lookit them men— you know what they wants well as me, an' I'm the only growed woman hereabouts."

"They asked for his daugher, Mama!" Ben whispered. "They know about the girls."

"It's Laurel they heared about, you fool!"

"She ain't here," Ben said.

"So it'll be me to suffer in her place," Mathilda said, "an it's gonna be all the worse iffen you spirit away them other girls."

Ben stood looking at his mother, blinking and frightened. "They'll kill Mary and Pammie iffen they get them, Mama."

"What about me?" Mandy howled.

"You're healthy," Ben said, his eyes still on Mathilda. "I'm gonna do it, Mama. I'm gonna take them through the window an' run fer the woods. I wish you'd he'p me by talkin' to 'em through the door." Ben picked up his baby sister and motioned for Mary to follow him.

Mary began to cry. She reached for Mathilda, clinging to her dress. "Mama, Mama, I'm scared. I can't run like Mandy. They're gonna git me, Mama."

"Come on, Mary," Ben hissed. "I'll he'p you. Hurry!"

Mary hesitantly took a step toward him. Mandy crowded close to her sister.

"You ain't leavin' me to face them alone," Mathilda said and reached for Mary. Ben grabbed his sister's hand and jerked her to him. Mathilda's grasping hand landed on Mandy's shoulder.

"No, Mama! Not me! Let me go. Ben, please, he'p me! Don't let her give me to 'em."

Mathilda shoved the girl closer to the door and yelled to the bandits. "Here's my daughter! I got her right here. You let my man be, y'hear? I'll send you the girl. Let my man come on in!"

"Mama! Let her come with us," Ben whispered.

Mathilda looked at her son, then back to the door. "Y'hear me out there?"

Ben hurriedly shoved Mary through the window, then climbed out after her with Pamela tucked under his arm.

"Come out here, woman!" the man shouted back.

"I ain't comin' nowheres! You send Harley in, an' the girl comes out."

The lead horseman motioned to one of the other men. "Mort, build us a nice, hot fire, an' le's see iffen these people don't start bein' a li'l friendlier."

Mort and another man called Grady dismounted and gathered wood and brush. From a bucket near the barn they got tar and put it on the pyre. The fire sizzled and smoked. Mort jabbed it with a stick and quickly had yellow flames licking upward toward the overhanging branches of the tree nearest the barn. "Be a real shame were that to catch fire. Most likely it'd run right to the barn roof, mebbe even the house. Be a damned shame."

"Woman, I got an iron here," the leader said and held it aloft. "An' I got me a big fire goin'. I kin burn you out or I kin stay right here an' have me a li'l fun with your man." He handed the poker to Grady. "Hot that iron up real good, Grady."

"My pleasure, Albee."

"Send her out!" Harley shrieked, his eyes on the heating iron. "They gonna brand my hide!"

Mort sucked air through his front teeth. "Now lookit that. What a shame. That durned ol' tree was jes' as dry as tinder. Looks likes the barn's gonna set afire."

Unable to help herself, Mathilda peered around the door. The lowest limb of the tree was shot through with a spiral of flame that licked and curled like a serpent, moving slowly toward the roof of the barn.

Albee, still astride his horse, laughed. "Send out the girl, woman. You ain't got nothin' to gain an' you ain't got nothin' to win. You done lost your barn. Nex' it's gonna be your man."

"You sons o' bitches! Come git her iffen you man enough! I ain't doin' nothin' fer you!"

Albee shoved his hat back on his head. "I'm a patient man, woman. I got all the time in the worl', an' I'm willin' to spend it." He nodded at Grady and Mort.

The two men forced Harley closer to the fire. Albee dismounted and motioned for the other man to follow him. Slowly he walked to the door, shoved it open and faced Mathilda. His musket was tucked under his arm and his thumbs were hooked in his belt loops. He looked Mathilda over from her head to her feet. "Well, if you ain't the ugliest, orneriest-lookin' woman I ever saw, I'll eat it."

Mathilda stood by the table with Willie on one side of her, smiling and clapping his hands for the stranger. Missy slobbered at Willie's side, her eyes unfocused and unaware. Mandy hid her face against her mother, her body heaving as she tried to stifle her sobs.

Mathilda spat at Albee as he moved toward her. He reached out and slapped her across the mouth. Mathilda grimaced, then drew back her lips and spat at him again through her teeth. "You hanker fer li'l girls. Don't s'pose the likes o' you could pleasure a woman—well, here she is."

"Better shet your mouth, woman, while you still got one to shet."

Mathilda sniggered, her voice low and filled with disgust. "Ain't you gonna take her? She ain't hardly bigger'n a stick, an' poor as we been feedin' her, she's mos' likely sickly too." She shoved Mandy forward and burst into hysterical laughter. "Hope you git your death from her."

"This ain't the girl!" Albee growled. "I ain't foolin' with you no more, woman. You done took all my time I'm givin'. Where's the girl?"

"This here's the girl. I'm her mother, ain't I? I oughtta know my own daughter, ain't I?" Mathilda shouted at Albee, her jaw thrust out, almost daring him to hit her again.

"Grady! This here's a lyin' bitch. See how much she cares fer her man."

Mathilda's eyes widened. She wanted to move so she could see out the door, but she didn't. She clutched the back of the chair, holding herself rigid. She'd run across men like Albee before, and she put all the hate she'd garnered over the years on this man's head. She cursed him with her mind. She cursed him in her heart. She cursed him with her eyes.

Grady moved around in front of Harley, taunting him, then walked to the fire and removed the hot iron. He waved it in front of Harley's face.

"You gonna let all the heat out, Grady."

"They's plenty o' heat. Hol' his han' out here."

Harley blubbered and pulled away from the hot iron. Mort's powerful hand closed over his wrist and slowly forced his hand down. Harley clenched his fist shut. Mort increased the pressure on his wrist until his hand was purple and the veins stood out like cords.

"Don' do this! I'll give you the girl," Harley sobbed. "Lemme go, I'll give you two o' my daughters. You won' hurt 'em. See, I knows. I'll git her fer you, I swear. Don' hurt me! You kin have her!"

Grady brought the poker down across his closed knuckles. The flesh sizzled and turned bright red, then black. Harley screamed and twisted in Mort's grip, his fingers opened wide, and Grady jammed the still-hot poker into the palm of his hand.

Ben, on hands and knees, was about thirty yards from the house when he heard his father's screams. Mary scrabbled behind him to catch up and cling to him. She began to cry again.

"Mary, be quiet!" Ben whispered.

"I'm trying, Ben," she whispered back and then began to cough.

Ben put Pamela on the ground and grabbed Mary. He pressed his hand tight against her mouth. Mary clawed at his hand and fought for air. Pamela began to whimper. Frantic and close to tears himself, Ben released Mary and stretched out, grabbing Pamela and dragging her nearer to him. He rocked her a little, then in desperation placed his hand over her mouth as he had done with Mary. "Be quiet, baby, please, they'll find us. Quiet, Pammie, please quieten."

"Let her go, Ben, she cain't breathe," Mary whispered, still fighting a coughing seizure.

Ben's blue eyes were wide and wet with tears. "They're gonna hear us! Cain't you hear what they're doin' to Pa? You want that too? Please, don' make 'em fin' us, Mary. He'p me!"

Mary nodded solemnly. "I'll he'p, Ben. Where we headin' fer?"

He looked at the top of the hill, which was nearly invisible in the darkness. It seemed miles away, but once they had gained the summit. . . . "I don't know. The woods. We'll be safe there . . . mebbe."

Under his hand, Pamela struggled, her small head thrown back, gasping for air.

Behind him, the barn roared as the fire engulfed it. Billows of smoke and ash shot up into the air along with the flame. Mary and

Ben could no longer hear their father's cries. The noise of the burning barn was all around them. Ben looked down. Pamela was quiet. She must have fallen asleep, he thought. Carefully he held her in one hand, her small legs tucked inside his open shirt front. He edged on hands and knees up the slope of the hill, Mary at his heels.

Laurel's side hurt as she started down the hill. The teasing color was no longer teasing. It was now a horrible brush of yellow flame and spark leaping high into the sky. She ran harder, her breath catching painfully in her throat. "Mama! Mary! Oh, no! Please, God, let them be all right. I won't leave them! I'll never leave them, I promise! Please!"

She ran as hard as she could down the hill, almost falling in her haste. She cried as she ran, calling to her mother and her brother.

Ben looked up, his face drawn and filled with fear. "Oh, no! Mary, it's Laurel. She's running right to them!"

Mary put her hand to her mouth. "Ben. Oh, Ben."

Ben handed Mary the baby and began to run across the hill toward Laurel, trying to cut her off. No longer thinking of himself, he called to her. "Laurel! Laurel, run! Run away . . . don't go home!"

The fire roared, and the sound of her own blood beat in her ears. Laurel's eyes never left the small house at the summit of the next hill. At the front of the cabin stood four horses, and in the yard she could see three men around the fire. Her father! One of the men was her father. She screamed his name, and all three men looked in her direction.

Ben sobbed and ran harder after his sister, breathlessly calling her name. Finally Laurel heard him and slowed. She glanced quickly to the side, then her eyes went back to the scene in the yard of her home.

"Laurel, they're after you!" Ben yelled. "Run! Run away!"

The men holding her father released him, and Harley fell to the ground. The larger man ran to the door of the house, and another man came to the door. The large man pointed, and the other ran from the house shouting. Then Laurel understood and turned back in Ben's direction.

"Hurry, Laurel!" Ben said, his eyes on the men below. They ran in confusion for their horses while trying to keep Laurel in view.

Ben bit his lower lip and hopped from foot to foot as he waited for his sister.

"Ben, what happened?" Laurel gasped when she reached him.

"Not now. I've got to go back for Mary and Pammie. Run, Laurel."

"Where's Mama?"

Ben kept looking back as he ran. He let out a strangled cry. "They're comin'!"

Laurel was running bent over, her hand clutching her side, her breath making harsh, rasping sounds now.

"Manning," Ben gasped. "They'll he'p." He made frantic motions with his arms. "Leave me!" He headed toward the spot he had left Mary. Laurel hesitated, not understanding; then she saw Mary and Pamela.

Mary sat huddled and crying, a silent Pamela in her arms. She burst into tears and coughing when she saw Ben.

"Get up, Mary! You've got to run! They've seen us. Hurry, you can't be weak! Run, Mary, run!"

They heard the sound of the horses' hooves behind them now over the sound of the fire.

"They're near!" Ben cried.

Laurel looked back and could see the bobbing silhouettes of the horsemen coming. She looked at Ben with Pamela, and Mary running barely faster than another would walk. She stopped running and stood exposed in the moonlight and the firelight. Then she veered off and ran back across the open hill, away from her brother and sisters. She ran and she ran. She thought she had been running forever, and she hurt all over. Would they never catch her? She couldn't fail. They had to catch her and not Ben and Mary and Pammie. They had to catch her soon. She couldn't run anymore. She gained the woods and raced down the paths she thought would make it difficult for a horse to follow. The sounds of the horsemen were all around her, and yet they didn't catch her. She couldn't see them. Where was Ben? Was he safe?

Behind her, close at hand, she could hear a horseman thrashing and cursing his way through the brush. Then she heard shouting and the unmistakable sound of Ben's voice. She fell hard as the night cracked with the sound of a musket shot. She saw black, unable to breathe, unable to think as she slammed against a fallen log.

Dazedly she sat up and looked into the face of one of the men she had seen in her front yard.

"You caused us a lot of trouble, girl. You'd better make yourself worth it."

She looked up at him, then fell back against the tree trunk, hardly caring what he said or did. She hurt so badly she could think of nothing else. She turned to her side, retching.

Mort dismounted and walked over to her. "Stand up, girlie. Le's git a look at you."

Laurel groaned and leaned heavily against the tree trunk. She looked up and saw that another man was there as well. His eyes were all she noticed. Even in shadow, even in the soft darkness, she could see his eyes, his dark, dark eyes.

"Where's my brother and sisters?" she asked faintly.

Mort laughed and licked his lips.

A third man joined them. He dismounted quickly and paced the small area nervously. "What are we waitin' fer? Le's git movin'. We di'n't kill them ol' folks back there. They's likely goin' to git he'p."

"I wanna git a look at her," Mort said.

"You cain't see nothin' in the dark," Grady said.

"You cain't see nothin' noway, Grady, you're as blind as stone. C'mere, girlie. Come to ol' Mort."

Laurel drew her legs up, hugging herself into a compact ball. She looked up when she heard the horseman's voice.

"Get up on the horse behind me."

Laurel blinked at him, startled at the authority in his voice.

"Now wait a minute, Albee," Mort whined. "We been chasin' this filly all damn day. You cain't jes' take her fer yourself like that. Let us fun ourselves a li'l first."

"You're goin' fun yourself right to the end o' a rope. Iffen they got Govey, they kin git us. Le's git outta here," Grady said.

Albee ignored both men. He looked straight at Laurel, his dark eyes showing only as recesses in the moonlight. "Get up here," he repeated to Laurel, indicating the back of his saddle.

"Let me go, please."

"Sure, girlie, after we spent a whole day huntin' you down an' a week afore that findin' where you be." Mort took her under the arms and hauled her to her feet. "Better git up on that horse. What Albee says goes."

"I'll be no good to you," she said in a stronger voice. "I'll do nothing you ask of me."

Mort laughed, but Albee remained stone-faced. "You'll be what I want you to be; you'll do what I want you to do. I'll tell you once more to get on the back of my horse."

Laurel stood stubbornly refusing to move. Mort's hands began to move along her sides to her breasts, then with a quick glance at Albee he thrust his hand between her thighs. "Ah, she's a meaty one," Mort breathed. "It ain't fair you gettin' her jes' fer the sayin', Albee. I want her too."

Laurel wrenched away from his groping hands and backed into Grady. She cried out as his hands plunged down the bodice of her dress.

Albee took his whip from his saddle horn and snapped it in the air. Both men stopped immediately, stepping back from her. Mort, Grady and Laurel all stared expectantly at the horseman.

"You'll learn obedience to me is best. The next time I tell you to mount my horse, you'll do it first off." He stared at her for a moment, then nodded at Mort and Grady.

The two men closed in on her, fighting over her, their hands digging and pulling at her clothing. She fought, twisting and turning from one only to feel the hands of the other under her skirts, tearing at her undergarments.

"Oh, God, she's makin' me daft," Mort panted.

"Git outta my way," Grady snarled. "Ain't nothin' goin' ta stop me." His rough hands snapped the remaining fasteners of her bodice. His open mouth clamped down on her exposed breast.

Laurel screamed, scratching and kicking, but her every move now seemed to aid them.

Mort shoved Grady aside and leaped full-length on Laurel. Her vision went black as she fought for breath. He released her hands to spread her legs and undo the packet of his breeches.

Regaining her senses, she clawed at his face, her fingers digging at his eyes. Mort screeched, grabbing her hands and pinning them to the earth. Stretched out on her, his face was inches from hers.

She breathed in the fetid tobacco wash of his breath with each lunging thrust of his hips. Mort cried and bleated as he worked himself into a frenzy. Sweat poured from his face onto her.

Grady, unable to wait any longer, grabbed Mort by the hair, pulling his head backward until he released his hold on Laurel and fell panting and moaning on the ground beside her. As Grady mounted her, Albee looked on with dispassionate interest.

At the snap of his whip the two men dressed themselves and carried Laurel to him. They thrust her over the rump of his horse and waited for her to struggle upright.

"You'll hold fast to me, woman, for if you fall off I'll leave you where you lay, injured or no," Albee said.

Laurel righted herself on the horse behind him and put her arms securely around his waist.

"Where's Bert?" Grady asked.

"We'll ride back by the cabin. Mos' likely he's thereabouts," Albee said and wheeled the horse around, nearly unseating Laurel.

They rode back toward her home, and she cried softly at Albee's back, trying to will herself not to look, knowing she didn't want to live remembering what she would see. But she couldn't help herself. She smelled the smoke of the still-burning barn, and she looked.

Bert walked toward the horsemen, a stupid grin on his fleshy face. Under one arm he dragged along the limp body of Mary. Her head hung down on her chest. Laurel gagged at the vision of one of the barnyard chickens after their necks had been wrung leaping into her mind.

"I thought I had me a girl," Bert said, grinning up at Albee. "Guess not." He shoved Mary away from him. She fell to the ground, her lifeless eyes staring unseeing into the night sky. "She wasn't much anyhow. They's better ones, ain't they, Albee?"

Bert mounted his horse, and the four men began the long ride to the new camp they had formed deep in the mountains, the only place they could go since the Rangers and Andrew Manning had driven them from the settled community.

19

Drew arrived at Riverlea on March 23, 1768, with Elizabeth accompanying him. They were both rain-drenched and cold when they were escorted to the house by the welcomer. Elizabeth was showing signs of the strain, as well as the wear of travel. Drew had tried to talk her out of coming with him, but she would listen to nothing.

"If you are determined to do this thing, I shall be there. The marriage agreement may be a custom that is ill advised in the colonies. Walter questioned it at the time your father and William made the agreement, so I am not totally against you, Drew. On the other hand, it is a matter of family honor, and whether or not it was an ill-advised agreement, it was made, and now it is about to be broken. And by a Manning."

Drew had looked down, murmuring, "Perhaps I should say nothing and allow the agreement to stand."

Elizabeth had looked at him with disgust. "You could, and should, if there was any possibility that you would ever honor the contract, but we both know you never will. There is no purpose to be served by adding a lie to an already grave situation. We shall go to Riverlea and salvage whatever honor we can." Then she had smiled. "Even our dishonorable acts shall be done with courage and integrity."

Drew had been able to say or do nothing to dissuade her, but the trip and the worry had taken its toll. Behind them, in Charles Town, they had left a Manning family as upset and divided as Drew's family in the Upcountry had been. Eugenia said adamantly that Drew would never again be welcome in her house. "I have been tolerant of Andrew, I have put up with coarse behavior from him for years, but this I shall not tolerate. With this act he has not only made a display of himself but has damaged and dirtied the good name of every Manning in the colonies."

Elizabeth had felt a terrible pain at what she saw as the cleaving of her family, but she had said nothing, for she could not argue with Eugenia. There was no reason that John and Eugenia and their family should be damaged by Drew's actions any more than could be helped. She could not in good conscience ask them to defend or even stand by Drew in this matter. He had chosen his own course, and it was not in accord with the family's best interests.

She could barely stand the thought of entering Riverlea under the circumstances. As the welcomer led them down the long, manicured road to the house, she felt more ill than she could ever recall. Ruth, William, Joanna, Meg and Gwynne would all be expecting a pleasant visit and perhaps even definite plans for the wedding. Instead, Elizabeth and Drew brought with them only humiliation, disgrace and disappointment. She could hardly bear it.

Drew was alarmed at the pallor of his grandmother. For the first time he could see clearly the mark of her years, and it frightened him. He carried with him a hard, cold stone of illness deep within him as the enormity of his decision to break the marriage contract unfolded. Nothing that he had imagined or thought had prepared him for the disappointment or pain he was causing his family members or for the terrible, encompassing sense of emptiness it was provoking in him. He had naively considered this a circumstance primarily involving himself and Joanna and only touching the rest of his family secondarily and indirectly, but that was not the case. He could see that now, but it was too late. There was no time left for circumspection or prudence. He was in the middle of a family crisis, and had no means to stop it or to correct any of his mistakes. And somehow he had managed to precipitate his loyal and courageous grandmother into the center of it, and she was being harmed.

He almost jumped at the sound of Riverlea's front door opening and Joanna's voice. "Drew! Elizabeth! I am so sorry one of us didn't meet you at the gate. Welcome! What a wonderful surprise!"

Drew helped Elizabeth into the house, Joanna walking at their side, looking concerned as soon as she noticed how ashen Elizabeth's face was. "What can I do to help, Drew?" she asked. "Cousin Elizabeth, shall we take you directly to your room?"

"Have you any smelling salts?" Drew asked as he helped Elizabeth through the entry hall. He moved nearer the staircase when Elizabeth held her hand up. "No, Drew, take me to the parlor. Joanna, would you please call your family. Drew and I must discuss a family matter, and it is best we do that immediately."

"Of course, Cousin Elizabeth, I'll do whatever you ask, but couldn't it wait until after supper? Your luggage could be taken to your room, and I'm certain you'd feel much better after a short rest. You look so pale."

Elizabeth shook her head. "This is not a matter that can wait, and please do nothing about our luggage yet, Joanna."

Joanna looked at Drew, questions in her eyes. He was nearly as pale as his grandmother. Joanna felt a finger of icy fear touch her. "Something terrible has happened, hasn't it," she murmured, her hand at her throat.

"Joanna, please, do as I ask you," Elizabeth said weakly.

Drew remained silent. He had never had much sympathy for swooning women, but suddenly he understood it quite well. He could barely breathe. The room seemed to close in, and he wanted to escape this horrible situation so much, he would gladly have fallen unconscious to the floor. He sank down suddenly, weak-kneed, on the sofa near Elizabeth. She glanced at him, sorrow and love in her eyes. She took his hand in her own cold, dry hand and held it tightly. She said quietly, "It must be done immediately, Drew—before our bags are brought in and before we accept hospitality that may no longer be extended."

"Oh my God," Drew moaned, his head down.

She patted his hand. "You have chosen your path. If you believe in it, Drew, then you must follow it to the end and do so with courage and stoutness of heart."

"I don't know if I believe in it, Grandma. I mean I do, but I'm not certain I understand what it is I claim to believe in. All I have done or meant to do was to say I preferred to marry one woman and not another . . . I didn't intend for all this other to happen."

Elizabeth smiled sadly. "I know, Drew. That is the tragedy of youth. A young man always knows what he believes in and has the courage to seek it, but he seldom if ever knows what his choice will cost him." She sighed deeply, her eyes watering. "And the tragedy of age is that we always know the cost of our desires and seldom have the courage to seek them. Life is not an easy matter, Drew. At every age we have our strengths and our weaknesses, and perhaps the greatest tragedy of all is that we human beings seem incapable of sharing our strengths. We seem capable only of criticizing each other's weaknesses. We see only the mote in another man's eye."

"What should I do? Should I tell Joanna we will marry?"

Elizabeth gave him another of her sad smiles. "Can you?"

Drew looked at her but said nothing, and Elizabeth nodded and looked toward the door, waiting for the Templeton family to gather.

One by one the Templetons came into the parlor, each of them eyeing Elizabeth with consternation. Seats were taken, quiet maintained, until everyone had arrived. William blustered in last. "Well, what is this, Elizabeth? Joanna tells me you aren't well . . . so why is no one seeing to you?"

"I am well enough, William," Elizabeth said. "If you will please sit down, I as the eldest member of the Manning family have some trying news to tell you. I think it best we discuss the matter immediately. There is no good way of saying this, so forgive me if I am merely blunt and to the point. My grandson, for pressing personal reasons, finds that he shall be unable to honor the marriage agreement made between yourself, William, and my son Joseph." Elizabeth tried valiantly to look directly at William but failed. Her voice cracked and she looked down at her hands. She was hideously ashamed.

The room was deathly quiet. No one spoke or moved for what seemed an endless time.

"I know what a shock this is to all of you. Drew and I shall do whatever possible to ease the consequences to Joanna. Naturally it will be publicly known that it was she who chose not to marry Drew. However you care to set that up, we will cooperate, should you want our cooperation."

William cleared his throat, began to speak, then fell silent again, only to erupt into angry unintelligibility a second later. "Hang it all, Elizabeth, what I have to say I will not say to a woman, particularly not to you. Get that damned mollycoddle out from behind your skirts and let me talk with him, if he is man enough to meet me."

"I'll be glad to talk with you, Cousin William," Drew said.

"This concerns all of us, William," Elizabeth insisted.

"Then why are none of the men of your family here? Where is

John? And for God's sake, where is Joseph? It was with him that the contract was made. If it is to be broken, then that is between him and me—not you."

"John had—"

"Don't excuse anyone, Elizabeth!" William roared. "They aren't here because neither Joseph Manning nor John Manning would ever countenance such a breach of trust!" He stalked about the room, his face bright red.

Joanna sat staring ahead of her, so still and motionless she didn't seem alive. When she spoke her words were so slow and soft, all strained to hear her. "Why are you doing this to me?" She didn't look at Drew but continued to stare at nothing.

"Could we talk about this later?" Gwynne asked, going over to her sister. "None of us . . . this is too much, too great a thing to deal with casually and at once. Joanna needs some time."

"I'm afraid there is nothing to discuss regarding the broken contract, Gwynne. That is done." Elizabeth fought back tears.

"And we have nothing whatever to say about this? You ruin my daughter's reputation and tell me I have no say!?" Ruth screeched. "Have you considered what this means to Joanna?" She glared at Drew. "William, are you going to allow him to stand in your house before your wife and daughters and say for his own personal reasons he will not honor a contract that affects the life and well-being of your family!"

"No, by God, I won't! I won't take this from you, young man. You never have fit into this family. You've been given too much and never asked to pay the piper for your bounty. Personal reasons! A *woman,* I suppose—that would be your caliber of personal concern."

"Yes, a woman. I'll marry Laurel Boggs when I return home."

"William, Drew, please . . ." Elizabeth began.

"No, I do not please! Andrew Manning has been allowed to run wild since he was a child! He has been permitted to think of himself before all others, and all events and all good reason. I hold you and Joseph responsible for this, Elizabeth! I hold the Manning family at fault. You—all of you have coddled and encouraged this young man in his ways, and now it is my daughter and my family that pay the consequence for his irresponsibility, his thoughtlessness, his arrogant assumption that his wishes come before all others. No, by damn, I do not please to keep quiet, nor will this contract be broken without just retribution."

"Perhaps Joanna would find one of her other cousins appealing, and one of them, too, might . . ."

"No, Elizabeth, no!" William shouted. "No Manning man shall ever lay finger on Riverlea or be welcomed as a member of this family."

"We are all family," Elizabeth said.

"I thought we were," Ruth cried. "But no member of a family would treat another as Andrew has my Joanna. Oh, my dear, what will we do? He's thrown her over for some backwoods trollop."

"If I could do it in good faith, Cousin Ruth, I would even now carry out the contract, but I cannot," Drew said.

"Dare you behave as though you do this family a favor by marrying my daughter? Are you so damned arrogant that you cannot see that no favor is being done us by your marriage? My God, Elizabeth, has no one ever told this pup that this contract was made to the benefit of Joseph, not the Templetons?"

"It was, Drew. Your father asked that the agreement be made so that he could ensure your future."

"I need no assurance," Drew said.

William laughed loudly and bitterly. "I don't suppose you do. How many times have you in your brazen ignorance told me you are more American than Englishman. Americans don't need assurance, do they, Drew. They always have their hills to roam in and their bear grease to slick upon their scalps. What need is there of art and honor, integrity or culture to such a man—no assurance at all, I'm sure." William's eyes watered in rage. "My God, what I have put up with from you these years! And for what?"

Drew stood up, his own face highly colored with anger. "Cousin William, I am sorry that this has come to—"

Elizabeth made a sound of deep pain and slumped quietly to the side.

Drew dropped to his knees at his grandmother's side. "Have you any smelling salts?"

Gwynne and Ruth rushed from the room. Gwynne returned with the salts and Ruth with the servants to take Elizabeth to one of the bedrooms.

William stood back watching the confusion. "We shall heed

Gwynne's advice belatedly. Take Elizabeth to rest and recover. With cooler heads we shall discuss what is to be done and how this contract is to be resolved." He walked quickly from the room.

The women hurried Elizabeth upstairs, their talk divided between concern for her and for the announcement Drew had made.

Drew found himself alone in the parlor. He didn't know what to do. He was aware he no longer had the welcome or freedom of the Templeton house. He didn't know where to go, so he sat down stiffly on the sofa. He started as he heard Joanna's voice. He had not known she was still there.

"I'll never forgive you for what you're doing to me, Drew." She still stared straight ahead, her gaze on nothing.

"Joanna, I know it is difficult for you to accept, and I am truly sorry that it cannot be otherwise."

"You lie, Drew. You are truly sorry that you are being caused discomfort, but you don't know what it is to care for others. You call me cold, but I am a burning white hot coal compared to you. And I shall never forgive you. If it consumes my life, I shall repay you for this. Remember that, Drew; it is a solemn vow. I would have been your wife. I am now, until death parts us, your enemy. Even to the cost of my own soul, I shall do you harm."

20

Drew was past startlement or surprise when Gwynne walked softly into the room; he merely girded himself for another onslaught, which he was only beginning to realize he deserved.

"I shouldn't be here," she said. "It is grossly disloyal to my sister."

Drew made a helpless motion with his hand. "Then you should leave. Why are you here if you don't want to be?" He felt deep sorrow. He didn't want to lose her or her friendship. And now it was too late to do anything about it. In some of his more nostalgic moments he thought of Gwynne visiting Laurel and him in the upcountry. He had been sure Gwynne and Laurel would like each other, and he loved them both.

Her eyes were beautiful and clear. In them he could see the sadness and hurt and confusion he had put there. She wasn't good at hiding her feelings, he thought; then he realized that she made no effort to hide from him what she felt. She never had. Gwynne, he believed, was the most honest person he knew. He looked away from her as he tightly said, "I wish this could be made easier."

Gwynne too looked away, her eyes sparkling with tears. "Oh, Drew, why are you doing this?"

He reached for her hand, and she pulled away from him and jumped up from the sofa. She nearly ran to the window, her back to him. Drew followed. He stood behind her, his hands raised to touch her shoulders, but he did not. "I don't know what to say, Gwynne. I didn't think far enough to see how this would affect you or Grandmother. I never wanted to hurt either of you."

She turned then, her eyes flashing bright, tearful blue sparks.

"You never think, Drew Manning! Never! As long as I've known you, you never think clearly about anything, particularly about women. And you do terrible things to those who love you!"

"Joanna doesn't love me, Gwynne. Please, we both know she doesn't."

She clenched her fists and shoved him aside, then turned back to him. "I'm not talking about Joanna! When you were engaged to my sister, I tried to be loyal to her and think of you as my Cousin Drew, who would one day be my brother-in-law. I forced myself to day-dream about being Aunt Gwynne to your children! Don't you turn from me, Drew! You listen to me! I've spent a lifetime making a fool of myself over you and keeping it hidden, and now I want to tell you. I want you to know!"

Drew was nearly whispering, "Gwynne, I don't want you to do this to yourself. There's no need for this. I could never have made it work with Joanna, not even before. Your parents wanted her to marry a Manning."

"You're not the only Manning! And I'm not talking about Joanna! Me, Drew, I'm talking about me! We could have worked if you hadn't been such a blind . . . stupid . . . fool! For years you insisted you'd do what was right by Joanna. No matter how anyone advised you, you always insisted, until I finally forced myself to believe it. Now, right when the time to marry my sister is at hand, you come riding in here with your buckskin fringes and your wildman's toma-hawk at your waist and tell us you are going to marry some back-woods girl none of us has ever heard of. You're going to leave your family, your friends and everything we value behind and go riding off into the Cherokee country."

Drew was staring at her in disbelief. "Gwynne, are you saying that you've always cared for me—I don't mean as a cousin, but—"

"Of course, that's what I'm telling you, and only a fool would have to be told! Any other man would have seen it years ago!"

"Gwynne, I'm sorry . . . I . . ."

"Don't touch me, Drew! Not now. This isn't the time." She backed away from him. "And I have no use for your apologies, either. They're cold comfort, and I don't need that."

Drew sat for a long time after Gwynne had left. He couldn't recall a time he had felt unhappier. Life could be a cruel and twisted thing, allowing a man to make a decision without knowing the fact, and then extracting from him consequences he had never considered. Gwynne. He had closed himself off from everything he had ever felt toward her. He had never permitted himself to think of Gwynne in the way she had confessed she had thought of him. He got up and paced around the room, then finally went outside and walked toward the woods.

He tried to clear his head and his heart of all the conflicting feelings but couldn't. So many accusations from his father regarding his youthful folly and inexperience came back to him. Comments that his uncle had made or even on occasion that his grandmother had made about his blind headstrongness came back to haunt him. Even Gwynne said he never thought clearly. Perhaps he didn't. What he did know was that now that he wanted the time to think through his feelings about his family and about Laurel and himself, he no longer had it. He had made a determination that would affect the rest of his life without being prepared, and he was no longer permitted a way out of it.

He wished he were anywhere but here, and that this were any time other than the one it was. He couldn't get Gwynne out of his mind. He had lost her without a thought or even the chance to know what he felt. And she was right. He never did think clearly. He followed blindly rules he didn't understand and then defied them stupidly when he could no longer stand the confinement. Now he had lost the safe harbor of his family, their care and support, and had again committed himself to a marriage that would dictate a certain kind of life with rules of its own. He was no more aware of what would be demanded of him with Laurel than he had been with Joanna.

Vaguely he began to understand his father's adamant adherence to what he called the rules of order. Perhaps the rules in themselves were not so important as the fact that those rules provided a sane and safe framework from which a man could progress. Drew had precipitated himself outside those safeguarding rules and now found himself alone and unprotected in a new, uncharted world that he wasn't sure he liked or wanted; but he could not go back.

He felt a terrible sense of loss and did not understand the meaning of it. He kept coming full circle in his thoughts back to Gwynne.

He couldn't erase the picture of her from his mind, nor could he control his thoughts of her, which seemed to have been suddenly released just today. He thought of her in ways he had never known possible. He moved restlessly through the woods, waiting, hoping for the balm of well-ordered nature to work its effect on him and knowing it wouldn't, for not even nature has room for the countenance of a disordered man.

As confused and hurting and restless as he had been when he left the house, he now returned to it. He went back to the parlor and sat down, waiting for the next step of his disgrace to unfold. As he sat there in silence and alone, his thoughts turned to Laurel. He wished he could see her. Nothing was ever complicated when he was closed away up in the wild Cherokee country with her. All the complicated concerns he now faced were irrelevant. There was no heavy responsibility waiting to be thrust on his shoulders. He had only to see her, have her put her arms around him, love him, and nothing was complicated.

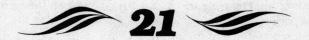

21

Drew had been at Riverlea for five days. They had been days filled with arguments, recriminations, accusations, anguish and anger. He was tired and miserable. Joanna was seldom out of her bedroom. William Templeton had vowed to work against the Upcountry cause in the Charles Town Assembly. Ruth was hastily putting together plans for a party to which the entire countryside would be invited so that she and Joanna could stage an incident over which Joanna could denounce Drew and refuse to marry him publicly.

Drew allowed himself to be carried along in the current of these angry and hasty plans, not knowing what he should do or even what he wanted to do. He had expected terrible scenes, but expectation and reality were quite different. He felt assaulted and trapped. But he also felt responsible for everything that had happened. They had right on their side, and all he had was his own desire to be free of the marriage arrangement.

Early on the morning of the fifth day, Drew went for a long ride, trying to clear his muddled feelings. It was an unfortunate choice of activity, for it gave Joanna the freedom of truth and logic when a special messenger delivered a letter to Riverlea.

"You don't need to worry. I'll see that Mr. Manning receives his letter," Joanna assured.

"I was tol' to put it right in his han'," the man said, still holding the letter.

Joanna's face grew colder. "Mr. Manning is not available. I have told you I'll see to the letter. You may either entrust me with it or you may leave Riverlea immediately."

"Don't look like you're givin' me much choice," the man said, shrugged and placed the letter in Joanna's hand.

Joanna stuffed the letter into her bodice and walked back inside the house.

"Who was that man, dear?" Elizabeth asked when she came back into the parlor.

"Oh, it was nothing of importance, Cousin Elizabeth. Daddy just sent a message home by way of a passing stranger. He will be late coming for supper, that's all." Joanna fidgeted for a bit, then excused herself and hurried to the privacy of her own sitting room. She read the letter. Laurel had been captured by a band of outlaws, and Georgina, in defiance of her husband's wishes, had written to Drew to tell him of it. Joanna smiled. She hadn't expected her first opportunity to repay Drew's treatment of her to come so soon. She crumpled the paper and threw it into her wastepaper basket. She sat down, reveling for a moment in the feeling of power she had gotten from the destruction of the letter. There was only a trace of guilt deep within her over the effect her action might have on another woman's life. She stared off into space. What was Laurel Boggs like? What kind of woman did it take to become so involved in a man's life that his actions as a Regulator would affect her very survival, as had happened to Laurel, according to Georgina. The outlaws had taken Laurel because they could not get to Drew directly. She couldn't imagine Laurel. She couldn't imagine any woman being so important to a man that this could happen.

She squeezed her eyes shut and felt cheated by Laurel as well as Drew. Why couldn't he have wanted her? She wanted to marry him. She wanted him forcibly to break the mold of propriety she herself could never break. He had robbed her of the only chance she had of changing. He alone would not become prey to the fears of not being accepted. He would do what he believed, and he would force her to do the same because he would leave her no other choice. Bitterly she realized that he was actually doing that now. By refusing her and laying her open to humiliation, he was forcing her to retaliate. She would do it. Instead of spending her life trying to support him and help him, she would spend her life hating him and causing him pain whenever she could.

She fed on the thoughts of damage he had done her. In some ways Drew had ruined both her and Laurel. That thought pleased her, for they would both suffer the same way, and at the bottom of it would be Drew. Drew was an evil, thoughtless man. All who saw Laurel for the rest of her life would look at her and know of her life with the outlaws. They would see her from the corner of their eyes and talk about her with motionless lips, just as they would about Joanna. She felt sick to her stomach, and her hatred of Drew grew larger.

Before she dared think of anything more, she went in search of her mother. Plans for the public denouncement would go on. It had to be soon. She wanted Drew publicly exposed as soon as possible. She stepped into the hall just as Minna, the upstairs maid, came along with her dust mops and cloths. "Be sure you go carefully through my dresses, Minna. There are several hems that need attention, particularly the green silk, for I want to wear it this Thursday evening."

She hurried on to her mother's room, and the two women spent the afternoon making plans.

Elizabeth remained apart from the activity. She could say nothing, no matter how much she hated what was taking place. She had not even been able to muster up a good anger at Drew for having gotten the family into such a horrible state of affairs. She just felt tired and old and wished the entire affair were over so that they could all calm down and hope that time would heal some of the wounds. She had just lain down on her bed for a short rest when Pelagie burst into the bedroom with barely a knock.

"Miz Lizzybeff! Look at this!" She handed Elizabeth the crumpled and stained letter from Georgina.

Elizabeth made a face. "What is that filthy thing, Pelagie?"

Pelagie's face shook in indignation. "It's a lettah to Mastah Drew. Ah knows his name when Ah sees it."

Elizabeth put her hand out for the letter, her eyes on Pelagie. "How did you come by it in this condition? Did Drew do this to it?"

Pelagie shook her head. "No, ma'am! Missy Joanna do this. Minna tell me, 'cause she see it in Missy Joanna's bedroom. Minna's jes' as curious as a chipmunk, an' she go see what Miz Joanna throw away. She cain't read an' throws it back into the garbage, but Ah sees it, an' Ah kin read Mastah Drew's name, so I brung it here to you."

"You did well, Pelagie. It seems any family, even ours, is capable of a great deal of intrigue, deceit and dishonesty when our wishes are thwarted by one of our numbers."

"Yes, ma'am," Pelagie said, shaking her head, but her eyes rested on the crumpled letter. "What do it say?"

Elizabeth smiled at her. "I don't know, Pelagie. The letter is addressed to Drew. I shan't read it without his permission. Would you please ask him to come to my room immediately? Perhaps he shall tell us of its contents. It must be important or Joanna wouldn't have bothered to keep it from him."

Elizabeth fidgeted with impatience as she waited for Pelagie to return with Drew. It was difficult for her to look at the narrow, upright script and not read the words that Georgina had written. She knew with every instinct she possessed that the message Georgina had sent to her son was an important one. With circumstances as they were, Georgina would not have written had she not felt compelled. Elizabeth pressed the letter to her breast and closed her eyes. "Pray God that if it must be bad news, it is bad with the promise of good to come of it," she murmured.

It was half an hour before Drew finally came to her room with Pelagie. Pelagie was more disturbed than she had been the first time she came to Elizabeth. "He was out galavantin' with Miss Gwynne, as if we don't have enough troubles to swallow already." She looked at Drew, her black eyes gleaming at him. "You was younger, an' Ah'd have you right over mah knee!"

"Let it be, Pelagie. Drew, this letter came for you some time recently, and for reasons known only to Joanna, it was not delivered to you. As it's from your mother, I think it has some import." She handed him the letter.

Drew held the crumpled letter for a moment, then sat down and smoothed it out on his knee. He had read for only a moment when his grandmother saw him pale. His hand was shaking when he handed her the letter and got up from his seat. "I must leave immediately, Grandma." He seemed in a daze and did not wait for his grandmother's reply, nor did he say more. He walked from the room, and she and Pelagie heard him running down the hall steps. He hadn't even packed or changed clothing. Elizabeth went to the window and watched him run around the side of the house toward the stables. Moments later she saw him ride swiftly down the Riverlea road. He was going to the Upcountry. She now returned to the letter, no longer wanting to read it, feeling hesitation and dread of its contents. "Oh, Pelagie," she said softly, "I think I am finally learning what it means to be old. I don't think I want to know what is in that letter. I am learning to fear what life may bring. I am learning to doubt that I am up to the rigors of its gifts."

Pelagie's face saddened for a moment. Then she put her hands on her hips and the bright, impish light returned to her eyes. "But you gwine read it, ain't you, Miz Lizzybeff."

Elizabeth smiled. "Yes, I am. I didn't say I was old, Pelagie, I said I was beginning to learn." She glanced at the first line, looked up at Pelagie frowning, and began to read it aloud. Looking up from the letter when she was done, Elizabeth trembled. "What manner of world do we live in, Pelagie? Georgina is very mild in what she says in this letter, but I know Georgina, and she is frightened. I am sure she just doesn't want to alarm Drew any more than the news itself will. That poor girl Laurel—and Drew—what he must be feeling."

"Mastah Drew woan gib up till he fin' her," Pelagie said staunchly. "What else she say?"

Elizabeth looked at her blankly for a moment, her thoughts far away, then she shook her head. "Oh, the rest is nothing, just sympathy for Drew and Laurel, and a closing." Elizabeth fell silent again. Pelagie waited patiently for her mistress and friend to speak. Finally Elizabeth's beautiful eyes saw her again. "Pelagie, something is brewing. It is all around us, and now it has touched our family directly."

"What you s'pose that is, Miz Lizzybeff? What would Mastah Waltah say?"

"I'm not sure," Elizabeth said slowly, "or perhaps more correctly, I don't want to be sure."

"Then you does know!" Pelagie said, her eyes wide and filled with foreboding. Anything that disturbed Elizabeth was of monumental proportions.

"No one knows, Pelagie—except the Almighty, of course—but if I were to guess from how I read the signs He sends us, I would say the colonies are finished with the mother country, and we are seeing the unrest that precedes it. Christopher Gadsen and the Adamses have said we'll seek independence for years." She was quiet again for a time, then said, "Drew is a man of the next era, Pelagie, and God willing, you and I will see what is to come in that new age. We are privileged or cursed, Pelagie. Not all people live at such a time."

"Ah sure do hope we's privileged."

"So do I, Pelagie, so do I, but privilege does not always bring ease or pleasure. For now we would do well to take to our knees and pray for Drew's safety and the return of Laurel—or whatever may be merciful."

22

Drew saw nothing but a blur before him as he rode with all possible speed from Riverlea. He cut across rice marshes, raising ducks in a flurry of perturbation as he went. Terns, egrets, herons and black skimmers flew, hopped and skimmed the water in disarray. He rode toward the Santee, thinking to follow it closely to the place where it split into the Congaree and the Wateree. He would then follow the Wateree home, stopping only when he and the horse could no longer go without food and rest. At each stop he would ask for information about any outlaw activity, any strangers in the area, any loiterers or low people who caused unease by their presence.

A great rage alternated with fear within Drew. He had a feeling of personal violation that he hadn't before experienced. He couldn't bear to think of Laurel herself. His own pain at the abduction was so great, he couldn't bring himself to enlarge that feeling of fright and hurt to include what she must feel. Yet he pictured her being frightened and trapped by the wild and reckless men he knew the outlaws to be. As quickly as the thoughts came, he brushed them aside. As he rode the long hours and the longer miles to home and grew tired, thoughts of Laurel and Joanna mingled and it became difficult for him to keep one woman separate from the other. Too tired to go another mile, he began looking carefully at his surroundings. He was somewhere near a plantation, and he began watching for the entrance. It was another weary hour before he saw the sleepy black welcomer dozing at the gate to Marshside plantation.

The black man came to attention as soon as Drew neared.

"Massa Trainah o' Marshside bids you welcome, suh! Ah's Bo, suh, an' Ah'm at yo' service."

"Run ahead, Bo, and tell Trainer that Drew Manning of Manning Plantation on the Wateree begs rest for the night." Drew handed the man a coin. Drew walked his horse slowly up the drive after the man ran toward the big white house that peeked through the trees. Drew smiled as he saw Bo stop about a hundred feet up the drive, whistle for a child and send the small messenger the rest of the way. Bo reached into the pouch he carried slung across his hip and took from it a piece of raw cane. The little boy smiled broadly and raced up the road, the sugar cane bobbing up and down with each pumping motion of his small hand.

Bo grinned as he passed Drew on his way back to his post. "Ever' body happy now. Good day to you, suh."

Mr. and Mrs. Trainer were a gracious couple who opened their house and their friendship to Drew. John Trainer met him on the front steps of the house.

"Welcome, Manning. Li'l Bo tol' us you looked like you'd come a long way. I'd say he's mighty right. Follow me, an' we'll bed down that horse of yours. He's a good-looking animal—you do any racing?"

"I've been known to try it on occasion," Drew said, smiling. "Almost any occasion that the horseflesh is promising and the stakes are good."

Trainer laughed. "Then you've made the right stop. We're having a race here on Sunday. After you've had a chance to rest up and get a cool drink in you, I'll show you my track. Had it built just last year, and if I've got to boast for myself, it's the best running track hereabouts. Be glad to have you join the field—there'll be about fifteen or twenty of the best South Carolina–bred horses in the area running."

Drew rubbed his horse down while John Trainer got a feed bag and filled it for the steaming animal. "I wish I could, John," Drew said sincerely. "But this trip is a little different from my usual. I hope you'll give me the opportunity to race on your track some other time. I come through here often."

John placed the feed bag over the horse's nose and stepped back. "Manning," he said softly. "Why am I familiar with your name? Manning . . . Manning . . . why, you're the fellow got himself known all over the county for chasing down Govey Black an' his ilk." He walked up to Drew quickly and put out his hand. "I want to shake your hand, sir. Me an' my family owe you a great debt. Those Black brothers near cleaned me out a couple o' years back. Maimed my bes' man while they were at it, too. Bo's daddy was my welcomer back then, an' them slimy bastards blinded him. Now I got to take care o' him till ol' age carries him off, 'n I cain't get a lick o' useful work outta him. Course it's worse fer him than me. He was a good man. I got the expense o' him, but he was a workin' man an' all he's got is idle days an' piddly li'l jobs we kin fin' ever' now an' again."

"Well, Govey Black won't be leading any more bands. I watched him hang myself, and I can't say I felt the remorse a man should feel when he watches another man die. But a remnant of his gang seem to be operating in spite of our efforts. These last few men are the reason for my haste. Have you heard of any unusual activity in these parts or seen anyone with whom you aren't familiar?"

John thought for a moment. "Haven't heard of anyone having trouble like there was before. Been a couple of robberies, but those are the work of the low people—been nothin' like you're talkin' about. An' you're the only stranger come through here in the last two weeks."

Drew looked out the open barn door to the hills beyond. "I didn't really have hope that they would stay so close in. My best guess tells me they're way up in the Cherokee lands."

John Trainer started to say something about good riddance, then correctly read the lost, sad look on Drew's face. He looked at the ground. "Guess you got yourself a good reason for needin' to hunt 'em down. Well, I can't say I'd like to be you, Manning, but I'm damn glad there are men like you willin' to clean out their rats' nests fer the res' o' us." He placed his hand companionably on Drew's shoulder and gently guided him in the direction of the house. "Come on in an' meet my wife. If I know Carrie, she'll have drinks waitin' for us an' something cold and good to eat. One thing about Carrie—she always knows when a man is needin' an' what to do to fix it. She's a good woman, my Carrie."

Drew spent the night at the Trainers' and slept soundly. Carrie Trainer had an enormous breakfast on the table for him when he came downstairs shortly after dawn. Her smile was bright. Her gold-enrod hair was tightly braided and wrapped around her head. Her eyes sparkled with zest for life. "John asked that I give you his regards and wishes for success in your search, Drew. He is already out with the men. Race week is a big time for him. He's not seen much around the house." She sat with him as he ate, then hurried him on his way with an enormous packet of food, and John Trainer had packed a similar bag for his horse.

Drew continued to push himself and his horse onward up into the hills. He watched the clear rivers turn dark with the stain of tannic acid from the cypress and other roots, and then finally they turned red. Heavily laden with the red mud he loved, the rivers sped along back the route he had taken toward the Atlantic. With the encouragement of seeing red in the river, he trotted briskly along the Catawba Trail, knowing that soon one of the curves of the narrow road would bring a view of Manning Plantation's outer border.

He rode up the drive to his home—the home he had thought he might never return to when he left to go to Riverlea. The night he had told his father that he would marry Laurel even if it cost him his inheritance, his family and everything he had ever known as home seemed long ago and no longer important. At this moment he needed desperately his brother Arthur's love and support.

Dismounting quickly, Drew ran up the front steps to his home. He was deeply stunned when Milo opened the door and stared at him as though he were a stranger.

"Milo! Stand aside. I want to see Arthur."

"I am sorry, sir," the black man said. "Mr. Arthur Manning is not in to you."

"Milo, damn it! This is my home. Step aside before I have you given a good thrashing."

Milo's expression never changed, nor did the cold impersonality of his voice. "I have been told, sir, that you are no longer part of this family and are not welcome here. You must leave, sir; those are the orders of the master of Manning. Good day, sir," he said and closed the door firmly in Drew's face.

Drew raced to the back of the house and came away talking to himself as he received the same treatment from Amma. He would not be given entrance to his own home. Thunderstruck, for the first time he realized that truly he had no home. He had no family. He needed them, and they were not there for him. He was frightened.

He didn't know how to behave when he was not permitted admittance to his own home, his own brother, his own room, his own parents. Why were they doing this to him? He would never have left them in such desperation. Never! But the wild, frightened thought didn't hold, for only now did he realize he had done just that. He had violated his father's word. He had abandoned his family and left them needing.

Storms of thought raced through his head. He began to understand and see a multitude of things he had simply not understood before, but overriding all this was his very real worry about Laurel. She had to be found. Above all his sins and their consequences, above all his cares and those of his family, Laurel's safety had to come first. He stood back and looked at the house. He walked around to the side where Arthur's bedroom was and began to scale the wall, relying on the strength of the ivy and the eave of the house.

The drape on Arthur's window was pulled closed and the window locked. Drew knocked repeatedly but received no response. He moved cautiously along the ledge to his own bedroom window and climbed through. He noted only briefly that all trace of his possessions and all those things that had made the room particularly and uniquely his were gone. It was just another bedroom in Manning House now.

He hurried down the hallway, thankful he did not see his parents or any of the servants. He knocked on and opened Arthur's door. "Arthur," he whispered. "Arthur, wake up!"

"Drew?" Arthur muttered sleepily. "What are you doing here? How did you get in?"

"No one knows I'm here—I climbed in the window. Arthur, please—I need your help. I've got to find Laurel. I know you won't want to help me, but she has done you no harm. For humanitarian reasons, please help me find her."

Arthur sat up in bed, rubbing his eyes. "I just came back in from thirty miles north of here, Drew. The men have been systematically searching every inch of this territory, expanding our limits north and west each time we search a new arc of land." He got up and awkwardly hugged his younger brother. "You should have known without asking that we would not ignore a woman's plight, Drew. But you must also see that I cannot support you openly. Manning deserves and will get my loyalty. I can't see my way to violate that. I'm sorry, Drew."

"But you will help me find Laurel," Drew asked.

"Yes, I said I'd do that . . . but not as your brother; only as another man. And I will not openly leave Manning with you, Drew. I'll meet you in a couple of hours—out in the open—on the road to Camden."

Drew looked at Arthur for a long time. Finally he said, "There's no chance that Papa will change his mind, or . . ."

"There's no chance, Drew. Even Mama can't bring your name up in his presence. He misses you sorely, but he said when a man's word is worthless, so is the man."

"It wasn't my word," Drew said miserably. "I didn't make the marriage agreement."

Arthur shrugged. "It was the family word. That is the way Papa sees it, and he believes there is no valid reason for your refusal. You could have had Riverlea, Joanna and Laurel—and most important of all, the honor of the family."

Drew sighed, and Arthur put his hand on his brother's shoulder. "There's nothing to be gained by going over this again and again, Drew. Let me clean up and we'll go out after Laurel. That is something we perhaps can do something about. This is not."

Drew left his house the same way he had entered. He rode out along the Camden road and waited for Arthur. About an hour later Arthur rode up beside Drew on a fresh horse. He handed him a sack. "I thought you might be hungry, seeing as how you expected to be coming home."

Drew thought of refusing it, then thought better. He was hungry, and he had counted on being welcomed back to his own home, at least given hospitality under the circumstances. He ate greedily of the meat and cheese and bread Arthur had packed, then they set out.

At Drew's suggestion, they rode far into the Cherokee lands beyond Manning. "I don't know where else they could go without attracting notice," Drew said.

Arthur shook his head. "I'm not saying this isn't a good possibility. I just can't share your certainty that we'll find them up here, even if this is where they took her. It's so wild we could go right past them and never know."

"That's part of the reason I believe she's here."

Arthur shrugged and rode on, looking from side to side, trying to read tracks and make sense of them. "What are you going to do now, Drew?"

"I haven't given it much thought. Go to Cherokee, I suppose, and turn it into the plantation I've always claimed it could become."

"Will you continue with the Regulators?"

"I don't know. I will if there is need, but from what I've heard, there is little outlaw activity. It may be the Regulators have come to the end of their usefulness. We always looked upon it as a temporary measure."

Arthur laughed. "The Regulators are still quite active and most likely will remain so. Sniff the air, brother, and tell me what you smell."

"Rotting carcass," Drew said.

"We have an abundance of those lately. Many of the low people have taken to hunting for the skins of animals, which is all to the good. However, rather than use the meat of the beasts they kill, they leave them to rot, drawing wolves and other beasts of prey to attack our sheep and cattle."

"And the Regulators are after them," Drew finished for him. "I suppose that means they've been to Harley Boggs."

"They haven't been as hard on him as they might have been because of Laurel. But it won't last, Drew. Harley is a stupid man and will soon lose the little sympathy he has gained. He has declared her dead in his mind if not in fact. Every day you can see him in the pubs in Camden, telling the sad tale of his daughter and how he was nearly killed trying to save her."

"Is it true?"

Arthur shook his head. "It's true that someone nearly died trying to save her, but it wasn't Harley. Ben ran from the house with Mary and the baby. Somewhere—apparently in the woods—he came across Laurel. The two of them tried to split up and lose themselves in the brush, but it didn't work. Laurel was taken, Mary was slaughtered, Pamela died and Ben was shot in the back of the head. He's still alive, though no one knows how. Maybe God does reward those few of us so courageous. I don't know, Drew. I hardly know what I think these days. Do you ever feel that way? So unsure of what is happening you can't even grab hold of your own beliefs?"

"I do, most of the time; but I never knew that you did. You always seem so set and sure of what you want and the right way of doing things."

Arthur rubbed his hand across his forehead and laughed. "I do know the right way to do things—if you want to do them as an English country gentleman. The problem is, Drew, that I don't know or can't seem to find where I belong at the plantation. Good Lord, I could no more plant a field like you can than climb a mountain on my hands. I wouldn't know if I had a good crop until it was all processed and ready to go to market. But is it necessary that I know such things? Is it requisite that I be able to plant my own fields? Can't I hire someone to do all that?"

"While you sit happily in your study, poring over those great tomes of knowledge of which you are so fond."

Arthur smiled. "Yes, I am comfortable with my books and theories, much more so than I am with the harsh and rather sordid realities that you so often delve into—like this search we are on tonight. I don't know whether I fear that we shan't find her or that we shall."

Drew was quiet for so long that Arthur thought he had taken offense and began to apologize.

"There's no need for apology, Arthur. I am quiet because I don't like my own thoughts. I have the same fears as you, but I haven't the right to them. I say I love Laurel, and I do, but I don't know what to say to her when I find her. What do I do? How can I look at her and not wonder about what she has lived through. I don't know, Arthur. I have only questions, and I'm happy for the opportunity to say so."

Arthur smiled, shaking his head in amused appreciation. "It's been a long time since you and I have bared our souls to each other, Drew. Do you remember how, when we were very young, we would stay awake half the night whispering the secrets of our lives to each other while Mama and Daddy would periodically come in threatening the hickory stick if we didn't go to sleep immediately?"

"Were things simpler then or does it just seem so now because we understand more?" Drew asked.

"A little of both, I think. I've spoken to some old and very wise men, Drew, here and in England, and none of them can make sense of what is happening. There are so many facets to the questions we face today that even they are not always clear on what must be done. Men speak of rights and freedoms that we have been given as subjects of the crown. If we have them as citizens of England, why then must they think of fighting to gain what they already have? But it is not just a right, it is that right in a particular manner. It is as if men suddenly want to be autonomous—that there is no need for the king. I find it frightening and feel that it can lead to nothing but anarchy, and that chaos must come after."

"Why are you so sure there must be chaos?" Drew asked.

"Look to yourself for a microcosm of that which we speak. What else could there be? What would we do without England's beneficence? How would we of all people survive if it were not for England's support of the indigo market?"

"We'd turn to a new crop," Drew said quickly and simply.

Arthur made a gesture of impatience. "You are hopelessly unrealistic. You think that all one needs is a change of mind, and then as if by magic, everything will come right."

"That's not so!" Drew said indignantly. "I have been making plans for some time. I may not be very wise, but I am canny to the mood that is around me, and I know unrest is within the hearts of all men, whatever their politics or beliefs. My Cherokee land will support nearly any crop I choose to plant on it."

Arthur's face remained set. He shrugged his shoulders, then looked at his brother. "Have you really planned that well, Drew?"

"I don't know, Arthur. I wish I did. I think I have, but then sometimes I just feel as though I'm fighting and I don't know what it is that I'm fighting against."

They stopped for the night in the open and lay side by side under a black sky studded with so many stars it was difficult to pick out the constellations. Neither of them spoke. They shared a quiet companionship during which they acknowledged each other's uncertainty and recognized that neither of them had answers for the other. It was said that there were a few men in every society who could anticipate change, and that they were like the leaves at the top of a tree, quivering in a breeze that could not be seen or felt lower down. Neither Drew nor Arthur knew what it was that they sensed, but the leaves of the tree were quivering, and they did not know what it portended for them.

Just before Drew fell asleep, he heard Arthur's voice coming to him in the darkness. "Perhaps you have planned wisely, Drew. Maybe we'll all wish we had Cherokee lands to run to. But have you ever thought how fortunate you are to be able to plan and execute such things? I cannot do what you have done. My life is already tied to Manning Plantation and to the indigo crop, and therefore to the king. If King James's influence is broken, then Manning is a lost plantation, and with it so am I. I cannot run to your red hills."

Drew had wanted to answer, to say that wasn't true, that there would always be a family, that the Mannings would go on together no matter what, but the black sky had lowered and closed in over his heavy eyes, and he knew the words were no longer true.

23

Drew and Arthur returned to Cherokee, Drew's plantation, in April of 1768, tired, hungry and without Laurel. The two brothers slept for the better part of two days, then Arthur went on to Manning, where Georgina hovered over him, ministering to him and coaxing nourishing broth and soft meats and delicacies into him.

"Was there any news of her, Arthur, any trace?" Georgina asked her son.

"Oh, yes, we followed one cold trail after another. Some said she was living with a man named Grady, and others said his name was Albee. Some said she killed her man and ran to the mountains, and still others said she was dead or the best thief the outlaws had ever trained. If she was ever near the Cherokee lands, she isn't now, or she is so well hidden we found nothing of her."

Georgina let the tears slip down her face unabashedly. She held fast to her son's hand. "Oh, Arthur, what can we do? There must be some way to find her. I keep thinking of her. She is with me, in my thoughts and in my prayers, even in my dreams. I see her face—that beautiful, innocent face, so full of life. It doesn't seem possible that something so terrible could happen to one we know. Why is it that we always expect tragedy to strike a stranger when it is all around us?" She sat quietly for a time, then looked up at him. "How is Drew? Is he well, Arthur?"

"He didn't expect Daddy to keep him from coming home. He is still very young in many ways, Mama. He thought he'd be forgiven. He's staying at Cherokee—that's what he's named his land."

"Is anyone with him?"

"Ned Hart arrived just as I left. I imagine he'll see to Drew. Ned is a good man. And," Arthur sighed, "knowing how Ned feels about Drew, I imagine Daddy and I can count on losing him as an overseer. I hope we find someone good, because I'll never be the planter Drew is."

Georgina smiled and kissed her older son, then went downstairs to her sitting room. She gazed out the windows and tried to imagine Drew as he would look if she could see him at Cherokee. At least Ned was with him. That was some comfort.

Ned Hart had listened to Drew's account of his search for Laurel. Little had been said about Drew's problems with his family, and Ned would not be the one to bring it up.

Drew was tired through and through, both physically and emotionally. "Have you heard anything more about Ben, Ned? Will he recover?"

"He's holdin' on fer dear life, but there ain't much change."

Drew gave a grim smile. "I suppose that's the best that can be said about any of us. But I'll take that bit of news as an omen. As long as Ben remains alive, I believe I'll find Laurel alive, too. From what Arthur told me, the wound Ben sustained would have been fatal to almost any other man, but Ben lived. It must mean something. I'm sure it does."

"Well, he lived, all right, but he won't never be the same, Drew. Some folks say he wasn't lucky at all livin' through it. Some say he'll never git well and'll wish he were dead."

"I thought you said you hadn't heard anything more about him."

"I wasn't thinkin' that'd be the kind of news you was lookin' for."

"It doesn't change how I feel, Ned. It is a sign of strength and of hope. I'll find Laurel, and whatever happens, we'll get through it. I have had my doubts about myself and her and what has happened, and I have found weaknesses and pettiness in myself that I loathe, but I can overcome it, and with Laurel's love, we'll come through whatever may come when she returns home."

Ned shook his head, but he smiled. "You sure are countin' an awful lot on one li'l backwoods girl, ain't you?"

Drew nodded. "And on myself." He laughed bitterly. "You may have heard, Ned, I've burned a few bridges behind me of late. I can't afford to fail now. I have to go on, and I have to do it well. I've given up too much and come too far to discover I'm wrong."

Drew joined with a group of the Regulators in early April, and expected to enlist their help in finding Laurel immediately. He found that there was going to be little or no help forthcoming. The Regulators had moved on in their interests, and for their purposes, the outlaws were a phenomenon of the past.

"We searched for her, Drew," John Haynes said. "I know how you feel. Laurel's not the only woman still missing. There are many of us who have lost loved ones, but we've got other problems to deal with. We can't keep looking for her. The low people have to be seen to, and reforms must be instituted now."

"Does that mean we no longer have time for people like Laurel?" Andrew asked.

Defensively John said, "You know I don't mean that! We'll all be on the lookout for her, and every damn time one of us is out we'll continue searching. All I meant is we can't keep organizing parties to scour this countryside for your sake or the sake of one woman. We're concerned with a whole population up here, not just one man or one family."

"So you become judge and jury to a bunch of poor people, dunk them in the rivers and put lashes across their backs, and allow a woman to remain lost?"

"Yes, that's it, because if we don't we'll have a new crop of outlaws, and a year from now we'll be in the same battle we just concluded. These low people will become productive members of society or leave, because the only other choice is for the rest of us to spend our lives raising crops and sheep and livestock so that they may steal and pilfer and not contribute anything."

Drew looked away from John and said nothing. John continued. "You haven't been gone long, Drew, but the past couple of months have made a big difference in you, and I don't understand it. Before you went to Charles Town and off with Arthur into the Cherokee lands, you understood where we were, you knew what the Regulators were trying to achieve and you were one of the most enthusiastic of us. Now it's as if this is all strange to you."

"Damn it, John! It is all strange to me. I'm not the only one who has changed in the last couple of months. So have you. You all have. What are we doing now? Going to war with the Charles Town authority?"

"Maybe so," John said, jaw jutted out. "Maybe so, and that's something else you were pretty much in favor of a few months back. It didn't bother you a bit when we all thought we'd march on the Assembly with our grievances."

"That was different."

"How so, Drew?"

Drew rubbed his forehead. "I don't know, John. Maybe it is me who feels differently about what we're doing. I don't know; I just don't seem to know anything. I keep . . . I want to find Laurel, and dunking a woman because she smiled at a man other than her husband doesn't seem as important to me."

"You just better start seeing the importance of that, Drew, otherwise we'll have new outlaw communities and new outlaw women. We got rid of one bad bunch, but that doesn't mean it is over and can't happen again. It can and it will, if we're not vigilant."

"I suppose," Drew said wearily, but his mind was no longer with John. He'd look for Laurel alone, but for the first time he faced the possibility that she might never be found. She had been gone for nearly two months, and no one had seen her, nor had he received any news of any new outlaw settlements.

He traveled the back roads of the Upcountry alone, stopping wherever he could find a plantation or farm and asking for information. He returned to Camden, and the knowing eyes of John Haynes defeated him there. John, knowing he had won his point, was kind with Drew. He put his arm across his friend's shoulder. "I know how you feel . . . don't you remember how I took on the night we all found Melanie Williams? Do you remember, Drew?"

"Yeah, I do, but John . . . it's not the same."

"I know that. What you feel for Laurel makes it worse, but at least I do know how you're feelin'. I couldn't make myself believe that something like that could happen to a girl I'd known most of my life. She . . . she wasn't Melanie anymore, and I still don't know who she was. She was a wild, fighting thing that hated us all. I wanted to find her for a long time, Drew. I knew it didn't make any sense. She was right there already found, but it really wasn't her. It was someone who looked like her, had her name, but it wasn't her anymore. It was like some other awful wild woman had slipped into her body and had her tongue and her thoughts, but Melanie was gone, and I wanted somehow to find her even when I knew I couldn't."

Drew looked pleadingly at him. "But . . . she . . . she was at least there, John. Even if she'd changed, she was there."

John shook his head, and Drew saw the real hurt and sadness in John's eyes for the first time.

Drew didn't speak, because he didn't know what might come from his mouth. He squeezed John's forearm and began to walk away.

"Drew," John called before he had gotten five paces. "You can't do it alone. Stay with us. We may not be perfect, but the Regulators have the right intention."

Drew went home that evening, but he returned a few days later, his resolve to work with the Regulators once more deeply set in his mind. He went to the meeting held in Camden and listened while the leaders discussed exactly how they should go about drawing up an acceptable and workable plan of action in curbing the habits of the low people.

Rob Williams and his father Thomas were there, and so was Peter Dobbs. That meant it would most likely be a no-nonsense meeting, Drew thought, and moved among the men until he came to a space made for him between Bart Cole and John Haynes. John smiled warmly at him. Bart in a raspy whisper said, "You shore as hell took your good ol' sweet time gettin' to the meetin's. Where you been?"

"Shut your mouth, Bart, an' lissen," John Haynes said.

Ned Hart stood up to be better heard. In his hand he had a sheaf of papers. He looked at the group of about twenty men and smiled as he waited for Bart, John and Drew to quiet. Then he put on a pair of spectacles that perched on his nose, stretched his arm out to full length and said, "I been doin' some lookin' up an' talkin' to Moses Kirklan' an' Ed McGraw an' Henry Hunter about our problems with the low people. Now, first an' foremost is the fact that other colonies take care o' low-people problems by means o' laws, mostly vagrancy laws. We in South Carolina ain't got no law like that." He laughed. "Not that it matters a whole lot, 'cause if we did have a vagrancy law, I'd sure like to put money on bettin' that it wouldn't apply in the Upcountry anyhow. What laws we got have a strange way o' gettin' exercised only in the Lowlands."

There was an appreciative smattering of quiet laughter.

Ned lowered his head and made another comical production of using his spectacles. "But jes' 'cause we ain't got a law of our own don't mean no one has. Mother England don't put up with low-people nonsense. She's got laws, and we can pattern ours on what she does. Now if one of our low people was to be in London carryin' on the way they do here, he'd be whipped or sent to the house of correction till the next quarter sessions. Mebbe he'd be sent to the workhouse or the almshouse an' wait there till somebody offered him work, an' then he'd damn better take it or he'd find himself at hard labor in the house of correction. Now we don't have all them houses of detention and correction and almshouses 'round here, but we sure do have a whip an' a dunkin' stool and stocks, an' if we need somethin' else we kin get it.

"For us the bes' example I could fin' of a law already workin' an' curbin' the kin' o' behavior we want to curb comes from our sister colony, Georgia. They got a law leveled at people who don't have property and don't seem to want it or want to work it if they do got it. People who live loose, disorderly lives or don't make a livin' except by huntin' an' leavin' carcasses behind, drifters, crackers and the jes' plain lazy aren't wanted in Georgia any more'n we want 'em here. So me an' some others decided what we need here is to purge the country of all idle persons, all that have not got a visible means of gettin' an honest living, all that are suspected of or are known to be guilty of malpractices, an' all those we know and see to be of loose or immoral character. These people are to be employed every day, exceptin' the Sabbath, in Regulation work. They will be paid the customary rate for their labors. Them that won't work will come under our lash, be dunked in the river or banished from here for all time." Ned looked up from his papers and peered at the group. "Anyone got anything they want to say or figger we left anything out?"

Thomas Williams stood up. "There's a peck o' men who don't do right by their families. I think you'll all recall the time Samuel Boykin came to the Regulators about Bennet Dozier. We all knew Dozier for the slothful man he is. He never did do right by his family. Half the time his wife an' kids didn't have the necessities. After

Boykin an' the Regulators made a visit to his home, talked to him, tol' him the way o' right, he's been doin' a whole lot better than before."

"It didn't hurt none that they stripped the sluggard, tied him to his own oak tree and plied him with thirty-nine persuasive lashes," Peter Dobbs added.

Thomas Williams, a severe man to start, looked disapprovingly at Dobbs for the interruption. "I think we should write clearly in our law that neglect of family won't be tolerated any more than vagrancy will."

"What's Governor Bull goin' to think of all this? He's never too partial to us makin' our own order," John Haynes asked.

"Who cares what he thinks," Bart Cole said. "He don't have to live here an' have his property an' kids an' women influenced by these people."

"The Assembly meets this month and will consider our proposals then," Ned said. "We'll find out what Charles Town thinks then. But meanwhile these are our rules, an' we'll abide by them. Is it agreed?"

He looked around the room, and with a chorus of yeahs and raised hands the Regulators agreed to clean the Carolina hills of low people. "Is there anyone who has a disagreein' word to put in?" Ned asked again.

There was no response. The men sat quiet, their hands motionless. An hour and a half after he had walked into the meeting, Drew left. It had been businesslike and efficient, almost a formality. The Regulators had known what they wanted before they came to the meeting.

It was the last quiet meeting of the Regulators Drew was to know. Later in the month news from Charles Town filtered back to the Upcountry. The Charles Town authority had once again taken exception to the Regulators' assumption of self-rule. Governor Bull declared that the Regulators were not authorized in any way to make or execute laws that affected their neighbors.

The Regulators gathered in small groups. At Cherokee Ned Hart, John Haynes and Bart Cole talked with Drew.

"Damn it all!" Drew blustered in frustration. "The Upcountryman does have the right to the protection of law—English law—and Charles Town does not provide it for us, in spite of our repeated requests. By lack of law they have made us victims of the lawless."

"Yeah," said Bart. "But what are we gonna do about all these li'l piss-ass low people who's bringin' lawsuits agin us? Somebody in Charles Town is sure 'nuf lissenin' to their grievances. Eight warrants have been issued agin the leaders to serve as examples. I hear they plan to prosecute. What the hell are we gonna do about it? Let 'em arrest our leaders?"

Drew shook his head emphatically. "There'll never be an arrest of any one of those men. The rest of the Regulators won't allow it."

John Haynes said what they were all thinking. "We've made our minds up and have vowed to stand by our leaders. Suppose Lieutenant-Governor Bull decides the same thing. If warrants have been issued and the attorney general is authorized to prosecute, are we gonna prevent the militia from taking those men? Aren't we gonna be declarin' war on our own Assembly if we do it?"

"Looks like we would be," Bart said cheerfully.

"That's nothin' to joke about," John said. "This ain't some lark we're all goin' out on. Seems like this is takin' sides in a serious way, an' it don't matter who wins—folk ain't gonna fergit it soon."

"No, they won't," Drew agreed. "But we're committed—if we remain Regulators. The challenge from Charles Town has been met and accepted by the leaders we'll have to defend. It wasn't too long ago, John, that you questioned my loyalty to the movement. Perhaps it is time you examine your own feelings about the Regulators now."

"God," John breathed. "I jes' hate gettin' in this deep, but I guess that's the way it's gonna be, ain't it?"

The summer of 1768 was a long, hot summer filled with tension and continual clashes between the Regulators and the Charles Town authorities. Drew was as much on call with the Regulators now as he had been during the time they were chasing down the outlaws. The Regulators rode wherever there was trouble, wherever warrants had been issued to arrest any Regulator leaders. Lieutenant-Governor Bull had intended only to make an example of a few leaders, but many of the provincial judges carried his intention far beyond and issued many warrants.

Late in June Drew rode with his Regulator group to prevent Provost Marshal Roger Pinckney's deputy John Wood from delivering twelve legal processes into the Upcountry. One of the processes called for the arrest of Moses Kirkland, Henry Hunter and Edward McGraw at the suit of Gilbert Hat, a magistrate who didn't like the Regulators and had made it known for some time.

Wood had managed to serve several of his processes before the Regulators caught up with him on June 27. Drew and five other Regulators came upon him with their guns and pistols ready. Wood backed away from them.

Drew looked at his friends and received an answering grin. With a flourish of his cutlass, John Haynes strode toward Wood, a ridiculously ferocious expression on his face. Wood was horrified, and Drew could barely keep from bursting into laughter. Another of the Regulators grabbed Wood by the throat and jerked him from his skittering, nervous horse. The Regulators fell upon him and bound his hands tightly behind his back.

"Now what do we do with the skunk?" John shouted, laughing wildly. He turned Wood to face Drew and gave him a mighty shove that sent him staggering into Drew.

"I don't want him! He's a real stinker! Give him to Rob." Drew turned Wood again and shoved him toward Rob Williams. The men taunted and insulted Wood for a long time, then, growing tired of their game, Wood was placed on his horse once more, his feet tied to the underside of the animal. Continuing to pummel and taunt Wood, they rode him to the Frazier house, the home of a Regulator leader on the Broad River. For the next five days they kept Wood chained to a post at the Frazier house.

Drew and John sat on the veranda of Frazier's house the last night Wood was kept captive there. They had been quiet for the last half-hour, enjoying the still warmth of the summer night.

"There'll be hell to pay over Wood," Drew said offhandedly, the long stem of grass he was nibbling on bobbing up and down as he spoke.

"Maybe it is a little out of hand, but I think we've got a ways to go before we're through with Mr. Deputy Wood," John said. Silence fell between them again. Crickets and owls and night birds chirruped in the tall grass and trees. A slow, easy breeze washed over them from time to time. "You know, Drew, livin' jes' ain't all that

easy. First we were chasin' the outlaws, an' Charles Town was chasin' us; now we're chasin' the Charles Towners while they're
chasin' us still. Think it'll ever come to pass that we all stop chasin'
after each other an' get back to our fields?"

"I've been wondering what will happen with the harvest this
year."

John made an agreeing sound. "My old man is doin' everything
this season an' hatin' every minute of it. You gonna stay home for
harvest?"

"Yes, I am. I'm committed to the Regulators, but not so much
that I won't be damn sure I have a crop to see me through."

Loud noises came from inside the Frazier house. Drew looked
over his shoulder toward the house. "Sounds like the boys have
been havin' a good ol' time with Frazier's corn liquor."

"Yep," John agreed. "That should mean trouble for Wood. Wonder what they'll do with him next?"

They found out half an hour later when the Regulators came
outside onto the veranda, ready to ride.

"Better get your gear, Manning, Haynes," Frazier said. "You're
gonna be left out o' the fun."

By the time Drew and John had their gear together and were
mounted, the rest of the men were already on the road, prodding
Wood on his way toward the Little River, a tributary of the Broad
and the location of Barnaby Pope's house. Barnaby Pope was a
crude man given to drama and loud boasts. "I'm gonna make this
pukey li'l process server eat ever' damn shred o' this wuthless
Charles Town paper!" He lunged at the bound Wood and shoved
the process into the man's mouth. Wood gagged and struggled as
best he could as Pope continued to shove the wadded paper into his
mouth. Finally in self-protection, Wood tried to chew the paper and
swallow what he could. Pope seemed pleased but not at all satisfied.
"Now we gonna give him the floggin' he deserves! Come on, boys,
le's do this right! One less process server and one more lesson to
those no-heads in Charles Town. We'll teach 'em who we are an'
that they better let us alone to mind ourselves."

Drew and John and two of the other men, aware that things had
gotten out of hand, convinced the group that they should move on
with Wood. They took him a few miles farther on to Thomas Wood-

ward's house. But the respite didn't last long. The talk and the revelry went on until the band of Regulators had decided to put Wood on trial and carry out whatever justice they decided upon.

Once more they mounted and placed Wood upon his horse. Drew and John brought up the rear of the party, straggling several yards behind the noisy, insulting group.

"I don't think I like this much, Drew," John said in a wary, singsong voice.

"You have company. I don't like it either. They've gone too far. They're losing the value of Wood as an example, and there will be no justifying our position if they actually put him on trial and do him harm. No one in the Charles Town Assembly will give us the time of day, let alone be sympathetic to our viewpoint." Drew made an impatient gesture, and his horse leaped forward. He reined in the animal, soothed him and dropped back near John. "We'll lose everything we've worked for if this continues."

"Whyn't you say something to them? Talk to them . . . make 'em lissen," John said. "Go on, Drew. You can do it. You're a good talker."

Ahead of them the group slowed down and then stopped. Wood's horse bent his long, graceful neck toward the water. Several of the Regulators let their horses water as well. Suddenly and without warning Wood's horse bolted forward and galloped at top speed for the woods. The Regulators, after momentary confusion and surprise, raced off after him. Drew and John spurred their horses as well.

"What the hell are we doin'?" John said and laughed. "We don't want to catch him, do we?"

"How the hell should I know. I don't know if it's worse that he get away and blab the whole affair in Charles Town or that we get him and do him in first. Seems to me we already hanged ourselves."

"So why're we runnin' with the pack?"

"Cause we don't want to miss out on the finale," Drew yelled and cut his mount hard to the left to avoid a broken tree limb.

Wood's direction was unquestionably east and his objective Charles Town. The man had the determination and drive of a pack of starving wolves. Without a moment's hesitation he plunged his horse into both the Broad and the Saluda rivers and swam them both. The Regulators gave up, knowing that, barring mishap on the trail, John Wood would gain Charles Town by Friday night, July the eighth.

Drew pressed his lips together, staring at the now-empty trail. "Maybe it's Friday the eighth that is bad luck and not the thirteenth."

The episode with John Wood did not dampen the Regulators' enthusiasm or fervor for battle with the authorities. The band did not break up, nor did they show any remorse or fear for what they had done. It was on to Mars Bluff, where there had been another report that trouble was to come.

Rumors were rampant, and the Regulators expected more difficulty and more citations from Charles Town daily, but it was relatively quiet. Drew left for home with the promise he'd return by the twenty-second or twenty-third of July. As had become his habit, he returned home by the longest route he could manage, stopping and asking about Laurel at every opportunity. Drew was tired and discouraged as he finally began the ride up Cherokee's dirt road. The lean-to looked ramshackle and in need of repair, but it was home. He missed Laurel and had the vague, nagging feeling that he was also missing that man he might have been had she not been lost to him.

Part Three

Nathaniel

24

Far away from Drew, but sharing some of his same thoughts, stood an Indian girl on another hill in the Carolina wilderness, wrestling with the unwelcome twists of fate life had given her. She, too, was alone and set on a path she didn't understand but from which she couldn't turn.

Star Dancer stood at the crest of a hill, her head thrown back, her face toward the night sky. She stared at the twinkling stars for which she had been named. The light from the moon glistened on her cheekbones and brought out the highlights in her long, sleek black hair. Star Dancer was a young woman, strong, proud and bitter. She couldn't bring back her man. Albee had killed him, and there was nothing left but his spirit. There was never going to be anything of him except his spirit. She kept her inner self quiet and felt his presence. Her memories of him were still strong, and she could even gain warmth from them, but it wasn't enough. It would never be enough. Albee would pay for killing Little Elk. He would suffer the loss of the woman who kept him warm in heart and body, as he had made her suffer the loss of her man.

She studied the stars awhile longer. The woman was vague about where she had come from. Star Dancer had only a few clues and the stars to guide her and the woman back to where she had once lived. Satisfied that she had oriented herself correctly, Star Dancer walked slowly back to the spot she had chosen for them to sleep this night. She sat quietly on the cool, dry earth, her dark eyes watching over the figure of the woman, whose long, light brown hair was spread out around her, her blue eyes closed. The woman's face was pinched and tired-looking. Lines of fatigue marked her under the eyes and around her mouth. She had never told Star Dancer her name. To Star Dancer she was only Albee's woman, and now mostly when she thought of her she was The Woman. She had come to like The Woman. There was a quiet strength in her that Star Dancer admired. However she didn't understand some other qualities. The Woman was a contradiction. She wanted to escape from Albee but did not want to go back home especially. Yet there was no other place of which she spoke. Star Dancer had to listen very carefully to the few bits of conversation The Woman engaged in; otherwise she would have had no idea where to take The Woman.

The Woman stirred in her sleep. She turned quickly, then moaned gently, her hands automatically going to her swollen belly. Star Dancer's eyes sought the black velvety sky once more. Her face barely changed, and yet there was a smile on her lips. "It's a boy child," she murmured to the sky. Slowly a tear found its way from her lid down her cheek. Somewhere up in that endless darkness, in among the spaces where the stars did not twinkle and shine, she could see Little Elk and the boy child they had wanted and dreamed about and who would never walk this earth with her.

Soon she would awaken The Woman, and they would travel once more. The Woman could not travel for long without rest, nor could she walk well in the heat of the day. The boy child was already active and large within her, and the summer was hot, and The Woman hadn't the caring within her that would carry her with haste back to her man. She seemed not to care about him at all. Those few times she would talk, she spoke of the man with great longing, and Star Dancer then thought she felt about the man she called Drew as Star Dancer felt about Little Elk. But that couldn't be true, for there was no mountain so high or sun so hot that it could stop Star Dancer from reaching Little Elk. It was at the times when The Woman said she would never return to the man Drew that Star Dancer didn't understand her and sometimes didn't like her for it. It was at those times she wondered why she helped The Woman. Why did she keep her alive? Why did she guide her? Her objective had been to take from Albee his comfort and warmth by taking The Woman from him. She had never intended to care for her. She still wasn't sure why she did. But there was a reason, a secret reason that spoke to her from the woods and rocks, the sky and in the spirits of the wind. They didn't tell her all, only enough so that she kept trying to find a way to bring The Woman back to her people and back to her man Drew.

She slept for a while, then awakened and sat quietly until the sky began to lighten in the east. She touched The Woman's shoulder, and as always, The Woman jumped, her eyes still filled with sleep, unseeing but wild with fright. The Woman was frantic, like a trapped animal, then her eyes focused on Star Dancer and she relaxed, her whole body changing. The Woman put her hand to her face, her head down. "I did it again, didn't I?" she said.

Star Dancer nodded. "You always awaken running from the evil spirit of the evil man Albee."

"Have we gone far from the camp?" she asked.

"We have come far," Star Dancer said. "Many hills lie between you, but not so many days lie between. You and I will walk the hills, but you alone must walk the days that take you from him."

The Woman laughed, but there was no laughter in her eyes, nor did her face show relief. "Perhaps I carry him with me. Perhaps there are no miles to walk and no days to separate."

"There are some who do that," Star Dancer agreed. "But you have two men to choose from. It need not be Albee that you carry. It could be the man Drew. His is a good spirit."

"Why do you bother with me, Star Dancer? I have seen it in your eyes many times that you do not like me. I don't believe as you do. You love your Little Elk no matter what, and no matter the pain or what the outcome will be, not even his death deters you, and I can't even think of Drew. I am nothing to you. I have no value. Why do you save me?"

Star Dancer's eyes went to The Woman's belly, but she said nothing.

"Is it the child?"

"It is a boy child. It is the man Drew's boy child."

The Woman buried her face in both her hands and sobbed. So often when the man Drew was mentioned she did that. It was not a happy crying. It was not the crying of a woman who knew she was coming home to her man. It was a bitter, hard crying that Star Dancer did not like. It was not right. "We must be on our way now or we will not have gone far enough by the time the sun is high and you must rest again."

25

Drew rejoined the Regulators on the twenty-third of July. There had been tension between the Regulators and an anti-Regulator justice of the peace named Robert Weaver. The tension grew and threatened to become an incident when Regulator leader Gideon Gibson led a band of Regulators and captured Lieutenant John Holland, taking him into custody.

By the time Drew arrived, Weaver had already issued a warrant and entrusted its execution to Constable George Thompson.

George Thompson was a captain in the militia, and he gathered a small party of militiamen to assist him. Thompson and his band of fourteen militiamen were on their way to Mars Bluff and the arrest of Gideon Gibson at the same time Bart Cole, John Haynes and Drew made their way toward Mars Bluff to join with Gideon's band of Regulators. None of the three of them was particularly enthusiastic to be involved in a repeat of their last venture involving Deputy John Wood.

"I can't see that this kind of campaign can serve us well," Drew said. "The very best we could hope to gain from the Wood affair is that Charles Town knows that we will not blindly follow their whims and wishes, but don't they already know that?"

"I don't know," Bart said. "Doesn't seem to matter much what Charles Town knows. Never have known them to be swayed by the fac's. Have you, John?"

"Nope, long's I can remember, no fac' ever tainted a Charles Town mind."

The three of them laughed and began to reminisce about times each of them had been in Charles Town and run across the attitude that Charles Town was South Carolina. "By God, they don't know there is a world outside here," John said, his voice getting lighter with mirth.

"Oh, they know," Bart disagreed. "Who protec's them from all them bad Indians they talk about, an' what about all them slaves that get away? There's not a Charles Town planter that doesn't quake in the night that but for us, all his runaways would come and slice his throat."

"Even that is an ignorance of fact," Drew said more seriously. "No one wants those damn slave ships dumping off their cargo here, but all the Assembly does is talk and complain. The ships keep landing and the cargo keeps getting sold. Why don't they stop it?"

John shrugged. "Why don't we have courts and law up here? They have passed the legislation, but we don't see no courts in action. Nothin's really changed. Maybe that's all these John Wood things is worth; jus' keep pointin' out that nothin's changed, an' we know it, an' won't sit tight for it."

On July 25, George Thompson; William White, a cooper; his father, James Taylor White; and his brother, Reuben White; and eleven other militiamen met Gideon Gibson and his Regulators on Mars Bluff. The Regulators were drawn up into two lines in front of the house where they had John Holland sequestered, waiting for Thompson and his men.

Thompson and four of his men boldly strode between the two lines of Regulators. A well-placed elbow, a few crude gestures and grimaces, and the lines of Regulators and militiamen were broken and men were on the ground fighting. Pistols were drawn, and in the men's faces showed all the anger and frustration that had built up on both sides through the preceding months. As they looked at each other they no longer saw friends and neighbors but only the face of the enemy.

"Shoot down Billy White!" Gideon Gibson shouted. "I have Reuben, and if you kill Billy we will manage the rest easy enough."

William White drew his cutlass and stood prepared to fight any and all who came at him. With men jostling and fighting all around him, it was only moments before he was knocked from his feet. From the melee a hand reached out to him. He grasped his father's hand and regained his feet. Realizing that he was in no position to battle successfully, he tried to escape in order to gain a more advantageous position. As he pushed his way through the men and ran, a musket ball ripped through his flesh. In a dizzying blur of color and grayed blackness, he fell to the earth.

The Regulators were well-trained fighters. They had fought Indians hiding in the bush; they had flushed frightened, enraged Negroes from every conceivable hiding place. They had run outlaws to ground and battled hand-to-hand men crazed by the wilds. Fourteen militiamen presented little problem to them.

By the time William White had come to his senses, the militiamen were subdued and contained. White lay on the ground and opened his eyes to a sweating, triumphant and mean group of Regulators standing over him.

"Shoot him through the head!" cried one of them.

"No, damn him! He can't live long. Let him feel himself die!" another shouted angrily.

Several of the men, Drew among them, carried White into the house and dumped him on the floor. White in a state of sickly panic watched his blood seep from him, to be lost and absorbed by the wood-plank flooring.

When Drew and the others walked outside again, the rest of the Regulators had several of the militiamen strapped to trees. Others awaited their turn as the Regulators administered fifty lashes to each.

Satisfied with their day's work, the Regulators left, but all of them knew that they had crossed some unseen but very real boundary this day, and this would not be the end of it. Charles Town could not ignore an affront to their authority such as this had been, nor could they ignore the outrage against law and order and the treatment accorded the men whom they had sent to enforce that order.

Drew and John and Bart remained near Mars Bluff, waiting, as did the others, for the next step to be taken. On August 10 Provost Marshal Roger Pinckney and George Gabriel Powell, one of the leading politicians and planters of South Carolina and a colonel in the Peedee militia, marched to Mars Bluff to arrest Gideon Gibson. Powell and Pinckney arrived in Mars Bluff with about twenty-five men and established headquarters in the house of Robert Weaver, the justice of the peace who had always been against the Regulator movement. At Weaver's house they were joined with fifteen men from Weaver's militia company. The following day twenty men from Colonel Thompson's company arrived to swell the ranks. With the reinforcements, among whom were Arthur Manning of the Wateree district and Leo Manning of Charles Town, however, came news that Gideon Gibson was well guarded by a large band of Regulators and could raise three hundred more men in an hour's notice.

Roger Pinckney and George Powell discussed the matter and decided prudence and reinforcements for the militiamen were in order. No one was fooling anyone any longer. The Regulators were at war with the Charles Town authority and all those who tried to enforce it. No more talking or bargaining was to be done. The battle was a real one; the muskets were loaded and the intent was to kill. Pinckney asked for reinforcements from two other companies. Waiting became the order. With the passage of each hour Arthur and Leo found their presence with the militia more difficult. They kept to themselves, both men acutely aware that for the first time the Manning family had split in such a way that members of the same family might be facing each other with guns. At any time one or both of them might do battle with Drew. It affected Leo as strongly as it did Arthur, for Leo and George had had a raging argument before Leo had left. He wasn't even sure that George had not done as he had and come to Mars Bluff on his own. Perhaps it would not be Drew he faced but his own brother George. The tension and doubt and fear had mounted in both men.

As new men came to Weaver's house and camped there waiting for word from Pinckney that they would move against Gibson, information filtered in. Among the pieces of news that came, there was one that gave Leo and Arthur hope that the whole situation could be avoided. It was said that Gibson had decided that the forces were too large and the stakes too high, and that he would surrender.

Pinckney and Powell looked at each other. Skepticism was deep in Roger Pinckney's eyes. "There is just enough of a chance that Gibson actually would be willing to surrender to save his men that we must honor it," he said.

Powell agreed but fell into deep concentration. "They have taken captive several representatives of the Assembly, with no regard of their authority, Roger." He looked at Pinckney, his brows knit, his hands pointed steeplelike to his lips. "They've never had an opportunity to capture someone of your stature. If we act upon this information, I believe that I should be the one to expose myself to them. If I was captured, it would mean much less than if it was you."

"I don't care for the idea of staying safely behind while you are at the front of the field, George, but I must concede that your point is valid. I suggest that we inform Gibson that we would like a meeting . . . a private meeting. Perhaps we can suggest that the two of you can speak calmly and clarify the situation between us. Do you think he'd agree?"

"If he is as able a commander as he's reputed to be, I think he could hardly refuse a reasonable man's request for a private interview over a situation as grave as this one is," Powell said. "I think I should make the request immediately."

Arthur and Leo conferred and decided to offer their services. "I would be pleased and honored, sir, if you would accept my offer to speak with Mr. Gibson. As you know, my brother is a member of the Regulators and is most likely in Commander Gibson's camp. I would have, in a manner of speaking, a friend in court."

"You might also become a valuable hostage, but I shall consider your offer heavily. Be assured I am most grateful for it, Mr. Manning. I have appreciation for what your position must cost you." He sighed and looked into the distance. "I fear more and more that we shall see terrible times in which brother will face brother on opposite sides."

Pinckney did discuss the matter with George Powell and decided to leave Powell as negotiator for the militia, as he was a more experienced man.

On Sunday, August fourteenth, George Powell set out to meet Gideon Gibson in the woods deep in Regulator territory for a conference. For an hour and an half the two men met and conferred. Powell emerged full of confidence and impressed by Gibson's sincerity.

"Roger, I think we have made great progress. Gibson is a most impressive man and is truly concerned for the safety of his men and the satisfactory conclusion of our difficulties. I think, with a modicum of caution, we can congratulate ourselves. Occasionally reason does win out over hot tempers."

"He has consented to surrender, then?" Pinckney asked.

"He has. He will give himself up at eight o'clock tomorrow morning. He requested this time to speak with his men, and I thought that a proper request. Not all men are capable of seeing as clearly as Gibson is. He shall have to talk to some of the Regulators in rather strong language, I would guess, in order for them to agree to giving him up and accepting a peaceful conclusion of this whole sad affair."

"So it would appear. However, though I know Gibson's reputation for good leadership, I must admit that I have a sense of wariness." Pinckney ran his hand through his hair, his eyes focusing somewhere far away in thought. "This has all come about a little quickly for my faith to be fully with it."

Powell looked miffed. "I felt that I had done a rather thorough job of negotiating with Gibson. We talked at length, and I feel I impressed him favorably and imparted to him the import of law being established in the Upcountry. I found him very reasonable and quite an astute man, concerned that this confrontation be resolved in the best possible way."

Pinckney, Powell and the militiamen arrived at the agreed-upon meeting place at eight o'clock the following morning. The men were lined up, their eyes alert and searching for sight of Gibson and his men, if he brought any with him. The woods were silent until they were near to giving up. Finally they heard the sound of a horseman. Boldly one of the Regulators rode up to Roger Pinckney and handed him a letter.

"From Gideon Gibson, sir," the man said with a smirk on his face. He rode quickly back the way he had come.

Pinckney looked at Powell, then, sighing, he ripped open the envelope. His brow furrowed as he read the missive. Then he handed it to Powell and said, "It seems Mr. Gibson has changed his mind." With an angry, jerky motion he commanded his men to follow him back to the Weaver house.

By ten o'clock that morning Claudius Pegues had arrived at the

Weaver house from the Cheraws, thirty-five miles north of Mars Bluff. Pegues was a highly respected magistrate throughout the Peedee region. But his presence gave Arthur pause. He moved closer to Leo so no one else would hear. "Something doesn't feel right about this, Leo. I'm not as familiar with the Regulators as Drew is, but I am sure this Pegues is the man I've heard Drew talk about often as a respected and strong member of the Regulators. I'm beginning to wonder if these men in general are militiamen or Regulators."

"Where does that leave us?" Leo asked, a worried look on his face.

"I'm not sure, but I think we should be prepared to ride out at the first indication of betrayal. Agreed?"

Leo nodded, and from that point on both men listened to all the talk circulating around the camp.

After Pegues, Pinckney and Powell talked they called a conference with the five militia commanders: Pledger, Hicks, McIntosh, Clary and Michael. The leaders had drawn their men up in a line about one mile from the Weaver house. Pinckney, Pegues and Powell arrived to be amazed at the number of men standing and waiting for them in formation. They had anticipated one hundred militiamen and were now faced with nearly three hundred of them.

First pleasure gave way to uncertainty. Powell went before the men and explained the situation to them and asked for the assistance he needed from them. He also made it clear what was expected of them.

Powell walked along the lines of men, talking, urging, cajoling, warning, slowly beginning to learn that it was a tenuous position he held. These men were Regulators, at least to the extent that they had on occasion ridden with the Regulators and in most cases sympathized with the Regulator movement. He turned to Roger Pinckney.

Pinckney, with little to add to what Powell had already said and satisfied that Powell had made their need and position clear, read the proclamation against the Regulators issued by Lieutenant-Governor Bull.

The men listened quietly and respectfully, then refused to aid Pinckney. "Gibson is one of us," a spokesman said. "And he has asked for our protection. He has it."

Desperate now, Powell and Pinckney thought that since the men had come in response to the militia call, there had to be some room for doubt. Rather than give up and allow Gibson to escape arrest altogether, they talked the men into going back to Weaver's house to be fed and to talk some more. The men, not above being given a free meal, complied with the magistrate's wishes and went with Powell and Pinckney. Here the two men hoped to talk sense into the militia leaders. After supper the talk began again, and again the men listened to what Roger Pinckney and George Powell had to say.

As the evening wore on and the militia leaders seemed to be enjoying themselves, Pinckney and Powell began to realize that the enjoyment was perhaps too thorough and too relaxed and confident.

Claudius Pegues had sat quietly throughout most of the evening, a pleasant, knowing smile on his face. With gusto and satisfaction, Lieutenant Clary introduced Claudius to his hosts in a new fashion. "Gentlemen, may I present to you the Regulators' candidate to represent St. David's Parish in the next session of the Assembly." Leo and Arthur quietly left, mounted their horses and raced for the safety of Manning.

Powell and Pinckney backed off and away from the wall of men who were no longer allies. Fearfully they stayed close to each other, no longer sure of their safety and knowing that the slim thread of authority they carried from Charles Town was no protection against the seemingly endless wall of Regulators. No matter where they turned or whom they trusted, no one seemed trustworthy. Regulators were everywhere. One could not be sure there was a man in the Upcountry who was not one. As soon as they were able, the two men retreated to Georgetown, making no further attempt to apprehend Gideon Gibson.

Gibson suddenly seemed invincible, and yet neither Pinckney nor Powell doubted for a moment that it was imperative that the power of the Regulators be curbed or broken, for the authority of the government in Charles Town was being challenged and for the moment overpowered. That could not happen. Powell, however, had fought his last battle. On the way back to Georgetown, he considered all he had been through, and at the end of his trip he wrote to Lieutenant-Governor Bull and gave his resignation as a militia colonel. "These disturbances seem to have so dismal a tendency that I am at a loss to guess where they may terminate."

George Powell ended his association and responsibility for the battle with his letter, but Pinckney went on, and so did Lieutenant-Governor Bull, for they had no choice. The Upcountryman was demanding rights he claimed as his own, and when they were not forthcoming, he was taking them. In a colony already rampant with new and different views of freedom and rights and demands for control and autonomy, the Regulators could not be ignored.

26

In the Templeton parlor Wiliam, Ruth, Gwynne, Meg and several guests gathered after dinner. It was a quieter gathering than most the Templetons hosted, and the conversation was not as light as it ordinarily was. There were few people in Charles Town and the Low country who did not follow the exploits of the Regulators in the newspapers.

"I just read in the *South Carolina Gazette* last week where three thousand of them gathered at the Congarees, and for purposes that could not be published in the paper without causing undue alarm. Anytime three thousand men of one mind and purpose gather together, the potential for danger is present. We are their stated enemies," William said. "What are they likely to do, is what I want to know. Why do they need so many if they haven't an invasion of the Lowland in mind?" He looked apprehensively at his friend and nearest neighbor, Alan Mitchell.

"I think they have in mind to march on Charles Town," Alan said. "What I question, and perhaps worry about more, is what will we in the Lowlands do when the attack comes. If we retaliate we are likely to end up in an all-out war with them, and if we do not retaliate, they will gain in strength and take more power and influence into their own hands. Either way, I cannot see how South Carolina as a whole can benefit from this movement."

"But is it not true that requests they have made of the Assembly are reasonable?" Gwynne asked. "When Andrew used to tell me of the Regulators, he said that all they wanted was what was guaranteed to all Englishmen and the protection of the law and English bounty that we already enjoy in the Lowland. Shouldn't they have these laws and courts and schools they ask for?"

Alan Mitchell and William Templeton exchanged looks of tolerant patience. Then Alan smiled paternally at Gwynne and spoke in a soft voice as if she could not understand normal English. "Now, my dear, you must understand that when men are vying for power, oftimes what appears to be the issue is not. The Regulators have been granted through the generosity of the Assembly the laws and means to end their problems. But as you can see from their recent behavior, it is not legislation that they desire, for they refuse to wait for these new laws to be put into effect. Instead they have gathered together large numbers of men and are preparing to take to the field. These are not the actions of honorable men, my dear. However, I am, and I'm sure your father is, pleased that you anticipate all men being as honorable as those to whom you have been exposed in this house."

Gwynne pushed her temper down. She sat looking off into space until she could gain control of the anger that had surged up in her. She had never cared a great deal for Alan Mitchell, but tonight she felt like dashing him with a bowl of cold water. "Then, of course, what you are actually saying is that my cousin is a liar and a dishonorable man," she said tartly and was rewarded with a scowl of disapproval from her mother.

"Gwynne, I don't think it wise to bring Drew into this conversation. We have all learned quite painfully enough the kind of man he is, and I hardly think *honorable* fits him."

Jemima Mitchell put her hand out to Ruth. "I was so hoping someone would mention him, Ruth, for I was so loath to mention his name myself, but I have wanted the opportunity to offer you my sincerest, heartfelt sympathy for Joanna. How is the poor darling?"

"Well, of course, she is prostrate over the entire matter. It was enough of a shock for her to have to face the fact that he would never make a suitable husband for her and then announce to the world that she could not bear to go through with the arrangement, but then on the heels of that shock to also discover that he is so integral a part of a gang of rowdy, unsavory rogues intent of harming the colony itself in order to further their own unjustified ambitions was more than she could bear. She took to her bed, of course," Ruth said, and dabbed her eyes lightly with a filmy lace kerchief.

Gwynne looked away, unable to watch her mother. Neither Ruth nor Joanna had behaved like themselves since Drew had run off for the last time. The difference was particularly noticeable in Ruth. Gwynne knew and loved her mother for being an earthy, positive person. But since Drew's abandonment of Joanna, her mother had taken to posing and posturing for effect as she was tonight, and Gwynne felt sick when she saw it. She didn't understand the transformation at all. She knew that her mother wished to do what was best to save the shreds of Joanna's reputation, and rightly so, but she did not comprehend how or why falsity made the efforts more effective.

As she found herself doing so often lately, Gwynne drifted off into her own thoughts. Those thoughts were almost always of Drew. As far back in her life as she could remember, she could recall being enthralled by him. He had always been a hero to her, even in the days when she was too young to join in with the older children. She had watched, and even then it had been Drew who had fascinated her. The worst day she could recall had been the day when she was eleven, when her mother had told her that it was planned that Joanna and Drew should marry when they were older. Gwynne had been crushed. All her dreams of being a wife and mother had flown from her mind. She had gone to her room and cried for what seemed to her days and weeks and months. She had done a whole lifetime of crying. It wasn't fair, she had told herself. Drew was hers. She didn't understand how, but she knew that somehow Drew belonged to her and not to Joanna—never to Joanna.

She came back to the present to hear Jemima saying soothingly, "In a way, Ruth, you must be grateful that she will not be linked to that man for the rest of her life. It isn't as if he were the only man interested in Joanna. She actually can have her choice. She is very fortunate to be such a beauty. It makes life so much easier for a woman if she is fair of countenance."

"I am glad that she is free of Drew, Mima, but it is so trying for her. I must say I think she has done well to keep her senses about her."

"Well, we shall just have to make an effort to convince her to be seen in society as soon as possible. It shouldn't be difficult. I know for a fact that many young people have been asking for her." Her eyes sparkled as she added, "There is one young man in particular who would give his eyes for the opportunity to court Joanna, and he is quite a comely gentlemen, too."

"You must mean Tyrus Kincaid," Gwynne said too smartly for her mother's taste.

"I do indeed!" Jemima said. "Has he been bold enough to ask your permission to see her?"

"Oh, he's been bold enough," Gwynne said before Ruth could open her mouth. "He has been here almost every day. The man doesn't know the meaning of the word no. If Joanna refuses to see him, which she always does, then he will sit with Meg or me and annoy us with his constant chatter of Joanna."

"You mustn't be so impatient, Gwynne," Jemima said. "After all, his persistence is merely a sign of his ardor." She glanced over at Ruth with a knowing look in her eye. "After you are a bit older, you will know that once a man has set his sights on the woman of his choice, he can be most annoying in his persistence. You will just have to be tolerant, dear. It is for your sister's good."

Gwynne smiled but said nothing more. She and Joanna agreed about very little, but neither of them could abide Tyrus Kincaid. He couldn't have been more obvious in his greedy desire to have control of Riverlea. Joanna hadn't been fooled by him, and she wouldn't be.

The difficulty was that Gwynne was no longer sure what her sister would do. Joanna was as bitter as she had ever known her to be. Drew had done the unspeakable. In his willingness to suffer the direst of consequences he had finally penetrated Joanna's defenses. For once in her life Joanna had questioned her worth as a woman. He had humiliated her publicly, it was true, but it was the private humiliation that had gone deeply into Joanna and that she would never forgive. It would be the public display that she spoke of, but Gwynne knew the real damage had gone deep and was private, a part of her feelings that she'd never speak about to anyone again.

Her mother was telling Jemima about another man who had come to request that he court Joanna. Gwynne listened and felt a trill of worry run down her spine.

"Bertram Townshend is a marvelous young man, and so gentlemanly . . . he makes me think of young men back home who'd come to speak to my papa from time to time." Ruth smiled with the memory.

"He is a lieutenant, is he not?" Jemima asked.

Ruth smiled and nodded. "He looks so attractive in his uniform. His coloring is quite appealing, and the red merely enhances it."

"And he is a young man with a brilliant future before him, from all I have heard," Jemima said with satisfaction.

Joanna Templeton moved slowly along the upper hall near her bedroom, listening to the conversation below. She was not prostrate; she would never allow herself to be prostrate over a man. None was worth it. But she was no fool either. It was best to play the game wisely, let all the women—and the men, too—talk about her, feel sorry for her, and when she finally did appear in public again, they would be nearly talked out, and for the most part none of them would have the nerve to say anything to her face; nor would they risk having her hear what they had to say behind her back.

She made a face as Jemima Mitchell spoke again. She could imagine how Jemima's eyes would sparkle as she talked, hoping to hear some tidbit of news that she could pass along to her friends tomorrow or the next day. She smiled as a moment later she thought of Gwynne and Meg sitting politely through all this, holding their tongues and tempers. Meg would do all right. Meg had a way of lapsing into total silence and daydreaming far away from what was going on about her if she didn't care for it. But Gwynne could not do that. Gwynne would listen to every disagreeable word and weigh all that was said with her own sense of importance. Gwynne would suffer for her concern always, and it gave Joanna a feeling of satisfaction. She could never get even with Gwynne directly, because Gwynne had never behaved overtly in any way with Andrew that could be criticized, but Joanna knew that Gwynne had always cared more than she should for Drew. She had known, and she had heard Gwynne talking to him the day before he left. She knew and she wouldn't forget.

She'd side against him in every way possible—even if that meant fighting King George if it came to that. She made a face of distaste as she thought of herself as a rebel. It wouldn't come to that, she assured herself. Drew was unlikely to side with the King. It would be he who was the rebel and she the Loyalist, but nonetheless she had to be prepared to do whatever she must to oppose Drew.

Joanna turned from the hall and went to her sitting room. She sat at her desk, took out quill and paper. She thought for a moment, then began to write.

Dear Bert,

I have considered at length the conversation we had during your last visit to Riverlea. I have concluded that you are correct. There is no reason or justification for isolating myself because I have discovered the sordid character of Andrew Manning. There are, indeed, many levels to any society, and painful though it may be, I must recognize that these divisions exist within the confines of my own family as well as elsewhere.

I should like it very much if you would call upon me and my sisters, as you expressed a desire to do. I believe you shall find me quite changed from your last visit, and having adopted a more mature and optimistic outlook upon the entire affair.

I shall be looking forward to a pleasant afternoon of conversation and perhaps a ride later at your earliest convenience.

Yours truly,

She looked the letter over again and found herself unsatisfied with it. She sounded too eager, too ready to capitulate to Bert Townshend. Then quickly she folded and sealed it. What did it matter what she appeared to Bertram Townshend. He wanted her, and more important, he wanted Riverlea and the prominence that went with it. Bert was a lieutenant in the British army, a position obtained for him by his father as a younger son. He would rise and someday make his fortune, but it would be a long time and a difficult road. Joanna Templeton and Riverlea would hasten that rise considerably and establish him in America as an English gentleman farmer.

They were well suited to each other, serving each other's ambitions and understanding the weakness of each other. Of course, they did not love each other, but Joanna believed fully now what she had always suspected. Love was a nearly useless affectation, unless it had a purpose, and then it could hardly be called love, at least not as the romantics thought of it.

She would see Bert Townshend as soon as possible and give him every bit of encouragement he needed to bring about a marriage soon. She didn't want to waste a moment in her campaign against Drew Manning, and her first need was respectability, position and a husband to enforce these things.

27

The day after Alan and Jemima Mitchell had visited, Gwynne found herself in a sad, morose mood. Nothing was wrong, and yet she sensed that everything about her life was wrong. Unlike her usual self, she moped about the house, listless and quiet. Ruth asked after her health and, receiving no response, she said testily, "Well, for heaven's sake do something with yourself! All we need is another prima donna floating about the manse."

"What happened to the sweet, misunderstood Joanna you described to Jemima last night, Mama," Gwynne said saucily. "Your tune certainly changes when no one is about, doesn't it."

"Yes, it does!" Ruth said sharply. "My private opinions are for the ears of this household and no others, and often those opinions, especially about you girls, differ markedly from what I say publicly."

"About me too, Mama?"

"Yes, about you too! I don't know how I had such children as you three! None of you is like me, and I'll be amazed if any of you makes a successful marriage! You'll all end up with riffraff, and everything your father and I worked to build at Riverlea will be frittered away."

"I'll marry," Gwynne said softly but firmly.

"Will you? Whom, may I ask? As far as I know, you've never met a man yet suited to what you call 'your needs.' As far as I know, no man has properly respected your mind and your capabilities, which don't happen to be those a woman needs to satisfy a husband!"

"You can be very cruel!"

"Can't we all!"

"No, Mama, not like you, because some of us don't pretend to be nice and agreeable when we're really not. You do, and it makes your comments very hurtful when they are finally heard."

"But your way, miss, is supposed to be better? How do you think a mother feels when faced with an obstinate young girl, so sure of her mind that she will look at no decent man and not consider suitors because they will not discuss politics with her or they look askance at her riding bareback like a common gutter snipe. No one wants a woman like that for a wife. I knew I should have stopped your tomboy ways when you were just a mite, but I didn't and I regret it, and so will you, miss, when you live with your mama and papa for the rest of your life and have no family of your own to care for and be proud of."

"That will never happen to me," Gwynne said, her beautiful eyes flashing, her small jaw set hard. "Never!"

"Hrmmmph," Ruth said in disgust. "We'll see."

"It won't happen to me," Gwynne said. "I know what I want and I'm going to get it."

Ruth's eyebrows raised, and she laughed sarcastically. "Oh, you do! Well, well, may I know what that is, or shall it be a surprise for us all?"

"You may know—at least part of it, Mama. Right now I am going to visit Cousin Elizabeth in Charles Town, and after that I'll decide what I'm going to do next."

"Cousin Elizabeth? What for, pray?"

"I want her advice," Gwynne said, and walked from her mother to the writing table in the sitting room. Ruth followed after her, her face full of questions. "As soon as I've received a reply, I'll be leaving for an extended period of time."

"And that's all you have to say? You think you're going to be allowed to walk out of your home to see Elizabeth, of all people, and then make a decision about your future based on what *she* has to say?"

Gwynne looked at her mother for a moment and felt a deep sadness. She knew she could not talk to her mother about Drew Manning. She had to leave home. Perhaps she would never be able to tell her mother what she wanted of life. Ruth might never know whether Gwynne had succeeded or failed. "I'm going to go, Mama," Gwynne said quietly, and turned her attention to the writing paper on the table.

It was nearly two weeks before Gwynne received a reply from

Elizabeth, and in that time she thought and considered how drastic a change in her life would be made if she decided to pursue the course she was contemplating. All her doubts and fears had surfaced by the time the letter from Elizabeth arrived at Riverlea, but it took only the arrival of that letter to dispel them. As she read Elizabeth's enthusiastic invitation for her to come to Charles Town and stay for as long as she wanted, she felt a surge of excitement pulsate through her. She felt airy and filled with life.

She packed her bags that day and was ready to leave the following morning. Her father stood by, baffled and confused at the bad feelings between his youngest daughter and her mother. He was also taken aback by what he thought was a sudden decision on Gwynne's part. Ruth had never told him of the discussion she and Gwynne had had two weeks before, and Gywnne had said no more to anyone about what she was doing. William Templeton discovered his daughter was about to leave on an extended visit to Charles Town when he happened to come around the corner of the house to see the carriage standing in front of his door, being loaded with Gwynne's trunks. Now he was discovering that this was the culmination of a long disagreement between Ruth and Gwynne.

"How long will you be gone?" William asked wistfully.

Gwynne looked at her father. She could see the hurt and confusion in his eyes. Her father was a good man, she thought, but he was not the kind of man she wanted for her own husband. She didn't want to be the kind of wife her mother was or to have the kind of family she had grown up in. Maybe her mother had been right. She was a disappointment to her parents. Gwynne stepped up to her father and threw her arms about his neck. She hugged him tightly, her face pressed against his thick, barrel chest. "I don't know how long I'll be gone, Papa, but I shall miss you, and I'll write often." She stood on tiptoe and kissed his cheek, saying, "Papa, I love you," then quickly got into the carriage and sat looking straight ahead.

William smiled. "My little mule, headstrong as always. Elizabeth will have her hands full, eh, Ruth? But she's up to it. You take care and watch for Leo and Rob and George. They've got an eye for the ladies."

Gwynne was crying in earnest by the time the carriage turned from the Riverlea drive onto the road to Charles Town. She didn't really know what she was doing, and she might be entirely wrong. She had never been away from her home or her parents before, and suddenly it didn't seem at all comfortable to be on her own. She felt miserable and a fool for even considering the idea that Drew would marry her when she knew perfectly well he wanted to marry Laurel Boggs, whoever she was! She had changed her whole life to chase after a daydream she had had in childhood. That was all it was! A stupid, impractical daydream!

28

Elizabeth was eager for Gwynne's arrival and ordered the guest suite to be readied for her. Eugenia was in her usual flurry of nervous tittering at the prospect of a guest staying in her house for an extended but unknown period of time.

"I don't know how you do these things, Elizabeth. How can I be expected to run a decent, orderly household with you upsetting everything at every turn?"

"Eugenia, my dear, you must learn to take unexpected turns of fate with a more relaxed attitude."

"There's no talking to you! I told John it was useless to say anything to you. You never consider my feelings . . . nor do you give me credit for having any wisdom! No one listened to my warnings about Drew, either." She turned on her heel and stalked out of the room.

Undeterred, Elizabeth had the guest rooms redecorated with new light curtains and a fresh coat of paint on the woodwork. Had she had time she would have changed the paper on the walls. By the time she was finished even John had a few comments to make about her extravagance.

"You do seem to be going a bit overboard, Mother. If this is just a visit from a cousin, why all the time, money and effort into her quarters? Could it be you're trying to ease feelings about your favorite grandson?"

"Just courtesy, John," Elizabeth said tightly.

John laughed and settled into a chair opposite his mother. He took out his pipe and slowly filled it, on his face an amused smile of great patience. "What are you up to this time, Mother?"

"Why, nothing! Nothing at all. It is hardly right that you should talk to your mother like that, John. Are you questioning me?"

"In a manner of speaking, I am. I am not questioning your right to do as you will do anyway, Mother, but I am asking what you are going to involve the family in this time. If for no reason other than to satisfy my own curiosity, I'd like to know what you are up to with Gwynne."

"Absolutely nothing. We're just going to have a nice family visit and that is all."

John laughed. "Forgive me, Mother, but I think you are evading."

"John! That is tantamount to saying I am telling an untruth."

"Is it?"

"It certainly is, and I never lie!"

"Then I owe you an apology, Mother."

"You do, indeed!"

"Shall I receive one from you when the repercussions of this visit are felt later on?"

"I cannot be held responsible for repercussions of anything, John." Elizabeth looked at him critically and got up from her chair with a great show of her displeasure. She took great bunches of her small rosette print skirt in her hands and daintily minced her way from his presence.

"Pelagie," she called as soon as she got to her room, "can you imagine that John has just accused me of doing something underhanded and covering it up by the telling of half-truths or perhaps even mistruths?"

Pelagie burst into laughter, her large stomach shaking merrily. "Mastah John, he say that? Mebbe he gettin' some sense aftah all these yeahs."

"Oooff!" Elizabeth said with another show of exasperation. "I see no call for these sudden attacks on my good character by those I love and who are supposed to love me."

"We ain't attackin', Miz Lizzybeff, we lovin' you, but we's wonderin' too what you gettin' ussin into."

"Either you have been talking to John or John has been talking to you. He said exactly the same thing. I am merely trying to have a pleasant visit with a favorite young cousin. Now what harm could possibly come of that?"

Pelagie giggled again. "Not one thing, Miz Lizzybeff, iffen that's all you're gonna do, an' you doan mention Mastah Drew's name, an' you doan 'courage Missy Gwynne into doin' nothin' headstrong."

Elizabeth suddenly sat down. Her eyes sparkled, and smile wrinkles formed around her mouth and eyes. "Do you really think Gwynne has enough spunk to go after Drew and run him to the ground, Pelagie? We may lose him, you know, if something very powerful doesn't bring him back."

Pelagie shook her great head. "She jes' like you was when Mastah Waltah was here. You never let him do nothin' you di'n't like, an' she ain't gonna let Mastah Drew marry no white trash girl from the hills. All she need is a li'l 'couragin' from you, Miz Lizzybeff. You knows that, an' I knows it, an' "—she began to laugh again— "Mastah John, even he knows it. They's gonna be fireworks at Ribberlea."

Elizabeth looked serious for a moment. "Yes, I suppose. Oh well, we won't worry about that." She smacked her hands down on her knees and got to her feet again. "Come, Pelagie, we'll see to the finishing touches of Gwynne's suite ourselves."

"We gonna do it all in a day?" Pelagie said, getting to her feet far more slowly than Elizabeth. She looked at her mistress and thought of their respective ages. Pelagie was not certain how old she was, but she knew that she and Elizabeth were very close in age. Elizabeth was far more sprightly, however. Pelagie promised herself she'd stay away from Cook's apple pie from that day on. Then she smiled and thought of the delicious odor of one of those pies just coming from the hearth and decided she'd avoid something less tempting, or maybe she just didn't have to be as sprightly as Elizabeth. After all, all that energy was very taxing on a person's body.

Pelagie was happier to see Gwynne's carriage come up the drive than Elizabeth was. She was tired.

"She's here, Pelagie!" Elizabeth cried, peeking from her bedroom window. "She's here! And she looks as beautiful as ever! Oh, Pelagie, come here and look at that little wasp waist of her, and see how her hair shines. She was made for Drew, I just know it. Hurry, we must go downstairs. I want to meet her at the door." Elizabeth hurried across the room, then slowed to a sedate walk in the hallway, muttering to herself, "Decorum, Elizabeth, decorum."

Gwynne clung to Elizabeth when the older woman embraced

her. "I'm so glad to see you," she whispered, then stood on her own and greeted Eugenia and John warmly. She had pleasant comments to make to each of her cousins and gracefully accepted the flowery compliments of the male Manning cousins. After a time, with George, Rob and Leo each trying to outdo the other, Gwynne turned her head to the side, looking up at them coyly. "Why, y'all are going to spoil me. You'll make me too vain to be tolerated, I swear. Tell them, Cousin Eugenia, they're going to spoil me."

"Well, I think I may be ill from all these speeches being cast about and none being directed toward me," Elizabeth said merrily. "And anyway, it was I who invited Gwynne, and I think I am entitled to a long, pleasant chat with her before the rest of you monopolize her time and attention."

Alone in Gwynne's sitting room, Elizabeth came directly to the point. "Now, young lady, what exactly is on your mind with this visit?"

Gwynne blushed, turning her naturally pink cheeks fiery red. "Why, nothing, Cousin Elizabeth . . . just a visit . . . some time to . . . to . . ."

"To what? The sooner we get this out into the open, the easier it will be for both of us, Gwynne. You have taken a terrible risk with your family, so I know that you have a purpose in being here, and I think I can guess what it is."

"You can?" Gwynne said, her cheeks still red, and she was unable to look Elizabeth directly in the eye. "Is it that obvious?"

"I think so . . . it is to me, if I'm correct," Elizabeth said, and laughed. "Of course, if I am wrong, it isn't obvious at all."

"What do you think it is?"

Elizabeth pursed her lips together, her eyes twinkling. "You'd prefer me to say?" She smiled openly at Gwynne's nodded assent. "Very well; I think that you are in love with my grandson Drew and have no intention of allowing him to slip through your fingers into the hands of the young woman he is currently panting after. I think you have kept these feelings quiet out of respect for your sister and your family, but now you feel that you would be wasting yourself and perhaps Drew as well if you do not try. I also think you foresee the potential tragedy to this family if the rift remains unhealed and mean to do something about it. Am I correct? I certainly hope I am, or you may never speak to me again."

Gwynne burst into tears and threw herself into Elizabeth's arms. "I have felt so alone, and . . . so . . . so stupid. I think I am the silliest, most foolish creature ever born, Cousin Elizabeth. If Drew loved me, or even thought of me as a man thinks of a woman, I'm sure he would have said something . . . or shown it in some way, wouldn't he? I am foolish, aren't I?"

"Not at all! Not at all, Gwynne. He has shown it. Many times, and in many ways, but Drew is a gentle man, if not a gentleman in the way our people would like. He would never have done harm to Joanna by showing his feelings toward you. He may not be fully aware of them himself, but they are there. I have seen them, dear. I have seen them often, and I have heard his affection for you in his voice. He cares for you a great deal. I would wager the rest of my life on it." Elizabeth looked impishly at her. "Some would say at my age that isn't much of a wager, but it is, my dear, and I would win."

Pelagie laughed in the background. "You kin be shore o' that, Miss Gwynne. Miz Lizzybeff nevah wrong when she talkin' 'bout man-woman things. She know. She look an' she jes' know."

"Then I'm not a complete fool?" Gwynne sniffed.

"No. How can one be a fool to go after with all one's might what one believes is the fulfillment of one's life?" Elizabeth said. "Can that be foolish? If it is, it is tantamount to saying it is better to be unhappy in this life than to pursue happiness. I could never believe that, could you, Gwynne?"

Through her tears Gwynne began to laugh. "How could anyone disagree with a statement worded like that, Cousin Elizabeth? But if I fail—I would—I would have nothing, no one."

"You will have me," Elizabeth said. "And you'll have Drew, for you won't fail."

Gwynne felt much better when she awakened fresh the following morning. She lay in bed sipping tea that Pelagie brought to her on Elizabeth's orders, thinking about her trip to Charles Town and the talk she had had with Elizabeth. Of all the men and women in her family, Gwynne knew of none she admired more than this old woman. She was honest and had the courage to back up what she said and to go after what she wanted. As long as she could remember, she couldn't recall ever having heard Elizabeth say she regretted any part of her life.

She wasn't at all sure she had Elizabeth's wisdom, but she did have the heart or the spunk to try to pursue her dream. She wanted to be Mrs. Andrew Manning, and she was going to do her best to accomplish that. If she failed she had no idea what would come of her. Perhaps her family would take her back. Most likely they wouldn't.

Gwynne finished her tea and with great deliberateness arose and dressed carefully for the day. She was not going to look back. Her mind was made up, and somehow she would deal with whatever consequences came. She was going into Charles Town, her first objective to learn of the current feelings about the Upcountry, the Regulators, the coming election for the new Assembly and about English rule. She knew nothing of the subjects, but she knew that each of these topics would affect Drew and the woman he lived with.

Dressed in a walking suit, Gwynne went into Elizabeth's room to bid her good morning and tell her of the day's plans.

Elizabeth was in her dressing gown, sitting at her writing table. "I am not at all certain I can reach Drew up in that wilderness of his, but I thought I would try," she said, smiling. "I didn't think you would object, and it does seem best if Drew is told you are here."

"Could he come here? I mean, would Cousin Eugenia permit him hospitality in this house?"

Elizabeth made a face. "It would be difficult, and I am not certain I would have my way in this, but we shall never know if we don't try, and it is yet to be seen if we can reach Drew. All our worries may be academic."

Gwynne laughed. "If there is a way to reach him, you'll find it. Neither Drew nor Cousin Eugenia has a chance with you on my side. But I am on my way to doing my own part—at least a first step. I'll be going to town. Is there anything I can get for you, Cousin Elizabeth?"

Elizabeth declined, and it was into a hot August morning that Gwynne walked as she left Elizabeth's house. As she walked past the Manning stable, Leo came around to the front. "Gwynne! Where are you headed for on foot? Let me call the carriage for you. We can't have our prettiest cousin walking on a hot day like this." He sniffed the air. "It isn't going to be a very pleasant day for walking anyway. The air is bad today."

"I'll be fine, Leo, and I choose to walk. Would you care to join me? I am going into town to have a good look around and to hear the news."

"You are in town."

"I mean to where the shops are. You must recall I am but a poor country cousin, likely to say things all wrong."

He took her arm, grinning. "Poor country cousin, my eye. I do believe the lady is fishing for compliments, when she has only to look in my eyes and see them reflected there. Where shall we go first?" he asked, offering his arm.

"I have nowhere in particular in mind. Let's just walk until someplace strikes our fancy. I'd like to pass by the Liberty Tree and see what is going on there, if anything."

"I am sure there is quite a bit going on down there, considering the mood of this town."

"And that is?"

Leo laughed. "Dread, mostly. Half the town lives in fear of an attack by the wildmen of the Upcountry—like Drew."

"George told me you have been in the Upcountry recently. Did you see Drew?"

Leo's mood changed instantly. He was somber. "No, I didn't, and considering we would have been staring at each other over muskets had we met, it was fortunate."

"The crisis has become that extreme?" Gwynne asked.

"It has. This morning's *Gazette* reported that two to three thousand Regulators are assembling again at the Congarees for 'very unjustifiable purposes,' and your guess is as good as mine what that means. Once they have taken the giant step of overtly disobeying Charles Town authority, there is little telling where they may draw the line."

"Do you think Drew is part of this gathering?"

"I do indeed. And to some extent what happened with Joanna had a bit to do with it. Drew has always been the rebel of the family, and I think it was only his loyalty to us that held him in check. Now he has no family. There is nothing to keep him in the mainstream."

"Perhaps, but Drew may have his mind on something else at the moment. The girl he wanted to marry hasn't been found yet, has she?"

"Not that I've heard, but then news of Drew isn't as frequent or as accurate as it once was. Joseph won't allow him near the house, so all news comes from a man who once worked on the plantation—Ned Hart, I believe."

Gwynne made a sound of sympathy. "Poor Cousin Georgina; it must be so difficult for her."

"I suppose so, especially since Drew has in effect barred himself from the family for no purpose. He shall certainly not marry the girl now, even if she is found. I'm sure he'll be kind to her and perhaps take care of her for a time, but to take her to wife under these circumstances—even Drew would balk at that."

Gwynne said nothing for a moment, considering Leo's comments and what she knew about Drew. She walked briskly, keeping up with Leo's pace. The streets were bright in the hot sunlight and filled with color. Charles Town was a bustling, noisy place. Conestoga wagons, with their hooped covered tops shaking, hurtled down the street from the north, constantly bringing new settlers. Gwynne liked the sight of them, with their gay red and blue bodies, and the bright red harness on the horse teams. Most had four to six horses to draw them and families perched on the seat and often peeking from under the canvas. The newcomers' faces were covered with trail dust and lined with fatigue but filled with curiosity and hope for their new home. It gave Gwynne a good feeling, one that corresponded with her own sense of starting all over again. She looked away from the busy street back to her cousin Leo. "I think you are wrong, Leo. I don't know if Drew will ever marry Laurel Boggs, but I don't think he'd change his plans just because she was captured by the outlaws."

Leo gave her a knowing smile, then said brightly, with great paternal affection, "You are a kind, innocent woman, Gwynne. It is good to hear you are free of the contaminating carnal knowledge some of our women seem so ready to take upon themselves."

Gwynne nearly laughed aloud. Instead she looked sweetly and coyly at Leo from the corner of her eye. "Why, thank you, Cousin Leo."

Leo noticed nothing insincere in her reply and took it as his just thanks.

Smiling, Gwynne returned to watching the activity on the street.

Two horsemen, riding abreast, raced down the middle of the street, nearly colliding with a freight wagon. One horseman swerved to avoid being hit by the wagon and crashed into the other. Horse and rider fell onto the pedestrian walkway with screams of pain. Instantly a crowd gathered several people deep around the injured man and the screaming horse. Someone in the crowd shot the horse, and for a moment there was a deathly silence. Then once more the background of people talking and whispering took up again, and the sounds of innumerable wagon and carriage wheels rumbling up and down the street rose again.

Gwynne shuddered, and Leo strengthened his supportive grip on her arm. "You mustn't let it alarm you too much," he said. "It is one of the hazards of living in a city. Can't be helped."

Gwynne looked at him in disgust. "Of course it can be helped. Neither of those men had any business traveling at such speed down a crowded street like this. Look at that street . . . it's filled with carts and wagons and . . ."

"My dear, you are used to your empty country roads. Believe me, it is quite different here."

"A child or a woman crossing the street could have been killed!"

"And quite often are," Leo said complacently. "One very good reason that you should not be on foot and never alone, especially as ignorant of the ways of a city as you are."

"If you're trying to frighten me with such reasoning, Leo, you are not. I will not be intimidated by the unreasonable behavior of men such as those two."

Leo sighed. "You sound like Grandmother."

"I'm glad," Gwynne said, and she glanced back to see the crowd parting and several men carrying away the injured man on a makeshift stretcher. Several onlookers helpfully called advice to the bearers. Leo quickly turned a corner, wanting to get her away from the sight. As they walked past the Dock Street theater, Gwynne's attention was immediately arrested. She stopped in front of the theater, looking at the large doors. "I must see a play once while I am visiting."

"I didn't realize you were such a theater lover," Leo said. "Do you enjoy Shakespeare?"

"I do." Gwynne was smiling, her hands clasped in front of her,

her eyes bright with memory. "The last time I came to the Dock Street theater was two years ago, with my father. He brought us into town, and we saw Mrs. Centliver's *A Wonder! A Woman Keeps a Secret!* Mrs. Cibber did the translation from the French, and the performance marked Miss Cheer's American debut. It was wonderful. Papa took us out to supper after, and we had a table right next to one Miss Cheer was sitting at with friends. Papa arranged an introduction. She was an enchanting woman. Oh, how I would like to have poise such as hers. The whole room became her stage. And she really didn't do anything. She greeted us, asked if we had enjoyed our evening and thanked us for our compliments, and yet it seemed as if there was nothing in the world so fascinating or important as the words she was saying. Don't you think it would be marvelous to be able to hold people's attention like that, Leo?"

"Provided one always had something to say," he said dryly. "I should guess it becomes quite taxing to have strangers hanging on every *bon mot* that falls from one's lips."

"I suppose," Gwynne grudgingly agreed and began to walk again, leaving the theater behind. "But I still think it might be nice to know, if only for a short time, what it would be like to have the self-possession to make people want to cling to every word and gesture."

Leo laughed. "You would be queen?"

Gwynne didn't laugh in return. "Yes, of my own chosen realm, I would be queen." She was quiet for a moment. "And I am going to seek out and conquer that chosen realm."

Leo looked at her strangely. "Whatever are you talking about?"

Gwynne smiled then. "Oh, nothing at all, Leo, just silly talk. Shall we stop for tea? And then I'd like to walk past the Liberty Tree and hear what is being said about the Regulators and about England."

Leo shook his head but resigned himself to doing whatever his peculiar young cousin from the country wanted. He had no idea what interest she could possibly have in speeches that were usually deadly dull harangues under the Liberty Tree, but he supposed this was what was meant by a tourist. Gwynne was undoubtedly overwhelmed by the importance and activity of Charles Town and was doing what she supposed all Charlestonians did. He had nothing better to do with his afternoon anyway, and it would please his mother to know he had kept Gwynne safe. He was quite certain one full day of walking and listening to endless talk would cure her of her wanderlust.

Gwynne was tired by the time she returned to Elizabeth's house late that afternoon, but Leo had been wrong. Her curiosity had not been sated, nor had her determination to learn all she could about the politics and events that were changing her world. With the minor exposure of one day, she could already begin to understand what Drew had been telling her and Joanna about the times they lived in. Even if the talk that sprang up from time to time about independence from England was no more than hot wind, it did herald a major change of some kind.

Gwynne had heard Drew talk of it, and today she had felt it for herself. She kept thinking of the words Christopher Gadsen had spoken at the Stamp Act Congress while he represented South Carolina: "There ought to be no New England men, no New Yorkers, known on the continent, but all of us Americans." She had no idea how often she had heard those words repeated or seen them written, but she had never had so clear a picture of what they meant as she did today. She knew what Drew meant now when he said he was an American.

She was excited and a little baffled when she said to Elizabeth, "I became an American today, Cousin Elizabeth. I don't know what I'm doing, but I have never felt more like Gwynne Templeton than I do right now." She paused for a moment, then went on. "I feel like a new person, and . . ." Again she paused. "I know that if I don't succeed in what I want with Drew, I'll never again be as I was in the past."

Elizabeth smiled, the pleasure etched deeply in her eyes and heart. "You won't fail, Gwynne. It will not be easy for you, but you won't fail."

In the days that followed Gwynne found herself so wrapped up in her new quest that she wasn't aware of the time passing until several letters from her mother arrived, asking about her plans to return home. Gwynne dutifully answered each of them, always begging a social occasion as her reason for staying a bit longer.

She had set a regimen for herself, spending part of each morning learning languages, history and philosophy. Gwynne's schooling had been minimal, and Riverlea had few books and less encouragement for such knowledge. Elizabeth's house was quite different. Elizabeth's library was quite extensive and varied in subject matter for a family collection of books, and Elizabeth herself provided a sounding board and an active participant in evening discussions of what Gwynne had learned that morning.

In the afternoons she went into Charles Town and listened to what people on the street had to say.

"I feel as if someone is walking past the powder magazine with a torch, Cousin Elizabeth. Something must happen. The talk is no longer confined to a few. The Regulators and the elections are topics on everyone's lips."

"I am sure it was so today," Elizabeth agreed and fished through a pile of papers for that day's edition. She placed the *South Carolina Gazette* for September 12, 1768, on the table beside Gwynne. "Have you read this letter that was published?"

Gwynne glanced at the letter quickly at first, then more slowly, reading more carefully. The Regulators were to meet in Camden on October fifth to draw up their grievances, which they would lay before the Assembly. These men would march on Charles Town, while twenty-five hundred to three thousand more of them were to gather at Eutaw, ready to proceed to Charles Town to pursue proper means of redress if their demands were not met. Gwynne looked up at Elizabeth. "We could . . . what would happen? There would be a war, wouldn't there? We would actually be fighting in the streets of Charles Town. But . . . but it says here they have assured that no person shall be harmed . . . that they want only justice and what is guaranteed to them as English subjects. What will happen?"

"I don't know, but war comes slowly to men. They talk about it and threaten it long before they are prepared to engage in it."

"But the Regulators have been talking about it and threatening for some time . . . and they have engaged in battle on many occasions."

"Yes, perhaps they are ready, but the Lowland is not. There must be two sides to make a war. We are still in a time of change, and all of us must remain vigilant to see and feel how the winds are blowing."

"But those terrible winds of discord are blowing," Gwynne said.

"Oh yes, Drew is quite right; they are blowing," Elizabeth agreed.

The events of the month seemed to have postponed what so many dreaded: an untenable position the Regulators would not tolerate. In the fall elections the Regulators managed to elect six men to the new Assembly. Moses Kirkland, Tacitus Gaillard and Aaron Loocock would all be strong new leaders who had the Upcountry interests in mind, and from St. Matthew's parish William Thomson would be heard. From St. Mark's parish Benjamin Farrar would speak, and in St. David's parish Claudius Pegues would be a loud, powerful voice. The Regulators returned to their homes well pleased with their accomplishment and looking forward to a better future.

November 19, 1768, four days after the new Assembly convened, it was dissolved.

Stunned by the turn of events, Elizabeth and Gwynne sat in Elizabeth's sitting room, silent, the same question bright in each of their eyes. What did this new event mean? What would happen now?

29

Drew walked slowly through the woods around his plantation. In his hand he held his musket. He had told the men he was going to hunt. But he had come here to the quiet depths of the woods to think. Perhaps it was more proper to say that he had come to the quiet of the woods to clear his mind. In recent months all he had heard from the lips of politicians, farmers, even the low people was talk of rights and laws and needs and politics. There was always one last demand the Upcountrymen had or the Lowlanders made. There was always one last battle to be fought, one last stand to be made. Drew didn't know what was in the wind, but he no longer believed that the unrest belonged to the Upcountry or was represented by the Regulators. Something else was happening. An unrest had entered into the colonies, and there wasn't a man, woman or child who was not responding to it.

Drew shook his head and forced himself to look at the trees and concentrate on the sounds of animals moving stealthily across the fallen pine needles. It took a long time to achieve the silence within that Drew craved. When he finally found it, and the thoughts of the Upcountry, the Regulators, the Lowland, the king, and the royal governor were all quelled, and the sounds of angry or excited voices no longer reverberated in his head, he found a place to sit. His musket beside him, Drew sat cross-legged, his arms over his knees, his face turned upward to the spear of sunlight streaking through the pines to shine on him.

He lay back against the warm, soft pine-strewn ground and let his mind and feelings float free. Thoughts and memories of himself and Laurel danced before his closed eyes. It had been such a long time since he had allowed himself to have thoughts and feelings such as these. Until today he had been too afraid of what he would feel if he let go of the feelings he had about her, but today he felt comfortable with himself and his dreams of Laurel. He didn't try to think of finding her. That was still too painful to contemplate. He no longer knew where to look, and everything he did know led him to believe that the outlaws had left the territory and taken Laurel with them. Thinking about trying to find her somewhere in the British Empire was too big an obstacle and too hopeless a task. He had to consider her gone forever. So he pushed aside those thoughts and dreamed about her, how she was before she left and how she would be when they were together again, whenever and however that would happen.

He fell asleep in the warmth of the sunlight and awakened a short time later, thinking about his land in the mountains and then of Manning and the indigo crop that had to be harvested. He hadn't been there to tend to the plantation this year. It had been left to Arthur and his inexperience showed. Most likely Manning would have the poorest and smallest crop they had had in years.

Drew remained sitting and quiet for a moment, letting a feeling of unease and dislike for himself grow, until he stood up and knew that he was ready to go back home and repay Arthur for searching for Laurel with him. He'd bring the indigo in, do it in secret so his father wouldn't know he was there. That much he owed his brother.

Drew first talked to Ned about his plan. "What do you think Arthur will say? It means he'd have to go behind my father's back as well."

Ned considered for a moment, scratching his chin. "Don' know fer sure, Drew, but I'm thinkin' he might take you up on it. He needs that crop, an' he don' know shit about harvestin' indigo."

Drew made a face. "So it boils down to whether Arthur wants to avoid me more than he wants his crop."

"That's my guess." Then Ned smiled. "But if he says yes to you, tell him I'm in as a bargain."

Ned went to Manning with Drew's message, and Arthur met

Drew at a tavern in Camden to talk over the harvest. With some reluctance Arthur agreed. "But Daddy is never to know you're there."

"He won't," Drew said. "This is just between you and me. I'll show you how to treat the crop as thanks for your searching with me for Laurel. A simple repayment of one brotherly act with another."

Arthur's eyes teared. "I wish it weren't this way, Drew."

Drew looked away. "So do I, but there is nothing we can do about that now. I'll see you in the morning, Arthur. If you can do it without giving the whole plan away, tell Mama I'm thinking of her."

Drew watched his brother ride back toward Manning and once again felt the acute loss of his family. Ned urged him back into the tavern and tried to distract him with ale and song, but it did little good. It was a restless, lonely night for Drew, one of many.

When Drew went to the fields the following day, Ned had already had the slaves gather the indigo. The blacks were tending to the huge barrels lined neatly before the indigo shed. Ned Hart, unaware of Drew's arrival, walked briskly from one barrel to the next, peering at the indigo stalks to see that they were soaking properly.

"What th'hell's wrong with you, Jobie? Your indigo ain't covered," Ned barked, and glanced up to see the black man smiling but paying no attention to him. "Wha—" Ned began, then turned to see what was holding Jobie's attention and causing him to laugh under his breath.

"You surely are a tough man, Ned. I don't know as I can work for a man like you," Drew said, his face serious.

Jobie burst into laughter.

Ned shook his head. "Don't even know if we're gonna get a crop outta this year. Arthur's a good man, you know, Drew, but he ain't no indigo man."

"Then we have a big job," Drew said, looking at the black men who waited to hear what he'd say. "Has it all been harvested?"

"No, suh," Jobie said. "It growed jes' like wheat this yeah, an' we tuk in only what we could do in one roun'. Res' is prob'ly too ol' to be wuth nothin'."

"Bring it in, Jobie. Let's see what we can do. Take five men with you, and for God's sake let's have a little song."

"Yes, suh!" Jobie said briskly. He pointed to five of the blacks, and they headed back toward the fields.

"You can't do nothin' about this year's crop, Drew. Let's jes' take what we can and call it a year," Ned said. "You're allus tryin' the impossible, boy."

"Come on, now, Ned, we don't know it's impossible until we try—and fail. And we're not going to do that." Drew walked along the line of soaking barrels as Ned had before him, peering into each and poking at the indigo inside. "Doesn't look too bad," he said.

"What we got ain't too bad. But that stuff still in the fields . . . You're not going to get the quality Manning's come to be known for."

"If it's that bad after it's been harvested, we'll let it go, but I want to look it over myself."

Ned shook his head. "If your brother had one tenth of your bull-headedness, he wouldn't need our help."

"Arthur's learning," Drew said casually. "Where is he?"

"He ain't come out yet. He don't take to these early hours. An' another thing, he don't handle blacks like you. Makes a big difference and I ain't sure you can teach him in one harvest.

"That Jobie, he's a proud devil. If he takes it in his head that he ain't bein' respected, he won't do nothin'. On t'other han', if he thinks he's valued, ain't nobody can outwork him." Ned scratched his head and stood looking at the slaves, who were singing and working. "Don't know 'xactly what to make o' these blacks mos' of the time, Drew. They sure do make a man wonder. Are they human bein's like we are, or are they jes' real smart animals like some say?"

Drew laughed. "Maybe they're a little of each. If I was to pick a man to help me out of a tight spot, I'd not argue against Jobie, but then I sure wouldn't want to be stuck with Mule over there. I've never gotten a bit of sense or anything else worthwhile from Mule."

"Yeah, Mule is a mean son of a bitch," Ned said. "But strong . . . Ummm is he strong."

Arthur arrived about noon and watched and talked with Drew about the techniques of what was being done to the indigo and with the slaves. Drew, Ned, Jobie and the others worked the remainder of the day sorting and soaking the indigo. Sunset came and went, and still they worked. Jobie and three other men made torches and lit the work area. They stopped only for something to eat and returned to the tending of the indigo. The indigo would be the master of them all for the next three weeks.

When Arthur finally went back to the Manning house, it was dark and had an empty feeling. Only one small light shone in the entry, left there by Georgina. The house was quiet, and all were asleep. Arthur walked slowly up the stairs, every muscle and bone in him aching with fatigue. It would be this way every day until the indigo was ready to be taken into Charles Town. He had never known the physical labor his brother had always taken for granted. He wasn't certain he could last the full three weeks.

Arthur awakened before the sun was up. He fixed something to eat in the empty kitchen and left the house before any of his family was up or stirring. He arrived at the fields at the same time his brother did, and as he had the day before, he worked and learned by his side until late at night, when he rode home too exhausted to do anything but fall into bed.

After the indigo had soaked for a week, Drew, Ned, Arthur and the slaves took the indigo stems and squeezed all the juice from them.

"Much as I love this work, I sure do hate this part," Ned grumbled, wiping his brow with the back of his wrist, careful not to smear the juice over his face.

"Lordy, it sho' hot," Jobie sighed.

Arthur watched in fascination at Drew working. He and Ned were the only ones who did not seem exhausted by nightfall. Arthur began to imitate his brother's motions. Drew worked mechanically, expending no unnecessary energy as he took the stems from the barrel, squeezed the juice and then put it back into the barrels to cure for another week. Periodically he shook his hands dry and walked the long line of barrels, checking each container of juice and the worker carefully. "Topper, get those stems from that barrel, y'hear." He continued down the line, Arthur following him mutely, saying to himself whatever Drew said. Soon he was identifying with Drew, and he felt as though he were actually running this harvest.

Drew and Arthur continued down the line, praising some, chastising others. Drew stopped back by Topper's barrel again, looking into the liquid, poking it with a stick and stirring up anything that had gone to the bottom. Topper put a face on, and Drew tapped his shoulder with his walking stick. "You're a good man, Topper. Don't show me bad work again."

As they passed Ned, the older man laughed. "You don't never give up. But this time you're beat. You ain't never gonna make an indigo man outta Topper. Topper don' want to do nothin'."

Arthur looked back at Topper. Drew said positively, "He will."

"Come the day o' judgment maybe," Ned said and laughed. "An' that's only if St. Peter talks nice to him."

Drew laughed lightly. "Don't you ever wonder about them—I mean what they were like before they got shipped over here?"

"Sometimes," Ned admitted.

"Topper said he was head of his tribe. Suppose he was. I expect that's like me being master of this plantation. I sure as hell wouldn't feel cooperative if someone stuck me on a ship and took me to Africa."

"No, I don't expect you would," Ned said, looking at the pouting Topper from the corner of his eye. "But I still don't trust the son of a bitch behind my back for a split second."

Drew laughed. "I can't argue with that . . . but I think it's because of his ignorance of our ways and not part of his nature."

Ned gave him a skeptical look, then stood up, stretching, his hand on his back. "Oh, Lord, is this day never gonna end?"

"My sentiments exactly," Arthur said fervently.

By the end of the second week of tending the indigo, Drew had Arthur giving orders. The slaves stood over the huge barrels and stirred the mixture throughout the day. Arthur had them working in shifts, and still their shoulders and arms ached by mid-afternoon. With each new step in the indigo processing, Ned proclaimed, "Much as I love this work, I sure do hate this part."

Drew smiled and continued to work by his side in silence. Occasionally he'd stop to watch Arthur, and he felt good. He could tell Arthur was beginning to like his position and to feel confident in it.

For the next three days the indigo sat in the barrels. Slowly the precious sediment separated and settled to the bottom, leaving the water on the top. By the fourth day Arthur, Drew and the men were ready to draw the water off and collect the settlings. During the next week the indigo was cut into small blocks to be used for blueing and dyes.

Arthur returned to Manning to make plans to take a wagon train to Charles Town to deliver the Manning indigo. He was tired and aching from a long three weeks, but pleased as well. He greeted his father with a broad smile. "We did it," he said grandly. "Manning has as good a crop as ever . . . but not quite so large. There was some that was harvested too late to be of good use, but what we have is top quality. It would even meet Drew's standard," Arthur said and blushed at the deception.

Joseph grinned and patted his son on the back. "Did you hear that, Georgina? He's done it—we have a superior crop. I always knew Arthur had it in him, given the chance."

Georgina's eyes teared as she saw Joseph with his arm around Arthur. She was happy for Arthur. So often in the past she had seen the look of jealousy and disappointment on his face when Drew took all the praise, but now, seeing Arthur with Joseph, she couldn't bear the feeling of loss she had for Drew. Joseph had told her to think of him as dead, but she couldn't. He was her son; no matter what he did, she loved him and would never stop missing him.

She hugged Arthur. "Will you also take the indigo to market, Arthur?"

"I plan to leave as soon as the wagons can be readied."

"You're not accustomed to the travel as Drew was. Perhaps you should consider letting one of the other planters take it this year."

Joseph frowned at her. "A Manning will see that Manning indigo gets safely to market. Arthur must get to know the agents, the sooner the better."

"I don't want to lose two sons, Joseph," Georgina said, more sharply than she normally spoke to her husband.

Joseph frowned at her. "Arthur is a capable man, as he has proven. You needn't worry. And anyway, he will have a full complement of guards."

Arthur agreed with his father in front of his mother but didn't completely share Joseph's optimism. And he wasn't at all sure he would get as good a price for the indigo as Drew usually did. He had gained a great deal of respect for Drew in the last month.

Two days before the wagon train to Charles Town was to leave, Arthur gave in to his doubts and sought Drew out. Again they met in the tavern in Camden. Arthur smiled as his brother came to join him at his table.

"This is unexpected. Nothing is wrong, is it? Mama, Daddy—they're well?"

"I thought perhaps we could do another round of one brotherly favor for another." Arthur put his head down, then said, "No, that's not the truth. I could never repay you for what you did for me. There would be no Manning indigo crop this year or any in the future if you hadn't come to my rescue. And even now what I really want is for you to come with the wagon train and teach me how to deal with the agents. God, Drew, I never knew how much we depended on you."

"I'll be there," Drew said quickly. "Ned can see to Cherokee."

Arthur took Drew's hand and shook it in both of his. "Thank you. Dear God, Drew, thank you. You may be the making of me yet, and I have nothing of real value to give you in return. All I can promise is that I'll do the best I can. I'm beginning to see what Manning meant to you. Fate is a cruel mistress. I should have been the one married off to Joanna, and you should have gotten Manning. God, I wouldn't care if she had two heads." He drank deeply of the cold ale the serving girl had set before him as he talked. "I do have one small bit for you. Mama received a letter from Grandma. Gwynne is visiting for an extended time, and for some purpose that Grandma hints at but won't say directly. Mama thinks it is because of you, or so she told me." Arthur looked closely at his younger brother. "Are you interested in Gwynne? I thought it was only Laurel."

Andrew sat quietly for some time, considering trying to tell Arthur everything that had happened at Riverlea. He decided that when and if he told him, it would be on the trail to Charles Town, when they both had plenty of time. Now he just looked at Arthur and burst into a huge grin. "I'm interested," he said. "And that news is more than a fair exchange for a ride into Charles Town and a lesson with the indigo agents. This brotherly bartering suits me well," he said, and clapped Arthur on the back at the same time as he called for more ale.

He felt light-headed and good when he left the tavern. For the first time in months he felt young and happy. He wanted to see Gwynne more than anything else he could think of at the moment.

30

Star Dancer looked into the night sky. The constellations had changed once more. On the horizon she could see stars that had not been visible before. Autumn was on the wane. The winter stars were coming into their season. There was already a chill in the mountain air that heralded cold days and colder nights. And the animals had begun to grow their winter coats.

Behind her, near the campfire she had built an hour ago, sat The Woman. Her belly was huge now, and the baby would come at any time. The Indian girl still did not know how to take her to her home. The Woman's time was imminent and still she did not care. She did not seem to desire the warmth and care of her home. Star Dancer was perplexed. She only knew if she left her to the cruel mercies of the wilds, she would not protest.

Star Dancer squatted by the fire and drew from her pack the rabbit she had caught earlier in the afternoon. She skinned the animal, cleaned it and put it on a spit. She stared into the fire as she patiently turned the cooking meat. Occasionally she glanced up at The Woman to see if the odor of cooking flesh tempted some sign of life or interest in her pretty, pale face.

The Woman's long light-brown hair was matted and filled with burrs, yet she didn't seem to care. Star Dancer had seen the look she saw in The Woman's eyes only in the very old of her tribe—that look came when they were ready to die. Seeing it in one so young frightened her. Her eyes went to The Woman's belly once more. She sat, her weight back on her haunches, her eyes returned to the fire. She was hypnotized by the flickering lights and colors of the fire. Slowly a peace settled over her. She felt as though a cool breeze had entered her and made all within her calm and peaceful. She would not leave The Woman until the boy child was born. If the woman wanted to die, Star Dancer would not interfere, but she would take the child. The child would look to life. If The Woman chose death, then Star Dancer would take the child.

Star Dancer ate her rabbit, her mind at rest, her path now known to her. For the first time she did not try to persuade The Woman to eat. She was free of responsibility for her. She ate her fill and lay back, sleepy from the satisfying meal. Her eyes were heavy. She closed them, rolled over on her side and fell into a light sleep.

The Woman was hungry and uncomfortable. She shifted her position, sitting up straighter. Star Dancer was asleep! She looked at her as if expecting the Indian girl to get up immediately and come to her. She glanced over at the dying fire. Part of the rabbit still lay against the warm outside rocks. It looked good. She couldn't help herself; her mouth opened, and she licked her lips. She leaned forward, her eyes devouring the rabbit. Then she glanced once more at the sleeping Star Dancer.

The Woman leaned back, her eyes closed, determined not to think of the rabbit or her hunger. She sat rigidly, her arms close against herself over her large belly. Then she moved quickly, almost angrily on all fours to the rabbit. She sat cross-legged by the fire, eating the succulent meal. The grease rolled down her chin, and she wiped it away with the back of her hand. Sounds of pleasure broke from her throat.

Finally satisfied, she went back to her seat by the rock. She leaned against its hard, comforting solidity in real relaxation, her eyes nearly closed, but watching the night sky. So often she had heard Star Dancer talking to herself about the stars and their position. She had never known much about the stars. Tonight she found them fascinating. They were not just beautiful, they were the guides that had brought them across the mountains and through so many empty valleys back toward civilization. She smiled when she thought of the many times she could have led Star Dancer right back to Manning and her own home. But always she had indicated a different way, and Star Dancer had obligingly stayed by her side and kept on taking one path after another, waiting for Laurel to say she recognized the terrain.

She touched her matted hair, and suddenly she felt sad. She began to cry so hard she couldn't stop. The sobs racked her body and made the child restless within her. She ached inside and out, and there would never be any help for it. She couldn't go back to Drew, and she couldn't stay in the wilderness forever. She wanted to die but could never bring herself to let go of life, and yet she couldn't face the ordeal of returning to her home and community to become the object of stares and curiosity and conversation and condemnation. The look on Star Dancer's face bespoke peace, but there was no place of peace for Laurel. There was no comfort for her to seek, and she thought there never would be again.

She thought of the times with her parents when they had had no place to stay. They called themselves homeless. They hadn't ever been homeless, she knew now. Homeless was what she felt tonight. Homeless was having no place within oneself to find warmth. Homeless was the limbo between life and death. It was the place of no welcome.

She looked at Star Dancer again. The Indian girl still slept, the slight smile gracing her face. Star Dancer was as alone in the world as she, yet she had a zest for living that Laurel couldn't find in herself. She had never given the Indian so much as an honest smile, and the girl had nonetheless saved her countless times, cared for her, tried to bring some of the joy of life to her. Why, she wondered. Why had Star Dancer bothered, and why tonight had she changed? She knew Star Dancer had changed. She had felt it as it was happening.

Laurel looked once more at the stars. Would she be left alone now? Would Star Dancer leave her? If she closed her eyes this night in sleep, would she awaken in the morning alone? Would she die? And the child with her? The child should die, she thought. If the child was Albee's child, he should die. She didn't want his child.

The tears flowed from her eyes again, and she stared through them at the Indian woman. She said the child was a man child, and it was Drew's. Could it be? Drew's child couldn't die. She wouldn't let him die. She awkwardly got to her feet and stumbled toward Star Dancer. She knelt at the Indian girl's side, her tangled hair falling over her face, her tears coming hard and loud.

"Star Dancer! Star Dancer! Wake up. You can't leave me. Please don't leave me now. I want the child. I do! Please don't leave me now." Laurel reached out tentatively and touched Star Dancer's arm. She had never done that before. She stroked her long, silky black hair.

Star Dancer rolled over onto her back. Her eyes opened slowly, full of sleep. "Woman," she said softly. "You touch me?"

"Don't leave the child and me . . . please."

"Your time has come?"

Laurel shook her head.

Star Dancer ignored her. She looked at Laurel carefully, then pushed her hair from her face, noted the puffiness of her skin, the tear and dirt streaks on her face. "You lie down," she said and got up. She led Laurel back to the rock where she had been, then, leaving her there, walked a short distance to the creek. She returned with a wet chamois and bathed Laurel's hot face. "Your time is near," she said firmly. "Tomorrow we will find the place of the man child's birth." She started back to her place across from Laurel, then stopped and came to lie down beside The Woman. They slept, and for the first time Laurel reached out in her sleep to touch the Indian girl.

The Woman cried and whimpered by her side for some time before she finally fell asleep. Star Dancer remained awake. She thought of the trails they had followed in the last months and tried to recall where she had seen or known of a place she could take The Woman to bear the child and be safe. Star Dancer knew little of white women; only what she had been told. She remembered, before she had been taken by the outlaws, the women of her tribe sitting around a smoking fire, giggling and telling the tales they knew of white women. Always the tales emphasized the superiority of the Indian. The girl now worried that perhaps all she had heard was true. Perhaps The Woman would fight nature. Perhaps she would make it difficult for herself. Perhaps her body was different from the Indian's and not so suited to bringing man children to the earth. Perhaps this was all something about which Star Dancer had no knowledge. Perhaps she could not help The Woman bring the man child to this land.

She tried to sleep but couldn't. Her dreams were not the beautiful adventures they usually were. Little Elk didn't appear before her eyes when she willed him to. She saw only the spirit of a small child, indistinct and uncertain. She couldn't tell exactly what he looked like, nor could she tell what he wanted of her. His small arms were outstretched. She didn't like the image she saw. It made her sad and allowed a sense of apprehension to invade her, which she fought back.

At dawn the Indian girl got up from her place beside The Woman. She built the fire up again, took some roots from her pouch and made a warm brew to start them on their way. She still had no thought as to where she should take The Woman, but she knew she had very little time. Higher in the mountains she could see snow, and she could feel the cold breezes moving down to the fall line in the night and hovering there through much of the day. And The Woman's time was very near.

Before they left the campsite, Star Dancer left The Woman and walked alone into the deep woods. She stood in the midst of a circle of pines, her hands by her side, her head bowed. She was completely still. Slowly she felt calm enter her, and she raised her head, and then her arms. She gave praise to the spirits that guided her life; she gave praise to the Great Father of all. She stood for a long time, and then when she no longer felt the spirit filling her being, she turned and went back to The Woman. The Woman had fallen asleep again, her right hand over her belly. Star Dancer looked at her, and for the first time saw the beauty of The Woman's face.

She awakened The Woman gently and helped her to her feet. It was getting difficult for The Woman to walk for any distance. They stopped often and rested. The Woman slept a great deal. At each stop Star Dancer racked her brain for knowledge of a place to make The Woman safe and could think of none within the distance they could travel. Each time she failed, she reminded herself of her lack of faith and went to a quiet spot to give praise. Each time she helped The Woman to her feet and walked in the direction her heart indicated. She did not tell The Woman, but they now entered trails that Star Dancer had never traveled before. She didn't know if friend or foe frequented them. She gave her praise to the Father of them all and trusted his guidance of her feet.

The deeper they went into the unknown territory, the more cautious Star Dancer became, traveling more at night than she had ever done before. They had walked far before Star Dancer reached an area she recognized. Her heart sang with gladness as she looked out upon the waters of a corkscrewing river she knew from her childhood. The Wateree River bent and twisted through the terrain. The sounds of its waters were the sounds of an old friend.

She left The Woman carefully secreted in a camouflage she had constructed. The Woman sank to the ground gratefully. She looked up at her companion and attempted to smile tiredly. "I couldn't walk another step," she said. "I don't know why you put up with me and care for me, but I am grateful. I am very grateful."

"I will find a place for the man child to come. Stay quiet. If one comes, you do not speak. You do not move."

"I won't," Laurel said, and lay down against the soft mat of dry leaves and reeds Star Dancer had made for her.

Star Dancer covered her with more of the reeds, then quietly made her way through the thicket of bush and limbs that she had made. She returned to the banks of the Wateree and walked south until she got her bearings. Not far from her was the settlement she knew as Pine Tree Hill and the white settlers called Camden. There were many scattered cabins nearby, from which Star Dancer could steal what she would need to keep herself, The Woman and the child alive through the winter. She thanked her spirits that had guided her feet in a direction she would never have taken had she not asked their guidance.

It was dark when she returned to the place she had left The Woman. The thicket appeared to have been untouched. Star Dancer prayed over the thicket before she entered, asking the spirits to remove all traces of her passage. The Woman was asleep. Her skin did not look good. There was the same puffiness about her face that Star Dancer had been noticing for the last two weeks. Her color, always pale and unattractive in Star Dancer's eyes, was more lifeless-looking than ever.

She waited patiently for The Woman to awaken. It no longer mattered how far into the night they traveled. Darkness was her ally now. She could reach the very edges of a settler's cabin without being seen or heard, and she knew that at this time of year most of the cabins would have hogs curing in the small building they all kept behind their cabins. The meat was nourishing and succulent. It would serve to feed her and The Woman for as long as they needed, and Star Dancer would no longer have to spend time away from The Woman hunting for their meat.

She glanced at the sky and smiled as she watched the twinkling stars. It was the time of the Archer. Perhaps it was the great Archer who had guided her to this area of white men and cabins. It was his bow that would slay the animals, and she had only to be his servant and collect the fallen meat.

The man child would be born under the sign of the Archer. The child she had saved so many times would be a hunter. His range would be the earth. He would know no bounds. She fell asleep thinking about the child—the hunter.

The following day Star Dancer found a cabin that had once been used by trappers. It was covered with dust and filth and was falling to ruin. Great cracks in the walls let in the cold night air, and sometimes the wind made eerie whistling sounds that frightened The Woman, but Star Dancer interpreted this as the voice of the Archer. The Woman begged her to fill in the chinks in the cabin to keep out the cold air and the noise of the night wind, but Star Dancer steadfastly refused. She was being guided by those sounds. She knew, too, that the Archer would merely have to talk louder, and that he would not be pleased if she made him make that extra effort. It would be disrespectful.

One day his voice began early in the morning and did not subside all that day. Star Dancer hurried that entire day. She didn't wait for darkness but braved the twilight as she approached the settlers' cabins to steal what she would need for the coming man child. As she scurried through the underbrush, her eyes and ears alert for all sounds, she came upon a huge cabin nestled in the woods by the Wateree. This cabin was unlike any she had seen, although she had heard of such places. Men who lived in these big cabins had taken many of her ancestors to work for them. They had been put in chains and beaten with rods and whips, but never had her ancestors worked. They had starved and some had died, but they did not do the white man's bidding. The day came when the black men came to free the red men. They worked, and Star Dancer's people returned to their woods and mountains.

She felt pleased that the Archer had directed her to such a place. On a rope near the back of the cabin hung cloth, wide blankets of cloth. She crept along the side of the house, edging her way along with caution. She stood under the window of the cabin and heard the voices within. They spoke too rapidly for her to understand them, but she heard Charles Town, and knew that was the big place of many whites near the ocean. Another sign. When The Woman and the man child were ready, she would take them to that place of white men.

Confident, she walked toward the rope with blankets on it and removed two of them. She folded them and tucked them inside her tunic to free her hands. She was reaching for a dress for The Woman when she heard a sound behind her. Star Dancer whirled around, grasping the dress in her hand. Twenty feet from her, no more, stood a man. His head was not turned toward her, but he was making noises. She stood still, like a deer at bay, ready to run, ready to fight, ready to do as she must.

The man was tall and well made. She thought of Little Elk. The man's shoulders were broad as Little Elk's had been, and his hips were narrow. His legs were those of a runner, or a horseman, or a man of power. His hair alone ruined her reverie. It was dark brown, but the sun made it shine red. It was like a flame coming from the dark brown of bark.

She began to move carefully toward the shadow of the house. He hadn't seen her, she thought, and then nearly laughed at herself. He had moved slightly. He had seen her. He was watching her. Star Dancer paused. Why didn't he stop her? Was he helping her? Once more he made a sound deep in his throat, and then he raised his hand and called a greeting to someone Star Dancer couldn't see. She questioned no more. She didn't understand, but the man was helping her. She turned and ran for the woods, knowing he would not prevent her. She was singing within herself when she returned to the trapper's shack north of the big cabin. It was the day of the man child. The day of the Archer.

Star Dancer came back to the trapper's cabin with her dark eyes dancing. She stood before The Woman and took from under her tunic the fresh clean blankets. "Tonight is the night the man child will come to us," she said. "I have seen signs and I hear the voice of the Archer louder than usual all day."

The Woman reached for the blankets and drew them around her.

Her hands were trembling, and she had to concentrate with all her might to follow what Star Dancer was saying. She ached all over. Her back hurt no matter what position she sat in. She was so tired all she wanted to do was sleep, but the malaise in her body would give her no rest.

Star Dancer hummed as she looked over her cache of stolen treasures. She had a kettle and swaddling for the child. And she had the new dress for The Woman. She kept it hidden, anxious to give it to her when the time was right—after the man child had come. She also had a comb and a piece of the glass that showed one's image. Those, too, she would save, giving them to The Woman only when the spirits told her the time was right. Content and certain that it would be hours before The Woman's time, Star Dancer prepared their supper from some of the pork and roots she had stolen from the cabins. She enjoyed the meal tremendously. Everything was heightened for her. She glanced at The Woman to see if she, too, was feeling the poignancy of this time. She couldn't tell. The Woman didn't look unhappy, but she was drawn inside herself.

Laurel was feeling the oddity of her own body. It no longer seemed to be hers. It was doing things on its own and outside of her control. She thought of Mathilda and all that she could remember of the time Pamela was born. It hadn't been that long ago, but she couldn't seem to remember. She did recall having plenty of water and keeping Mathilda and the new baby warm. She wished Mathilda were with her. It wasn't often Laurel could recall wanting the closeness of her mother, but she did on this awful night. She pulled the blankets closer to her but couldn't stop the shaking. She was terrified. She was tired and wanted to close her eyes, but she dared not. She might die tonight. She might indeed die. She might be punished for wishing her life away so many other times while she was with Albee, and after, while Star Dancer was trying to save her. She couldn't get from her mind the terrible wishes she had made so often and her lack of cooperation with Star Dancer. She could be in her own home with Mathilda at her side if she had just helped guide the Indian girl. Now she might pay for that. There might never be another day for her.

A wave of pain gripped her, and she bent to it. She tried to be silent but couldn't. A gasp of pain escaped her lips and alerted Star

Dancer. She moved the stolen kettle she already had sitting over the edge of the hearth to the main body of the fire. Methodically and with a little apprehension, Star Dancer gathered the cloth she had for the baby's swaddling. It felt smooth and soft to her skin, and the smell was of fresh air and sunshine.

The two women waited for several hours, Laurel drawn within herself and only occasionally looking at Star Dancer with pleading eyes, asking for help and relief she knew couldn't be given.

As the hours passed her fear grew. She didn't know what would happen to her with the birth of this child. She knew so little about babies. She remembered her mother's telling her of her aunt's death during the birth of a child. She remembered every word she had ever heard about the terrible things that could befall a woman. Her teeth were chattering with tension, pain and fear. She lay flat on the pallet as she had seen her mother do. She was terribly uncomfortable. She raised her knees also as she had seen her mother do in bearing Pamela. She began to cry as she thought of Pamela and Mary. She had promised Mary she would look after her and that this winter she would not be cold or want for food. She thought of the small house at the top of the valley and all the hopes and ambitions she had had for her family. She had failed all of them. She didn't even know if she still had a family.

A great wave of pain rolled across her back and belly, causing her to double up and cry out. Once more she tried to position herself on the pallet as she had seen her mother do.

Star Dancer got up and came to her side. She gently touched The Woman's forehead. "You cause yourself more pain than needed," she said.

Laurel turned her face from Star Dancer.

"Do not lie flat," the Indian girl said.

Laurel looked at her in annoyance. "What are you talking about? What else would you have me do? Squat like the field hands do and drop the baby to the earth?"

Star Dancer nodded her head. "Nature did not give us the birthing bed, the white man did; and all know that the white woman gives birth in great agony. Come beside me—here. I will show you."

Star Dancer squatted near the bed, demonstrating to Laurel. Laurel turned from her again, a look of disgust on her face.

Thoughts of the low people flashed through her mind. She would not give birth to her child in that fashion. She would not fall that low. The pain rolled through her again. The minutes passed, and then became hours. She struggled and worked to near exhaustion and still the baby had not come.

Gently and quietly Star Dancer repeated, "Come with me. Squat as I do and the child will come." Star Dancer looked through the open chink in the cabin wall. The night of the Archer was nearly over, and the man child hadn't come. Star Dancer felt a cold fear creep across her skin. She turned to The Woman with renewed determination. "You come beside me and bring the man child forth! You come here now!"

The Woman would not look at her. Star Dancer stood up and went to the pallet. She took The Woman by the hands and dragged her to a sitting position. The Woman began to scream and cry, pulling against Star Dancer with her greater weight. The Indian girl called upon her guides, planted her feet firmly and pulled against the white woman. "You do as I say or I split you like a rabbit and take the man child!" she said through clenched teeth. "You do as I say!" She released The Woman's hands abruptly, and she fell back to the pallet. Star Dancer came at her again, this time taking her by the shoulders and forcing her up and off the pallet.

The Woman scooted away from the Indian girl, her hand clutching her abdomen. Wherever she went in the small cabin to escape the Indian, Star Dancer was right there. Finally, in fear and exhaustion, The Woman did as Star Dancer asked, imitating her position exactly. Less than an hour later the cabin was filled with the sounds of a healthy baby squalling in protest against the cold and harshness of his new environment.

Star Dancer took the small boy child and washed him carefully in warm water. Then she bound him securely in the swaddling. The Woman lay on the pallet, watching her with the child. She said nothing, but Star Dancer knew that she wanted the child beside her. The Indian girl held the baby close to her, feeling its small movements and listening to the sounds it made. She thought of Little Elk and closed her eyes against the whiteness of the child's skin. Then slowly she got up and took the child to his mother.

The Woman smiled as she took the child into her arms. A look, completely private, crossed her face and closed Star Dancer out. Star Dancer walked outside the cabin. The dawn was approaching, and the stars were not so easily seen in the east now. The night of the Archer was over. Tears silently slid down her face.

After a time she returned to The Woman and the warmth of the cabin. She began to clean and empty the water, replacing it with fresh to warm over the fire. She collected more wood and made the fire flame higher. The cabin grew warmer, and the baby slept peacefully against his mother's breast.

Star Dancer's eyes kept seeking the sight of the sky through the open chink in the wall. She didn't understand life or why it had led her to the place she had come. In all ways she knew, she was superior to the white woman, and yet it was she who served and would always serve. She bowed her head for a time, unable to look at the sky because she was unable to accept what the guides had given her as her lot. It took her a long time, standing still, her head bowed, before she could stare at the sky and feel blessing and thanksgiving in the Father and the spirit guides for having brought her to this night. There must be, she thought, something greater in us than the gifts of our life and our superiorities and inferiorities. There was only one thing of which she knew and that was life itself. Perhaps she had been led upon her path, and to this night of birth, to be told by the Archer that life was the true praise of the Father and the spirits. With that she felt whole and filled with warmth. She gave thanks to the Father, to the Archer, for life, all life.

The Woman slept, and Star Dancer felt alone again when her thoughts returned to the cabin. Her moment of enlightenment had been fleeting, and she wondered if it had happened at all. She sat motionless, her eyes fixed on the patch of sky that shone through the cabin wall, when she became aware of The Woman watching her.

"I wouldn't be alive if it weren't for you," she said, her voice soft and filled with affection. "Neither would my baby. I want to thank you, but I have nothing, Star Dancer. My words are nothing, and I own nothing." She fell to silence, her teeth over her lower lip.

Star Dancer couldn't speak. Had The Woman read her thoughts and her doubts and her fears? Or was the Archer once more guiding her and affirming that life was the ultimate praise of God?

The Woman thought for a long time, then said, "Would you be offended if I named the child after you? You gave him life as much as I did, and I'd like him to carry part of you with him always."

Star Dancer could barely speak. "You give him an Indian name?"

"I would like him to be known as Nathaniel Dancer. May I?"

The Indian girl shrugged, for she was incapable of anything else. She was filled with a feeling she couldn't fathom. Then she burst into a smile and laughter. "Nathaniel Dancer." She came over and touched the sleeping child's cheek. "He is of restless spirit . . . the Archer's spirit . . . he is powerful. His name will be known and his deeds will be legend, for the spirits shall always be with him. Nathaniel Dancer, the blessed one."

31

It was a clear, cool morning when Drew left Cherokee to meet the Manning produce train three miles below Manning. He saw Arthur looking for him before Arthur saw him. Drew smiled as he saw in his brother the apprehension and uncertainty he himself had suffered on his first train. Arthur's face broke out in a smile of relief as Drew hailed him.

Drew rode up beside his brother, greeted him and then with no nonsense moved to take his place at the side of the lead wagon. Almost immediately the wagons of the train straightened in their lines and the men guiding the heavily loaded, awkward wagons came alert. Arthur followed his brother's lead and watched all Drew did. Behind them stretched twenty other wagons filled with goods to be marketed in Charles Town.

At the noonday rest Arthur indicated to Drew that he would like to speak to him alone. Drew shook his head. "Not now; we'll talk tonight. Meet all your drivers and identify your possible trouble-makers and those you can count on should there be trouble or an accident."

"But you already know all of them," Arthur said.

"I'm not in charge of this train, you are, and you don't know them, nor do we always look for or want the same qualities in men. Go find out for yourself who you are traveling with."

With a deep sigh and some annoyance, Arthur walked off to join a group of men sharing their midday meal.

That night when they had made camp and the guards were set for the cattle and livestock and Arthur was nearly too tired to think, he was finally able to bring out the lists of goods the planters in the area wanted brought back to Camden. He handed them to Drew. "What do I do about these? I think everything is to be negotiated through a different agent or factor. I can't see all these men. The only reason I accepted the lists was because I knew you always did, so there had to be a way to do it all."

Drew quickly read the papers and smiled. "You're going to have near a full load returning."

"Not if you're about to tell me I have to contact each of those agents myself, because I'm not going to do it."

"That's one of the best reasons I know for getting to know these men. Divide the list among them and make certain each man is purchasing for the planter he is most responsible to or to whom he owes something. The job will be done well that way. The only purchasing you may want to do yourself is for Manning, and even then you may want to assign it."

The following morning Drew and Arthur rode about a mile in front of the train. Drew taught him what to watch for in the road—ruts, unevenness that might cause a wagon to break an axle or a wheel, which would cost them valuable time. In covered, protected areas Drew led Arthur off the road, his pistol drawn as he scoured through the bush and underbrush for runaway Negroes, Indians or stragglers looking for easy prey. As the daylight began to wane, he turned his concentration to finding a place with grass that could be cleared for the cattle that night.

The men of the train dismounted, leaving only a couple to watch the train. Laughing and talking as they worked, brush was cut down, limbs of trees were hewn, and within a short time a penned-in area was constructed for the cattle. Nearby, others were at work on the campsite for the men.

Fully sated with grits, pork and corn bread, Drew and Arthur lounged on their blankets, feeling sleepy in the flickering light of the fire. The night air was heavy with the sounds of the men singing softly the songs of the campfire.

Two weeks later the men had crossed the hills and saw the difference in the running and color of the streams. The terrain changed, and the smell of the air carried salt with it. Drew, Arthur and the others felt the familiar quickening that meant they were near the end of their journey. Thus far it had been an easy, uneventful trip.

Arthur lay on the soft, sandy ground near Drew. "We'll be in Charles Town tomorrow," he said softly, then added, "I almost hate to see the trip end . . ."

"I've been thinking the same thing," Drew said. "It's this trip. There's something easy about it—no fights, no disagreements among the men, no hard times . . . it's like . . . well, it's been easy."

"And it's probably the last time you'll make this trip for Manning. The only time we'll have done it together," Arthur said, his head propped up on his elbow, his eyes staring into the hypnotic brilliance of the campfire.

Drew didn't want to think of that, so he said, quietly, "We all have our time to move on."

The two men fell silent until they went to sleep.

The next morning dawned sunny with the promise of real heat by midday. They squinted against the white sheen of Charles Town as it lay before them. As always they straightened in their saddles and felt the thrill of the wide-eyed stares the Upcountrymen always drew from the bustling throng of people along the streets.

A street urchin dashed from behind a building, his face wide with a smile. The small boy raced ahead of the train, yelling, "Tra-ain comin' in! Upcountrymen! Comin' in!"

Drew looked at Arthur, then back at the urchin, and smiled, touching his hat as several women looked in the direction of the train. He turned in his saddle to look behind him. Nearly without exception every man on the train looked like a rooster in a new hen yard. It wouldn't have surprised him to have heard all of them break into war whoops. He chuckled and thought Charles Town was in for a big night tonight. He and Arthur would be busy tomorrow getting some of the boys out of the jailhouse. And Dillon's Tavern might be in for some repairs. Amused, he wondered how Arthur would take to this part of the duty of bringing produce to town.

Near the warehouse the train broke up, with men taking their wares to their favorite agents. Drew and Arthur went to take the cattle and crops to Benjamin Smith's warehouses and holding pens. As they were put into the pen, each of the Manning animals was examined from hoof to mouth for injury, imperfection or sign of illness. The new man, Marv Townes, chafed at the need for such care, and Drew gave him a tongue-lashing that stunned Arthur's ears and properly impressed Marv to good work.

With the Manning goods stored, Drew headed straight to Smith's office, with Arthur trailing behind, trying to remember all this trip entailed. Once again he was impressed and a little overwhelmed with all that Drew oversaw and what he, Arthur, was taking upon himself.

Walking among the warehouses and going through the familiar actions reminded Drew of his last visit to Smith's office. He had been full of questions and wonder about what the future would bring. He had heard that day about Governor Montagu's proclamation against the Regulators and had felt a defiance from which he had never recovered. He thought briefly of all that had transpired between that day and this, and it was filled with his own history. He brushed the red trail dust from his clothes, adjusted his hat and walked into the front entry of the office a different man than he had been when he last saw Benjamin Smith.

Smith jumped up from behind his desk as Arthur and Drew entered. "Both Manning brothers! Arthur, good to see you. Drew . . . what can I say? This is a delightful surprise. I'd heard you wouldn't be coming with the Manning train."

Drew looked carefully at the man and saw the difference in Benjamin Smith. The easy friendship was no longer there. He was unsure what to make of Drew's presence here and wasn't going to commit himself until he knew where Joseph, the Manning money and orders stood. Drew put his hand out to shake Smith's. "I'm not here officially, Ben," Drew said. There would be no more Mr. Smith. That, too, had gone with so much else this last year. "I'd appreciate it if you would forget that you saw me."

Arthur shifted from one foot to the other uncomfortably. "I am new to this and needed help, to be honest."

"But Joseph doesn't know you two boys have gotten together."

Drew frowned. "Now that we have that cleared away, shall we discuss price on the Manning crop and cattle?"

They concluded business as quickly as possible and then stepped out into the blinding sunshine.

"What will you do now?" Arthur asked. "I know you want to see Gwynne and Grandmother . . . but how are you going to do it?"

Drew put his hands on his hips and squinted against the glare. "I've thought about every way I can come up with and none is going to work very well, so I've decided I'm just going to Grandmother's house and trust to the fates—maybe I'll get lucky and Pelagie or Grandmother herself will come to the door."

Arthur rolled his eyes into his head. "My God, Drew, if you're wrong, and the wrong person decides to come to the door and slam it in your face, you'll never see either of them."

"What else can I do? Meet them at Dillon's?"

"No, but a tearoom or a hotel would be appropriate. Send a messenger telling them you're in town, and ask them to meet you. That way if there is a problem it can all be handled quietly—no catastrophic family scenes."

Drew laughed. "You should have been the one bound to Joanna. She would appreciate you, and I'm beginning to see why she didn't care much for my ways."

Arthur cleared his throat and smiled at Drew. "You tend to be overly direct."

Both men laughed. "I'll send a messenger," Drew said. "Are you going there right now?"

"Nooo-o," Arthur drawled and stretched. "I am going to a hotel—take a long hot bath, have someone shave me, and change into fresh clothing. Then I am going to rest, have the best dinner in town and go to my cousins' house tomorrow."

"The proper man." Drew grinned. "Then we'll part company."

"Wait!" Arthur said suddenly. "Where will you stay—in case I need to find you?"

"I'll camp with the men and wagons as long as they remain. After that, I don't know."

Drew wrote a hasty note and sent it to Elizabeth by a small black boy. He went to Dillon's, cleaned up and shaved in the back room, then went to the tearoom Arthur had suggested to wait for Elizabeth and perhaps Gwynne. As he entered the tearoom, he became aware of a tension in himself that was not entirely unpleasant. He ordered sandwiches and tea but couldn't keep his mind on the food despite his hunger. Repeatedly his eyes sought the front door. In his imagination he played over and over the sight of Gwynne coming through the door. He was captivated by the sense of what her hand would look like, the soft whiteness of her skin, the unforgettable deep blue of her eyes. He realized he had been staring distractedly at the door and turned to concentrate on his food in embarrassment.

As Gwynne and Elizabeth stepped through the door there was no need to hunt among the tables for Drew. He was the focal point of the room—a big, broad-shouldered man in Upcountry garb sitting among small tables covered with white lace tablecloths and set with delicate china. Elizabeth and Gwynne laughed as they watched him pick up and bite with some revulsion into a small watercress sandwich.

Drew looked up and met Gwynne's eyes. He couldn't look away. It was as though everything had stopped and he were looking at her for the first and only time in his life. Gwynne, too, moved as though she were in a trance.

Elizabeth watched her grandson and young cousin and was warmed by the spirit that now filled the room. Most people called it love, she thought, but then many things were called love, and seldom did the caller know what he was talking about. She thought of this more as recognition: a man recognizing in a woman the completion of himself and a woman recognizing in a man the completion of herself. She had no specific name for it and didn't want one. It was enough that she was once more in its presence and was deriving a deep and satisfying pleasure from it. Seeing Drew in Gwynne's eyes and her in his was somehow an affirmation of Elizabeth herself. She walked up to his table and watched him pull his attention from Gwynne to stand and greet her. Drew kissed her and put his arm around her briefly as he guided her to her seat. Seated, Elizabeth watched his hand linger at Gwynne's shoulder as he seated her. This was a happy day. Everything she had hoped for these two specially loved children of hers, she was seeing today.

"I'm sorry I had to ask you to come meet me, but I was afraid I'd cause a real brouhaha if I came directly to the house." He smiled and looked impishly at his grandmother. "Actually that is exactly what I was going to do, but Arthur talked me out of it and suggested a message as an alternative."

"Arthur is in Charles Town? Then you have not come in response to my letter—and how is it that you and Arthur come to be together? I thought there was no communication between you."

"What letter?" Drew asked. "Arthur told me of a letter you had written to Mama. I came because . . ." he paused, glancing quickly at Gwynne. "I came because Arthur needed help. He and I have a more or less secret agreement to help one another. I worked the harvest with him and then came to Charles Town. He's never done the harvesting alone, nor has he ever led a wagon train. It is rough to do your first time alone."

"And in return for your favors, Arthur told you of my letter, is that it, Drew?" she asked, her eyes twinkling mischievously.

Drew colored slightly. "Something to that effect," he admitted.

Gwynne and Elizabeth ordered tea, and the three of them spent the next hour talking of small things and catching up on the events in each other's lives. As she listened to Drew and Gwynne talk of the king and the Liberty Boys and the Regulators and all the issues that were becoming more and more well defined to the general public, she decided that whatever it cost her in family dissension, she was going, somehow, to have Drew as a guest in her home. Perhaps she was getting old and was no longer as observant of the laws of propriety and family loyalty as she should be, but in that case her family would have to tolerate her aged peculiarities. After all, eccentricity was a hallmark and privilege of the old age she seldom relied upon, but was fully entitled to.

"Drew, are you still feeling that a bit of family battling is acceptable to you in order to see Gwynne and me?"

"Always," he said, and took her hand in his. "And more than that. I'd defy armies to reach you."

Elizabeth laughed. "I should know better than to ask you for a compliment. Imp that you are, you drown me in my own begging. I would like you to stay at the house."

Gwynne's eyes widened. "Cousin Elizabeth! This is going to cause more than a little family battling."

"Yes, I am sure it will. It may be a rather full-scale battle. I have neglected to tell you one bit of information. Joanna is visiting at the moment."

Drew burst into loud laughter, and everyone in the tearoom turned to look at their table. Gwynne moved self-consciously. There were going to be family battles in any case, for to be sure, news would return quickly to Joanna and Eugenia that she and Elizabeth had been seen in public with Drew.

"Grandma, you cannot actually want to bring me as your guest into the house while Joanna is staying there."

"But I do. You are my grandson, and I want to see you! Even if you were not my own flesh and blood, I would want to offer you the hospitality of my home, and I shall. In fact, that is exactly what I shall do! As a stranger, cast out by decree of my son, I shall invite you as my guest."

"Perhaps you should consider this a bit longer, Cousin Elizabeth," Gwynne said.

"Well! I certainly never expected you to be fainthearted."

"I'm not!" Gwynne said. "I only said that you might want to consider it a bit longer. If that is what you wish to do, I would not think of standing in your way or trying to deter you."

"Then we shall proceed. Drew, please arrive in time for supper, and do not be late. Gwynne, you and I shall go home now and break the news."

Drew saw them to their carriage and gave Elizabeth assurances that he would arrive on time for dinner. For once he was sorry he had not brought the proper clothing. He would have nearly an hour and a half before he would arrive at Elizabeth's, so he went to Arthur's hotel and told him of Elizabeth's decision.

Arthur shook his head, then finally smiled. "Well, we now know for a certainty where you got some of your headstrong traits, don't we? Why don't you try on one of my suits? I doubt it will fit you, but it can hardly look worse than you do now. Perhaps tomorrow, if Grandmother has her way, we can shop for a suit for you here. I know an excellent tailor, and I am sure he would hurry if I told him what an emergency it was." Arthur moved quickly around his room, sorting through clothing and selecting garments he thought might fit Drew, who was considerably broader than he. He collected an outfit and handed it to his brother. "Are you sure you want to do this, even if Grandmother wishes it? It is going to cause a further division in the family, Drew. We're already seriously drawing apart. I didn't tell you this before, but Leo and I were at Mars Bluff with the militia. I assume you were with the Regulators."

"Yes, I was. Why didn't you tell me?"

"It would have made no difference. You would have remained on your side and Leo and I on ours, but the point is that we are brothers and cousins, and it was fate alone that kept us from facing each other on a battlefield. I don't want to be responsible for shooting at my brother or my cousin, Drew, not even if it is by chance and not deliberation."

"And my going to Grandma's is going to worsen that, you think."

"It cannot do otherwise. George already leans toward radicalism, and it will most certainly be in the open that Gwynne and Joanna are divided. I know you've been the one to bear the brunt of the marriage contract and now the breach of it, but my God, Drew, where is all this going to end?"

"Perhaps it need not be as you describe at all, Arthur. Perhaps Grandma has something else in mind. She is a shrewd old fox, you know. It may be in her mind that if she brings me back into the midst of things, we'll all fight it out and the Mannings will once more try to find their common ground."

"I am sorry to be the pessimist, Drew, but your own words have made me so. It is too late. You've been right all along when you were telling the rest of us that something was in the air—that change, radical change, perhaps even revolution was in the air. It is, and already the family is beginning to split between Whig and Tory."

"Then my visiting won't change anything, Arthur. If it has already happened, I can't stop it; nor can I make it better."

"You're going, then?"

"Yes, I am." Drew picked up the clothes Arthur had laid down and began to dress. The vest stretched tight across his back and strained at the front, and the jacket barely went across his shoulders.

Arthur looked at him in dismay. "Perhaps your buckskins do look better. Whatever you do, leave the waistcoat open all night, and do not stretch forward or you will split the whole thing down the back. You are not a fashion plate."

Drew shrugged. "I never was. Wish me luck, Arthur." He walked to the door, gave his brother a jaunty wave and left.

Elizabeth herself answered the front door of her house. "They are like a pack of trapped, hungry wolves," she said, "but I have had my way for the moment. This is not going to be easy, Drew, but it may be important."

"Grandma, you cannot bring the family back together this way. I know your heart is in the right place, but this will not accomplish the impossible."

"We'll see," she said, and patted his hand. She was still patting his hand as she walked into the parlor, a broad smile on her face. "He is finally here," she said to the group of Mannings and Templetons gathered there.

Talk in the room quieted to an awkward silence. Drew said nothing but looked from one family member to another. George, Leo and Rob were like a trio of stunned monkeys, their mouths open, each of them turning to their mother for a cue as to how to behave. Eugenia tried to smile but succeeded only in making her upper lip quiver unattractively.

Gwynne alone seemed pleased to see him. Her dark blue eyes shone, and while she did not greet him, a smile was in her very beautiful eyes. Drew sensed a renewal of the closeness they had experienced that afternoon and was warmed by it. She was so vitally and vibrantly alive.

He finally looked at Joanna. She sat poised and attractive. Her hair was coiffed in the latest fashion, and she wore a lovely cream-color lace afternoon gown. He admitted to himself that she was magnificent. He raised his eyebrows, nodded to her and, releasing himself from Elizabeth's gentle grip, walked across the room, took her hand and kissed it. "You look lovely, Joanna. I am happy to see you so well."

A glint flashed in Joanna's eyes. "You are being very kind, Drew, and quite out of character with it. I don't believe you have met my fiancé, Lieutenant Bertram Townshend. Bert?"

Drew looked into the face of a man nearly his own height, well built and wearing his well-fitting uniform as a badge of accomplishment. Bert Townshend stood rigidly straight, his hair, mustache and beard carefully clipped. His features were regular and bespoke breeding; his eyes were a cool gray, and his gaze was direct. After a slight hesitation he put his hand out to Drew and greeted him, smileless. His only comment was, "Joanna has told me a great deal about you. You are quite the . . . rebel of the family, aren't you?"

Drew's eyes gleamed, and a smile was on his lips. "As far as I know, I'm no longer a member of the family at all. I am merely a guest."

Before Townshend could say anything, Joanna asked, "Very clever, Drew. Did you think of that or did Cousin Elizabeth? How long shall you stay?"

This time the hostility in her eyes was unmistakable, and Drew met it with anger of his own. "As long as Mrs. Manning extends her hospitality," he said clearly and deliberately. The effect was instantaneous. Joanna put her teacup down with a clatter Drew noted with satisfaction. "Cousin Elizabeth!" she said, then got better control of her voice and her temper. "Surely Drew will not be staying here—in this house."

Elizabeth looked innocently at her. "Where else would he stay, my dear? He's my guest, and in the city to visit me. Where would you have him put?"

Joanna was speechless. She sat back in her chair. Bert moved protectively behind her chair, his hand on her shoulder.

"Perhaps Drew could stay with the grooms," Leo offered. "That would solve the problem. He'd be here, but not . . . . not . . ."

"The stable?" Elizabeth asked him. "You are suggesting we ask a guest to stay in the stable while he visits us?"

"Perhaps it wasn't such a good idea," Leo blustered. "I was just trying to think of something . . . anything that would offer a solution."

"It may not be such a bad idea, Leo," Elizabeth said sweetly.

John looked at her with consternation. He knew trouble was afoot when his mother's voice took on that deceptively sweet tone. With all his heart he wished his son had had the good sense to keep quiet.

"It may be that you have offered us the best of all possible solutions," Elizabeth went on. "In New Orleans, I have heard many of the great homes have a building behind the house that is kept strictly for the unmarried male guests of the house. We could temporarily have our own *garçonnière*. Does it seem agreeable to you, Drew?"

Drew didn't dare look at his cousins. He kept his eyes directly on his grandmother. "That is agreeable with me."

"Rob? Leo? George?" Elizabeth asked.

"Us? Live in the stable?" Rob said weakly. "But why . . . we all have our own rooms . . . there's no need for us to . . ."

"Well, of course, we'd no longer call it the stable," Elizabeth said reasonably. "We'd call it the single male accommodations."

"But why must we . . . it is only Drew who . . ." Leo said.

"Are you not male and single?" Elizabeth asked.

"Of course, but . . ."

"And was it not your suggestion?" Elizabeth pressed. "Then it must apply to all single male members of the family and guests, must it not? John, is that not the way it should be?"

John looked at his mother, then at his sons. "It is the way it will be. I suggest you round up some of the servants and start them to making it clean and habitable for tonight."

The Manning cousins sat in cold, angry silence for a moment, then excused themselves and left to have their new men's quarters put in order. Leo paused at the doorway, looking back at Drew, waiting for him to join them.

Elizabeth frowned at her grandson. "Leo, Drew is our guest. Be off with you!"

Drew walked over to his grandmother. "I would enjoy helping, Mrs. Manning." He turned to the others in the room. "Ladies, gentlemen, if you would kindly excuse me . . ."

They had not reached the rear of the hall before Leo was complaining bitterly. "God, Drew, wherever you are there is trouble. Don't you ever get tired of having half the world mad at you at any given time and the other half just waiting in line for their turn? What the hell are you doing here? Jesus Christ! And Joanna right here!"

Drew started to say something, but Leo was fired up and went on. "This time you've really done it! You've put us right out of the house with you. Do you think Rob and George are going to take this lightly?"

"They sure as hell aren't!" Rob said from the end of the hall, his arms folded over his chest.

As Drew neared him, he broke into a smile and put his hand on Drew's shoulder. "Discomfort aside, it's good to see you. I haven't had a broken nose since your last visit."

George joined his brother. "I think I understand why you left Joanna sitting on her knitting," he said. "I thought Grandmother was one always to get her own way—and she is—but that Joanna is not going to have herself thwarted in anything. I don't envy Bert Townshend."

"Bert is getting what he wants," Rob said and winked at Drew. "I happen to frequent the same areas of town Bert does, and I know his mistress—a very pretty actress. In the meantime Joanna has managed to create a reputation of bravery and dashing glamour that has him the most sought after up-and-comer in the city. Don't feel sorry for him; he has the best of everything, and I think he's Joanna's match in getting what he wants. It's my opinion that they are a perfect couple."

"Forget about Bert and what he wants for now. What are we going to do about us? Have y'all forgotten we'll be sleeping with the damned horses, thanks to our 'guest'?" George said.

Leo stood to the side, watching. "Y'all may think this is a lark but I don't. Drew, you have no business here. Grandmother has no right to force your presence on us. The rest of you may do as you please, but I'm not staying in a stable or under any roof with him," he said and stalked off.

"Why don't we head for Dillon's and forget about sleeping and my brother?" George suggested.

"Better still, let's get the darkies working. This might not be all bad. There are eight or nine rooms up in the top floor of the stable. With no one keeping too close an eye, we can do as we please up there, and it just happens I know a very pretty lady who delights in giving parties for a small fee. And considering the delights of the evening, it *is* a small fee," Rob said, his eyes shining.

The three men went to the upper story of the stable to examine their new quarters. They quickly approved the long, high-ceilinged, heavily beamed room and set the servants to work.

"You make sure there are linens out here, y'hear. I don't want muslin against my skin," Rob said fiercely as though the black man would give him an argument.

"And a table," George added. "Bring a table and a stock of liquor, and have one attending to the need to serve us later tonight."

With that the three of them did leave the stables and head for a more exciting part of the city.

It took a great deal of time before the women relaxed enough to say anything after George, Leo, Rob and Drew left. Joanna stared at Gwynne with malice close to hatred in her eyes. Gwynne stirred uncomfortably and looked at Elizabeth for support, but even Elizabeth was at a loss.

"It certainly has gotten quiet with the men gone," Eugenia quailed. "It'd make their heads swell were they to know how we need them for entertainment."

"Why, Cousin Eugenia, I think a certain absence has improved the group. I find Cousin John and Bert quite enough male companion for all of us," Joanna said, then glared at her sister. "Gwynne, why don't we have some music? Would you all like that? Gwynne sings so beautifully, and so does Bert." She got up and walked toward the piano. "Come, let's all gather 'round. We'll have a good sing." Joanna took Beth by the hand. "You'll be my assistant and we'll play together."

32

Nathaniel Dancer lay back in his mother's arms, his small mouth still working in sleep, a drop of milk on his lips. Laurel looked at the small, compact body of her son. She thought she could never learn to love this child, so great was her fear that he was the son of the outlaw Albee, but she was no longer sure. She didn't know whom Nathaniel belonged to.

Star Dancer hovered nearby, her eyes moving about the room but always back to the child. She envied The Woman her child. She moved quickly about the small cabin to keep at bay the terrible thoughts and wishes that had plagued her day and night since the child had been born. Little Elk and the child they would have had together had been much on her mind since Nathaniel's birth. Sometimes it seemed to her that the boy rightfully belonged to her. The Woman would have died long ago, had it not been for her. It was she, Star Dancer, who had assured the child's birth. It was she who had led them mile after mile across the mountains and open terrain to safety and the place of his birth. Even The Woman herself had acknowledged her right when she had named the child Nathaniel Dancer after her. Why would it be wrong to take the child? Could she take him and leave the mother behind? What would the spirits who guided her do if she took that course? She had praised them and offered her time and her soul to them, hoping for an answer. But the answer she had received had not been what she expected. The Archer had not given her the child but instead had given her to the child.

Since the night of the Archer when the child had been born, she

seemed unable to achieve the closeness with the spirit of Little Elk
or with those unknown spirits that guided her that she had had as
she traveled across the mountains. She knew it was because she had
not submitted to their blessing. She glanced over at The Woman
and saw her looking back. She had been watching. For what? Did
she know the thoughts that had been going through Star Dancer's
mind? The Woman's eyes were a deep gray today, and they were
losing the tired, ill look that had been so long in them.

Star Dancer's heart slowed to a normal beat, and she smiled at
The Woman. Occasionally, in moments like these, there was something about The Woman that Star Dancer liked. Right now, without
the worry or the fear clouding her eyes, The Woman was someone
she cared about, someone who would care about her and young
Nathaniel Dancer. Star Dancer looked away. Perhaps submission
was the way. Perhaps serving would be her fulfillment. Perhaps her
spirits had not tricked her. Perhaps Nathaniel was hers in a way, and
that way was through The Woman. Perhaps in some fashion her
love for Little Elk and the children they would have had rested in
the man child of The Woman.

"Are you hungry?" she asked The Woman.

"No," Laurel said softly. "You love the child very much, don't
you, Star Dancer?"

"The child's spirit was given to my trust," Star Dancer said
proudly, her head up, her chin thrust out.

"He wouldn't be alive if it weren't for you," Laurel said, then
looked down. "And neither would I."

"You don't want to see the days come and go," Star Dancer said,
her voice brittle and edged with resentment.

"I know." Laurel's voice was barely a whisper. She brushed her
hand gently over the sparse, downy hair of the baby. It was dark, a
nondescript color that could become similar to Albee's coarse black
hair or to Drew's wavy chestnut hair. Tears came to her eyes. Even
if Nathaniel was the son of Albee, she could no longer hate him. In
the few days that she had had him, that he had lain at her side,
suckled at her breast, she loved him. He was her son, only hers. She
held the baby close, holding in the sobs that threatened to break
free and awaken him. Star Dancer said nothing. She stood as she
had been and watched. She watched Laurel so often, Laurel had

come to feel lonely and uncertain when the Indian girl was not present. She fell asleep with Star Dancer's eyes on her.

Star Dancer took the infant from his mother's arms and laid him in the cradle she had fashioned from a hollow log. She carefully wrapped him in one of the blankets she had stolen from the line of the big house. She thought often of that day. She thought of the man and how he had looked at her. She knew that when he had first seen her he had been going to stop her. She wondered why he hadn't, and then with the same feeling she had had that day, she knew he hadn't stopped her because he had sensed she needed that blanket and that her mission was meant to be. The Archer had been her guardian that day and must have talked to the man as he had talked to Star Dancer.

She squatted by the side of the cradle, her hand on it, gently making it rock. The infant slept. The Woman slept. The Woman slept often. Star Dancer did not know the ways or weaknesses of white women; she knew only that had she herself had the baby, she would have died by now or she would have been on her feet tending to her child. The Woman slept and remained weak. She did not die, nor did she get to her feet to tend to her child.

Laurel continued her slow mending process, and with the healing of her body came a revitalization of her spirits. It was difficult for her now to sit in empty contemplation of a single cloud or to stare blank-mindedly for hours at the ground or a tree. Her curiosity was once more aroused, and her desire to do things was returning. She had complained so often about the cold winds blowing through the loose chinking in the cabin. Now she got up, went outside, fashioned a mud cement of straw and wet soil as she had seen Ben do and filled in the joints between the logs. Proudly she asked Star Dancer if the cabin was not warm and cozy.

The Indian girl nodded, smiling, and to show the extent to which she meant it, loosened the swaddling around Nathaniel. "You have done well, Woman," Star Dancer said. "You rest for a time, and then we eat."

"You always call me Woman," Laurel said.

"I know only Woman."

Laurel stared at her. It couldn't be true that in all this time, with all they had been through, Star Dancer did not even know her name. They had come so far that it was difficult for Laurel to recall that while she had been with Albee and after she had escaped, she had wanted no one to know who she was. She had never mentioned her name to anyone. She had refused to answer when the outlaws had called her Laurel. Even now it was difficult for her to think of the time when eventually everyone in the camp called her Woman, for she would respond to nothing else. "My name is Laurel," she said to Star Dancer. "I'm Laurel Boggs."

Star Dancer looked at her but said nothing. She got up from beside the baby's crib and, still saying nothing, stirred the fire to make dinner.

Periodically Star Dancer would leave the cabin for a hunting and stealing trip to replenish their supplies of food. The stronger Laurel became, the longer the trips were and the less frequently made. Star Dancer seldom missed stealing something from the big house where she had seen the man. Somehow she felt that she had a right to take from that house, that the man had given her permission. She was never greedy, but she always returned with vegetables, or linen, or smoked meat from the big house. To her what she stole from him always tasted the best. She also hunted for rabbit and squirrel and occasionally tried her luck at bringing down a small deer.

Laurel now took over the task of cleaning and preparing Star Dancer's catch. They ate well that winter and developed a companionship that Laurel thought of as being forever. Her mind could not conceive a time or place without Star Dancer. And yet even in her most idealistic and optimistic time, she knew that they couldn't stay there forever.

Star Dancer, too, grew fond of Laurel. She had still not used her name aloud, but in her mind she had come to think of The Woman as Laurel. At night when she would go outside to pray and to look at the sky, searching it for signs, listening to the voice of the wind and trying to hear the sounds that would guide her, she asked about Laurel. She watched the sign of the Goat move across the sky for his time and then vanish. There was no sound or sign to indicate to her that it was time for Laurel and Nathaniel to leave the cabin. Star Dancer decided to stay. She knew the woman Laurel would not object.

Star Dancer busied herself with the child. She made a board for him and carried him upon her back. Only his small head and arms were free of the binding carriage. Daily she took him for walks in the deep pine woods. She crooned the songs of her people to the child and talked to him as if he understood every word she said. She told him of the signs in the sky, the voices of ancestors and spirits that came to one in the cries and songs of the wind if one was wise enough to listen.

Star Dancer, too, found herself wishing that these tranquil days need not end, but even as she thought it, she could feel how few the number of these days would be in the whole of her life. But the Indian girl was wise in the ways of such things and did not plague herself with thoughts of loss until loss came. She treasured these days and used each minute. When the child was in her sight, she memorized his every feature, his expression. How he was right now was something she wished to carry with her all through her life. As young as he was, she showed him the nests of birds and held up to his bright, dark eyes the eggs she took from the nests. She pointed out to him the burrowed holes of small animals, the lair of the fox, the print of the deer.

The air was frosty, and the Goat gave way to the Water Bearer before Laurel began to join them on their walks. She learned quickly and became an eager pupil to her companion's tutoring. She was never as adept as the Indian girl at reading signs or recognizing patches of edible roots or mushrooms, but she learned and had little doubt that if she was ever pressed again, she could make her way through a wilderness and survive. It was during this time that Laurel realized that in most circumstances she would survive. Before Star Dancer had come into her life, she had always felt the need of depending on someone else, perhaps because she had never been without another person. Only with Albee had she known what it was to be alone, and she had thought she'd rather not live. She now knew that no matter what happened, she did want to be alive. She, too, wanted to hear the songs of the pines and see the stars move across the sky in formation, each with its own time of the year, with its own messages to be seen. She wanted to live to see her child become a man, and even now, though he was an infant, she could see he was going to be an outstanding man.

She still could not bring herself to think of leaving, but as Star Dancer knew, Laurel also knew that the time was coming.

Part Four

Gwynne

33

Drew was persuaded by his grandmother to stay in Charles Town for the Christmas holidays. On the silver tray in the hall were stacks of invitations to Christmas balls, evenings of carol singing, and dinners from which he was always excluded. The entire household was busy from early morning until late at night. The women had the local seamstress in daily, and there could be heard the moans and squeals of delight as each new gown was tried and fitted.

The men were concerned with far more serious stuff, they said. The Yule log had to be selected and plans made for the green hunt, not to mention the hog killing and day-long search for the greenery to decorate the house.

"Have you noticed there's always a lot of shooting at Christmastime?" Rob said with some amazement at the dinner table the evening before they were to go out looking for the Yule log and mistletoe.

"Have you no idea why that should be so?" Bert asked.

"It's quite a lot of fun," Rob offered lamely.

"It's quite a lot of superstitious nonsense, actually," Bert said in all seriousness. "We think we are sophisticated and very aware of things, but we are in fact quite barbaric and not a great deal further along than the ancients. We still think Merlin will pop out of the tree trunk and give us a scare."

"I'm certain we do," Rob said, "but what has that to do with the shooting of guns at Christmas? But ignore the question; I shall answer it myself. We eat too much and as a result have a great deal of hunting to do. We also do a great deal of kissing and have a great deal of hunting to do to facilitate that as well."

"Fertility and sacrifice," Bert said, wiping his mouth carefully. "It all comes back to that, if you are still interested in a serious answer to your question."

"Most things do come back to that," Elizabeth said tartly. "And I for one am glad they do. Keeping the old gods happy has never harmed us. It's good for the soul. And as for fertility . . . the small homages we pay that are indeed pleasurable."

The following day Drew and his cousins saw to the task of killing the hog so that it would be ready for the Christmas Day feast. It was an all-day task, for Elizabeth would hear of no part of the hog being wasted. Even the hog bladder was in demand as a balloon to be blown up for the children to play with.

All work, except that dealing with Christmas, had come to a halt. The day after the hog was readied for the feast, the men took to the woods on horseback in search of the Yule log. The women followed more sedately in the family carriages and carts. Eugenia was bundled up to her nose, a scarf wrapped completely around her neck and lower face. At her side was a basket filled with chicken, puddings, egg nog and mulled wine, cheeses and huge, freshly baked rolls.

When the women arrived, the men were racing through the woods, showing off their expert horsemanship and having far more fun shooting mistletoe from out of the trees than they were looking for a log.

Leo dug his heels into his horse as he saw the carriages drive up and stop, making the animal rear and paw the air. With a flourish of the mistletoe in his hand he raced over to the carriages, dismounted, and held the mistletoe high over the head of Gwynne.

Gwynne blushed and giggled. "You are cheating, Leo. The mistletoe is supposed to be hung someplace and stood under accidentally, not carried about to be put over the head of whomever you choose."

"Whose rules are those? Did the king order it? I shall have the Assembly change the rule immediately," Leo said, and dived for her mouth.

Gwynne deftly moved, and Leo stumbled forward. "You don't back away from Drew," he complained.

"You must be sporting, Gwynne," Eugenia said quickly. "He's got you."

From the corner of her eye, she saw Drew walking his horse up to the group standing by the carriages. Looking at Leo warily, she turned her cheek to him. He kissed her, then placed his hands on her shoulders. "The next time you will not get away so chastely, Cousin. And there will be a next time . . . many next times, for the Christmas season has just begun. By the end of it you'll know the better man, and so will he," he said, looking at Drew.

Eugenia, her mouth buried in the folds of her scarf, went into a fit of nervous giggles. "Oh, would you listen to him. What a rogue he is! My son! I do believe he's in love!"

"It's just the season, Cousin Eugenia," Gwynne said acidly.

Leo let out a guffaw. "So you think!" He gave her a hard look, then mounted his horse and rode away from the group.

"I saw that!" Rob shouted, and came running with his own sprig of mistletoe.

George, laughing, was right behind him. "Drew, come join in!"

Gwynne began to laugh and blush, dodging the playfully amorous advances of her cousins. Soon the men were racing through the carriages, holding the mistletoe over the heads of all the women.

"Drew," Elizabeth said, "if you continue to stand here like a wart on a toad's back, I shall kick you in the shins."

The others were dancing about the carriages, playing seek and find. Squeals of delight were heard from the women and roars of triumph from the men. Gwynne came running past Elizabeth and Drew with George close behind her, his mistletoe held high. Drew glanced at his grandmother, then spun on his heel, reached out and caught Gwynne by the waist. He swung her around, lifting her into his arms, and deftly poked his mistletoe into the band of her hat. He leaned forward to kiss her, and as she had been doing, she turned her head.

"No kiss for you," she said coyly. "You have no mistletoe, and strong arms don't count."

"I don't need mistletoe. You are under it, and therefore I not only get a kiss but a full and proper one."

She laughed. "I am under nothing of the kind. Put me down, Drew."

He tapped her hat. "See for yourself."

She felt the brim of her hat, then worked up to the ribbon. She looked at him wide-eyed as her fingers closed around the stem of the mistletoe.

Drew's dark brown eyes were filled with warmth as he moved slowly nearer her face. He held her, his mouth no more than an inch from hers. Gwynne held her breath, then closed her eyes. Still he did not kiss her. She opened her eyes and began to squirm nervously. "What are you doing?" she whispered. "This is very embarrassing. Please put me down. Everybody is looking."

He smiled and remained so close to her she could feel his breath and the warmth of his skin. "No one is looking."

"Drew, please!"

His eyes grew warmer. "You want me to kiss you?"

From custom she began to protest, then she relaxed. "Yes, I do. Now, please." She put her arms around his neck and brought her lips to his.

Her mouth was warm and pliant against his, and she smelled of spices and flowers. Drew's arms tightened around her, and his kiss grew more ardent. Gwynne's lips pulled away from his. Her tongue flicked out and ran across his upper lip. She leaned back, away from him. "Merry Christmas, Drew Manning."

Breathless, he looked at her, his eyes full of questions and desire.

She smiled again, her eyes dark blue and wickedly mischievous. "You'd better put me down. The others are watching—and disapproving."

He felt Elizabeth's cautionary tug at his coat sleeve and let Gwynne slowly to the ground until her feet touched. He still had one arm around her and held her against him. "As Leo said, there will be a next time, Gwynne. The Christmas season has just begun."

"So it has." She turned to the others. "Are we ever going to find the Yule log? I'll wager I can find it before any of the rest of you." She ran toward the woods, the rest of them following. Even Eugenia ran, her scarf held closely with both hands.

Elizabeth and Drew followed at a more sedate place. Elizabeth was clucking at him as they walked. "Either you stand about as though you are above such nonsense or you make a public spectacle of yourself. Have you no sense of proportion, Drew?"

"You are jealous that you were not kissed," he said, and swung her into his arms as he had Gwynne. Without benefit of mistletoe, he soundly kissed his grandmother, and when she protested, kissed her again. Elizabeth finally gave up and laughed. "You incorrigible hedonist! Put me down. You will have me the scandal of Charles Town! Oh, my dear heavens, that is the Kincaid coach coming and I'm sure they've seen us. Drew, you must put me down immediately! Whatever shall I say?"

"That you have sprained your ankle."

Elizabeth patted his shoulder. "Oh, that is marvelous."

Drew walked to the Kincaids' coach, Elizabeth looking pained and clinging to him. "Good afternoon, Mrs. Kincaid, Tyrus. It is so nice to see you. I suppose you all are out for your Yule log, as we are? I am afraid I am a casualty of the day . . . I sprained my ankle." She was talking too fast and knew it, but she wasn't accustomed to lying and wasn't at all sure why she felt compelled to now.

Mrs. Kincaid got out of the carriage with her son's help, then turned back to usher her younger children out. Tyrus stood nearby, watching his younger brothers and sister run for the woods in search of their log.

"Drew, I think if we are careful, I could manage to stand now," Elizabeth said sweetly.

Drew placed her feet upon the ground. "How does it feel?"

She looked up at him and nearly laughed. "I think it will do well now. I feel hardly any pain. Why, I'd be hard pressed to say I sprained my ankle at all. Thank you, dear. I think I can walk on my own." She let go of his arm and walked along with Mrs. Kincaid toward the others in the woods.

Drew fell back and walked with Tyrus. The two men had always been rivals and not always friendly ones, particularly when it came to Joanna Templeton. Now Tyrus looked at Drew and asked, "I thought you were crossed out of the family Bible."

"I am," Drew said and laughed. "I am Grandma's *guest*."

Tyrus laughed and asked, "Is it true Joanna's visiting, too—in the same house?"

"Yes, she's here. She's with Bert Townshend . . . looking for the Yule log," Drew said.

"Perhaps I can catch her while he's looking the other way. You and I have not always seen eye to eye, Manning, and I think you deserve to hang for what you did, but I'd rather see her with you than with that snooty red-coated bastard."

Drew laughed. "Perhaps we are not so far apart in our views as we seem to be. You were under the Liberty Tree and so was I."

"For entirely different causes, my friend," Tyrus said.

"Not so different. If you would place the Lowcountry in all the spots I referred to the Upcountry, I can guarantee that you would easily have given the same speech as I did."

Tyrus laughed. "I concede. It's too bad you aren't in Charles Town more often, Drew. We could use you. Matters are not calming down; they are getting worse. Good old Mother England repeals one set of duties and replaces it with another, which in itself might not be so disturbing to us, but the high-handedness with which she trespasses on our rights is reaching a point beyond tolerance."

Drew took a deep breath. "I may be here more than I have been." Drew tapped Tyrus's shoulder. "If you look that way, I think you may see someone of interest temporarily alone in the woods."

Tyrus smiled at him and hurried off to see Joanna before Bert was once more at her side.

Elizabeth and Mrs. Kincaid were soon at Drew's side. "Drew," Elizabeth said, "I have volunteered you, dear. I hope you don't mind."

Drew smiled and looked at Mrs. Kincaid, an amused expression on his face. "What have you volunteered me to do?"

"Tomorrow you and Gwynne are collecting the pine and holly to decorate the house, and as Mr. Kincaid is laid up with gout and Tyrus is unable to help tomorrow, would you and Gwynne mind gathering enough for the Kincaid house as well as ours—and a tree for them, too?" She turned momentarily to Mrs. Kincaid. "We're having a holly tree. Would you like the same, Roberta?"

"It'd be my pleasure," Drew replied with a silent chuckle of disbelief at his grandmother's seemingly neverending scheming.

Gwynne and Drew were gone the entire day hunting for the pine boughs and holly. It was nearly dark by the time they cut down the second holly tree for the Kincaid house.

"Which one shall we give to the Kincaids?" Gwynne asked.

"The second one—the one we picked for them," Drew said.

"But I think it is slightly bigger and perhaps has a better shape. What do you think? The first one for us or the second one?"

By the time they delivered the tree, it was so dark neither of them was certain which tree they had actually given away. Elizabeth's house was bright with candlelight when they came home. Joanna and Eugenia and Elizabeth had spent the day purchasing the largest and most beautifully colored candles Charles Town had to offer, and now they were set in the parlor and the dining room, blazing with color and warmth. The entire family greeted Drew and Gwynne at the door, and made over the holly tree.

Rob ran outside and brought in a huge tub to plant the holly tree in so that it would stand upright for the season. They placed the tree in the parlor, and though they had planned to complete the decorations the following day, no one wanted to wait. Amid singing and foolery, the Mannings pruned and placed pine boughs and mistletoe and holly around their house.

Drew and Leo were put to weaving a wreath of pine and holly for the front door. Without causing a scene, Leo couldn't refuse, but he complied sullenly.

"You son of a bitch, Drew. I saw you with Gwynne yesterday. What is it—you need to put your stamp on every attractive female in the family?"

"Leo, I—"

"And then today you go ferreting off with her to the woods!"

"Grandmother arranged that," Drew said defensively. "I didn't say anything to Gwynne or anyone else about collecting the pine boughs."

Leo looked at him disbelievingly, then asked, "Why you? What reason would Grandmother have for choosing you—and Gwynne?"

Drew shrugged. "You'll have to ask her. I don't think she had any reason. I was just there while she was talking to Mrs. Kincaid, and she asked me if I'd do the Kincaids' collecting and ours as well."

"I don't believe you. I can't think why Grandmother would pick you. You're the pariah of the family—not even supposed to be here. I can tell you one thing: you'd better watch out on the turkey shoot tomorrow. A man just can never tell when his eyesight will play tricks on him."

"I do hope you're joking, Leo."

Leo stared at him. "I'm not sure, Drew. One day or another we'll find out."

The next days were spent in a variety of activities. Elizabeth's house was filled with the comings and goings of guests, and her table overflowed with Christmas fare, plum puddings, fruit of every sort and variety available, succulent hams, poultry and home-baked breads and pies. The mistletoe, which had been hung from every portal, was used frequently and with great relish. Often in the evening after supper, the doors would be opened wide to allow the children of the neighborhood in to carol. The family joined in. Drew was reminded of the Christmases he had had as a child. On Christmas Eve, with each family member secretly hiding gifts beneath the tree for the others as was their custom, Drew sat in a large chair in the parlor, watching his cousins and grandmother enter stealthily, deposit their gifts and leave. He stayed there, in the shadows, unnoticed until Gwynne came down.

She tiptoed into the room, looking to her left and right, and then, kneeling, reaching far beneath the red and green holly tree. Her long white nightgown pooled around her, and her dark hair hung loose down her back.

Drew smiled to himself, enjoying her excitement, her love of the feast. She leaned back on her legs, her hands clasped in front of her, pleased with her handiwork. She had been there for some time when he softly said, "Merry Christmas, Gwynne."

She turned at the sound of his voice but did not get up, or try to cover the fact that she was clad only in nightclothes. In the muted light her smile was broad and filled with pleasure at seeing him. "I'm glad you're here. I've been hoping for a chance to talk with you alone and despairing of ever finding it."

"It sounds serious and very important."

Gwynne came close to him, and then before he could say or do anything she sat on his lap. "It might be, or it might be nothing at all."

Drew's arms slipped easily around her. The pleasure with which he noticed the shape of her surprised him and caused him some discomfort.

Gwynne smiled, and there was a knowledge in her eyes that

caused him further discomfort. "You know how I feel about you, Drew. I should be coy and tease, but I don't have any desire to do so. I have told you of my feelings, and I haven't changed in that. I have decided that since I have come this far, I shall take yet another step, probably to my own ruin. I want to be your wife. I want to live with you, love you and have your children."

His discomfort changed to alarm. He had never heard a woman talk like this before. He wasn't sure what it meant or what he was meant to do about it. "Gwynne, I haven't—"

"I don't want you to say anything right now, Drew. I'm not finished with what I have to say. You have never led me to believe that your desires match mine. I know you were planning to marry Laurel, and I imagine you still love her. But life has a strange way of altering our plans, thwarting them or sometimes hurrying them along. I want you to know what I feel, and I have told you."

"But Gwynne, I don't know what I feel or what I want to do. It is unlikely I'll ever see Laurel again, and if I did . . . if I did, I think I'd still marry her."

"I know that, and in part it is why I have made my second decision. Jemima Mitchell and her family are going to visit England this spring. Joanna is going with them, and I have decided to go too. I'll be gone for some time, and perhaps by the time I return both of us will better know what we want and if perchance that should include each other." She paused, her eyes focused on her hands. "Or is it that you could never think of me in that way, Drew, and you are merely too much of a gentleman to tell me to keep quiet?"

Drew's eyes were filled with wonder and admiration. He stroked the side of her face, then ran his finger across the soft skin of her lips. "You're an endless surprise to me, Gwynne. No matter how long I know you or how well I think it is, I don't know you at all."

She smiled. "You haven't answered my question, or is this again a polite way of telling me there could never be passion between us."

"Oh, no, I'm not telling you that. There is passion between us—there always has been. I am telling you only that I don't know what to do with it . . . I have already caused your sister great pain, and the family. I wouldn't do that to you."

Gwynne put her arms around him and leaned against him. "Oh, Drew, I thank you for protecting me, but please don't love me so that I never truly know your love. Don't guard me so safely to an empty bed."

Drew held her, his eyes closed, his mind and emotions reeling. She felt so small in his arms, and a rush of desire fought with the instinct to protect she had spoken of. He wanted her, but the greater his desire ran, the greater was his wish to keep her from the harm he thought he'd inflict on her. His mind was a welter of thoughts. She was young and beautiful. Many men would want her, and she could take her choice of whoever she wanted. She had no need of a man like him, who was filled with vague ideas of justice and freedom and rights but who couldn't seem to organize his life into any practical pattern. The thoughts curled into smoke with the dizzying warmth of her lips against his.

34

Laurel, Nathaniel and Star Dancer stood on the outskirts of Camden in April, 1769. They had been walking steadily since early morning, Star Dancer carrying the five-month-old child in the carrier on her back. Now the two women stopped. The expression on Laurel's face hardened. So often she had thought of returning home, and to the talk and attitudes she would find. During the last few months, as she had learned to live and enjoy life as Star Dancer did, all of that seemed far away, but now looking at the neat houses, the shops lining the streets of Camden, it was Star Dancer's way of life that seemed far away, nothing more than a memory of her past.

She stood still, staring at Camden, unwilling to go on. "I hate to come back, Star Dancer," she said wistfully. "You won't like it here."

"We will not go there," Star Dancer said.

Laurel, her mouth tight and turned down, laughed. "I would like that. There are so many of them in those houses who will do nothing but condemn and talk and even glory in my falling, but I want—need—to see my family. I don't even know if they are alive. What happened to them? I must go on."

The Indian woman nodded and started walking again. Laurel took her by the arm and stopped her from moving toward the town. "We do not need to go there; that can be put off for a time. We'll go through the woods to my home. Come, I'll guide you for a change."

They came to the final hill, the one Laurel used to love, for she could come over the rise and see her home, the smoke rising from the chimney, often her younger brothers and sisters running in front of the cabin, and occasionally she could match her time so that Ben would be coming in from the fields as she came home from working at Manning. Now as she looked across the sloping green expanse, all was quiet. She saw no activity in the front yard, nor was anyone mounting the hill from the field. For a moment fear clutched at her. Supposing they were no longer there. She had been gone a long time. She had just assumed her family would remain here, but they had a history of moving on. Mathilda had lost other children and left to begin again in a new place. Laurel stood paralyzed, staring at her home. "They're gone," she breathed. "No one is there."

Star Dancer pointed to the back of the house. Laurel followed the direction of her hand but saw nothing. After a moment Mandy came into view, struggling with the weight of a full bucket of water. Laurel's heart thumped with excitement. She laughed, her hands pressed to her mouth, her eyes full of tears. She turned to Star Dancer. "Give me the baby. I want to carry him the rest of the way." She unlaced the baby from the carrier and took him in her arms. Nathaniel gurgled with pleasure at being free and immediately entwined his hands in his mother's long, honey-colored hair.

Laurel pushed open the cabin door and walked in. Mathilda stood by the window, her hands automatically paring potatoes, her eyes vacantly staring. "Mama," Laurel said, barely able to speak.

Mandy looked up and shrilled, "Laurel! You're home! Laurel!"

"Laurel?" Mathilda said unbelievingly. "Laurel, is that you?"

Mandy ran to her and stopped as she noticed Nathaniel in her arms. The baby began to howl as the new, unfamiliar women rushed at him. From above them, in the loft, Laurel heard Willie's delighted nonsensical squeal. He clambered down the ladder. He was smiling as always, but she knew he didn't know who she was. Once more she heard steps on the ladder rungs and looked up to see Ben. She began to cry. "Oh, Ben! You're alive . . . I didn't know. I didn't know what happened to you."

Mathilda looked over her shoulder. "He's alive all right, but he ain't worth much no more; never will be again. Where'd the young'un come from? Your'n, I expect."

Laurel looked from her mother to Ben, not knowing what to say first. "Yes, he's mine . . . Nathaniel . . . but what do you mean about

Ben? Ben, what does she mean?" She frowned at her mother. "Why would you say that, Mama?"

Ben blushed and looked down at the ground. "It's true, Laurel. That night . . . the night we were attacked, I was shot . . . it did something to me." His face was scarlet red, and his eyes filled with pain.

"It's his head," Mathilda said. "Doc said a part got shot away, an' he ain't right no more. Has fits."

Laurel paled. "Fits? What do you mean? What does he do?"

"Mos' anythin'," Mathilda said and went back to paring her potatoes. "Like as not he'll tear the house apart, an' anybody gets in his way."

"Oh, Ben . . ." Laurel cried. "I'm so sorry. It's all my fault. Nothing would have happened to you if it hadn't been for me."

"If it hadn't been for that Manning fellow, you mean," Mathilda said. "He's the cause o' all this. Our lot's hard enough without him an' his Regulatin' makin' it worse. He come sniffin' aroun' here a few times, askin' iffen we'd seen you, but he didn't do a blamed thing for us." She looked at Laurel over her shoulder. "You be stayin', I suppose. Her too?"

Laurel took her attention from Ben. "I was going to, Mama, but if you don't want us . . . don't you want to see your grandson?"

Mathilda made a face, then her eyes bored hard into Laurel's. "Looks like he been eatin' good. More'n I kin say fer us. My babies was never fat like that."

Laurel choked back her anger and disappointment. "Star Dancer is to be thanked for that. Both Nathaniel and I would be dead if it weren't for her. She hunted for us and fed us and took care of us. Nathaniel's last name is Dancer—after Star Dancer."

Mathilda still did not soften. "Who's he supposed t'be named fer?"

Ben rubbed his hands across the back of his neck. Mathilda looked alarmed. "You all right, Ben? Iffen you ain't feelin' right, you tell me so's I kin git outta here."

"I'm all right," Ben said as he moved toward Star Dancer. "You took care of my sister?"

Star Dancer's eyes were dark and kind on him. She showed no fear or apprehension and took his hand as he offered it to her. "She tell me many stories about her brother Ben," Star Dancer said. Ben smiled at her, then turned to Nathaniel. "Will you trust me to hold him, Laurel?" he asked diffidently. "I can always tell when one of the fits is comin'. I get a terrible pain first. I'd not hurt him."

"He like to kilt your papa t'other night," Mathilda said.

Laurel handed the child to her brother. Nathaniel's dark brown eyes danced with curiosity at this new person on his horizon. He poked his fingers into Ben's mouth and pulled at his eyebrows. Ben began to laugh, a rusty, unaccustomed sound even to him. It had been a long time since he had felt like laughing. Most of his days and nights were haunted by the memories of Mary's body, of Pamela's cold little figure pressed into the cold soil of the hillside, and of Laurel's screams—or perhaps they had been his in that last burst of gunfire and darkness. It was a good, vital warmth that he felt in Nathaniel Dancer, Laurel's child. A strong healthy child.

Star Dancer caught his eye and motioned to the door. Ben smiled and said to Laurel, "We'll be just outside the cabin. It's time he saw his home."

Laurel watched them walk outside and envied them. "I can do the potatoes, Mama," she offered. "I'd like to."

"Think you kin walk back in here all full of yourself an' take over agin, do you?"

"I didn't mean that. I thought you'd like the help. What do you want me to do, Mama? I can leave again if that's what you want. Is it?"

"I thought you was dead, like the others," Mathilda said pathetically.

"I was afraid to ask," Laurel said. "I guess I knew."

"They did awful things to Mary, Laurel," Mandy said, her face white and pinched. "I saw her . . . right out there in the yard . . . she was all bloody and awful. I ain't gonna let no man come near me ever. They was shoutin' an' yellin' an' killin' Mary." Mandy began to tremble and sob. Laurel sat next to her sister and held her close. Mandy continued to cry until she was vomiting.

Mathilda tossed a rag onto the filthy floor. "Ain't been nothin' the same since that night. Yore pa cain't hardly work fer nothin', an' them damned Regulators allus is nosin' 'roun' here mindin' our business, tellin' him what to do or they gonna whup him. You brought trouble down on us like we never seen before when you hooked up with that Manning fellow."

"What's thet damned Injun an' her papoose doin' out there with Ben?" Harley said as he pushed through the cabin door. He stopped short as he saw Laurel sitting on the cot with Mandy. "I'll be damned! That you, girl? Thought you was dead."

"The Indian in the yard with Ben is Star Dancer, my friend, and the child is your grandson," Laurel said sharply, and stood up.

Harley looked at Mathilda. "Jee-zuz, she come back from the dead more uppity than she was when she got took. Whose brat is it?"

Laurel looked away.

"Belong to one of them raiders?" he pressed.

"I don't know," Laurel said quietly.

Harley guffawed. "Mebbe it's Manning's. Damned bastard caused us the miseries. He's the fault of all our troubles. Give the brat to him. Let him worry about what to put in another mouth. You stayin' here an' wantin' to eat too, I 'spect."

"I'll see to the food Nathaniel and Star Dancer and I eat."

Mandy squeezed Laurel's hand. "I want you to stay, Laurel."

Laurel looked at her and hugged her. "Good. 'Cause I am staying, at least for now."

"You see you work your share," Harley said, hitching up his pants and looking authoritarian.

Laurel laughed nastily and walked outside to Ben and the child. Behind her, Harley and Mathilda spoke in hushed tones. Like so many things, she had not remembered them clearly, or her home, or her need for them. When she had wanted to die of pain and fright the night Nathaniel had been born, she had longed for her home and her mother. Now she had her mother, and the woman would not even look at the child. Her father thought of him only as another mouth to feed. Yet she had insisted on remaining here. Why, she asked herself. She could say it was for the benefit of Mandy, Ben and Willie, but it wasn't. It was for herself. She didn't know how she could benefit from staying with her parents, but they still had something she needed—or needed to rid herself of. She wasn't sure. She and Nathaniel and Star Dancer would remain here as long as she chose. No one would drive her out, she vowed.

Ben put his hand on her arm. "Sorry it was like this," he said, then shrugged. "Some things never change."

"It has always been like this, hasn't it, Ben," Laurel said.

Ben looked at her as if he didn't understand.

She laughed bitterly. "I had forgotten—or maybe I never knew before. Lord, Lord, I was an awful dreamer. I thought the Boggses would be something special one day. I remember when I first started going to Reverend Fowler's cabin to clean and learn to read. I thought we'd be like the Mannings if we all worked hard."

Ben's eyes filled with sympathy. He shook his head slowly, then brightened. "You want me to tell Drew you're home again? He done a lot o' lookin' fer you. Everybody else gave up, but not him. He was out in the brush all the time, swearin' by all that was holy if you was alive he'd find you."

"He did?" Laurel asked, her eyes bright. "He really looked for me?"

"For months. For all I know he's still lookin'. Folks 'roun' here thought he was crazy. They all said he wouldn't find you, an' if he did he'd be sorrier than if . . . Oh, God! Laurel! I'm sorry, I—"

"Don't be, Ben," Laurel said crisply. "I'm no fool. I've been here when other girls were taken. I remember what people said and what they thought. I remember how those girls were treated, too. There's no sense in trying to hide the truth from me."

"But it's not fair! I know that now . . . it wasn't your fault. You couldn't help what happened that night—no one could."

Again Laurel laughed bitterly. "I know that, Ben, but I also know the 'good' people, and their rules. Evil is evil, an' now that they think I tasted it, they're going to think I like it and can't ever be any other way."

Ben looked down at his feet. Again he rubbed the back of his head. "What's wrong with folks, Laurel? They read the Good Book, they talk of God an' followin' His ways. He didn't tell us to judge nobody like this." He looked at her, but all she could do was bite her lower lip to hold back tears and shrug. "Drew ain't like that. I'm goin' to tell him you're home. He'll see to you an' take care o' you. He won't let no one say bad things about you."

"No, Ben," Laurel said quickly. "Please, I don't want you to say anything to Drew. I don't want to see him, and I don't want him to know we are here."

"He's gonna find out, Laurel. You know he will. People's most likely already talking. You cain't keep a secret hereabouts. It ain't fair to let him learn from strangers, not after all the lookin' he done for you, an' he helped me too. There wouldn't have been no doc if Drew hadn't brung one here for me. You oughtta let me tell him. I don't feel good not tellin' him."

"You can't tell him, Ben, please, you've got to promise me."

"Why do I gotta promise? You was gonna marry up with him."

"That was before," Laurel said urgently. "I can't see him now, I just can't."

"Why not?" Ben persisted.

"I don't know exactly. The baby . . . we can't marry now, and I . . ."

"What about the baby? Is it Drew's baby?"

Laurel looked at him with great pain. "I don't know, Ben. He could be, but I don't know, and there'll never be any way of knowing."

"He looks a little like Drew, don't you think?" Ben said and turned the child to face him.

"Oh, Ben, he doesn't look like Drew. He doesn't look like Albee either. Please don't tell Drew I'm here, Ben. I don't know what to tell you. I just don't want to see Drew now, maybe never."

Ben stood where he was, saying nothing. Finally he sighed and said, "I ain't given you my word on it, Laurel, but I won't tell Drew nothin' right now."

"Ben, please, you've got to promise."

"No, I ain't got to do nothin'. I'm gonna take me a nap now." Ben chucked the baby under the chin and smiled at him. He touched his forehead to Star Dancer, then went into the house.

35

Ben worried about telling Drew. Each day Laurel was home, he saw her move about the house and slowly bring order to the Boggses' cabin again. Ben's clothes were aired and washed, the floor was swept, the suppers they ate were hot and well cooked. But she didn't belong here, he decided. He liked having her and he didn't want her to leave. He hadn't been so cared for or felt so good since she left, but there was something about her caring for her family that seemed dishonest, like they had all stolen something from Drew Manning they shouldn't have.

Several times he walked toward Cherokee, but he always turned back. Laurel didn't want him to go. He knew she meant what she said. She wasn't teasing or playing coy. He didn't understand her at all, but she really didn't want Drew to know she was home again. He was on his way back to the cabin when he crossed paths with Star Dancer returning home with three fat rabbits.

He waved at her, knowing she would remain silent and drawn within herself if he did not. "Looks like you had a good day. Mebbe I can go with you nex' time an' he'p you out." He laughed self-consciously and scratched his head. "I might be embarrassed, though. I don't remember ever bringin' three rabbits home by this time o' day."

Star Dancer smiled. "I'll teach you. You've been over near the man Drew's house again?"

Ben looked at her, feeling guilty. "How'd you know where I went? You follow me?"

"No," Star Dancer said without apology, her eyes directly on him. "I know. You are troubled that Laurel will not talk to him. You think it is right that he should know of her return and the man child."

Again Ben found himself smiling self-consciously. "Cain't keep many secrets around here."

Star Dancer walked on, allowing Ben his strange custom of toting the catch for her. She finally decided he carried for her so that the family would think he had done the work. She could fathom no other reason that he would not allow the woman to bear the burden.

"I think about how many times he went out after her and allus come back empty-handed, and his face as sad as an ol' houn's. An' I think o' all the times he come 'roun' astin' me iffen I had heard anythin' about her. He'd talk fer long times, tryin' to think like them outlaws would think. He thought he might figger out where'd they take her iffen he could figger out what he'd do iffen it were him on the run. He seen me through a couple o' my worst fits ever. I don't git them so often now, but in the beginnin' I wasn't no good to be 'roun' atall. He got me the doctor, an' stayed with me. Weren't many'd do that. Mos' folks jes' wanna git outta the way."

"You should follow what your spirits tell you," Star Dancer said.

"I ain't got no spirits like you do to tell me things. I jes' know what I'm feelin', an' that don't tell me nothin', either."

Star Dancer put her hand on his arm and stopped him. She waited until he looked directly at her and their eyes held. "In the heart of us what we feel is the voice of the spirit guide. You listen, for he speaks to you and tells you truth."

"An' what about Laurel? She ast me not to tell Drew. What if her spirits is talkin' to her? Whose spirits is right?"

"Spirits don't tell untruths. If your voice is strong, then it is not her spirits talking to her and telling her to hide but the fear that comes and hides the truth. In many ways you have the old man's wisdom, Ben; use it."

Ben remained silent for a long time. "Somethin' inside me is strong an' wanted to walk right over those hills there to Cherokee. My feets jes' itchin' to go there."

Without saying anything Star Dancer began to walk to the top of the hill. Ben paused for a moment, then ran after her. "Hey, wait up! I di'n't say I was gonna do it, I jes' said I was itchin' to."

Star Dancer continued walking and did not stop until she was at the top, looking over another expansive valley. Far in the distance, mostly hidden by trees, was another large hill. Beyond it lay the big cabin of Cherokee. Her heart beat faster. She knew that place. She knew it very well. She thought of the blankets that had kept her and Laurel warm last winter; the blanket that she had wrapped the newborn Nathaniel in. She thought of the bushels and bushels of roots and vegetables she had hauled away from that big cabin. She thought of all the things she had stolen, because it was always so easy there. It was almost as if someone was helping her, and indeed she had thought it was the Archer who had led her. She still did. "The man Drew lives there?" she asked, a picture of a tall young man in her mind's eye.

"Yep," Ben said, smiling, his thumbs hitched into his belt. "It sure is a nice place. He's as good a man as comes. An' he's got substance an' such a back fer work you'd never know he weren't one o' the plain folk like us."

"You listen to your spirits. They tell you truth. You must listen," Star Dancer said urgently.

Ben looked from the hills to her and back again. "You look like you're seein' a ghost. What do you see down there?"

"I see no ghost," Star Dancer said, and she turned quickly and walked away toward the cabin.

Ben came after her. "You're a strange lady, Miss Star Dancer, an' I don't know what you're talkin' about half the time. An' folks say I ain't sharp as I used to be since I got shot, but I ain't so slow I don't know when someone's seein' somethin' I ain't. I'm gonna think some more on this spirit thing, an' iffen I keep feelin' like it, I'm gonna see Drew. Soon."

Laurel had been home nearly a month, and Nathaniel was beginning to move about the cabin, hitching along on all fours, when Ben decided he was indeed hearing spirits and that they were telling him the truth. Drew Manning needed to know that Laurel was at home, and he needed to see Nathaniel Dancer.

Ben left early one morning, hoping he'd be back before the others in the house would pay any attention to his absence. Since his injury, he enjoyed a great deal of latitude in his behavior and often took advantage of it. It was a pleasant walk, and Ben made no effort to hurry. Since Star Dancer had come to live with them, he seldom hurried so fast that he didn't have time to enjoy the world around him. He hadn't had a fit in a long time, and the one that he had had since her coming had been mild. She had brewed an herbal tea for him that had soothed him and eased the pain that made him clench his jaw till his teeth hurt. He hadn't hit anyone or anything, and after it was over there had not been the usual broken pottery and furniture scattered around. He had never been around anyone like Star Dancer before. He liked it. She made him feel whole and alive.

Cherokee loomed up before him before he was ready for it. He cleared his mind of thoughts of Star Dancer and walked to the door.

Ben found Drew in the rambling cabin he had built, leaning over a wicked-looking brew he had on the open fire. As he stood in the open doorway, Drew looked up and smiled. "Ben! Good to see you! Come on in. What brings you up here?"

Ben walked in and stuck his head over the dark, murky liquid boiling in the pot. "This your supper, Drew? It shore don't smell good. I got some vittles in my bag I think you'd like a whole lot better." He glanced over at Drew. "I'd be glad to share with you."

Drew put his arm around Ben. "I'll take you up on it. This is not supper, but it is the pot I need to cook supper. This, my friend, is going to be a year's supply of beautiful dark blue ink."

"Ink?" Ben repeated. "That's a lot of ink."

"Just let me add this indigo and we can sit a spell and talk."

The two men sat on straight-back chairs on the stoop of Drew's house. Ben unpacked the pouch of cheese, pheasant and bread that Star Dancer had packed for him. She had included a jug of cider, which Ben and Drew both lamented had not yet begun to ferment. "Well, I guess she didn't know how we'd like it bes'," Ben said, happy the small talk was prolonged.

They talked for some time of Drew's place and the work he had done to it. "It will be a long time before it's worth much or I have the money to hire someone besides Ned to help me, but I figure I can get at least twenty-five to thirty acres under cultivation." He made a face. "It's a lot different from Manning. But it's mine, and that makes a difference, Ben, don't let anyone ever tell you different. It makes me feel like I'm my own man." He wondered how many times he'd have to say that before it felt true.

Ben grew more and more silent the more Drew talked. He was no longer certain he should tell Drew anything. He sounded as though he had finally begun to work things out for himself, and hearing about Laurel now might not do him any good at all. It might bring back all the unrest and uncertainty of the previous year.

"You're getting pretty quiet, Ben. What's on your mind?" Drew asked, and waited through several more minutes of silence, during which Ben began to rub the back of his neck. "I know you didn't just happen by, Ben, and though I like to think we're friends, I don't see a horse. It's a long walk for a hello."

"Now I'm here, I don't know as I should be, Drew. Tell the truth, I'm not too sure of nothin' right now. That Indian girl I tol' you about—she got me to thinkin' about spirits an' doin' what's in your heart."

"Sounds like good advice to me. Where'd you meet this girl?"

Ben rubbed his neck again. He started to speak several times, but couldn't find the words.

Drew watched him closely now. "Ben, have you heard something about Laurel? You'd tell me if you had, wouldn't you?"

"Well . . . the trouble is, Drew, she don't want me to," he said, trying to tell Drew without telling him.

Drew looked at him open-mouthed. "What do you mean she doesn't want you to . . . you've seen her? God, Ben, she's not home, is she?"

Ben nodded. "She's been home fer near a month. I woulda tol' you right away, but she made me promise. But then it didn't set well with me, an' Star Dancer said to follow my heart an' here I am."

Drew just stared at him. "Why? Why did she ask you not to tell me? Doesn't she know I searched every bush and rock in these hills for her? Doesn't she know I want her back?"

"She knows. Says that's why."

"For God's sake! What sense does that make?" Drew shouted and got to his feet, pacing back and forth in front of Ben.

"It don't make any sense to me, but that ain't all my news," Ben said, and again he couldn't find the words. He hadn't thought how difficult it would be to tell Drew. He had only thought how much Drew wanted news of Laurel, but never that the news might be hurtful to him. Now he felt as though each word he delivered was a blow, and Ben was full of sorrow. His head felt like it was going to pull apart. He hadn't meant it to be this way. Now Laurel was going to be angry with him, and Drew was being hurt by the news. He hadn't wanted this at all. This was not what was in his heart. The spirits were misguiding him.

"What more?" Drew pressed. "Did they harm her? Is she all right? Is that why she doesn't want to see me? Did they do something to her?"

"No, no, there ain't a mark showin' on her. She . . . she come back with a . . . a baby . . . a baby boy. She called him Nathaniel Dancer, 'cause she says he ain't got no pa. She give him the Indian's name, 'cause she said none of them would be alive if it weren't fer the Indian."

Drew sat stunned, his eyes on Ben but not seeing him. It was some time before he could speak. "Is it my child, Ben, or . . . or does she really not know?"

Ben, too, found talking difficult. "I don't know, Drew. I think she's afraid to think much on it. If I was to say, I'd say he's your son. He always puts me in mind of you, but I don't know nothin' neither." Ben looked down at his hands. "What you gonna do?"

Drew started to speak, then closed his mouth. He got up and paced back and forth. He looked at Ben, his face grim and tense. "Why does she want to avoid me? There must be more to it than you know. Is she . . . is she in love with this outlaw?"

"Lordy, no!" Ben said with disgust.

"It's happened before. Why else? We were going to be married, and now she doesn't want to set eyes on me. Before . . . before she was taken she would have come to me for comfort . . . understanding. I would have been the first she'd turn to. So why would she turn away now if there weren't more to it than you've told me?"

Ben said weakly, "Y'better see her, Drew. You got a lot of straightenin' to do with my sister. You could come home with me now."

"No, Ben, not now. I've got to think about this. I don't understand it."

"You went all over this country lookin' for her, Drew. Now I'm tellin' you she's here right in her own home, an' you say you gotta think on it? Mebbe it's you who've changed. Mebbe Laurel's got somethin', wantin' to keep it all from you."

Instant denial leaped to Drew's lips, but he said nothing, for thoughts of Gwynne were there, too. He stood looking at Ben. "It may be, Ben. I have changed, but Laurel has no call to keep this from me—not if that's my son."

"What if he ain't?"

"He might be. Why don't you stay here tonight? I'll take you back in the wagon tomorrow."

Ben thanked him but refused. "Star Dancer is waitin' for me. She won't go back till she sees me comin'. I'd better be startin' out now."

Drew sighed. "Help me hitch the wagon. I'll take you to the ridge. It'll save you a little."

When they reached the ridge, Ben and Drew parted company with little to say to each other. As Ben dismounted from the wagon, he glanced up and saw Star Dancer waiting for him, a string of game dangling over her shoulder. "Well, it's been good seein' you, Drew. I thank you fer the ride—saved my feet. She's waitin' fer me. I bes' be goin'."

Drew was staring at the Indian girl. "Is that Star Dancer?" he asked in a hushed voice.

"That's her."

"I know her," he said in the same hushed voice. "That's the girl who came to the house . . . I know her."

Finally Ben listened to him. "When did you meet Star Dancer, Drew. You couldn't . . . she's been with Laurel all the time. You got her mixed up with someone else."

"No, last winter she came to the house. Ask her," Drew insisted.

Drew remained in the wagon, staring after them. He had the same strange feeling of familiarity he had had the first time he had seen her. He had helped her then, and now it was she who had told Ben to come to him despite Laurel's wishes. It was she who had talked to Ben of spirits and guidance from within. On a sudden impulse he started the horse in the direction of the Boggses' cabin, then slowed and stopped again. He couldn't see her now. It finally came to him that he was afraid to see Laurel. But afraid of what? That she wouldn't care for him anymore? That the child was his? Or wasn't? Or that he no longer wanted to marry her?

He needed time to think. He had once more come to a crossroad in his life. One path led to Gwynne, the other to Laurel. He was only one man, and so he had to choose.

***

It was a full week later that Drew came back down from Chero-kee. He went directly to the Boggses' cabin and knocked on the door.

Mathilda, her hip stuck out, her hair falling from her topknot, opened it. She looked at him wide-eyed, then squinted, her face closed and hostile. "You here for the Regulators? He's workin', y'hear. Y'ain't got no call to meddle into our business.."

"I'm not here for the Regulators, Mrs. Boggs, I'm—"

"What do you want? I ain't got time to be socializin'. We're hardworkin' folk here."

"I was told Laurel was here. May I see her?"

"Well, you was tol' wrong. An' even iffen she was here, she wouldn't wanna see the likes o' you, not after what you Regulators done to her pa." She closed the door in his face.

Drew walked to the edge of the crest, where the hill made a sharp descent to the fields below. Fifty feet away, the Indian girl sat. A baby was crawling in the high grass. Drew could hear his high-pitched squeal as the grass tickled him. Slowly, his heart pounding, he began to descend the hill, his eyes always on the child.

"You are Star Dancer?" he asked as he neared her. "I am Drew Manning. Is this . . . Laurel's child?"

"He is Nathaniel," Star Dancer said. She showed no surprise or discomfort at Drew's presence. "He was warm in his first moments of life because you helped me."

"The blankets were for the child?"

"And the woman." She stared out across the hills for a moment. "I believed the Archer had sent me to a kind house, but I did not know for certain. It is difficult to follow the silent voice of the spirits. But I know now; I was guided. Could it be otherwise, when I was led to you?"

Drew said nothing, and Star Dancer looked up at him. "You do not believe in such things?" she asked.

"Until recently I had never thought of such things," he said. He continued to watch the child play. "Would it frighten him if I held him?"

"He fears nothing, this little warrior. Perhaps his boldness comes from his father."

Drew came nearer the child, then knelt. The infant stopped crawling and sat up. His eyes were dark brown and bright. There was no fear or strangeness in them, only a lively, warm curiosity. Drew smiled at him. Nathaniel liked that, and to show his pleasure and desire to share, he pulled grass with both tiny fists and held the trophy out to Drew. Drew reached down and picked the baby up. Nathaniel immediately began exploring his face with inquisitive little fingers. "He is a husky boy," Drew said, amazed at the pleasure the presence of Nathaniel's small body next to his gave him.

Drew suddenly realized that he wanted to take the child away. He wanted privacy with him, for what he didn't know, but his joy in the child was all-encompassing. With a glance at Star Dancer, who seemed to understand without his need for speaking, he walked toward the copse of trees at the side of the hill. As they neared the woods, Drew stopped and let the baby touch the dogwood, pulling at the pink and white petals, tugging at the small limbs. Slowly he moved from one tree to another. He was soon talking to the child as he would to another adult, telling him the lore of the woods, pointing out the moss on the trees and holding up to the sunlight various leaves, pointing out the different shapes and colors that each had.

He had been gone for some time and realized he'd have to take Nathaniel back to Star Dancer. As he suspected, she had begun to wonder at their absence and met them at the edge of the woods. He smiled at her but did not offer to hand Nathaniel back to her care. He walked at her side. "I could become a doting father."

"It is good when a son is with his father. That is the way it was meant."

"I wish Laurel felt as you do. Can you tell me where she is?"

Star Dancer nodded. "She is in town with her brother. It is the first time she has gone."

"Camden?"

"Yes, Camden, but it is not good for you to see her there."

Drew laughed. "Do you always read others' thoughts so easily?"

"I have seen you with the child. You want him. Her wishes will not mean so much to you now."

Drew raised his eyebrows, then relaxed. He handed her the baby. "Would you please tell Laurel I will be back tomorrow? I am going to see her and talk to her. Please make certain she understands that she can delay our meeting, but she cannot stop it."

***

Star Dancer relayed the message. Laurel was excited and angry. "Who does he think he is? I don't have to see him if I don't want to. I won't see him! I don't want to talk to him, either, and I'm not going to."

"What's he so all-fired eager to see you fer?" Mathilda asked. "I chased him outta here oncet today. I thought that'd be the end o' him. He mus' have somethin' mighty special on his min'. What is it?"

"I don't know and I don't want to talk about it, Mama," Laurel said and quickly busied herself changing Nathaniel's napkin.

"Don' you try puttin' me off, girl. What're you hidin'?"

"Nothing, Mama!"

Laurel took the baby and went to the far corner of the room to feed him. Mathilda was right after her. "You ain't exactly the pick o' the crop—not after what happened—so why's he sniffin' 'roun' iffen he don' have a pretty good reason? Tell me that, girl; tell me why he's after you."

"I don't know. He's not after me, he just wants to see me . . . probably wants to know that I'm all right, and that's all."

"Then why don' you jes' see him? Why you runnin' an' him chasin'?" Mathilda stuck her face into Laurel's. "Cain't fool me, girl, y'hear? I'm wise to you an' all your tricks. You're jes' like me when I was a girl—all full of secrets an' schemes. I know, an' I kin wait to fin' out." She stood straight and folded her arms across her bony chest, looking at Laurel. Then she smiled smugly and sat in the rocker by the fire, humming. Every now and then she'd glance over at Laurel, the smug smile fixed on her face.

Laurel was silent. She wouldn't look at her mother or anyone else in the room. She stroked the baby as he fell contentedly to sleep.

She saw Drew the following day as he rode over the crest of the hill, his hair ablaze with red highlights in the bright sun. She ran from the back of the house to the woods. She couldn't see him. If he didn't want her as a result of her abduction, she didn't want to know it, and if he would take her out of pity and a sense of responsibility, she didn't want that either. She couldn't even bear the dream of him still loving her. Even that wouldn't work, not with Nathaniel. She ran until she could no longer see the house. It was near dusk when she dared return.

Late that night Laurel walked outside. Tired and confused, she sat on the big log outside the house where she and Mary used to sit and tell each other about their dreams. It wasn't cold, but she hugged herself as if she were.

Star Dancer walked silently into the yard. She stood beside Laurel before Laurel realized she was there. "This is no good. You cannot hide from the man Drew. He will keep coming until he gets what he wants."

"And what is that?" Laurel snapped. "You always know so much. What makes you think you always have the answers?"

"He wants the child. I have seen it in his eyes."

"He can't have Nathaniel! He's mine. Mine—no one else's."

"That is not true," Star Dancer said simply.

"It is true!" Laurel shouted, then clapped her hand over her mouth, her eyes fearfully on the cabin. More quietly she whispered, "It is the truth."

"You will have to see him. It is better to do it now. He is a good man, but he is not a patient man with such things. You will arouse his anger."

Laurel put her head down. "I can't see him, Star Dancer. I don't want him feeling sorry for me."

It was mid-June when Laurel finally met with Drew. As always, she saw him ride over the hill and come toward the house. She was waiting for him in the doorway when he tied his horse to the hitching post.

She found it wasn't as difficult as she had imagined. Faced with him, she felt a cold, hard, prideful anger that allowed her to say coolly, "Hello, Drew. I hear you've been wanting to see me. Well, here I am."

The warmth left the expression on his face. "So I see," he said. "May I talk to you, or are we going to play hide and seek for another month before we accomplish that?"

"Talk. Talk all you want. I'm right here, and my ears work just fine."

He put his leg up on the stair of the stoop. "I searched high and low for you. All I could think about was seeing you again, making sure you were safe . . . and being with you. Are you angry that it wasn't I who found you? I tried."

"No, no, I'm not angry with you about that . . . or anything else, Drew. It's just that everything's changed. I'm not . . . I don't feel the same way I did before."

"About me?"

"About you, about everything, mostly about me." She took one more step outside.

"I want to talk with you," he said. "And not like this. Can't we go somewhere?"

"I don't have anything to say, Drew."

"I want to know about the child. Is he mine? Do you know?"

Laurel quickly came down the steps. "We'll go somewhere. I don't want to talk about that here." She kept looking back at the cabin. The curtains stirred in the window. "Please, don't say anything more. I was stupid. I should have left here as soon as I saw you coming."

Drew followed her agitated glance. "Your mother?" he asked softly. "Has she something to do with your not seeing me?"

"No. I've made my own decision, but I don't want her overhearing anything. She'll mix in just like always. She's always at me."

They walked quickly away from the house, going to the woods, for Laurel refused to mount his horse with him to go anywhere else. They found a pleasant spot among the pines where they could sit. Laurel, straight-backed and uncomfortable, perched on the edge of a log. Drew sat near the other end of it, equally uncomfortable. "I feel as though we're complete strangers . . . this is worse than strangers. At least with a stranger there is the possiblity of finding a friend, Laurel. What happened to change you so completely?"

She laughed bitterly. "I was abducted by outlaws. I was the woman of one of them, and I now have a child. It gave me a new perspective on things."

"Not a very pleasant one," Drew said.

"No, not very pleasant."

"You're making this difficult if not impossible. How am I supposed to talk to you with you answering like this? I feel like an inquisitor."

"I told you I have nothing to say, Drew. I don't want to talk to you about anything. I'm here because you've insisted. I can't keep you away from my door, but I don't have to talk."

"Nathaniel may be my son!"

"*May be,* not is!"

"All right, granted, but that still doesn't change anything. I love, you, Laurel."

She turned to him, her face a mask of anger and hurt. "You don't even know me! As you said, we're less than strangers, and it's true. I'm not the same woman I was before. I know things . . . I know . . ." she stumbled over the words. "We cannot go back to the way we were then."

"I don't want to go back, Laurel."

She laughed bitterly. "You want to go on with another man's whore and a bastard for a son? Is that what you call love?"

Drew looked away. "I don't call it that, or feel it." He was quiet for a time, then spoke again. "I believe Nathaniel is my son, and that we belong together."

36

During the second half of 1769 the political unrest in South Carolina continued to grow. The Regulators actively sought out the low people and made it their business to ensure that all men of the area were diligent workers, even if that meant they had to flog them to it. Slowly the rift between authorized government and the headstrong vigilantes grew. Several Regulators had been put in jail and languished there. Lawsuits were cropping up from many incidents as the victims of the Regulators fought back. But beyond the discord that raged between the Upcountrymen and the Lowcountry government, a new unrest was gathering force. The Lowlanders were beginning to talk of rights—English rights, and the means by which Parliament was trespassing on those rights.

Bart Coleman, John Haynes and several other of Drew's friends were in the forefront of Regulator activity and excited about the unrest in the Lowlands.

"My God, Drew, they sound jes' like we did in the beginnin', an' the damned fools don't even know it." Bart slapped his hand against his knee, then nudged John Haynes. "Tell him, John."

John shrugged and moved a few steps away from Bart's lethal elbow. "You tol' him enough. When you gonna start ridin' with us agin, Drew? It ain't the same without you."

"We need all us together," Bart added. "We was the best unit in the Regulators. You an' me an' John an' Will an' Rob . . . nobody could outride or outshoot us. Nobody! Remember that first time we all were together, chasin' down Govey Black an' his gang? We was *sooo* green! Man! Seems like a long time, don't it? Sure have been some changes hereabouts."

"So you gonna ride with us agin?" John asked. "Why'd you stop, anyway? Some say you don't like our methods anymore. You ain't turnin' on us, are you, Drew?"

"No, I'm not turning on you, John, but it's true. I don't like riding around the countryside chasing down low people. It seems like an awful waste of time to me."

"We got us a work force by doin' it," Bart said. "You know how hard it is to fin' a man to work the fields. We got 'em now; never been this good before."

"But it does the Regulator movement no good. Lawsuits abound, some of our men are in jail, and to some degree it violates the same rights we organized to preserve. Where are the courts the low people can go to?"

Bart laughed. "We're their court, and their jury, and their sentencers."

"And that's justice?" Drew asked.

"It's as just as their thievin', stealin', no-count ways is. We don' have the problems we used to have."

"Then you ain't gonna be with us no more," John said. "Sorry to hear that, Drew. We need cool heads, an' that you got."

"I didn't say that, John. I haven't turned my back on the Regulators, but I won't be riding for the sake of riding anymore."

"Well, now," Bart said pugnaciously. "What makes you think we want someone who's gonna pick an' choose which detail he'll take? We allus shared the good with the bad."

Drew shrugged. "Maybe I won't be wanted, Bart, but that's the way it is."

"If you ask me, all this hasn't got so much to do with you likin' or dislikin' what we're doin'. I heard Laurel Boggs showed up back home with an Indian an' a papoose in tow. Couldn't be you're off ridin' after skirt instead o' shirkers, could it?"

Drew said nothing.

"Awww, let him be. He tol' us his feelin's on things, Bart. Let it drop," John said.

Drew looked gratefully at John. "Thanks, John. I'll be around, and you can count on me."

Bart put out his hand. "No hard feelin's, Drew. You know me, I'm allus shootin' off my mouth when I oughtn't. I don' mean mos' of it

. . . I jes' miss havin' you by my side."

As Drew watched them leave, anger swept through him. Bart had come too close to the truth when he said he was riding after skirts. He spent day and night thinking about Laurel and the child, yet they had not come to any agreement.

He went quickly to the stables, mounted his horse and rode harder than usual to the Boggs house. "Tell Laurel to come out here now, Mrs. Boggs," he said.

"Well, now, doesn't seem like my daughter wants to see you, Mr. Manning. Whyn't you go pesterin' after someone else?"

"Either you get her or I'm coming in to get her myself."

Mathilda backed up a step. "No need to get all riled. I'm goin', I'm goin'." She turned slightly, still holding onto the door as though he might charge forward if she didn't bar the way. "Laurel! Laurel, caller fer you. Better come. Laurel!"

Drew moved impatiently away from the door. He reached down and pulled a piece of long grass and stuck the end in his mouth. Mathilda stood watching anxiously.

"She's tendin' the baby," she offered, then tried to fill the ensuing silence. "I called her, but she takes good care o' that baby. Spends a lot o' time, though. Don't think he needs all that time." Nervously she looked behind her. "Laurel! Come on out here!"

Laurel stepped out of the house and onto the stoop. He put his hands out for the baby, and without comment she handed Nathaniel to Drew. She followed his lead. Drew walked toward the woods to the spot they had gone the first time he'd tried to talk to her.

"There's a home for you and him waiting up at Cherokee, Laurel. It has three rooms now, and I plan to start the main house yet this summer—if you and Nathaniel are there to fill it. Will you be?"

Laurel sat quietly, her hands in her lap. The silence dragged on. She could feel him looking at her. Suddenly she put her hands over her face and began to cry. "Why are you doing this, Drew? Why won't you just leave me alone?"

He put his arm around her and pulled her close to him. She tensed but did not pull away. "My God, Laurel, I don't want to leave you alone! I want you with me."

She began to cry harder. Drew didn't know what to do with her. The baby sat on the ground, his small chest heaving in preparation to cry too. His eyes were big and dark as he looked at his mother. Drew scooped him up in one arm and frantically patted Laurel with his other hand.

"Laurel, please," he said softly, "I'm sorry. I didn't mean to make you cry like this . . . I—"

"Oh, yes, you did!" she sobbed. "You've been after me ever since you found out I was back. I didn't want to think about us or the house at Cherokee or anything about us. I was doing fine . . . I was taking care of the baby and I felt good until you came 'round pesterin' me, wantin' to dig out of me all my feelings."

He turned her face toward him. "I have to know. You must understand that. It isn't just your life, Laurel. All my plans are wrapped up in you. I wanted you to be my wife. I want you to be my wife now. By now I thought we'd have a house, and I'd have my first tobacco field ready to be harvested soon, and . . ." he looked at Nathaniel, "a child like this running around our front room, and maybe another on the way."

She looked at him with pleading eyes. "But everything has changed, Drew. Nothing is like we planned it. You can't have someone like me for a wife, and . . . and Nathaniel—people would never accept him. They'd look at me and at him and always wonder if he was Albee's child. And they'd call you a fool. You know what people say about women like me. Once a taste of evil, always drawn to it. I wanted to be someone, someone special."

"You are someone special to me, Laurel. You always have been."

"No. I mean really—to everyone. I wanted to be able to hold my head up and be proud of being Mrs. Manning. I thought I'd never have to feel gratitude that someone would have me as his wife . . . I even thought I could make you proud that I was the one you had married. Now I'd always be an object of suspicion, and you of pity . . . and I don't even know what they would say or do with Nathaniel."

"Do you think it will be better on your own, with no man?"

"No. It will be just as bad, maybe worse, but at least Nathaniel will be able to understand later on. He will clearly be . . . no one will expect him to be anything, coming about as he did. If we were with you, Nathaniel would look upon himself as your son, he'd know you as his father, and he'd never understand why people talked of him as they will or treated him as though he were something less than you. And if we had other children, he'd always be singled out. We're better off alone, Drew."

"Is that the way you want it?"

"No, but that is best. I can't change what's happened, and I am trying to learn to accept things as they now are."

"As soon as people know you, they'll understand. You have to give them a chance, Laurel."

The tears streamed down her face again. "Oh, Drew, you know so much, but sometimes I think you know nothing. People always make excuses for those they know, but I can never know all the people in Camden, and what of Charles Town? Those who don't know me will always judge; they will always look for someone to talk about. That is the way of people. You are a Manning and perhaps have never experienced it, but I was born a Boggs and have heard it all my life. I know how people are."

Drew listened to her. And he admitted to himself that she was right. People were eager to find someone to talk about, someone to condemn because evil was recognizable and definable in that person. He could recall from the days he had had tutors the philosophers he had read. So many of them had said that we recognized goodness only because we could recognize evil. Perhaps that was at the heart of what Laurel meant. If a finger could be pointed at her, then those who pointed could identify what they thought was their own goodness in contrast to what they assumed was evil in her.

"And what of me?"

"What about you?"

"Am I, too, supposed to walk away from you? Do I just forget you and my son?"

"He's not your son!"

"He is my son! I'll always think of him as my son, and it doesn't matter that it can't be proved."

"Oh, Drew, we're going around and around in circles. This is no good. I feel one way and you another."

"Then listen to me. At least try it my way. Let me take care of you and the child."

"You have heard nothing I've said," Laurel said.

"I've heard everything," Drew said, and pulled her close to him again. Nathaniel squirmed between them, and Drew put the child back on the ground in the soft pine. "What you have told me may all be true, but it isn't right, and it is trying to foretell the future, and that is not right, either. The future is not to be foretold, it is to be created—by us."

Laurel looked at him, her eyes still moist and filled with tears. "I wish it were so," she whispered.

"Make it so!"

"I don't know . . . I don't think I can. I'm frightened, Drew. I can't give in to thoughts like these. This is why I didn't want to talk to you. I knew you'd do this to me. I have to put these things away from me." She paused, and he took her in his arms and kissed her softly on the lips. She turned her head from him. He felt more than heard her ask him not to confuse her more. "I can't stop," he said. "One of us must have his way, and the other will lose. I can't allow it to be me, Laurel. I've come too far. I want you and the child with me. Tell me you'll at least see me willingly."

She still said nothing, but he could see in her eyes that he had won. He turned his attention to Nathaniel, who had crept several feet away from them and was busily teething on a pine branch. He had sticky sap smeared all over his cheeks and hands and was making a terrible face at the taste of resin.

Drew picked him up and wiped his mouth with his handkerchief. He laughed and looked back at Laurel. "Come on, let's take him down to the stream and let him wash the taste from his mouth."

She got up and walked by Drew's side. She felt differently walking beside him now. She had known to avoid this kind of talk with him. He had done what she feared most. He had shattered her resistance and had made a place at his side for her.

Drew knelt at the side of the stream, dipped his handkerchief into the water and let Nathaniel suck the liquid from it. Laurel stood back and watched him with the child. Nothing seemed real. This was what she had dreamed of so many times and what she had cried over when she was with Albee and thought it was lost to her forever. Now she was standing right next to a stream not a mile from her home, watching Drew take care of her child, possibly their child. For a moment hope flared in her. Perhaps Drew was right. Perhaps they could be together and live as though none of last summer had happened. Perhaps.

37

Laurel was happy, if still unsure of herself, and her joy was reflected in the harmony and accord that came to the Boggs household. Ben and Star Dancer were little seen, and those times they were a part of the family, they were constantly in each other's company. Laurel had noticed and made mention of it to Drew.

"Star Dancer has more sense than you," he said, not unkindly. "She would have as much difficulty with the opinions of others as you think you would have."

"Nothing has been said yet. I may not even be correct in thinking they are in love, and it is different with Star Dancer, in any case. No one expects anything from Ben."

Drew frowned at her. "What does that mean? Because people expect much from me, I am not permitted to marry the woman of my choice? Or that Ben, because nothing is expected, need not pay heed to what the rest of our society values? Certainly you can't hold a view like that."

Laurel looked away from him. "But I do. It may not be as things ought to be, but they are that way, Drew. You are free to do and say many things Ben could never say or do because you were born a Manning, and yet there are many things Ben is free to do and say that you may not because he was born a Boggs. Whether we like it or not, that is the way the world is."

Drew said nothing for a long time. Sometimes she made him feel hopeless and helpless. This was one of them, and he didn't like the feeling. Before, it had seemed that together they could do anything, achieve whatever goals they had set. They had seemed to be of one mind and heart and courage. Now, whatever he said, she seemed to have an impediment to offer. It wasn't that what she said wasn't true or that he wasn't aware of such things, but her objections were the kind that impeded a man from going forward. No progress could be made if great attention and obedience was given to such unwritten laws. Once more Gwynne came unbidden to mind. She would note the truth but not offer the impediment. Quickly he changed the direction of his thinking. He couldn't think of Gwynne now.

He looked at Laurel. She was lovely. The sun lit the soft down on her face and made her skin glow. Her long, waving hair glowed golden and brown, and her eyes were clear and blue. He wanted her, but did he love her? He had repeated to her that he wanted her as his wife, and yet something had changed. He no longer needed her as he had before she had been taken by the outlaws. This was a realization he had recently come to and had avoided thinking of too deeply. He didn't want to confront that fact yet, nor did he want to reckon with the fact that Gwynne was too often in his thoughts.

He finally looked at Laurel again. "It doesn't matter if what you say is true or not. We will do what is best for us regardless. We don't live with society in our home. There we live unto ourselves, not with the rules or expectations of anyone else." He paused for a moment, then went on. "I want my son, Laurel."

"Drew, please, let's not go through that again. I don't want to talk about something for which I have no answer."

"I don't want your damned answers! I want my son. Why is that so difficult for you to understand? Why can't you see I don't need your answer? I feel he is mine, and I love him."

"I can't believe that this altruistic feeling of yours will last indefinitely. You'll have to pardon me if I sound unfeeling or cold, but I have learned it isn't wise to count on the goodwill of people or expectations that may be impossible to meet even if we wish we could."

"I'll never argue again that you have changed. You have," Drew said coldly, and walked away from her.

That evening when Star Dancer and Ben returned to the house, they proudly displayed a line of fat fish caught in the mountain stream. Star Dancer insisted on cooking them outside over hot coals. Drew went with her to dig the pit and collect rocks.

For a while Star Dancer worked in silence, then she looked at Drew. "She has tried your patience."

"Yes, she has tried my patience. If you are her friend, you'll tell her that all men are not the same. That boy is my son, and I don't care about her uncertainties. I want the child. And if it comes to a choice between her and the child—I shall have my son."

Star Dancer looked down, attending to the setting of the logs and rocks, a smile on her face. She had been right about the man Drew. She had told Laurel she should have faith in his love for his son. He would be strong and take care of both of them.

Soon the others came from the house and joined Drew and Star Dancer. The fish crackled on the hot coals, and the Boggses gathered around, watching as though some mighty show were being performed before their eyes. Ben began to sing, and soon all had joined in. They ate happily, each of them relishing the taste of the fresh fish, and Star Dancer was complimented profusely for her catch.

"Wait a minute here," Ben protested. "I had something to do with this. I caught some of these fish. She didn't do it all."

"How come we never had dinners like this before she came?" Mandy piped up.

"Mebbe I wasn't of a mind to go fishin' then," Ben said, grinning. He walked over to Star Dancer and sat down beside her, taking her hand in his. "How'd you all like to have dinners like this more often?"

He delighted in the chorus of yeas. "Well, you unnerstan' I'd need a helper. So Star Dancer an' me decided we'd see Reverend Fowler an' make ourselves Mr. and Mrs. Boggs."

"Did ya hear that, Harley? Ben's gettin' married! The first of our brood's gettin' married." Mathilda turned, laughing, to Laurel. "He's gonna git married ahead o' you, an' you the eldes', Laurel. What do you think o' that?"

Laurel had stood with her mouth open. She had expected something of the sort, and still she was surprised when it came. She burst into a smile, and went to her brother and Star Dancer, putting an arm around both of them. "I'm so happy for you. Are we going to have a wedding?"

Ben blushed. "Naaw, we though we'd jes' go see Reverend Fowler an' git it done an' over with."

"And then we can have a party back here." Laurel looked at her mother. "We could, couldn't we, Mama?"

"It'd surely be nice," Mathilda said.

"Then we'll have a wedding!" Laurel cried. "A real wedding! That's another first for the Boggses."

When she came back to sit beside Drew, he said softly, "We could make it two weddings in one day."

"No," she whispered. "Don't say anything . . . not yet . . ."

Mathilda had leaned closer to the two of them. "That sounds like a good idea to me. What's holdin' you back, Laurel? When the man's offerin', seems only fittin' you should accept." She began to giggle, her eyes on Drew as though they shared a secret.

Drew smiled weakly at her and put his arm protectively around Laurel. "How about going for a walk in the moonlight?" he asked her.

Without answering, she got up and began to walk from the fire. As soon as they were alone, she turned on him. "I've told you to say nothing in front of my mother! Why can't you ever do as I ask?"

"I'm sorry. I wasn't thinking about her; that's why I asked if you'd like to walk. I thought you'd want to avoid anything further."

"The harm is already done," Laurel said nastily.

"What harm? She is difficult, but what is she doing, Laurel? When we marry, she will have to know. I don't see the point in hiding something that is fairly obvious anyway. She knows why I come here. She knows how I feel about you."

"I can't explain . . . she . . . she twists things."

"If you said yes to me, we'd be living at Cherokee the day following the wedding. You'd need to hide nothing then."

"You don't know my mother, Drew," Laurel said with great import, but she didn't know how to explain what she was trying to say.

She wished that he were around to hear Mathilda later that week, when she came at Laurel, her face ugly with bitterness and her mouth full of venom. "What's the matter with you? I heard you talkin' to him. You near as tol' him to git away from you. You lissen to me good, girl, 'cause I'm tired o' prettyin' 'roun' with you. I jes' about wore myself out with all this smilin' an' courtesyin'. That man wants you, an' you cozy up to him ever chancet you git. Ain't many men be willin' to take soiled goods like you, an' you got one that's got money to boot. You tell him you'll marry him fas' as the preacher kin say the words over you."

"I'm not going to talk to you about it, Mama."

"No, you ain't, I'm doin' the talkin'. Your pa ain't ever been worth nothin' an' he ain't never gonna be. He cain't work and he cain't think good. Somebody's got to look out fer us. You're the only one o' my brood worth anythin', an' the only one got a chancet to put us on Easy Street. You're gonna do it. Don't cost you nothin'. You git a husban' an' give your family a good life. You owe us, Laurel, an' I want it from you. Nex' time that man comes 'roun', you slither all over him till he's ameltin' from the heat, y'hear?"

Laurel was standoffish the next time Drew was there with her family. She was jittery and uncomfortable all evening long, refusing to sit beside him, or go for a walk after supper. Mathilda glared at her whenever she thought Drew wasn't looking, and then she tried to compensate for her daughter's coldness. "Laurel jes' talks about you all the time, Drew. Why, we cain't git a word in edgewise fer her jabberin' about all the plans you two have. Looks to me like she's real anxious to be with you permanent. Jes' look at her . . . cain't sit still a minute fer bein' jittery that we's all here with you all." She nudged her husband. "Harley, looks like you an' me an' the younguns oughtta go to bed an' let these two be alone." Harley scratched his belly and looked disinclined to move, so Mathilda grabbed him by the arm, giving him a mighty tug. The children ran for the loft.

Laurel sat bleakly in the nearly empty room. Her shoulders slumped, and she said nothing.

Drew also sat quiet. He didn't know what to say. He no longer knew what to do. When he could catch her eye, he motioned silently to the door. She nodded, and they walked outside to the warm night.

He looked up at the night sky and appreciated more than usual the clearness of the air, the beauty of the night. He still didn't know what to say. There was no use telling her he was sorry it had happened or that he understood. He wasn't sorry because he thought it was Laurel's fault that they were in the situation they were, and he did not understand. She said she loved him, but there were other things to consider. None of it made sense to him. He might have told her he was no longer sure he loved her but wanted to marry her nonetheless, and it didn't matter that there were other things to consider. Nothing made sense—not him, not her, nothing.

"You're sick of them, aren't you?" she asked quietly, not looking at him.

"Is that what you're trying to accomplish? Are you trying to demonstrate to me what a difference there is in our backgrounds, so that I will see we could never marry?"

"I don't know. Maybe it's me I'm trying to show."

"Then why do you prolong this? I told you we'd be at Cherokee. There's no need for any more evenings like this one. I'm going to Cherokee tonight. You can join me there, or I will see you the day of Ben's wedding."

She sat outside long after he had left. She knew Drew didn't understand her family, especially not Mathilda. He thought it was courage she was lacking, and perhaps it was, but there was also a hidden bondage to a heritage he would never see or understand. Mathilda saw in him a way to live without working. Drew would support the entire Boggs family, and that need would grow and the demands would grow. She knew Mathilda. Once Mathilda had food on her table, she'd want a better home, and better furnishings, and better clothes, and soon it would be a carriage, for the mother-in-law of Andrew Manning couldn't be seen in town on foot. Whatever Harley's excesses were, she'd expect Drew to handle the consequences. No matter how long she thought, she could continue with the list of demands she knew would come. She could walk away from her family, but what Drew couldn't understand was that Mathilda would always follow. She was also aware that Drew no longer felt about her as he once had. Some of his coolness came from the circumstances in which they now found themselves, but it went deeper than that.

She stared out at the darkness and found that it matched the darkness within her.

38

Drew returned to Cherokee and tried to assuage his restless dissatis-faction in work. He cleared a new field, struggling with stumps and sawing the logs into long, neatly hewn lengths suitable for building another room on his house. He hadn't really been thinking about building another room on the small house. It wasn't necessary. If he and Laurel lived there, he'd begin immediately on building what would be the manor house. They would not use this cabin for any length of time. It would become his foreman's house, a place only to house hired help when the time came. Four rooms were not neces-sary, he thought as he continued working on the logs like a man possessed.

By the time Star Dancer and Ben's wedding was to take place, Drew had the new room under roof. With some regret he put down his tools and prepared to return to the Camden area for the wed-ding. He had not been to the Boggses' house since the night he had left Laurel sitting morosely in the front yard. He had thought often of visiting but never had, and he admitted readily to himself that the greatest reason for going there was to see the child. The boy gave him a sense of permanence and continuity at a time when he felt his whole world was crumbling about him.

The talk coming back from Charles Town had become more and more ominous. The number of men who talked of breaking free of England was increasing daily, and even those who had no wish to be independent spoke critically of England's highhanded and cavalier manner of treating the individual English subject's rights.

He had received a letter from Elizabeth at the beginning of

August. She had had many words of caution and advice for him, as well as information. The letter more than anything else warned him to be prepared for change. He trusted his grandmother completely and respected her ability to read the signs of the times far better than most of the men he knew. Her letter was already worn and ragged, he had read it so often.

"My dear Drew," Elizabeth had begun, and he could hear her voice coming through the fine handwriting.

> The colonies of New England keep sending missives to our people. There is barely a day that the *Gazette* does not publish something of their activities and complaints against the English Parliament, usually with some substance. However, what is becoming apparent to us and is being more frequently mentioned by the men who gather under the Liberty Tree is that the despotism of which they complain is of an implied nature, while those of us who inhabit the Upcountry are experiencing it in fact. I suppose this is a form of apology, Drew; we should have listened to you years ago. You and your Regulators were telling us of things to come. I fear we are now in the midst of conditions that may well lead to the colonies seeking independence.
>
> Already we have signs that action is to replace talk in the colonies. On the twenty-eighth of last month nonimportation resolutions were agreed upon and accepted. Only eight days later the *Gazette* published the import figures. This was not to be merely another threat, we all realized. The merchants had to agree to observe the resolutions. On the twenty-second of July our suspicions were confirmed. Under the Liberty Tree a meeting of the committees was held. The merchants, the planters and the mechanics were each represented by thirteen men. A nonimportation agreement forbidding the import of many items from England, Holland and other places was agreed upon.
>
> Specifically there will be no importation of slaves. The Lord does work in mysterious ways. We are thankful for the curtailing of this dreadful traffic in slaves. So many times in the past we have tried to prevent such traffic, and here, now, on the brink of war, it has been accomplished.

My purpose in writing to you is not merely to keep you abreast of the news in Charles Town but to beg you to look deeply into your own heart and know what you believe and to what you will be committed in the months and perhaps years to come. Aside from the events that are taking place daily, a more significant and perhaps dangerous trend is developing. One can walk down any street in Charles Town, and in one house the family is staunchly Tory. In the next house a family of Whigs live, and often in the same house there is a great division of feeling and belief among the members of the family. Ours is no longer the only one so afflicted.

I believe we shall come to separation with England, and that most likely will mean we fight a war. Should that come to pass, Drew, there will be an awful rift among families. Friends we have known from childhood will become our enemies overnight. I fear for our family. I believe you would fight for independence. Think carefully, Drew; be certain you wish to take up arms against your father and brother, for you would have to do so.

I beg your pardon for writing such a cheerless letter, but I felt it was a necessary one. I have saved my one piece of good news until last, and even that I am not sure will bring you joy. Gwynne writes to me often, never failing to inquire about you and send you her warmest regards. You are ever on her mind. As always I long to see you. Please apprise me of your next planned visit to Charles Town.

At the bottom was her name, written in full. He ran his finger across the writing. She was a rare woman.

When he had first read the letter, he had been tempted to jump astride his horse and ride directly to Charles Town, leaving all other concerns behind. He had not. In a cooler moment he took her advice and began to think practically about what a war for independence from England would mean. It would not be a ride with the Regulators. It would change his life and that of his children, even of Nathaniel's children. Elizabeth was correct; the time had come for him to find what he believed to the point of battle. It was one thing to speak an opinion and quite another to say one was willing to stake one's life and future on that belief. He was relieved that he still had time and edgy that he did not know how much time. Was it a week, a month, a year?

He was anxious to return to Charles Town, and quite suddenly his thoughts went to Gwynne. She thought about him and he of her. She was in England with the Mitchell family. Would she ever come home? Or would she stay, leaving him and all that represented a discontented colony behind? And did it matter, for his life was already committed to another woman and a child.

Ben's wedding took place in mid-August, 1769. The small family group stood in the tiny main room of the Boggses' cabin. The Reverend Fowler stood before his small community, his face severe, his voice deliberately made as deep as he could manage to indicate the gravity of the step Star Dancer and Ben were taking. As always, he took advantage of his captive audience to speak at length. Even here, in this setting so far removed from Charles Town and politics, the ideas of rights and independence crept into the text. "A man cleaves to his wife, and shall bear fruit for the future," Fowler said, his chin nearly swallowed by his collar in an attempt to make his voice still deeper, "yet his duty to God and country must never be forgotten. Each of us, insignificant as we may be, has his role in the scheme of God's world. The protection of those rights God has given is left to us! We must not fail. A man is bound by all that is holy to preserve that which the Creator has given. A woman is beholden to support and aid her man in that mission. Today we have united in marriage one of God's warrior for justice, with the woman who shall nurture and be his helpmeet in all that mission may entail. . . ."

Drew lost the thread of Fowler's words after that. He was thinking of Elizabeth, his wise and surprisingly worldly grandmother. There was a time when he had thought Laurel would be for him what Elizabeth had been for his grandfather. He no longer held that illusion. He snapped to attention when Mathilda let out a cry as Reverend Fowler proclaimed Star Dancer and Ben husband and wife. He clapped and laughed with the others as Star Dancer shyly tried to hide her face in the shoulder of her new husband.

Harley, feeling good for once, and the center of attention, brought out his hidden cache of home brew. The entire Boggs family went to work. Laurel brought out sweet cakes she had baked, and

Mathilda mustered up the energy to place cups and other crockery on the table for those who did not wish to drink from Harley's jugs. The merrymaking continued throughout the afternoon, getting more boisterous as the home brew disappeared.

At twilight, Ben and Star Dancer slipped out the door and into the waiting packed wagon in front of the house. At Star Dancer's insistence, they were going to her country before they settled on the land they had claimed but had yet to clear.

Star Dancer looked over to see Drew standing on the stoop, watching them. In his arms he held Nathaniel. She couldn't resist and jumped from the wagon to hold the child and kiss him good-bye.

"You must take good care of him while I am away," she said.

Drew leaned over and kissed her on the cheek. "You have no cause to worry about Nathaniel. I will watch over him. When you get back, Ben, we'll get to work on that cabin of yours."

Ben smiled gratefully. "I sure do appreciate it, Drew. You're a good friend." He blushed profusely as he continued, "Mebbe soon we'll be brothers . . . I'd sure be proud o' that." He hurriedly made himself busy helping Star Dancer onto the wagon. He waved a quick good-bye and laid the whip across the oxen's backs. The creaky old farm wagon groaned into motion and rolled off across the uneven meadowland.

"Are they gone?" Laurel asked from behind him.

"Yes, they just left. Why don't you come outside—it's nice out here."

She came to stand beside him. She patted the side of the baby's cheek, then watched his small, chubby fingers curl around hers. "I'm very happy for them. I didn't think Ben would marry—not after his—his accident. Star Dancer will take good care of him."

"They seem very happy," Drew said. "I think she will do much more than just take good care of him."

Laurel smiled. "Yes, you're probably right. I wonder what it will be like a year from now."

Drew grinned at her and gave Nathaniel a chuck under the chin. "This little fellow may have his first cousin."

"Oh, I wish!" Laurel said passionately, then looked at Drew. "Do you know what I have come to realize? I am afraid of good things. I was listening to Reverend Fowler today talk of what a husband must do, and the duties of a wife, and the future Ben and Star Dancer will make together, and I was thinking I couldn't do that. I was thinking that if I tried, it would all be taken away from me. I was only thinking and I was afraid."

Drew shifted Nathaniel to the side of his hip and pulled Laurel close to him, his face in her hair. It was thick and soft and clean, smelling of fresh soap and herbs. "The fear will go as soon as you begin living with hope and expectation of good again. You'll lose that feeling, Laurel."

"Can I believe that?" she asked into his shirt front. "I want it to be like that, Drew; I really do. I'm just so afraid to believe it. Something will happen . . . it always does."

"No, trust life, Laurel, trust me. We'll work it all out. I'll make Cherokee as safe as a fort for you and Nathaniel. We can have a good life, but you have to . . . you have to want it, be an active part of it. I can't give it to you. You must take it in both your hands and make of it what you want."

"You know what I want, what I've wanted ever since I met you," Laurel murmured and turned her head up to him, her lips parted, her eyes closed.

Drew kissed her and tried holding her closer, which proved impossible with Nathaniel in his other arm. He kissed her again, then rested his head against her hair. "Take it, Laurel. Come with me to Cherokee."

"Yes," she whispered, and felt the immediate tightening in her stomach she had had for so long now whenever she dared dream of a better life. "Yes," she said, stronger.

They went inside and put Nathaniel into his crib, then went back outside. They talked as they hadn't since before she had been captured. She promised to come with him as soon as he was ready.

"It will be before fall is over. The new room will be a kitchen. As soon as the furnishings arrive from Charles Town, you and Nathaniel will move in."

"When will we be married?" she asked. Then the fear returned. She looked up at him. "Will we be married, Drew?"

"Of course we'll be married . . ." he paused, not knowing how to say what he wanted to say. Laurel waited for a moment, and Drew wiped his hand across his mouth. "We'll be married," he repeated.

"But . . ." Laurel prompted. "You have something else on your mind. What is it?"

"Nothing of importance," he said and smiled at her.

She looked away from him. "You don't want to be married as Ben was today, with my father drunk and my mother making crude jokes."

"I told you it was of no importance. All that matters is that we get married, go to Cherokee and begin to live as we wish. Nathaniel is going to need a little brother to play with."

She smiled. "A brother?"

He nipped at her ear. "Sisters can come later."

When she went into the house that night, she was happier than she could remember. She went to sleep thinking of Cherokee. She hadn't seen it in over a year and had never seen the new room. A four-room house with a loft. That was larger than what her parents had now. She smiled in the darkness, a trace of the old Laurel shining in her eyes. "Maybe I'll be somebody after all. Can't hold all the Boggses down." Quite suddenly she thought of Mary. She could almost hear her younger sister's voice adoringly saying, "You'll do it, Laurel. You always make everything special."

39

During the next few days Drew and Laurel made plans and talked about their future together. When the excitement and relief of having found themselves once again in accord waned, practicality once more became their main interest. For the time being Drew would return to Cherokee, prepare the house, build the additional room and outbuildings and, most important of all, see to the fields. Too often they thought of Cherokee in terms of the future. In fact, it was a plantation in name only. The fields were not prepared to produce the volume of tobacco that was necessary to secure financial solvency for the coming year. Without that income they would not survive. Drew and Ned had a monumental task before them to prepare Cherokee to bear the burden of the young Manning family in years to come, before Drew dared place all their hopes and reliance on it.

Laurel, too, had an enormous task before her. From her parents' house she would have to think about and purchase or make all the things they would need to live through the fall and winter to come. There was bed ticking and quilts and blankets, clothes for Nathaniel and herself and shirts for Drew, all of which meant hours and hours of stitchery. There were household goods to be ordered and delivered. The list of necessities was endless, and they had never thought of them before because they had always relied upon Drew's family to provide whatever was needed, but that family was no longer there for them, and everything they would have to begin life at Cherokee would come from their own labors or from the suppliers in Camden.

A week after Drew left for Cherokee, Laurel took Nathaniel and went to visit Ben and Star Dancer on the land they had claimed and were clearing. Ben proudly greeted her as she drove up in the cart Drew had left for her to use.

"Jes' look at this, Laurel," he said, gesturing toward his small house. "Our neighbors done this fer us. They all come over one day fer rail splittin', an' 'fore I knew it Star Dancer an' me was in a house with a roof over our heads an' had a pen fer our cow. They even give us a start with a ewe an' a ram. Ain't that the darnedest thing ever? Nobody ever did that fer Pa."

Laurel hugged him. "They like you, Ben. People sense the good heart in you. They know you'll work this place and have something good here."

Ben's smile grew broader. "You think that's it? Mebbe I better start some learnin'. Sure be nice t'be somebody folks looked up to. A man gets mighty tired allus bein' at the bottom o' the heap."

"Well, you aren't anymore." She looked around. "Where's Star Dancer?"

The Indian girl came out of the cabin. "I fixed a place for young Nathaniel Dancer." Her arms were out for the child as she neared the cart.

Star Dancer took the baby, and Ben helped Laurel down from the cart with her bag.

Once inside and seated at Ben's table, she told them of her coming marriage. "You were right all along, Star Dancer. He doesn't pity me, and he isn't marrying me out of obligation. He won't stay away no matter what I do." She smiled at them, then grew serious. She was no longer aware of Ben but looking intently at Star Dancer. "There is something different, though, Star Dancer. I can feel it in him. He is not the same, and I am not so sure he cares for me now as he did before. Did your guide tell you anything about that?"

Star Dancer shook her head but said nothing.

Laurel thought for a moment, a frown persisting on her face. "I . . . I am afraid sometimes that he is marrying me because of Nathaniel. I know that is nonsense . . . men don't have such feelings for children . . . that's a woman's thought, but sometimes it seems that way to me." She suddenly cheered up, as though she had thrown off her concern. "Well, we will be with each other for life, and there will be many more children, I hope, and Nathaniel will blend in with the others. Perhaps we will all be able to forget his origins."

"Sure," Ben said. "Give a man half a dozen younguns an' he cain't even keep their names straight. There ain't nothin' fer you to worry about."

She stayed with her brother and Star Dancer for two weeks. As she began her journey back to her family home, she tried to imagine what Drew would be doing at Cherokee. She imagined him felling trees, clearing fields, working on their house. Her daydreaming made the trip home easy.

Fall blazed with unusual beauty that year, and Drew stood on the stoop of his house, looking out across the acres of Cherokee. To the west the mountains rose steeply, carving a chunk out of the blue and white-clouded sky. The trees to the north were thick with red and brown and golden leaves, the pines forming a mighty dark green curtain against which all else flamed in brilliant glory.

Nathaniel would celebrate his first birthday at Cherokee and would never remember that it had not always been his home. Drew looked to the south at the plowed but uncultivated fields. A feeling of mild remorse came with the sight. He had done nothing this year with the land other than clear it. In the field nearest the house was a small stand of white corn, nearly gone now, and sweet potatoes that would be ready for digging by the time Laurel would arrive. In the pen were two fat hogs he had chased out of the woods and kept for hog-killing time. He'd have a smokehouse ready by then, and he and Laurel would see to a meat supply for the winter together. He looked again at the corn patch and got up, wheelbarrow with him, to collect the ripe ears still left on the stalk. He'd get those to soaking for hominy. His mother was known for making the best hominy around. She had the same touch with that as he had with the indigo. He smiled as he thought of the similarities. Both of them knew how strong to make their solution and sensed when the exact right time to stop came. She probably would have made a great planter. Arthur should ask for her help. He'd do better with Manning.

He hadn't gone home for the harvest this year. Arthur hadn't asked him to. It was the first time since the Mannings had come to the Upcountry that he hadn't at least participated in the growing and harvesting of Manning indigo. He wouldn't be leading the wagon train to Charles Town, either. Arthur would take charge alone this year.

Drew moved methodically through the rows of corn, taking the remaining ears and placing them in the barrow. Until today he hadn't thought a great deal about how radically his life had changed in the last two years. He was going to miss this trip to Charles Town. He wondered if Gwynne had come back from England. He still thought of her too often and in the wrong way. He wanted to see his grandmother and have a long talk with her. He even found he was terribly thirsty for a cold beer at Dillon's Tavern with his cousins. He had been separated from his family for a long time now, and the ache didn't lessen; it grew. Only through Nathaniel did he have a sense of his own continuity; of belonging.

As if memories of pleasant days lost reminded him, Drew began to move faster. He quickly finished with the corn and went back out to the woods and nearby swampy area, collecting roots, barks and leaves that Laurel would use for dye. He felt as though he were just awakening from a long night's sleep and found that he had an enormous day's work before him. He hadn't realized how much he had let go untended this year until now, as he was thinking about Laurel and Nathaniel living in the house.

He still had time in the afternoon to go to the woods to try to gather the forty sheep he had let run. He had found ten of them with the ear notches that marked them as his by the time daylight was giving way. He herded them into their pen and went into the house, cooked a utilitarian meal of pork and roast potatoes and fell asleep.

The entirety of the next week was given over to the sheep. It took him another two days to locate all of them, and not being an accomplished shearer, he managed to shear no more than seven sheep in a day. At the end of the week he stared tiredly at the pile of heavy, greasy wool that lay on his barn floor. He built a huge fire and put the kettles on, watching carefully that the water didn't boil and ruin his wool. He remembered well the quantity of ruined wool he had had from his first experience and wanted no repeat of it. He added the lye soap and washed the greasy oil from it. Batch by batch he took it out and spread it on the warm rocks to dry in the air. Every night he brewed his mountain herb tea, ate dinner and fell into his bed half-asleep before he hit the mattress. Finally he had two big storage bins filled with clean wool waiting to be carded. He stood back, satisfied with his handiwork, a job well done and not needing repetition until next spring.

His last task in preparation for Laurel and Nathaniel's arrival was to bring in the small amount of tobacco he had planted in the first two fields he had cleared. He had not yet settled on the crop he would specialize in. He had planted two varieties of tobacco—a light, sweet variety and a medium-weight tobacco named Pryor. He was leaning toward the Pryor, thinking the sweet was not as well suited to his land. As he moved through the fields, taking the leaves to be hung from the rafters in the tobacco barn, he was aware of how soon he would have to have help. One man could not properly manage more than fifty acres, even with the help of someone like Ned Hart, and if Cherokee was to become a prosperous plantation, over a thousand acres would be in cultivation. The work before him seemed endless as he thought of the building of cabins to house his people and the miles and miles of tobacco he'd oversee. Today it seemed overwhelming to him, but underneath the fatigue was an exhilaration he hadn't felt for a long time.

He wanted his hands in the soil. He liked feeling the sweat roll down the side of his face and body. He liked the fatigue that came at the end of a day, and he liked the days whose labor was so demanding that every sinew, every muscle screamed at the accomplishment of the tasks. He had been born to the elite, but he was a common man. Elizabeth's letter flashed into his mind and with it came the full realization that he was an American. He was not a colonist, not an English subject. The rights he fought for were not those due every Englishman. They were exclusively, uniquely his as an American man. He felt like letting out a war whoop, a victory cry, and did. Like a madman he ran across his fields, shouting and whooping until he was breathless. He fell to the ground and rolled, laughing, feeling free and insane and sure of who he was and what side he'd be on when the war Elizabeth had predicted came about.

At home Laurel knitted, spun wool and prepared the blankets and linens for her new household. Drew had made certain she had a supply of everything she needed, with a surplus for Mathilda's grasping hands. Young Nathaniel had never eaten so well or been dressed so warmly as he was now. At least twice a week Ned Hart stopped by the Boggses' house to see if she needed anything from Camden or Cherokee. He always brought a note for her from Drew, and occasionally a gift.

Laurel's confidence grew. There was never a sign in action, word, gesture or attitude that Ned disapproved of her or of Nathaniel. He always took time to play with the baby and occasionally brought him a toy.

As Laurel thanked Ned for some blocks he had brought, he shrugged. "Drew an' me had nothin' to do of an evenin', so li'l Nathaniel here gits the benefit." He stood back and watched the child pick up the blocks, bang them on the floor and then throw one tentatively, watching in amazement as it bounced. "He sure does like 'em. Makes a man feel like he done somethin' good."

Laurel chatted with him awhile longer, then went to put Nathaniel into his crib for a nap. Ned waved good-bye from the door, promising to stop by in a few days.

He walked down the hill aways to where he had tethered his horse. From the house Mathilda slipped out, edged her way past the door and hurried down the hill after him. "Mr. Hart, Mr. Hart," she called in a hoarse whisper. "Kin I speak with you a minnit?"

Ned turned and smiled. He touched his hat. "Howdy do, Miz Boggs. What kin I do fer you?"

"Well," Mathilda said with a trace of coyness, "seein' as how I'm jes' about kin to Drew Mannin', I was wonderin' iffen you could see fit to bring us some firewood? Harley's back ain't too good sincet them Regulators beat him, an we're runnin' real low. I know Laurel ain't likely to ask fer suchlike, her bein' so humble, but we sure could use it. P'or li'l Nathaniel sure do git col' in the middle o' the night, when we jes' ain't got enough to keep the fire up. Would ya tell Drew fer me?"

Ned nodded, his mouth pressed tight. "I'll bring you some next visit."

Mathilda frowned, biting her lower lip. Then she sighed. "I sure do hope that p'or li'l baby don't take a fever afore you git it here." She looked pleadingly at him. "You couldn't see yere way to bringin' it tomorrah, could you? I sure would hate fer Drew to worry his li'l boy'd sick afore the wood come."

Ned looked hard at the woman, fighting with himself to keep his mouth closed. She was probably not lying about the firewood, and it was probably true the baby would be cold in the night because Harley was too damned lazy to do a lick. He stood for a moment, wanting to tell the woman to kick her lazy husband out into the yard and hand him an ax, but he knew Drew wanted peace at any cost until he could get Laurel and Nathaniel out of the Boggses' house. "I'll bring it tomorrow," he said curtly, and mounted his horse without looking at her again.

He heard her laugh as he rode off. Then she yelled after him, "I sure could use a pair o' good shoes! Tell Drew it don't look right his kin runnin' about near barefoot!"

Laurel noticed none of Mathilda's acquisitions until she began to demand household furnishings. When a chair, a new bed and a mirror of good quality appeared on the back of Ned's wagon one visit, Laurel held her tongue until he had left. As soon as Ned was out of sight, she went to her mother. Mathilda was busy arranging her haul.

"Mama, how much have you been asking Drew to give to you?"

Mathilda looked at her blankly. "I don' know what you're talkin' about. He jes' give me a few things fer the house. They look mighty purty, too."

"You have no right to ask for things."

"'Course I have a right. Mannin's is my kin now—almos'. Ain't fittin' that we should live without nothin' when we got kin that throws out better'n we got."

Laurel closed her eyes. "You didn't buy those shoes like you told me, did you, Mama? You asked Drew for them, didn't you?"

"What if I did?" Mathilda asked. "It don' hurt nobody. What are you squawkin' at me fer?"

"You can't ask these things of Drew, Mama. Please, you can't do this. You'll ruin everything for me."

"He don' care! It ain't nothin' to him. Them Mannin's got cash money peelin' off their wagon wheels. Why, I could live a year on what he loses from holes in his pockets."

"What you're doing is wrong, Mama! You're taking advantage of Drew because of me."

Mathilda put her hands on her hips and looked her daughter over. "You are the mos' ungrateful, selfish thing every birthed. What's wrong with you? You don' wan' your mama to have shoes on her feet? Your daddy ain't good enough to sit in a Mannin' chair that they was throwin' away anyhow?"

"You don't know that, Mama, and that isn't what I mean. I'll help you and Papa whenever I can, but it has to come from my butter and egg money, not from Drew."

"Why? He ain't ever said no to nothin' I asked o' him."

Laurel fought the tears that threatened. "He never will! He'll do for you because of me and Nathaniel, but it is wrong of you to take advantage! Mama, please, I know you understand!"

Mathilda sneered at her. "You're a damned fool. Folks got to look out fer themselves. Drew don' miss none of what I take off him. Till he tells me I cain't have nothin' with his own mouth, I'll keep right on atakin' whatever I kin git, an' that's all to be said. Now git outta my way. I got a min' to take a bath in my new bathingtub. I ain't never bathed in nothin' fancy like that afore."

"Oh, Mama, I know you want nice things. I understand that, I really do, but can't you see what you're doing to me? Please, don't do this! Please!"

"Quit your whinin', girl. Nobody's doin' nothin' to you."

"I'll have to stop you, Mama, if you won't stop asking for gifts on your own. No matter what I have to do, I won't let you and Papa take advantage of Drew like this. I know you. If you get away with it now, you'll never stop."

"You make me want to puke, girl. We're your family. What's so bad about sharin' a li'l o' your bounty with us?"

"It isn't bounty, Mama! It was to be my life . . . my husband . . . my family, not some 'thing' we divvie up."

"I'm gonna take my bath. You kin stay there an' watch iffen you're of a min' to, but I ain't talkin' to you no more." Mathilda loosened her skirt and began to unfasten her bodice. She glanced triumphantly at Laurel sitting listless, head down.

The demands and parade of gifts to Mathilda and Harley continued. Ned dutifully delivered everything she asked for because those were the orders Drew had given him, but he no longer took the time to come into the house or visit with Laurel, and he did not make toys for Nathaniel. He behaved as any delivery man might, politely tipping his hat and greeting her if he happened to see her, but otherwise having no conversation.

Laurel couldn't stand it any longer. She ran after him one afternoon. "Ned! Ned, please wait a moment," she cried, and came panting to the side of the wagon as he slowed it down.

"Somethin' else you're wantin', miss?" he asked, his mouth turned down, his eyes hard and unfriendly.

"No! I want you to stop bringing all this. I appreciate the thought, and I know Drew is trying to take care of us, but you can't listen to my mother. Ned, I don't know how to say this kindly—I don't think there is any way. My mother will bleed Drew dry. Please don't honor any of her requests. No matter what Drew says, please don't bring more. I tell him in my letters, but he just doesn't understand my parents. Please, help me. I know you understand. Will you do that?"

"No, ma'am, I won't," Ned said flatly. "She'll git ever' damned thing she asks fer as long as I'm drivin' an Drew's orderin'.'"

Laurel looked at him in puzzlement. "Ned, why? I thought you were Drew's friend. She's taking terrible advantage of him."

"I am Drew's friend, li'l lady, an' that's jes' why I'll let her take advantage of him fer now."

"You don't understand. If Mama gets what she wants now, she'll think she can always do that and it will go on and on and on."

"Stop her," Ned said. "You're her daughter. Drew's gonna be your husband. Stop her. You gotta stan' up to her sometime, an' you're the only one who can."

Laurel looked down. She said quietly. "I can't. I've tried, but I can't."

Ned spit tobacco, squinted his eyes and looked at the horizon. "That's jes' what I figgered. Now you want me t'do it fer you. An' that's jes' why I ain't gonna do it. Mathilda will git her hooks into ever' store clerk an' every delivery man in these here parts, tellin' them she's Drew Manning's kin and would they bring her such an' such. Bes' Drew knows what it's gonna be like afore he gits into it up to his boot tops. What I cain't tell him mebbe I kin show him."

She was nearly crying, but she had to ask. "You don't think I should marry Drew, do you, Ned? You think I'll be trouble for him."

Ned's look softened. "You're a good girl, Laurel. You allus have been. But you come with the damnedest, meanest family I ever did see. Mebbe if you'd a gotten away from them it'd be different, but they're comin' right along with you, an' you don't have it in you to rid yourself of them."

She turned away from him and went back to the house. She took note of every corner of the cabin as she moved slowly across the room. Mandy had set the table for supper. The broken and cracked crockery was no longer to be seen. In its place was china bought at the general store in Camden and showing evidence that the Boggses had access to England just as well as any fine family in the area. The table on which it sat was not the warped board table Harley and Ben had made. This one had been made by a craftsman and brought to the house by Ned. On the hard-packed floor was a rug. All of it looked ridiculous in the poorly built, tiny cabin, and Laurel could see that it wouldn't take Mathilda long to complain that they simply could not live in this place any longer. She could almost hear Mathilda's voice saying it wasn't fitting. She could imagine the workmen Drew would send over to raise the new cabin, which would be better and larger and need furnishing. She could look further into the future and see that the list was endless. Each step would lead to the next, and there would always be a next with Mathilda. And Drew would never refuse, because of her.

She sat down on one of the new chairs and stared out the window. She thought of what Ned had said. And she thought of her own efforts to curtail Mathilda's demands. She would never be able to stop her mother. She wasn't strong enough to command her. Mathilda overwhelmed her. She couldn't fight as Mathilda did; she simply didn't understand. To her, caring and loving someone meant trying to help the loved one, trying to make life good, enjoying the good fortune. But to Mathilda, her daughter's good fortune was merely an opportunity for herself. She was using Drew's love and would continue to do so until she was stopped or until there was nothing for her to use. Laurel already knew she couldn't stop her, but she could take away the opportunity. She sat for a long time, pain deep within her as she thought of leaving home, of leaving Drew, of leaving everything she had ever known or wanted.

She got up and busied herself washing the baby's clothing. She couldn't decide right now. Then she laughed bitterly at herself. She had already decided. What she was unable to do was make herself act upon that decision. She didn't want to leave.

40

After his next trip to the Boggses a week later, Ned Hart awaited Drew's return from the fields with some trepidation. He had no idea how Drew would react to the turn events had taken.

Drew came in, surprised to find Ned asleep in the chair on the front porch. He shook Ned gently, and as the older man opened his eyes, he smiled. "Make yourself at home, Ned."

Ned jumped to his feet. "Drew! I been waitin' fer you."

"Come on in. I don't suppose you got supper started? I heard a little news that could be good for us. I heard from John Haynes that there's going to be a regular inspection and proper facilities in Charles Town for tobacco—soon. That means the money men believe tobacco will make it here as a major crop, and when they think it, it is so. We've got to be ready." Drew talked fast as he sliced, cut and tossed dried beef and vegetables into a pot.

"Drew," Ned interrupted. "There's something I got to talk to you about."

Drew took out two glasses and a bottle of home-made peach brandy. He gave the stew pot a stir and led Ned back to the main room. "Do you have a letter for me? Did Laurel send out that load of blankets and linens she was working on?"

"Everything's still in the wagon. An' here's your letter," he said, and handed him a folded piece of paper covered in Laurel's over-large scrawl.

Drew smiled, lifted his glass to Ned and began to read.

"Aww shit, Drew, I cain't sit here drinkin' with you till you let me tell you what's on my mind. I sure wish I di'n't have to tell you, but I do—looks like me an' my big mouth had a hand in it."

"Are Laurel and Nathaniel okay?"

Ned shook his head. "Don't know nothin' about them." He sighed, then told Drew of the conversation he had had with Laurel the previous week. "An' it looks like she jes' packed up her stuff an' lef'. Mathilda's about to go crazy—says you won't treat her right without Laurel. An' that li'l sister o' hers—Mandy—she said they jes' woke up one mornin' an' Laurel was gone with the baby an' the cart you lef' fer her."

"What about Ben? Did you talk to him?"

"He don't know nothin' either, nor Star Dancer."

"Somebody's got to know something! Why did she do it? Why now? All our plans are made . . ."

"Well . . ." Ned turned away, rubbing his chin with his hand. "That's the part I ain't feelin' too good about. Mebbe I had a hand in makin' her run off. I di'n't mean to, min' you, but I mighta." He sat down again on the edge of the chair, his elbows resting on his knees. "I was takin' all the stuff they wanted over there jes' like you tol' me, an' it di'n't take long fer Mathilda to see she had a prime opportunity an' start usin' it. Well, I could see right off that this was somethin' that was goin' to go on fer a lon' time to come. She had me ahaulin' tables an' chairs an' rugs an' china sets, even a porcelain bathtub over there." Ned looked at Drew's face. He was staring at the floor somewhere near Ned's feet. There was no expression whatever. "She's a mean, graspin' woman, Drew. She woulda run you right to ruin, given the chance."

"Go on with what you were saying, Ned. I already know what Mathilda is like."

"That day after I made my delivery, I was feelin' purty fed up with Mathilda an' her graspin' ways, an' I lef'. Laurel come runnin' after me an' asked what was eatin' at me, 'cause I hadn't stopped to play with li'l Nathaniel like I usually do. I jes' tol' her what I was thinkin' about her mama. I tol' her she oughta do somethin' to stop her. She tol' me she'd tried many times but couldn't do nothin'. She asked to me stop deliverin' to Mathilda, but that don't solve it. We talked a spell, an' she was purty upset about her mama an' her ways. She tol' me she'd see me nex' time, but when I went there today, she had packed up an' left. No one knew where." Ned rubbed his chin again. "If it was what I said to her that caused her to go, I'm mighty sorry, Drew, and you got my word and my time in pledge to helpin' you fin' her."

Drew shook his head. "It's my fault. I shouldn't have left her with Mathilda. I should have brought her here, no matter how difficult it is. She never could stand up to her mother."

"She ain't like that family, but can't git away from them, either."

"Her family couldn't have touched her once we were married. She knew I'd protect her."

Ned shook his head. "You're wrong about that, Drew. Even if you coulda kep' them from ever seein' her agin, which is doubtful, she couldn'ta protected you from them, an' that galled her. Mathilda an' Harley wouldn'ta stopped usin' your name to git them what they wanted. They woulda foun' some shopkeeper who woulda taken their account charged to you. She knew that, an' so do you. An' what could you do about it? Take Harley to court? Put your own father-in-law or mother-in-law in jail? Naw. She knew there'd be no end." He looked up at Drew. "You gotta give her somethin' fer pride. Folks bein' what they are, it wouldn'ta taken long afore they was sayin' she made a fool o' you—married you to keep her low-down family." Ned stuck some tobacco into his mouth, chewed for a moment, then said, "I'm buttin' in where I don' belong, I 'spect, but why don' you leave it alone, Drew. Leave her be."

Drew was getting up from his chair and shaking his head at the same time. "Oh, no! I'll find her. I'm damned angry, and damned fed up." He picked up his deerskin jacket and threw it down again. "What in hell is she doing? What does this accomplish?"

"Mebbe she knows she cain't win an argument with you any better'n she can with her folks. This way she don' have to say nothin'. You understan' what she's sayin'."

Ned ladled the bubbling stew into bowls and cut bread, placing it on the table in front of Drew, and Drew sat down again. For the most part the two men ate in silence, and after dinner they sat sipping from Drew's jug of peach brandy until neither could speak clearly. Drew's temper grew progressively worse, a side of him Ned had never seen before.

Bleary-eyed, he looked at his younger friend. "You need a good fight. You're askin' fer one . . . beggin' fer one. What we need is some good ol' outlaws to track down. Sure bet you'd be hell right now."

Drew grinned crookedly at him. "You'd win that bet. Feelin' like I do right now, Ned, I'm a whole regiment by myself. Mebbe I'd better take Bart's advice an' get back with the Regulators. Why do I care about the Boggses? What'd they ever do for me? Tell me that, Ned, what'd they ever do for me?" He leaned too far forward and had to catch himself with his hand before he fell off his chair. "I'll tell you, Ned. They di'n't do anything! Anything worthwhile!" he said and burst into laughter.

"That's right, Drew!" Ned said, holding his sides and rocking in his chair. "Tha's why we call 'em wuthless trash, 'cause they don't do nothin' wuthwhile!" Ned laughed harder. " 'Spose they call us wuthwhile trash?"

Drew got serious. "We're not trash, Ned. That's one thing no one can say about us. We're the ones who make this land fit to live on. We cleared it . . . plowed it . . . made it grow things . . . things those worthless low people want for nothing."

"Tha's a fac'," Ned agreed. "Bible says the poor we allus got; thing it di'n't tell us was that they like it that way. Them low people ain't jes' poor, they got it in their heads that they don' need to work long's there's fools like you an' me to take care o' 'em."

"Yesss," Drew hissed. "They sit all season long, and come harvest they start crying that they'll starve if we don't take care of them." He looked down into his brandy glass. "You know what, Ned—up till now I always thought we should take care of them."

"We learn in our time, boy, yes," Ned said profoundly. "We learn in our time." He cackled and finished the brandy. "Mebbe if they teach enough of us, they'll run out of fools an' have to go to work theirselves. Cain't you see ol' Harley iffen he had to work or really starve? Jes' think what it'd be like seein' him waitin' fer his dole, an' there ain't no dole to git."

Drew stared at him glassy-eyed.

"Why, he'd set right down an' cry big horse tears!" Ned howled with laughter, and two minutes later he had passed out.

The two men awakened the following morning with sore, over-sized heads and foul humors to match. Drew offered breakfast grudgingly.

Ned growled. "Make me puke, boy. Iffen you got a li'l more brandy it'd be a lot kinder."

"We drank it all up, and you don't need it. You don't need a damn thing except some sense. Why'd you let me drink so much?"

"I don' recall forcin' anythin' down your throat. I gotta be on my way afore you an' me git into it." He picked up his saddlebag and walked out on the porch, squinting against the sun. "Sure does pain a man's eyes. Snow in the air—smell it, Drew?"

Drew stuck his head outside, his hand shading his eyes. "No. You're still drunk."

"I ain't too drunk to remember the advice I gave to you. It still stands in the light of day. Leave her be."

Drew shook his head. "I won't let her be. There aren't too many places she can go with a child. I'll figure it out sooner or later, and then I'll bring them here where they belong."

41

The waterfront of Charles Town was like nearly any waterfront in any thriving city in the world. It was lined with warehouses, heavily trafficked, cargo on the docks waiting for loading or customs or processing. Carriages and drays were parked wherever their drivers stopped, clogging still more the busy area. Upcountrymen in town with goods to trade, seamen in port with a ship, clerks, longshoremen, warehouse men, customs agents, factors and businessmen all hurried into and out of the buildings and among the cargo, adding to the bustle and confusion.

Off the main business street and dock area, small inns lined up against boardinghouses, most of which provided temporary lodging and other services for men who'd be in port only a short time and hardly knew or cared what city their ship was anchored in this time. They were hardened, tough-looking and -acting men who frequented the waterfront, walking along the planked prominences with a strange rolling gait that marked them as men of the sea.

Laurel stood in the narrow doorway of her new lodging, watching. Her eyes were bright, and there was excitement dancing in them. The tall masts cut across a cold blue and gray sky, so many masts she couldn't count them all. The hulls of ships rubbed against the wharf. Men stood on deck, shouting orders to those ashore. Lines of black men hoisted rice, barrels of molasses, tobacco casks, cotton bales, every known product of South Carolina—even crates marked neatly with the Manning indigo label. It reminded her that she had not run very far from Drew and was living in an area he would frequent. Every time he came to town he would be right here, right in this dock area, possibly in Benjamin Smith's warehouse, which she could see from where she stood, possibly in half a dozen others. It hardly mattered which one it was; she was close to all of them.

She now called herself Mrs. Dancer and claimed that her husband was at sea on a long voyage to the cold waters around New Zealand and on, searching for whale. Upon his return, he'd collect her and his son and settle in Carolina. She was pleased with her fiction. It would keep her safe and relatively respectable for two years, the length of a normal voyage, and perhaps longer if she decided to claim his ship had come in but he had died at sea. In the meantime she offered her services as washerwoman and seamstress. She had a small flat with two rooms on the third level of this narrow building. She had loaded her wagon with as many of the treasures Mathilda had begged for as she could manage. She had never stolen so much as a scrap of bread before, but taking from her mother those things she had taken from Drew had felt good. There had been a balancing of a scale in that act for Laurel, and she felt no guilt or regret that she had stripped Mathilda of her dream. It was just. And it was final. She'd never see her family again—except perhaps Ben.

With a sigh she turned and walked back up the stairs to her flat. She had a pile of mending to do and several washings. She had been surprised at how easily she was able to get work almost from the moment she had let it be known she was there. She not only would be able to keep herself and Nathaniel but most likely could save a little money as well. Not all her customers were seamen. Many women in the area who earned their keep in quicker, more pleasurable ways brought their gowns to her to be refashioned or hemmed or mended. And in the last couple of weeks, a servant from one of the big houses in the better part of town had brought linen to be cared for, washed and ironed. She liked the big black woman, who always seemed cheerful and friendly and respectful of her. In fact, Pelagie had done more to restore her own self-respect than anything else. Pelagie made her feel as though she were somebody— perhaps not a Manning but certainly not an Upcountry Boggs. She once more had the feeling that with work and effort she could be somebody. She could climb out of and away from what her family was, to something decent and worthwhile. At that thought, at least, she felt good. She was daydreaming again about the house she would one day purchase in a nice section of town, and of her neighbors, who would like her and call her Mrs. Dancer and admire her son as he grew to manhood. Her neighbors would think her courageous, raising her son alone with a husband lost at sea. But she'd be respected, and no one would ever know about Nathaniel's background. All that would be left behind her in some nightmare that no longer was. She smiled, knowing finally she had freed herself of her family. She no longer felt responsible for them. She wouldn't look back.

She hurriedly finished the small amount of mending she had left to do on the lace border of one of Pelagie's tablecloths and then heated up the iron. She worked carefully but quickly, always aware of the time and fearful she'd not finish before Pelagie arrived. She heard the lumbering footsteps of the old woman as she made the last fold in the tablecloth. She added it to the bundle she had ready and then heaped fresh ironing onto the board. She didn't want to appear lacking for work; otherwise people might not think she was in demand and therefore not good. She always made certain she appeared to be overworked, even if it was her own clothes she piled on the board.

Pelagie was puffing when she knocked on Laurel's door. "It sure is a lon' ways up," she said, and gladly fell into the seat Laurel indicated.

Laurel looked concerned and gave her a glass of fresh lemonade. "Perhaps I should bring the laundry down to you hereafter, Pelagie. I hadn't thought about the steps, and I should have. You always have difficulty with them. We can establish a time, and I'll have the laundry downstairs for you."

Pelagie smiled at her. She liked Laurel very much and could well see why Drew loved her. "You're a kind lady, Mrs. Dancer. There ain't many who'd think of an ol' mammy like me."

Laurel blushed. "As soon as I'm able, I plan to get a place at ground level. I don't much like hauling the water up here either." She sat down opposite Pelagie, glad for someone to talk to. For all her feelings of good fortune, she often got lonely having only Nathaniel to share her thoughts and plans with. She missed Drew terribly and occasionally dreamed that someday she'd go to him as someone she could be proud of being. "I have been doing very well, so I think I shall be able to move soon."

"It would be a lot easier on you," Pelagie agreed. "What do you hear from Mr. Dancer?"

Laurel glanced away from her, then looked back, a smile on her face. "I don't hear much these days, Pelagie. He's at sea, you know, and the mails are not reliable." She helped Pelagie out of the chair and took the bundle of clothing. "I'll help you down with this. Be careful on these steps. They are very steep."

"I'm sorry I didn't get to see li'l Nathaniel today. You give him a big hug special from his Pelagie. I don' wan' him forgettin' me. You make sure he remembers his Pelagie, y'hear?"

"He won't forget," Laurel said with a laugh. "He loves you."

Pelagie reached the street, stood for a moment catching her breath, then said good-bye to Laurel. "I be back soon. We gonna get these linens in the bes' shape they ever been in with you workin' on 'em. You take care o' yourse'f." She walked down the street.

Laurel stood in the doorway for some time, watching the heavy-set old woman trudge away. For the first time she realized that she had never seen a carriage or cart pick Pelagie up. She was always on foot. It had never seemed strange to her until today. She shook her head and reprimanded herself for foolishness. People did not treat their servants that well, nor were they concerned about the effort it took for an old woman to carry a bundle and walk distances. She went back upstairs to her flat and the pile of mending she had yet to do. It was so much easier if she could complete it while Nathaniel was napping.

Pelagie was aware of Laurel watching her. She tried to walk slowly and evenly, but as soon as she turned the corner she started hurrying. Her flat feet turned outward, and she was puffing and hustling as fast as she could go, her eyes steadily on the Manning carriage. Elizabeth was looking from the window and scolding the driver for not backing up.

Pelagie rolled into the backseat, barely able to breathe. "My word, Miz Lizzybeff, I'm sure gonna haf to give up my sweets. I jes' got too fat to move."

"How is she?" Elizabeth asked, her bright eyes twinkling.

"I got to catch my breath," Pelagie gasped, and made a to-do over fanning herself. She loved having Elizabeth unable to do anything about her curiosity until she, Pelagie, wanted to tell her. She tried to draw the suspense out longer, but she burst into laughter as she watched Elizabeth. "You jes' fair to bustin', Miz Lizzybeff," she said with a chuckle.

"Well, tell me how she is, you old coot!" Elizabeth said, and began to laugh too. "We are two ornery old women, Pelagie. It's no wonder my son John doesn't trust a thing I say or do."

Pelagie laughed harder, her whole body shaking. "Some folks say we be meddlin' in where we don' belon's."

"Old stuffed shirts! It's no fun being where one belongs all the time."

The two women leaned back and slowly stopped laughing. Elizabeth asked again more quietly, "She is doing well, isn't she?"

"She jes' fine. She say she can get a place that ain't upstairs soon—praise the Lawd!"

"Did you see my great-grandchild?"

Pelagie shook her head sadly, as though she had failed. "He was down for his nap, Miz Lizzybeff. I tried stayin' a bit, but he stayed asleep."

"Drat!" Elizabeth said, and made a fist. "I must devise a way that I can see my great-grandson. Perhaps she would permit you to take him for a walk? Would she trust you to do that, Pelagie?"

"She like me . . . I think she say yes, but you sure you wants to do that, Miz Lizzybeff? Even Mistah Drew say he don' know fo' sure if that's his son."

"He thinks it is," Elizabeth said firmly, "and it would take me five minutes with the child to be sure."

"How you gonna do that?"

"He must have some of his father in him, and if it's there, I'll know it. I know Drew, and I knew Walter. They were cut from the same cloth. From what Drew has told me and written, this child is too. He's ours, Pelagie, I just feel it in my bones." She tapped on the top of the carriage and instructed the driver to take her home. "I'm not going to ignore this. That child shall be raised a Manning."

"How you gonna do that? Miss Laurel don' wanna marry Mistah Drew, an' Miss Gwynne gonna be comin' back any day from

Englan' thinkin' she has your blessin's to marry Mistah Drew, an' he ain't nevah said he wan's to marry her—how you gonna do all that?"

"I don't know. It has gotten a bit tangled, hasn't it," Elizabeth mused. "But there is a way! I'm sure of it. The answer is merely a trifle elusive at the moment."

"You usin' them big words I don' know again," Pelagie complained.

"I am using them, Pelagie, to cover the fact that I am not at all certain of what I am saying either. I have never understood why life does not arrange itself as it would seem best for all concerned. If it had been Gwynne who had had Nathaniel, we could unite everyone. Of course, it would cause a terrible schism in the family. However, at the bottom of it all remains the one fact that I will not have my great-grandson raised to think he is anything but a Manning."

"Miss Laurel say he's named Dancer. She won' like that."

"Oh, don't be shallow! A Manning comes from within! She may call him whatever she pleases, but he is my great-grandson and as such shall have the qualities that have made the Manning men strong. No, Nathaniel Dancer is a Manning, and I shall never forget it, nor will I allow Drew to forget it."

42

Elizabeth did not rest easily with her deceptions, and she had accumulated quite a few. Despite the letters she received from Drew, she had never told him she knew of Laurel's whereabouts. She wrote letters to him sympathizing with his worries and his earnest desire to find her, but she remained mute on the subject of her washerwoman. She continued to see Nathaniel whenever Pelagie was able to talk Laurel into allowing her to take the child for an afternoon, but she never revealed herself to Laurel, nor did she explain to John or any of the rest of her family why she was so interested in the washerwoman's son. She was merely surprised that no one of the family noticed the resemblance to Drew.

Her last and, in her mind, worst deception was to Gwynne. She had encouraged Gwynne repeatedly to express her love for Drew, and now she held her silence about Drew, Laurel and, most important, Nathaniel. In her worst moments she told herself that somehow everything would work out, but she didn't believe it. For the moment all was being held in abeyance, but it would not last much longer. Drew might come to Charles Town at any time and discover Laurel and Nathaniel, or Gwynne might return from England expecting to go to the Upcountry and see Drew. No matter what happened, both Drew and Gwynne would find out that while she had not lied to either of them directly, she had omitted those parts of the truth that most concerned them in every letter she had written.

"I have done a terrible thing, Pelagie," she said miserably. "But now that I have done it, I don't know what is best to do. If I tell Drew about Laurel, he'll come right away and take her—as his wife—to the Upcountry, and then what will happen to Gwynne? If I arrange for Gwynne and Drew to be together . . . what will become of my great-grandson? We would lose him." Elizabeth gazed unhappily out her window. "To make it all worse, I like Laurel."

In late March she received a letter from Drew filled with news of the Upcountry and Cherokee. He told of the many towns and villages he had gone to looking for Laurel, and concluded that the only place he had not searched was Charles Town itself. "He'll be coming here after planting is complete," she said to Pelagie. "I suppose I should accept this as a blessing. It takes all the soul-searching and worry from my hands. When he arrives, I'll make my confession and tell him where to locate Laurel and his son."

"What you gonna do about Missy Gwynne? She gonna be lef' with nobuddy."

"I know, Pelagie." She got up and paced nervously about the room. "At least I can tell her I did not lead Drew to Laurel, and I am not to blame for bringing Nathaniel into the circumstance. I just wish there was something I could do to ease her burden. Oh, Pelagie! I sometimes think Walter is the lucky one. He does not have to see the trials that come to the young. It is so easy for the old to forget the pains of the young. We see them so full of promise and want them not to make mistakes. But they are no different from us—they do make their mistakes, and those are painful to all of us. I do not want to think of this any longer. I am going shopping. It may not solve anything, but it will occupy my mind with harmless trivia."

When she came downstairs, her son John and her grandsons were in the parlor.

"My word, gentlemen, what is all the excitement about? Good afternoon, John," she said and presented her cheek for a kiss.

Leo came to her and kissed her as well. "It is nothing to trouble your head over, Grandmother."

"I have no intention of troubling my head over anything today, but I would like to know what has all of you so full of talk and good cheer."

"We were merely discussing the possible good effect Lord North might have on colonial politics. It is quite possible he could convince Parliament to be less restrictive in policy and taxation."

As John spoke, a messenger came back from the docks. He handed John a packet, bowed respectfully to all in the room and left.

John held the packet aloft, then began to open it. "Is anyone interested in mail? I seem to have something here for Elizabeth Manning straight from London, several newspapers, two letters for myself and—here, what's this?" He held up a letter. "Wilfred Magee—he seldom writes to me," John mused.

"Who is Wilfred Magee, Father?" Rob asked. "I don't recall ever having met him."

"I doubt you have. I knew him as a young man when we were growing up. Fred studied law and went to New York, where he lives now. We write one or two letters a year to each other, but of late he had been quite chummy with Sam Adams and his ilk." John opened the short letter and read, frowning. He looked up at his sons, his expression grave. "Lord North may be too late to do anything to stop or slow the course of events."

"I think not!" George said and got up, paper in hand. "Look at this," he said, pointing to one of the columns. "North has gone before Parliament, urging them to repeal parts of the Townshend Acts. It says that the feeling in London is that there is a good chance that the tax measure will be repealed with the exception of the tax on tea, for Londoners feel strongly that they should not have to pay more for tea than the colonists."

Rob laughed. "I suppose there is justice in that."

"It may not be enough now," John said dourly. "On March 5 a group of the king's soldiers met up with a group of Boston citizens. There was disruption, during which the soldiers fired indiscriminately into the crowd, killing several of them." He looked at the stricken faces of his family. "They were massacred," he said weakly.

"Can that be true, John?" Elizabeth asked, her hand at her throat.

"Of course, we'll get verification, but I see no reason that could possibly . . . I mean, why would Wilfred lie about something like this? George, look through those other papers. I believe there should be one from New York. If there has been a massacre, any newspaper would carry it. Do you see anything?"

George shuffled through the stack of newspapers, dropping some of them to the floor. "Yes, yes! Here it is, New York . . ." He handed the paper to John. "Philadelphia reports of it, also. It is true! What fools! How could something of this magnitude happen?" George looked at his father. "Loyalty to the king is one thing, but having our people slaughtered in the streets is quite another!"

Leo tossed the newspaper he'd been reading onto the sofa and looked with disgust at his brother. "As usual you take one quick look at a situation and jump to conclusions. Read the newspaper I just read. The people shot at were rabble out on the streets harassing the king's men, throwing snowballs and rocks as well as epithets and other radical nonsense. These were people trying to create an incident, and they did—much more so than they bargained for, I imagine."

George whirled to face his brother. "You are a cold man, Leo. You have no passion. There are Bostonians lying dead at this very moment, and they have died at the hand of the king's troops, whom we quarter and feed. They are here to protect us, not to murder us in our own streets!"

Leo clapped. "Have you become a rebel, George? Was your dramatic ride with the Regulators just a harbinger of greater things to come?"

"I haven't become anything, but I shall not be a party to action such as this. If that means I must join Christopher Gadsen and his Liberty Boys, I shall. Perhaps the radicals are right in at least one regard; neither Parliament nor the king is going to listen to us by request. Something must be done to gain their attention, and if that means threatening independence, perhaps that is exactly what we should do."

"All right, George, suppose I say I agree with you to that point," Rob said. "What happens when England accepts our threat of independence as a declaration of war, or perhaps treason. That word is being heard more and more often."

"Is it less treasonous to betray the country in which we live and that provides us with a very extravagant way of life? Think about that for a minute, Rob. Drew has been saying this to us for over a year, and we've all laughed it off as coming from a hotheaded Upcountryman. He may have seen months ago what we're only beginning to understand now. He's always said we should have more compassion for what the Upcountry suffered, for it was but a microcosm of what the rest of us were entering into. Suppose he's right. Suppose we will have to fight for rights we have always assumed were ours to have."

"The Upcountry is a far cry from Charles Town or any part of the Low Country," Leo said. "The Regulators are no more than backwoods politicians grasping for power they could never acquire by ordinary means."

"In some ways that's true, but that's not all of it. Any citizen of Britain has a right to trial and access to the courts. The Upcountry hasn't had that. And their representation in the Assembly is present but very weak. Is that so different from our dearth of effective representation in Parliament? Aren't decisions that affect us made daily without regard to the welfare of the colony? Isn't it the empire's concern and well-being that is tantamount?"

Leo stood up and moved toward the door. "I've heard all I choose to hear. We *are* the empire, brother dear, and what is good for the empire will, in the end, be good for us. There are and always will be times that are difficult and perhaps not entirely fair. However, our time for favoritism shall come, and some other part of the empire will have their turn at complaining at the squeeze on their resources." Leo nodded at his father, kissed Elizabeth once more and said, "I shan't be home for supper." He grinned, eyebrows raised. "I have a special invitation to a family dinner at the Miltons'. Wish me luck. I believe the honorable Mr. Milton is not at all certain I am fit to court his one and only daughter. I am off to win him over."

Elizabeth laughed and patted his sholder. "Charm the mother. Elise Milton can never resist a handsome, courteous young man." She turned back to her son. "Well, John, we may be having several weddings this coming year."

"Does Gwynne say anything about her return or when Joanna's wedding will take place?"

Elizabeth raised her hand with the letter in it. "Good heavens! I had forgotten all about this. I haven't read it." She tore open the envelope and smoothed the paper. "Well, well, it seems we are not to have the pleasure of Joanna's wedding at Riverlea. Bert Townshend has returned home and they are going to be married in England this May at his father's estate. Gwynne says she has no idea of when they shall return here, but she will arrive here in about a month." Elizabeth put the letter down on her lap.

John smiled. "It will be nice to have her back. I know you've missed her company. But does she give any indication if there are other reasons for Joanna's change in plans? Joanna and Bert do intend to make their home here?"

"They are coming back," Elizabeth said somberly. "The political situation must be more serious than we had thought, John. Bert's father is opposed to Lord North, claiming he is too liberal in attitude toward the American colonies. Gwynne says he impresses Joanna and Bert daily with the necessity of having active, loyal Englishmen settled here and influential in our government. Joanna was presented at court and is dedicated to doing all she can to further Bert's political career when they return."

John stared at his mother for some time. "Why does this upset you? It all sound like good news to me, Mother."

Elizabeth shrugged. "It is, John. I am uneasy. I dislike the feel of all the news we have had today. Perhaps I am having an attack of old age or fright. I don't know; I am simply not comfortable. I wish Walter were here to see us through the times to come. Our family is already divided, with Drew disowned and the differences I see in your boys and in Arthur. I am very much afraid the dissension over English policy may tear our family into factions that may never heal. Drew will almost certainly side with the rebels, if it comes to that, and Joanna with the Tories; Leo as well. And now George seems to be choosing sides. Drew has told me Arthur is adamantly opposed to the radical cause. If this continues to the point of a war of independence, John, we could well be viewing our own family members as traitors and enemies. That would be a tragedy. I'm not certain we would survive a division so great. We are already struggling with dissension among us."

John sat beside his mother, her hand in his. "We cannot borrow trouble, Mother. So far this is mostly talk."

"What of the massacre?"

John hesitated, then sighed. "I'm worried, too, but there is nothing we can do but wait and see what is going to happen. But do not doubt we shall survive whatever we must."

Elizabeth smiled. "You are a good son, John. I shouldn't fuss at you as I do."

"I enjoy it, Mother—most of the time. Weren't you going shopping?" He hugged her and brought her to her feet. "Be on your way or you shall come home late for supper and upset my Eugenia, and we may not survive that."

During the next days Elizabeth regained her sense of security about her family, but she viewed each of them differently than she had before. It reminded her of the time her own sons had been young children. She had encouraged John and Joseph to explore their infant worlds, delighting in the efforts their small, rotund bodies would make and knowing that with each success they moved away from her and took yet another step in growing up. Even when they were infants, she had been aware of the men they became. As she watched and enjoyed the members of her family now, she was aware of them drawing away from each other in subtle ways. She was ever aware of the Whigs and Tories and Rebels each of them was becoming.

"But I've accepted it, Pelagie," she said. "Because I cannot prevent it. Each of us must be tested. Our family is no different. We shall all fight for what we believe in, as we should as Mannings, and we shall fight each other."

Pelagie shook her great head. "I sure hopes I'm not aroun' when that happens."

"Nonsense! We shall both be there and in the thick of it, choosing our own sides," Elizabeth said, then waved away further talk of it. "Hurry now, help me dress. Pitt's statue is arriving, and I want to be there when it is first seen."

"You ain't goin' to those docks, Miz Lizzybeff!"

"I certainly am! He's been the champion of the colonial movement. He deserves my cheers! Broad and Meeting streets will look marvelous graced by his figure. This is quite a historic time, Pelagie. We are actually honoring one of our heroes."

Elizabeth joined the large assemblage of citizens to greet Pitt's statue. An air of vibrancy was evidenced by all who came. With the repeal of the Townshend Acts, many people believed the drive toward liberty and independence would begin to slow, but Elizabeth looked at her friends and neighbors and saw the lively excitement in their faces and heard it in the cheers they raised. Perhaps many of them weren't aware of what was happening, but she had lived long enough to recognize nationalism when she saw it. These people were becoming South Carolinians. The years and the land had made them a unique people, of a unique country for which they would fight and for which many would die. Again she felt the strange urgency to be with them and appreciate them now, for she might not have many more chances.

43

Drew hired five men and convinced Ned Hart he would make a better tobacco man than an indigo man. With seven working, Cherokee began to take the shape and look that Drew had always dreamed of. He had nearly six hundred acres under cultivation.

Near the house were stacks of lumber and the framework of the tobacco house. It was becoming a long, narrow building with rows and rows of rafters from which the tobacco would hang and be dried by the newer method of artificial heat.

Drew stood back, hands on hips. "I was beginning to think I'd never actually see the day this would be in operation, Ned." He laughed aloud, his head thrown back. "From this year on Cherokee is going to be known!"

Ned smiled. "It's been a long time comin', but it sure is beautiful, Drew." He looked out across the fields. "It sure makes a man proud to know he's had a hand in it. Ain't many things can give a man that feelin'. An' ain't it strange that most of them have to do with work. You wouldn't think it'd be that way, would you, seein' as we're always thinkin' we're gonna have so much fun when we ain't workin'."

"You should have been a philosopher, Ned."

"Seems to me he is a p'losper," Ben said and laughed as he came to join them. In his hand he had a banjo, complete except for the strings. "It's lookin' purty good, don' you think?" He showed it to both men.

"Eben teach you how to make that?" Ned asked. He ran his hand across the well-worked wood.

"Can you play it?" Drew asked.

"Not like Eben can, but I kin make it talk a little. One of these days I'll make it sing an' holler like him. We'll have us a good ol' contest. I tol' Eben he better watch out. Ben Boggs means to be the bes' from here to the Virginia border." He played on imaginary strings.

"How long do you judge it before we've completed this tobacco house, Ned . . . three more days?"

"Three, mebbe four," Ned agreed.

Drew smiled but said nothing. Word spread quickly that there would be a get-together at the end of the week. The day before the Cherokee tobacco house was finished, wagons filled with country people began to pull into the yard. Women and children spilled out and ran over the house and yard. Drew greeted neighbors he saw regularly, some that he hadn't seen in months and others he was meeting for the first time. The men as a matter of course rolled up their shirt sleeves and went to work on the building. The women selected their own area and, amid laughter and the soft hum of talk, the tables went up. Young boys raced back and forth from wagons, hauling what their mothers demanded. Provisions were taken from the wagons, pits for fires dug and pots put on to boil.

Drew looked around. There must have been fifty or sixty people milling around his house and barn, he guessed, and he was sure there would be more to come. From the corner of his eye he caught sight of a covey of quail happily sunning themselves and smiled. Three days of good weather, he thought. He looked back to the people in his yard. "I sure hope it's true," he murmured, and went at a trot back to the tobacco barn. He joined a crew of men carrying the long side planking to those acting as carpenters.

In the late afternoon Bart Cole and John Haynes arrived with three other men and their families. Cherokee was taking on the look of a camped wagon train, but no one seemed to mind. Ben, with the help of Eben Watts, strung his banjo and began to tune it up. Within minutes fiddles, mandolins, banjos, harmonicas and Jew's harps came from pockets, saddlebags and wagons. John Haynes, long, lanky and not eager to get drawn into roasting the pig, proved to be an excellent dance caller. Looking like a huge daddy longlegs, John stood amid the musicians, clapping his hands and tapping his foot. "Find your partners, folks. Come on now, fellas, get that bes' gal an' form a circle, form that circle . . ."

Calico skirts swirled, and Drew moved from one group to the other. The music grew faster, and neatly pinned hair curled hotly around the flushed faces of the women. It had been a long time since Drew had been to a get-together like this one, and it made him think of Laurel. He had heard nothing of her. It was as if she had walked out of her house, gotten into his wagon and disappeared. The only two things of which he was certain were that she was nowhere in this area and that somehow he'd find her. Just as Star Dancer had told him of the strange and special knowledge she seemed to have had about him, he now knew that somehow, someday he'd find her.

By the start of 1771 Elizabeth Manning could no longer justify her continued support of Laurel Boggs while keeping it a secret from Drew, even for the short time remaining until his visit. In every letter he wrote to her, he mentioned Laurel, his efforts and failures to find her and his determination to do so.

"Pelagie, I am a meddling old woman. I am afraid I have made a situation which will hurt both of the young people I love most. I must tell Drew of Laurel's presence here now. I should never have withheld it from him."

Elizabeth took paper, quill and ink and wrote Drew a letter, then gave it to Pelagie and sent her to town to give it to one of the wagonmasters going back to the Upcountry. It was a terrible day for Elizabeth, one of the few in which nothing could cheer her. She felt as though she had lost both her grandson and her niece. She had always been aware of how much she loved them, but never before had she considered how alone and empty she'd feel if they were not near her. She hadn't felt so devastated since the day her husband had died. She put her hands over her face and cried. Pelagie found her like that when she returned.

"I have only myself to blame, Pelagie. It is all the worse for that, for I am helpless to undo what I have done. I thought he loved Gwynne. I was so certain, and look at all the confusion and pain I have caused with my arrogant pride!" In a fit of anger she threw her hairbrush to the floor. "Arrogant, stupid old woman!"

Drew received Elizabeth's letter and was stunned at her revelation. "My God, Ben, she's known for months where Laurel has been. She's watched after her, supported her . . . why in hell did she keep it from me?"

"Mebbe she's one who thinks you shouldn't marry up with Laurel after all that's happened. You know, Drew, much as I love my sister an' all, I gotta admit there aren't many right-thinkin' folk who believe you should marry her."

"It's no one's business but ours."

"That's so, but it never stopped folks from thinkin' or talkin'. I ain't no different, neither. I never been respectable in my life before . . . an' now it's easy fer me to see my family is a wuthless bunch. But I di'n't know that till Star Dancer made me take a claim fer my own place. I allus thought Pa was plagued by bad luck, Ma too; but it ain't so. They make what they are deliberate like. Now me, bein' a man, kin walk off an' start fresh on my own. I ain't got the tender feelin's o' a woman like Laurel has. I don' much care if I ever see Ma an' Pa agin. But Laurel's allus feelin' sorry an' tryin' to he'p them. She don't see it ain't he'p they want but a handout. I don' wanna talk agin my sister's interests, Drew, but you're my frien', too, an' my ma an' pa'd be after Laurel all the time. It ain't no good." Ben stood up and walked to the doorway and back. "You wanna hear one o' the terriblest thoughts I ever had? Ever since them outlaws come that night, I get to dreamin' an' wishin' it'd been my pa they'd shot an' that he never come outta it. Doc said it was a miracle I come through. Pa mos' likely wouldn'ta."

"Your pa was lucky he wasn't killed."

Ben made a face of disgust. "He weren't lucky. He was pissin' his pants he was so skeered. Had he known Laurel's whereabouts, he'd of given her to them. He was all willin' to hand over li'l Mary. He don' care about none o' us. Onliest thing my pa ever cared about was what he could git from us. Laurel was his plum . . . allus tryin', dreamin', allus doin' her bes' to make life good fer us. Even at that he run her into the groun'. Nothing she did was good enough."

Drew listened closely to Ben. He had never heard Ben talk about his family at all. He had never even suspected that feelings such as these were hidden away. "Why are you telling me this now, Ben? You never said anything last fall when I thought Laurel and I would marry. Why now? Are you saying that you too don't want our marriage?"

"I ain't sayin' that. I ain't too sure what I'm sayin'. I'm jes' tellin' you I never knew no other way of livin' till Star Dancer an' me got our own place near fifty miles from my folks. We Boggses never had to live like we did, allus scratchin' fer ever'thin'. Long as I remember, it's allus been like that with my pa an' ma. Now I see they's jes' too damned ornery to work fer anythin'. Mebbe your gran'mother sees the same. I know Ned sees it that way—him an' me've talked about it. You marry my sister an' you got my whole wuthless family on you."

"Not if they know nothing about it," Drew said.

Ben suddenly smiled. "Now there's a thought. But how you gonna get Laurel to come with you?"

"I'm not going to ask her," Drew said and grinned.

"I thought you jes' said you wanted to marry her."

"I don't just want to, I'm going to. Your sister seems unable to take what she wants, so I'm going to take her to it."

"You ain't makin' no sense atall!"

"No, I'm not, In plain English—do you want to help me abduct your sister and my son?"

Ben stared at him. "I'm s'posed to be the one ain't right in the head."

"Will you help me or not?"

"Go to Cha's T'wn an' grab my sister an' Nathaniel an' run fer the hills?" Ben laughed.

"That's right."

"When do we leave?"

"In the morning." Drew got up and left the house in search of Ned. "I want a preacher here when I get back—not Fowler but someone who doesn't know the Boggses. Better give me six weeks. Ben and I will make good time going, but we'll take it easy coming back with Nathaniel. Can I count on you to have everything ready here? Most important, keep the Boggses ignorant of the marriage."

"I'll be damned! I allus knew you was a crazy man. What if she don't want to come?"

"I'm not asking her, Ned, I'm telling her. Will you help me?"

"I'll help you. You named this place right. Cherokee is gonna be as ornery an' woolly as the Indians it was named fer. God be with you, Drew. It'll be good to have her back."

Ben and Drew left at dawn the following day. They rode hard

each day, the empty wagon bouncing along behind them on the rutted roads.

"I think my tailbone's gonna come through my neck afore we git there," Ben complained. "What's your big hurry? She don' know when we're comin'."

"I don't want her getting it into her head to move on or something, and then I would have to start looking for her all over again. I might not be so lucky this time. Not even Grandmother can know everything all the time."

They were on the outskirts of Charles Town ten days after they had started the journey. Ben was exhausted, and his head was throbbing.

"We'll rest for a day," Drew said. "Grandmother can take care of you, and I'll spend the time finding the house Laurel lives in and figuring out how we can best take her." He turned the horses toward Legare Street. It was becoming a habit to drop in on his grandmother unexpectedly. He laughed aloud.

"What the hell can you fin' funny?" Ben growled. "I hurt from my hair to my toes."

"I was thinking about my grandmother. From the tone of her letter, she's going to be quaking in her boots when she sees me. And well she should be, keeping this from me for so long," he said.

He strode to the front door and knocked. Pelagie peeked from the hallway as Drew entered. He smiled as he watched her run up the stairs to his grandmother's room as fast as she could go.

"Miz Lizzybeff! Miz Lizzybeff! He here! An' he look like a madman! He hair is all on end an' he's jes' civered wiff mud from head to foot."

"Dear heaven, Pelagie, calm down, I can barely understand you. Slow down and speak clearly. Who is here?"

Pelagie was still breathless, and her eyes rolled in her head, always in the direction of the door. "He don' look happy! He lookin' wil'. He—"

"Pelagie! Who are you talking about? Who is here?"

"I am here, Grandmother," Drew said from the doorway.

Elizabeth's eyes widened. He looked enormous and formidable, his shoulders nearly filling the door frame. His face was burned a coppery bronze by the sun, and his hair curled riotously around his head. He wore the Upcountry suede shirt, and around his waist was the lethal-looking tomahawk. His brown eyes shone as he looked at her.

Meekly, Elizabeth said, "You received my letter, Drew?"

"Yes, I received it. I assume you also received mine, telling you of the time and distance I took trying to find Laurel?"

"Drew, I . . ."

"If you are about to apologize, Grandmother, I think it is too late, and of little value to either of us. What I would like from you is an explanation of why you chose not to tell me until now."

"I didn't know what to do. If I told you about Laurel, I felt disloyal to Gwynne, and by not telling you, I was disloyal to you. So I did nothing."

"Except support Laurel. Does she know who you are?"

"No! I have been very careful to keep myself a secret. She has never even seen me. I only did that to ensure the safety and well-being of my great-grandson."

Drew was quiet for a time. "Tell me about Gwynne. You said part of the reason you didn't tell me about Laurel was because you felt by doing so you'd be disloyal to her."

Elizabeth gazed at her folded hands on her lap. "Gwynne has told me she had informed you of her feelings, so I shall not be talking out of turn. Gwynne has also told me how she feels about you and what her hopes are. I, too, have hoped for a long time that you and Gwynne would . . . find your way to each other. I have seen . . . thought I saw in you a certain special response and feeling for Gwynne." She began to say more, then stopped and looked up at him. "Was I wrong, Drew?"

"No, you weren't wrong, but it can never be, Grandma. I can't turn my back on Laurel now. I did that once with Joanna, and I don't regret it, but I can't do it again."

"And if Laurel tells you she prefers to remain here and not go with you, then what of Gwynne, Drew?"

He shook his head. "It makes no difference. I am not asking Laurel to return with me; I am taking her. Laurel's reasons for avoiding me are good ones and kind ones, Grandma. I've asked her to be my wife, and she has my son. I am going to carry out that promise I made to her."

"But Drew, as fine a woman as Laurel is, she is simply not your kind. Laurel is . . . of a different class than we are, Drew, and while that may sound narrow to you, dear, there is sound reasoning in it. Class is not merely a matter of good or bad fortune but of years of training and breeding. That you cannot make a silk purse out of a sow's ear is not so far wrong, Drew. Just as you would not enter one of your plow horses into a thoroughbred race, you cannot ask Laurel to instill in Nathaniel or any other children you might have qualities she knows nothing of, ideas and attitudes that are not part of her own upbringing or heritage."

"She'll learn what she needs to know."

Elizabeth shook her head. "I wish it were that easy, but culture is not something one just learns at one's own convenience. It is not a thing to be partaken of at will and discarded when other qualities seem more useful. Culture is an evolutionary refinement that requires years, centuries of living it and breeding it into the very nature and ambitions of human beings."

Drew smiled questioningly. "In other words, I belong with one of my own kind. And then does it also follow that Laurel should be with a man of her father's ilk?"

"Nothing quite so simplistic, and I am insulted that you implied it. Laurel has gone beyond her family, from what you tell me of them, but that does not mean she has become the woman to best serve you as wife; nor does your position assure that you can best serve her as husband. Being too far beyond your mate can be as devastating and detrimental as being too rustic. It works both ways, Drew, and the class differences most often are not mere snobberies but protective devices that aid in assuring that human nature shall continue its halting progress toward civilization."

"And if I admit that I understand what you are saying, and perhaps even that I agree with you despite the fact that I learned too late, will you try to see that, regardless, I am going to marry Laurel and feel I must?" Drew asked.

"I understand, and I pity you, Drew, but I am also your friend as well as your grandmother. I will do whatever I can. I would ask you a favor, however. Gwynne is due to return home at any time. We are sending messengers to the docks for news of her ship daily. Would you please talk to her and tell her what you have told me? Do whatever you can, Drew, to allow her to understand why you have chosen as you have."

"I cannot stay here now. I am going to get Laurel as quickly as possible and take her to Cherokee, but I am planning to come back to Charles Town with the first sizable crop of Cherokee tobacco this fall. I will talk to her then, and I promise you, Grandmother, I will tell her all that I have told you, and . . ."

"And?" Elizabeth prompted as he paused.

Drew smiled. "And some things that are only for her ears."

Elizabeth laughed. "I do believe I am being told to mind my own business."

"I don't think I'll answer that. For the moment I think I shall beg your hospitality in the form of a bath, a place to rest and something to eat. It has been a long, hard trip. And—one other favor. Could I borrow Pelagie's services for a while. I brought Laurel's brother with me, and he is feeling poorly. I'd appreciate it if Pelagie would look after him. I can think of no one who could do him more good." He went on to tell both of them of Ben's wound.

Pelagie stood up immediately and with a glance at Elizabeth left the room. Ben would be enjoying her special tea for headaches in a matter of moments.

44

The evening of the following day Drew repacked the wagon, making the bed of it as comfortable for sleeping as he could. With Pelagie's help, he raided Elizabeth's kitchen, taking baskets of succulent meats, vegetable pies, pastries and containers of wine, lemonade and tea.

"If you are determined to do this, why must it be tonight? You could stay for a time and have a pleasant visit. You only arrived yesterday, Drew." Elizabeth handed him a tin of coffee.

Drew tweaked her cheek. "I left a new crop with Ned in charge, and two hands short. We are already short-handed when we're all there. By the time I get back to Cherokee, it will have been nearly a month."

"What will you do if she doesn't want to stay?" Elizabeth asked.

"I don't know, Grandma. I think she will want to. I don't believe she really wanted to run away in the first place and wouldn't have if it hadn't been for her mother and a confused way of looking at her abduction by the outlaws. If I am wrong . . . I don't know . . . as you once said, I can't keep her prisoner."

It was dark when the wagon was packed. Drew kissed Elizabeth good-bye and promised he'd write.

"And I want to meet her soon, Drew. I have only seen her and looked after her, but it was Pelagie who actually talked with her. I am feeling terribly left out. I think I am jealous," she said.

He hugged her. "You have my word we'll visit, and if you're up to the trip, I'll bring you to Cherokee for a visit. You've never seen it."

Ben had just completed hitching the horses when Drew came

out of the house. The two men mounted the wagon and started out of Elizabeth's drive. Drew took the time to drive slowly through the streets, pointing out places and houses to Ben. He drove around the new statue of Pitt at Broad and Meeting streets, took time to pass the Liberty Tree and then headed for the waterfront. They moved slowly along, Drew peering at the houses and flat-fronted buildings until he spotted Laurel's. He pointed to a back window in which a light shone. "She must be working," he said to Ben.

Ben gave a false shudder. "She's gonna be worse'n a hive of angry bees when she sees me. Drew, you sure we wanna jes' haul her off?"

Drew reined in the horses and handed the reins to Ben. "Wait here till I get her. You'd better drive."

"I don't know how to get out of town! You drive."

"And have you let her go? You'll find your way." He disappeared into the darkness, and Ben didn't catch sight of him again until he ran past the lighted window he had pointed out earlier.

Drew tried the door carefully and found it locked. He moved back around to the window. It too was locked. He stood for a moment and then went back to the door. He knocked boldly. From inside Laurel called out, "Who's there?"

"Laundry!" he said in a muffled voice.

There was a pause. His heart beat faster as he feared she might not open the door. The time he stood there seemed endless. Then finally he heard the bolt slide back. He stepped aside, realizing she was not going to open the door fully. She remained in the protection of the flat. "Who's there?"

"Laundry, ma'am," he repeated, his hand covering part of his mouth.

She leaned her head out the door. He quickly stepped back again, and she took another step. "Show yourself! Who are you?"

Quickly he moved forward, grabbed her by the shoulders and stepped into the flat with her.

She gasped, her eyes wide. "Drew! Drew! What are you . . . how did you find me?"

He ignored her and looked around the room at her belongings. "Gather up anything you want to take with you, Laurel."

"I'm not going anywhere, Drew. My mind is made up, and while I didn't think you'd find me, now that you have I can tell you—"

"I'm not here to talk with you, Laurel. I'm taking you and Nathaniel with me. If you want your things, gather them up. Otherwise I am simply going to put you over my shoulder and carry you out of here."

"You wouldn't dare!" She glared at him, then stepped back, unsure at the hard look in his eye. "Drew, please, you can't . . ."

He glanced at the partially open door to the next room. He walked over to it. Paying small attention to what he picked up, he gathered stacks of neatly folded clothing and dumped them into an empty basket sitting by her washtub. He dumped into the basket small bric-a-brac he saw sitting around the room, any odds and ends he thought a woman might treasure.

Laurel stood cowed in the corner of the room, watching him with horrified eyes as he dismantled her home. "Drew, please, you can't do this! I'm not going with you! I don't want to go with you!"

He stopped for a moment, the words hurting. "You truly don't want to be with me?"

She hesitated for an instant, then said, "I said I didn't want to leave here."

He smiled then, and began to move faster. "Get Nathaniel, or must I carry you?"

"I'm not going, Drew," she said firmly, her face set, her eyes frightened.

He strode across the room, bent and grabbed her at the hips. With a yelp Laurel was over his shoulder, her head hanging down his back. He walked out the door with her kicking and yelling. He took her to the wagon, stopping to touch his forelock as a man passed by. "A wife needs a firm hand on occasion," he said graciously, as though nothing were amiss.

"Stop him!" Laurel screeched, beating on his back. "He's taking me against my will!"

Drew dumped her into the bed of the wagon. "Keep her here!" he said to Ben and whirled to go back to the flat. He brought out the basket of her things and went back the third time for Nathaniel. The small boy was sound asleep. Drew picked him up gently. The child stirred, then settled down against Drew's shoulder, his arms hanging limply. He carried the child back to the wagon to find Laurel giving Ben a tongue-lashing and struggling to get off the wagon.

Drew took her arm and held it firmly. His eyes bored into hers. Very quietly he said, "Hush, woman, and take the child."

Laurel's eyes flashed. She opened her mouth, ready to argue. Drew's grip on her arm tightened until she winced with pain. "We are not playing, Laurel. Take Nathaniel and keep your mouth closed." He carefully transferred the boy to his mother's arms. Laurel glared resentfully at him over Nathaniel's head, but she said nothing.

They drove through the night. By midday the next day Ben was drooping, and Laurel was asleep in the back. Nathaniel was perched happily on Drew's knee, his hands on the reins with his father's.

"Ain't we gonna stop?" Ben asked. "You ain't let us do nothin' but feed our faces since we lef' Charles Town. I thought you said we'd have an easy ride back."

"It will be easy as soon as your sister decides to be cooperative. Get in the back, Ben. You can catch some sleep. There's room."

"I don' want my head bounced aroun' like a mushmelon," Ben growled.

"Then tell your sister to stop her carping. We'll stop for rest as soon as I can trust her."

Ben threw his leg over the back of the driver's seat and climbed into the bed of the wagon. He shook Laurel's shoulder roughly until she awakened. "I ain't gonna be bounced all the way to Cherokee, so you got to start actin' right!" he yelled at his blinking sister. "Gimme your word!" he yelled.

"Leave me be, Ben. Why are you shouting?" She pulled a blanket closer around her and tried to get comfortable again.

Ben shoved her again. "Tell him you ain't gonna give him no trouble!"

"No!" she shouted back. "Leave me be, Ben! I don't have to talk to you, you traitor!"

Ben knelt down, sticking his face into hers. "I ain't no traitor! Now you tell him, Laurel. I ain't gonna be bounced no more on your account. Tell him!"

"He'll stop. He'll get tired, too."

"He don't git tired!" Ben howled. He grabbed his hair and began pulling it. He looked at her from the corner of his eyes. She hadn't noticed. He howled again. "Hurrrts, Laurel, ohhh!"

"Ben! Ben, are you having a . . . Drew, stop the wagon. Ben is taking a fit."

Ben hadn't had a fit in nearly a year. Drew glanced back at him and caught his wink. "Blame yourself," he said to Laurel. "I won't stop until I know you'll stay put and behave."

"You heartless . . . miserable . . ."

Drew whipped up the horses, and the wagon gave a forward jolt. Ben held his head and howled like a mad dog. Laurel's eyes were frightened and filled with pity. "I promise! I promise, Drew! Stop the wagon! Please! He's in terrible pain."

Drew pulled the wagon off the road where from many trips he knew the location of a deep grove of trees near a bubbling stream with a pool suitable for bathing.

Ben continued his charade and crept under a tree with a blanket to sleep while Drew set up camp alone. By nightfall he had made a shelter for them and corralled the immediate area so Nathaniel was free to wander about its confines safely. With the last stake in place he came to the campfire, where Laurel cooked dinner dutifully and sullenly. "Are you as angry as you seem?" he asked as he sat down near her.

She said nothing. She didn't look at him.

"You promised to be cooperative," he reminded her.

She glared at him and snapped, "I promised to be quiet and to behave."

Ben joined them. They ate in uncomfortable silence. After supper Laurel put Nathaniel to sleep in the shelter but did not return to the fire. She ignored the shelter Drew had made and took a blanket to the bed of the wagon. She curled up in the corner and tried futilely to find a soft spot. Determinedly she closed her eyes. They wouldn't stay closed. She found herself staring blankly into the night sky, playing out scenes of angrily assaulting Drew. She saw herself magnificent in her righteous anger and him bristling with masculinity in his desire for her. Restlessly she turned on her other side, then sat up, and finally, unable to stay still any longer, she got out of the wagon and paced around the corral. She was careful to stay at the perimeter, away from the fire and its light. She marched, arms folded, the anger reigning supreme in her, her eyes always seeking the sight of the man sitting near the campfire. She saw Ben get up and go to the shelter, but Drew remained sitting as he had been. She no longer took her eyes from him. She stood still, staring at him, her anger building so that she thought she might explode. As though propelled, she came hurtling out of the darkness.

"Why did you come get me?" she demanded.

He looked up at her, his brown eyes looking black in the firelight. "I wanted you," he said simply.

"I don't believe you! You wanted my son and had to take me to get him. I saw you with him today. You want him, not me!" She stamped her foot. "Tell me, Drew! Tell me why you came!"

He stood up and pulled his shirt off over his head. Then he stood in front of her barechested and reached for the front of her bodice. "I want you."

She grabbed the front of her dress and stepped back, eyes wide, mouth open. "No," she squeaked, all fire drawn from her.

Drew took another step toward her. She looked around frantically and began to run, scurrying like a trapped rabbit around the corral. He began to play with her, cutting off each escape route, his arms out, ready to catch her. She became more and more aware of him. The anger was gone, and play started. She darted and dashed about, evading his capturing hands. She tried but couldn't suppress her giggles. Panting, she darted to her left and ran headlong into his arms. He held her tight for a moment, then picked her up and carried her out of the corral to the edge of the stream. He laid her gently on the damp, soft ground and undressed her. Laurel's hands ran over him, her fingers tasting the texture of his skin. It had been so long, she thought she had forgotten, but it wasn't true—she remembered him as though he were part of herself.

Drew kissed her tentatively at first, then, as she responded, more fervently. His hands roved over her body as he had dreamed so many times. He felt the creamy smoothness of her flesh against his. Her embraces were strong and filled with warmth. He lowered himself down on her. She held him so tightly he seemed to melt into her.

They lay together, locked in each other's embrace, half dozing, half wildly awake, wanting each other again. With a sudden smile Drew clasped her tightly and rolled, plunging them both into the icy chill of the stream. Laurel gasped and screamed, then was captured by Drew's arms and drawn under into the deeper water of the pool. They swam and splashed and played until they were warm again.

Ben lay awake in the shelter, hearing the laughter and squeals, the silences and the running of feet. It was all he could do to keep himself inside the shelter. They all awakened late the following morning. Ben poked his head out of the shelter, a tentative smile on his face. Laurel looked up from the fire, saw him and grinned. She threw her cooking towel at him. "I'll still never forgive you, traitor!"

Ben laughed. "Don' look like I need it. Drew said he'd keep you busy."

"That's enough," Drew said from the stream. He came into the corral carrying fresh water. "Don't set her to thinking again."

But Laurel did think, and for the first time in his life Ben told her how he felt about their family and her misguided loyalty to them. He spoke aloud for her all the things she had felt from time to time but had put aside as being sinful or unworthy or cruel. She had never really thought of keeping her whereabouts hidden from Harley and Mathilda. Even now with the thought of living with Drew fresh and pleasurable to her, she knew it would be difficult to keep from her parents.

"Worse'n never seeing Drew?" Ben asked. "It's gonna be one or t'other."

Laurel looked at Ben for a long time, then nodded.

Drew and Laurel were married at Cherokee in April. None of her family, except Ben and Star Dancer, was there, and no member of Drew's family. But the yard was lined with tables of food, and fiddles played, and children laughed and ran in all directions, and her neighbors were there in abundance to wish her and Drew a good, long life together. Drew allowed it to be known that she was Mrs. Dancer, a widow, and no longer Laurel Boggs he was marrying. Even those who knew all or most of Laurel's story accepted what Drew said and made no mention of the outlaws or comment about Nathaniel. No one doubted that Drew Manning would be an important man in the district, and he was certainly not a man one wished to be on the wrong side of. If he wanted his wife to seem more respectable than she was, then it was small price to pay for his friendship and aid. No one could always bring in a good crop.

45

Laurel was radiantly happy in her new home. She could barely understand why she had fought so hard to avoid Drew. She had not seen or heard from her parents, which meant they didn't know she was nearby or that she was married. It bothered her a little that she didn't feel bad about turning her back on them. But she gave it less thought each day as the duties and demands of her own household grew. Drew had kept his promise. She was so busy she hadn't time for discontent—or rest.

She finished setting the table and stepped onto the porch to ring the huge supper bell Drew had installed. For the time being all the men who worked on Cherokee ate at the Manning table. She stood on the porch watching them walk toward her, talking, laughing, playfully punching each other like children as they came in from the fields.

Ned came rushing by with the farm wagon. He leaned over, sniffing the air. "What do I smell?" he asked, grinning.

"Taters an' beef!" Laurel called back.

"Ya-hoo!" Ned cried and threw his hat into the air. "I'm bear-eatin' hungry." He was still yelling as he entered the cavernous barn.

Laurel shook her head and took the stance of a guard on the porch. With her cooking spoon in evidence, she pointed to the stand and washbasin in the front yard. "Not a bite to eat until you are clean—face and hands!" She laughed and waggled her spoon at the men.

Drew, with Nathaniel walking manfully at his side, his small hand tucked in Drew's large one, came in last. She still looked carefully at Nathaniel from time to time, wondering if he was Drew's son and fearing she would see some sign that would mark him as Albee's. Every time he misbehaved or threw a temper tantrum, her throat tightened with fear that she was seeing the evidence of bad blood in him. Drew, on the other, shared none of her worries. He never questioned that Nathaniel was his own son. And she had to admit she had never seen Drew happier or more content. Cherokee was all Drew had promised it would be—a happy home filled with people, children and laughter. She wasn't certain yet, but she thought she would be telling him there would be one more occupant of Cherokee soon.

Drew and Ned and his crew of men worked the tobacco fields, driving themselves harder and harder as harvest neared. The tobacco barns were completed, and even before the planted fields were harvested, Ned and Drew were sectioning off the new land to be cultivated the following year. Both men knew that in order for the plantation to support them, it had to have a high-quantity yield as well as top-quality tobacco, and that took acreage and skill. Despite their efforts and the hiring of new men, most of Cherokee remained forest land.

Drew was exhausted when he returned to the house each night and knew that Laurel expected little of him. He did nothing to alter her expectations. He played with Nathaniel while she cleaned up after supper and often took the boy for long walks in the reddish-purple haze of twilight. When Nathaniel was put to bed for the night, he and Laurel spent a quiet, pleasant time together. Her talk was always cheerful and filled with the small amusements and tragedies that occurred each day.

Drew enjoyed watching her sew as she talked. They had concluded that she was definitely going to have another child, and he imagined nightly that he could see her belly rounding a little more. Laurel laughed at him and nearly lulled him to sleep with more of her humorous and endless tales of her day. It was her voice he listened to rather than her words. She spoke with the soft drawl and easy twang of the Carolina hills. Her speech was far better than her parents', but it was nonetheless different from Drew's. It was during these pleasant evenings he spent with her that Drew began to realize how badly he missed his own family. It had been over a year since he had sat at the Manning table and participated in the lively talk of politics and philosophy and art and music that Arthur, his father and mother and he had engaged in nightly. He missed the repartee and the facile play with words and thoughts.

And women—he missed the women. He thought of his cousin Beth, and of the Templeton sisters talking and fussing over the qualities of satin versus sateen, velvet or silk, chiffon or brocade. He missed seeing the heavily laced sleeves draped over well-creamed and scented hands and wrists. He missed the scented kerchiefs being wafted deftly and gracefully for his appreciation. Elegant, well-tutored, graceful women—yes, he missed them a great deal. And despite himself, he missed Gwynne. He had told his grandmother he'd talk to her when he came to Charles Town with the harvest. His promise had seemed reasonable then, and a long way off. But the time was approaching, and he no longer felt so reasonable. Laurel was now his wife. He was looking forward eagerly to seeing Gwynne, but he was also apprehensive, for he didn't know what he would say to her. Nothing was clear to him now, not even his sense of duty.

There was great excitement at Cherokee on the last day of harvest. The barnyards were bustling with activity as the tobacco was put into the sheds to dry. Drew couldn't stay away. Even in the night, after supper, he'd return to the long, narrow sheds to look at the tobacco, to check the color of the drying leaves, to feel the texture, to smell the aroma as it developed and began to fill the rooms.

Finally the day arrived when the tobacco was cured and crated in preparation for the trip to Charles Town. Drew was impatient and excited as last-minute checks to the loading were made. At last he kissed Laurel and his son good-bye, took from her her list of goods to be purchased in Charles Town, and he and Ned mounted and shouted orders for the wagons to begin their journey. Drivers hawed and geed, getting horse teams into proper formation. Drew and Ned rode ahead. Drew felt good, free and alert in a way he hadn't been since he last rode for the Regulators. He noted every twist and turn in the path they called a road, sending back instructions to the drivers about particular dangers to be aware of and when to take particular care of axles and wheel rims. There would be enough time spent in the repair of wagons from normal wear and tear, and he wanted no unnecessary wasted moments.

Elizabeth had shown Gwynne the letter she had received from Drew telling her he was coming to Charles Town with the Cherokee crop. She was looking forward to seeing her grandson, but this was not going to be an easy time for anyone. She looked across the room at Gwynne, who was staring moodily out the window. Gwynne had been very quiet for the past few days—every day, in fact, now that the time was near that Drew could be coming in with the wagon train.

Gwynne had said very little to Elizabeth about Drew or her feeling since the day months ago when Elizabeth had met her at the docks upon her return from England. That had been a day Elizabeth wouldn't forget readily.

Gwynne had been dressed in an off-white afternoon suit trimmed with black piping, a large, wide-brimmed hat with a veil covering a good portion of her face but hiding none of her beauty. Elizabeth hadn't been able to keep a smile from her face or tears from her eyes. She hadn't been able to look at Gwynne without thinking of Drew. She hadn't been able to accept that they didn't belong together. She had beat her small fist on the arm of the coach seat. "It isn't right!" She had thought it then and still did. She leaned back in the chair and let the memory play before her closed eyelids.

She had stepped from the coach as Gwynne disembarked and walked gracefully onto the wide planking of the pier. Gwynne waved as she caught sight of Elizabeth, her smile broad and bright. Even at a distance Elizabeth was aware of the bright, clear blue of her eyes. Elizabeth walked toward her, her arms outstretched. "Gwynne! I have missed you so! It's good to have you home again."

"I've missed you too, Elizabeth . . . and home. The last month I was in London, I thought I would die of homesickness." She giggled. "You must never tell Joanna I said it, but Bert's family is so stodgy, I took to talking to myself in my room. I was the best company I could find."

"It did your sense of humor no harm, I'm pleased to see. What shall we do to make up for your long absence? I'm not sure what is playing at the theater, but we can certainly find out easily enough."

"Oh, no, Elizabeth, that is one area in which London excels. I have seen every play one could wish to see and many I wish I had not. I would most like to sit with the family and hear what is happening right here. Have you seen my mother and father lately?"

"Your family is well. Your mother is put out, of course, for being deprived of Joanna's wedding. She was all set to have the social event of the year at Riverlea, and then it was taken from her. I am sure she will never permit Joanna to hear the end of it. The truth is, it gave Mima Mitchell something to crow about when she returned from London, and it is so seldom that Mima has one up on Ruth, she has played it to the hilt."

Gwynne laughed; then both women fell silent. Elizabeth held her breath. Before Gwynne said anything, she knew it would be about Drew. Gwynne couldn't look at her, and her voice was rigidly controlled. "How is Drew? I haven't heard from him for several months now."

"He's . . . he's well, I believe," Elizabeth said hesitantly. "Oh, pshaw, Gwynne, you know perfectly well something is amiss or I wouldn't have been at the dock, and you wouldn't be asking in this fashion. Drew is married to Laurel."

Gwynne looked quickly away, unable to talk, tears in her eyes. She allowed Elizabeth to guide her to the carriage.

Elizabeth chewed on her lower lip and directed the driver to take them to the park. She told Gwynne all she knew of Laurel and what had happened. "I could not in good conscience keep the information from him any longer. I wrote to him, and he came to Charles Town immediately and took her back with him. I had hoped he would see you again before I had to tell him about Laurel, but it didn't work out that way. I am so sorry, Gwynne. I encouraged you to pin your hopes on Drew when I had no right to say anything. And now I can do nothing to ease it for you. I have been a stupid, foolish old woman and have nothing but an apology to offer—cold, useless comfort."

Gwynne's face was ashen, but she managed a trembling smile. "Don't fret, Elizabeth. I am a stupid, foolish young woman. I can't very well criticize you, can I?"

"You couldn't have known this would happen, and perhaps you would not have been so courageous had I not been filling your head with my ideas of his love for you."

Gwynne's laugh was harsh and brittle. "Oh, you no longer believe in that love, Cousin Elizabeth?"

"Oh, my dear, don't do this to yourself. What can I say that will not hurt you more?"

"You might tell me what you think. What difference can it possibly make now? He is married. I am not. I can do nothing, and I doubt anything could give me greater pain than what I have already heard. It might make it easier to think that I had deluded myself all these years." Gwynne blinked back tears. "You see, Cousin Elizabeth, I, too, thought he loved me. I didn't think I could feel so much for him and have him feel nothing for me. At least if he never cared, I could now write this experience off as a romantic notion of no substance—part of the painful path to true womanhood. But if he does love me and has still married her, what then am I to think? How then could he do this?"

"I think it was the child," Elizabeth said quietly.

"He married her because she had a child? He doesn't even know who fathered the child! What madness is that? Drew has never expressed a passion for children."

"Drew believes he is the father of the child and so do I."

"He could have had other children!" Gwynne moaned.

Elizabeth winced. "One child can never replace another. Nathaniel is his firstborn son. Had it not been for the child, I doubt he would have come after her. I think it was primarily that he wanted the boy raised as a Manning. He could not have been certain what would have become of him if he had been left to his mother alone."

"Could we go home, Cousin Elizabeth . . . I feel quite ill. I'd like to lie down," Gwynne said, her coloring gray, around her mouth a ridge of white.

Elizabeth had said nothing to Gwynne about Drew coming to Charles Town with the harvest until some time later. Gwynne had had little reaction to that news. She spent much of her day thinking quietly, staring, although not vacantly, at something only she could see or understand. Elizabeth made no attempt to question her or be made privy to the thoughts Gwynne was having.

Gwynne mourned her loss of Drew to begin with, mourned the children she had dreamed of having with him and now never would. She had once thought her own child would be his firstborn son.

Later she put that aside and thought of herself. Drew had taken something precious from her and had neither recognized it nor valued it. She would never again be able to love in quite the same way she had loved Drew. There had been an innocent fervor to that love, a devotion that comes only rarely. The purity of her devoted passion belonged only to him. She resented his ignorance of it. It was a quality a woman has to give only once, and only to one man. A deep, glowing sadness welled up in her as she thought of the loss and came fully to realize that her ability to love purely and innocently was gone. She would not even be able to give it to Drew were he here to receive it. It was no more.

Still later, Elizabeth had told her that Drew was going to visit her when he brought the harvest from Cherokee into town. Her immediate reaction was that she didn't want to see him, but since then she had considered many possibilities. She had come a long way and had risked and changed her whole life to love Drew Manning. His not valuing that did not change it. There were other ways of loving a man and being with him than being his wife. That would be a major step for her and a departure from all she had been raised to believe was moral and proper. If she became his mistress she would be taking a radical and irrevocable step. She wondered: would she do it? For days she considered the possibility and came up with no answer. The closer the time came to Drew's arrival in Charles Town, the greater the question loomed in her mind.

46

The first few minutes of the meeting between Drew and Gwynne were tentative and awkward. All those things which should be said by way of apology, explanation and consolation were already understood between them without words. They both were aware of it, but neither knew how to bridge the gap between where convention placed them and where their minds and hearts had taken them.

Elizabeth had graciously and wisely had them meet alone in the privacy of her sitting room, but even with that their time was limited. Soon they would have to join the rest of the family. Each of them would be thrust into the mainstream of conversation and concerns that focused on the whole. This time was theirs and into it they had to fit and find a way to say all those things each of them wanted to say, and to resolve their feelings for each other.

Gwynne looked at Drew, her vulnerability weighing her down and keeping her speechless. She had removed herself so far from her mores to tell him she loved him; now she did not know how to step even further outside the custom of her upbringing to tell him that she wanted to be his mistress if she could not be his wife.

Drew, too, found himself without words. He had no means to tell her the truth. The facts of what he had done would imply a lie. He would sound as though he did not love Laurel at all and had married her out of a sense of duty and to gain control of his son—all of which was true, but not wholly. He did love Laurel and probably would until the day he died, but that love seemed to lack the depth, breadth or passion of what he was coming to feel for Gwynne. As difficult as it was to face, he was beginning to see what his grandmother had always seen—that he and Gwynne were as water to soil, sunshine to flowers, stars to the sky. But the time had passed. It said in the Bible that there was a time for everything; but it did a man no good to sow in the time of reaping; neither could he reap when it was time to sow. Yes, there was a time for everything, but everything had to be done in its own time. He had lost with Gwynne. He could not offer her his name, for he had already given it away. He couldn't offer her his protection, for he would not be near her to exercise it. And now he did not even have words to tell her what he felt for her.

He looked at her. She was very small and fragile-looking. Her dark hair was carefully pinned atop her head, her dark curls framing her face. Her eyes shone a brilliant blue, but in them was a knowledge and a hurt he had never seen there before. She had changed in some subtle way, but it served only to deepen the qualities in her that he already loved and knew and counted on. He wanted to stride across the room and take her in his arms and tell her of every thought and feeling he had ever had about her. Instead he shrugged and smiled diffidently. "We're not doing very well with this conversation."

"No, we're not, but I don't suppose that is surprising. It is as difficult to speak when one has too much to say as it is when one has nothing to say—perhaps more so."

Drew looked away from her. "When I first told Grandmother I wanted to see you, it seemed that what I wanted to tell you was clear cut, reasonable and relatively simple."

"What happened to change that?"

Drew glanced at her and then away, uncomfortable. "I don't know exactly."

"Oh, I think you do. I think it is the same thing that keeps me from saying aloud what I am screaming inside my head."

He moved closer to her, then stopped about a yard away. "Why did you agree to see me, Gwynne? You didn't have to . . . this cannot have been a meeting you looked forward to."

Gwynne looked at him as though he were a small, unruly boy. "You want me to lay bare my soul before you say anything, Drew, but my time for that was last Christmas Eve. This time you must freely open yourself to any criticism or rejection I might wish to render you before you know what it is that is in my mind. Tell me, Drew, why is it that you are here? Tell me why after you have married Laurel you felt it necessary to talk with me privately. Did you hope to save my feelings by coming here? Or is it that you seek something more from me? And Drew, please don't lie to me."

Again he looked away from her. "Leave it that I wanted you to hear from my own lips that I have done what I felt I must and that I believed at the time that it was best, and still do believe that. That is not all of the truth, but it is true, and whatever more I might think or feel can do you no good and perhaps could cause you more hurt."

"As you said, I have already been hurt by the truth of your actions, but I do wish to know all of it. I have tendered you an honorable request for the truth, Drew, and while I might be able to forgive your actions, I cannot and would not forgive your deliberate deception, even if it is by omission."

He took her hand. "Sit down with me." He led her to a small love seat near the window. The sun shone in, lighting up the richness of her skin. Her hair gleamed black in the bright light.

"Do you love me, Drew?" she asked, her eyes directly on his.

He couldn't break away from her gaze, nor could he speak. Finally he managed to look down. "And if I did? What good would it do either of us for me to say it? Laurel is my wife. Her children are my children. I am bound to her—willingly bound to her."

"Do you love me?" she asked again, her voice soft but sure.

"Why do you persist, Gwynne?"

"Because I need to know. Do you?"

"Yes, I love you," he said and looked up at her, his eyes filled with remorse and longing.

She leaned toward him. She stroked his cheek, her hand smelling of perfume. Her skin was soft and cool against his skin. "I once held my tongue and my heart still and lost you to my sister, or thought I did. Perhaps if I had not been so reticent then, you would not now be married to Laurel but to me. My family would have been wildly upset had you and I expressed a desire to marry, but the outcome would never have been so extreme as your breaking of the contract in order to marry Laurel. Most likely your father and mine would have sat down and amended the marriage contract and all would have worked out peacefully in the end. But I didn't do that, and now

. . . now we are at the impasse of today." She kissed him lightly on the cheek. "I'll not make that mistake this time, Drew. I may not be able to be your wife, but there are other ways that a man may be with a woman. I want to be your mistress, Drew." She took a deep breath. "Ahh, now it is said."

Drew was speechless. Then he took her in his arms and held her close against him. He felt the smallness of her and sensed the strength of her. She stirred in his embrace and lifted her lips to his. His mouth brushed against the warm softness of her. He could still not believe he had heard her say what she had said. Before he realized what she was doing, she had unbuttoned the bodice of her shirtwaist and lay back in his arms, her eyes sleepy and inviting. Drew touched her neck, then his hand moved downward. He marveled at the creamy whiteness of her skin, the rounded firmness of her form. She smiled at him, then laughed softly. She got up and took his hand, leading him to his grandmother's bed.

Drew's senses were reeling. He hardly believed any of what he was experiencing. He tried hard to reestablish his conception of his cousin Gwynne, but he couldn't. She was the woman he wanted and loved. There burned in him a passion he had never felt before. He lay on the bed beside her and sank into the dizzying splendor of that passion.

Gwynne was triumphant and happy by the time they dressed and prepared to leave Elizabeth's room to join the rest of the family. "Tomorrow we shall hunt for a flat that you can rent and use when you are in Charles Town," she said cheerily as she redid her hair in front of Elizabeth's mirror. "Of course, we must make certain that it has a completely private entrance. I shall have to be discreet."

Drew came up behind her and put his hands on her shoulders, looking at her in the mirror. "As much as I'd like it, I can't allow you to do this, Gwynne. It would only be a matter of time before we were discovered, and you would bear the brunt of public opinion."

"Not if we're careful, and as I see it, I haven't an acceptable alternative. I don't like the prospect of living alone for the rest of my life, Drew, and if you are thinking I should meet and marry some nice acceptable man, please stop. I don't want some nice acceptable man. I want excitement in my life. I want . . . I want passion." She turned on the vanity bench and put her arms around his waist, her face buried in his waist. "Don't try to protect me from you, Drew, please. Protect what I feel for you, cherish it, nurture it, keep it safe."

"It is no life for you, Gwynne."

"And if you refuse me this little I ask, what kind of life is there for me then? You are what I want for my life, Drew."

The following day they went hunting for a flat that Drew could rent ostensibly for his own lodgings while he was in Charles Town on business. No one questioned his desire, for most all of Charles Town knew of his disinheritance and of the difficulties his presence in Elizabeth's house caused with the rest of the Manning family.

During the following week Drew led the kind of life he thought had been left behind him forever. In the mornings and afternoons he and Gwynne searched tirelessly for exactly the right flat. It needed privacy, an entrance she could use without being observed and many windows—for Gwynne liked the sun and fresh air racing through her home.

In the evenings there were dinners filled with lively talk and argument and discussion of politics, philosophy, literature and drama. Elizabeth and Gwynne and Drew went to the theater twice that week and heard a concert at St. Cecilia's Society. The day before he left he filled the order of goods Laurel had requested and had the wagon he would take back loaded. He set up a bank account for Gwynne in his grandmother's name, for he didn't dare use her own for fear it would become public knowledge that the source of her income was him.

She met him at the nearly empty flat the last night he was going to be in town. A smile on her face, she stood in the center of the room and looked around her, noting the fine gleam of the hardwood floors, the detail of the woodwork. "The next time you come here, you won't know it is the same place, Drew. It will be furnished and decorated, and it will be ours—a special look that it will have will mark it as 'us.' "

Drew took her in his arms and held her, rocking back and forth to the rhythm of some inner music.

"I wish I could stay here with you tonight. You know that is what I want to do, don't you? I don't want to leave you, nor do I want you to leave me tomorrow morning. I don't want to be separated from you for so long a time as it will be until your next trip to Charles Town."

Drew kissed her forehead, then leaned back from her, looking into her eyes. "That is the main reason this is not a good or equitable arrangement for you, Gwynne. It gives me the best of both worlds, but what does it give to you? You have so little."

"I have you. Do you consider that so little?"

He shook his head. "You have me when I am here, and I will not be here enough for you—or enough to satisfy me."

Gwynne gave him a wicked little smile and released herself from his embrace. "I shouldn't tell you this, but I intend to make you want to spend more and more of your time with me—and I've considered visiting the Upcountry. Surprised, Drew? Or worried? No one would need know I was there, except, of course, you. I could stay in Camden."

Drew looked at her, amusement and thought showing in his eyes, but he said nothing.

Gwynne sashayed around the room, viewing him from the corner of her eyes. "That is certainly one way to find out just how much you love me, Drew. I said I wanted to be your mistress, and I do; but not *just* your mistress, and not one to be used as a convenience." She came close to him, then darted away, teasing, as she smiled and blew kisses at him. "Are you worried?"

47

Drew returned to the Upcountry with his head whirling. He never remembered having had a better time in Charles Town. He was filled with memories of dancing, laughing and making love. Gwynne seemed to have become a part of himself. As he drove the wagon, it was as if she were there beside him. He recalled so many of their times together and had the feeling he was once again sharing it with her.

Ned met him as he drove up the road to Cherokee. One look at his friend and Drew knew something had been afoot in his absence. Almost as if by magic all thought of Charles Town and his life there vanished, and his mind shifted to the Upcountry. Ned rode at the side of the wagon right to the front door of the house. At the sound of the wagon and the dogs barking, Laurel came out on the front porch. Her hair had sun-bleached streaks in it, and she was smiling, her eyes alight with love and joy at seeing him. Behind her, young Nathaniel came at a headlong race to his father. Drew climbed down from the wagon, scooped Nathaniel into his arms and embraced Laurel. Nathaniel squirmed and laughed at being squashed between them. Drew kissed Laurel's face all over and then Nathaniel's, sending the child into peals of laughter again.

Ned stood to the side of the family scene, not interrupting but leaving no doubt that he wanted to talk to Drew immediately.

Drew motioned to Ned to follow them as he and Laurel and Nathaniel went into the house. Laurel hurried to the kitchen to fix Drew and Ned something cool to drink and cold meat and cheese to eat. Then she went outside to look at the goods she had ordered and whatever surprises Drew had brought back for her.

"You look about to burst, Ned. What's been going on since I left?"

"Something's in the wind, that's for sure. I cain't say yet if it bodes good or ill. Jes' about two weeks ago a band o' Regulators got wind o' a shipment o' munitions bein' sent to Governor Tryon in North Carolina—he's been a real pain in everybody's ass—an' they decided he di'n't need no more munitions to do harm to our cause, so they hied themselves up there an' attacked his wagons and ruined the whole damn wagon train o' stuff."

"Were there any repercussions?" Drew asked.

"Well, I ain't heard o' none, but you can bet that Tryon ain't gonna let that pass without doin' somethin' back. This fightin' the royal government is gettin' to be an everyday thing, Drew, an' I have the feelin' we're gettin' into somethin' real deep before we even know what the hell it is."

"I have the same feeling, Ned, and it is something one can sense in the Lowlanders as well. No one is exactly saying anything; the feeling comes more from what is not being said. There are too many doubts and uncertainties, and too many questions being directed toward royal authority."

Two days later, as Ned and Drew were working in the fields, they both stopped work in alarm as the porch bell was ringing frantically. "'Spose somethin's happened an' she's havin' the baby?" Ned asked, dropping his hoe and running with Drew toward the house.

Drew's heart was pounding. The bell was still ringing harsh and insistent. He ran as fast as he could across the uneven ground back to the house. His heart was thudding against his chest, and there was the taste of fear in his mouth as he imagined fire or trouble with the new baby or an accident. The house stood whole and serene-looking when it came into view. Laurel was on the porch, ringing the bell herself. Nathaniel was clinging to her skirts. Drew was breathless as he leaped to the porch by her side. Ned was two paces behind him.

"John Haynes just rode in," Laurel said. "Drew, something awful must have happened. He's injured and very ill—he won't talk to me or let me do anything for him—he says he wants to talk to you."

Drew nodded. "Get someone to see to his horse, Laurel. The poor animal is about to fall." With foreboding he took the few steps across the porch and entered his house.

As soon as he came into the room, John got to his feet. He was smeared with black soot, his clothes were in tatters and his left arm hung limply at his side. Blood seeped through his trousers at his thigh.

Drew put his arms around his friend before John fell. He sat him down again, took the empty glass that had been on the table, sniffed the contents and refilled it with brandy. "Let me see to your wounds, John. You've lost a lot of blood."

John slurped at the brandy, his hand shaking violently. "Tryon got us at Alamance Creek, Drew." John said and squeezed his eyes shut against the memories still so fresh, the sounds and smells went with them. "Bart's dead . . . hundreds are dead."

"Regulators?"

John shook his head.

Drew stripped the filthy, tattered clothing from him and brought a pan of water Laurel had already drawn and heated near John. He washed the gash in John's arm and the musket fragment in the fleshy meat of his thigh. By the time Laurel came in again, he had John dressed in a voluminous nightshirt. John kept up his constant repetition of what had happened, but his words were unintelligible. All Drew knew was that Bart Cole was dead and that he and John had been riding with the Regulators in North Carolina and had battled with Governor Tryon's troops. He washed John's face again and pulled his chair near the bed he had dragged into the middle of the room.

Only when she walked in the door did he realize Laurel had been gone a long time.

"How is he, Drew?" Ned asked, and came immediately to John's side.

"He seems to be sleeping pretty well. You might take another look, Ned. I think I have gotten the wounds clean, but you're a better hand than I. It looks like a saber cut and a minie ball to the leg. I don't know about that arm. It doesn't look good . . . a lot of muscle has been cut."

"From the sounds of it we've got a dirty business this time. Like we said the other day—Tryon's on the warpath after the Regulators. Laurel and I talked to a couple o' fellas riding through here on their way south."

"Do we know them?"

"I seen 'em before—North Carolinians—but I don't know 'em. They said mos' headed up to the hills in Tennessee. Tryon's out fer blood, an' he's got men scatterin' all over."

"What happened?" Drew asked. "Did Tryon just flush them out or was there a battle?"

"Di'n't he tell you?"

"I couldn't understand most of it. He did tell me about Bart. It hasn't sunk in, Ned. Bart can't be dead. He's always so full of orneriness . . . ready to argue, fight . . ."

"There'll be a few faces we won't be seein' anymore. Fellas told me a couple hundred at least were shot down, and they hanged six on the spot . . . more taken prisoner." Ned reached for the brandy. "They been takin' gun shipments from Tryon, more'n I knew about, and he come after 'em, like we thought he would."

"Did he take them by surprise? The little John said made it sound like a massacre."

"Nobody seems too clear. Seems like they had near two thousand Regulators massed up near the creek, an' Tryon an' his militia come up. Them Tarheels mostly wants local grievances righted, so maybe they thought they was gonna parley, but Tryon came in shootin' an' whoopin'. He scattered the Regulators every which way. They musta been expectin' him to talk, else they'd a never stood there an' got shot up. Them North Carolinas ain't the quality we got in our group, but a lot o' our men was up there too, an' you know, Drew, you don't get no Regulators to bust apart an' run if somethin' isn't wrong."

"Do you know who was hanged?"

Ned shook his head. "Not yet, but I aim to afore the day's out. Mebbe we better be on guard here. Soun's like this is over, but it's hard to tell. Mebbe those fools in Cha's T'n's gonna take it in their heads to come up here."

For the rest of that day and night they all sat tensely waiting to hear news and watching over John Haynes. They took turns sleeping when they were all too tired to remain awake, and still no messenger came.

Bart's body was brought home, and the Manning household of Cherokee went to the funeral, hands folded in front of them on a gray, drizzling day. Drew could not get himself to accept that it was really his friend Bart Cole in that pine box sitting on the ground. The last time he had seen Bart on one of his trips into Camden, Bart had been laughing and full of talk about his young wife Miranda. He and Drew had laughed about how they had met at the grave cleaning and how she was supposed to have been Drew's girl, but that Drew had ended up with Laurel and Miranda had been his.

Drew looked at the box sitting so sterile and impersonal on the ground and his mind fought against what he knew. It had to be someone else—a mistake. He held his hands tightly, fighting down an irrational desire to rip open the box and shout to all present, "See! It isn't Bart! It's not him!" A sound of utter desolation startled him, and he looked up to see Miranda, looking younger than her fifteen years, curl over and pitch into her father's arms. Laurel stood beside Drew, her hand pressed against her mouth to keep her sobs quiet. Reverend Fowler talked in a slow, almost sleepy voice. He, too, seemed too stunned to be able to take this occasion for the glory of his own eloquence.

A pall of empty silence fell over all the men from Cherokee. Not a word was spoken as they drove back home. Drew went into the house to take his turn at John's side. It was dark with the gloom of the rainy day, but he lit no lamp. He sat down in the chair, his hands once more folded across his stomach, held quiet and inactive. There was a vague feeling of apprehension throughout him. Something about Alamance Creek kept running in his mind. Alamance Creek. Was it the beginning? Was the battle of Alamance Creek one that would leave its mark and lead to the next battle and then the next? All last year he had thought about and even awaited the inevitable confrontation over English rule and American rights. Just recently he had returned his attention to his own life and begun to build Cherokee into what he had always dreamed. Would it end so soon? Did he have months and years to enjoy his family and farm, or would it be only days?

He looked carefully at John. Satisfied that he was breathing easily and sleeping soundly, he got up and walked into his and Laurel's bedroom. Her hair was spread across the pillow, her hand out and touching the place where he would sleep. He stood unmoving in the darkness. Bart Cole was dead. Bart Cole was dead. One instant he had been belligerently alive, and the next he was dead. How quickly that last battle had had to come upon him to catch him. How unexpectedly. One day separated from the others by an eternity.

He undressed hastily, tossing his clothes behind him and got into
bed with Laurel. This day was not his day. This day he had to live.
He didn't know about tomorrow, but he had what was left of this
day and night. He stroked Laurel's face. She moaned softly and
opened her eyes. He took her into her arms, holding her closely,
gently, feeling and warming himself with the life of her. He kissed
her and looked at her, enjoying as he never had before every sensa-
tion that came through his fingertips as he touched her, the sound
of her breath passing his ear. The air in the room tingled with their
vitality, and Drew knew as he never had before how much he
wanted to be alive.

He clung to Laurel, and after she had fallen sound asleep, he lay
awake in bed, listening to the sounds of the night. Some time before
dawn he fell asleep and the sounds turned to the marching of feet,
the distant British drums far away and insistent. He awoke, sitting
bolt upright to the sound of a piercing scream. He ran to the front
room to find John panting and breathing heavily. He was covered in
sweat, his fever broken. "I was dreaming," John gasped, and fell
back on the bed. "My God, I thought I was back there—at Alamance. I thought it had begun all over again. My God, Drew . . ."

Drew washed him down but said nothing. He looked carefully at
John's wounds and sat beside him until John fell asleep again. He
went outside to a bright, sunny day. His mountain was brilliant with
green. His fields cut dark patches in the verdant expanse. It was
peaceful—so far removed from the dream he had last night—yet
the sounds of drums continued like a haunting melody in his ears.
He walked the entire property then returned to the house. Laurel
stood in the kitchen, the house filled with the good odors of breakfast cooking. It was so familiar, yet it made him feel like crying. He
hugged her and kissed the back of her neck. He went to his son's
bedroom and looked down on the sleeping child. Unable to resist,
he picked the little boy up, cushioning his sleepy head against his
shoulder.

His eyes sought the window and the brilliance of the sunlight.
There was no acrid smoke of musket fire marring the air. There
were no drums, nor screams; no marching feet or assembling cav-
alry. This day was his.

48

Drew took his crop to Charles Town, as usual, in the late fall of 1771, just in time to hear the news that Lieutenant-Governor Bull had issued pardons to the South Carolina Regulators who had been sitting in Charles Town prisons. Bull had claimed that after investigation of the conditions of the Upcountry, the Regulators had illegally but deservedly punished the criminals who had ravished their lands, their homes and their families.

Drew looked at Gwynne, a frown on his face.

"Doesn't this please you?" she asked. "The Charles Town government is finally verifying that you had a right to do what you did. They are recognizing the problem and giving it proper weight."

"Yes, finally. But it comes too late for some very good people."

"You're thinking of Bart Cole?"

"And of Laurel—and Miranda. And Bull is just one man. His pardon is not going to have much influence on men like Governor Tryon. Yes, to answer your question, I am glad someone had finally publicly admitted that our grievances are real and our methods the only ones open to us, but it has come too late." He sat quietly for a moment, then said softly, "Much too late."

Gwynne felt a tightening in her throat. "That seems to be the mark of our times—everything happens too late. Why do you suppose that happens? Is it the times, or is it us?"

"You are asking the age-old question, Gwynne. Is man the product of his times or are the times the product of man. I doubt either is the answer; both are most likely true." He leaned back on the sofa she had bought and had delivered in his name. "It wouldn't change anything even if we did have an answer."

"Perhaps not, but it would make me feel a great deal better. I feel so uncertain of everything. I can't seem to keep control over what is happening even in my own daily activities. I go to a tea, and it may be as harmless as a hundred others I've gone to, yet it may just as likely end up with some of the women leaving, angry because of some political remark. I can hardly tell my friends from those who not only disagree with me but may overtly oppose me because of some view I hold."

Drew watched her for a moment and saw the unease that was in her eyes and had caused the tiniest line to form on her forehead. "You are having a difficult time. I wish there were something I could do . . . some way I could be here for you, help you."

Gwynne sniffed back a threatening tear and smiled. "But you can't. And I won't have us ruining what we do have by dwelling on what we can't have. We're together, Drew. We talk, and we love, and we know each other in secret ways that make us something very special."

Drew got up and took her in his arms. "My God, I love you."

She laughed, but her voice caught, and it was nearly a sob. "I know, Drew, I know you do, but we are creatures of our times. We discovered our love too late. Too many things were decided even while we were still in our cradles."

"The marriage contract my father made with yours."

"Yes, it did start there, didn't it? Had I not respected Joanna's claim to you as her future spouse . . . had you not accepted me only as your sister . . . what would have happened, Drew?"

He kissed her gently, then playfully. "I would probably have tried to catch you unawares in the hay mow."

She laughed, too. "You might have caught me, but I doubt it would have been unawares." She tilted her head to the side. "However, in different circumstances I might have wished you to think it were unawares. As it was, I had to turn myself into a hussy even to get your attention."

"Never that. You are very brave."

"Oh, Drew, do something to make me stop thinking. I keep wanting to cry out to whatever powers that be that it isn't fair that Joanna should have been designated to be your wife, that it isn't fair that you should have met Laurel, that it isn't fair that she should bear your children. It isn't fair, Drew, when it is I who want you to be by my side so badly." She buried her face in her shirt. "Drew, hold me and make me stop thinking."

During Drew's stay in Charles Town, he and Gwynne stayed together most of the time, seldom leaving the flat, seldom attending the theater or participating in any of the Lowland Manning functions. Elizabeth worried about their constant seclusion but said little. But she was not the only one who noticed how frequently Gwynne was going out and alone.

As Gwynne left Elizabeth's house one afternoon to meet Drew, George fell into step with her as she walked swiftly down the street. "Let me come with you today, Gwynne," he said.

She gave him a look of pretended surprise. "Go with me, George? Whatever can you mean? I am only going to do a little shopping and then to visit a friend for a bit."

"I know whom you are going to visit, Gwynne, and believe me, I am not judging you. I've known for some time about you and Drew. I don't know how to view it. He's married, and I can't see any good in it for you. I don't pretend to understand, but I know better than to try to stop either of you. I just want to protect you a little. You see him too often, and always alone. Let me protect you this little, please, Gwynne."

She stopped walking and turned her face from the street. She stood near the wall of a building and covered her face with her hand. "Oh, George, I feel such a fool, and so ashamed, but I can't stop. I want to be with Drew no matter what."

"Will you allow me to accompany you at least part of the time?"

She wiped her eyes with the handkerchief he handed her and nodded. "I'd like you to come with me. Drew would like to see you, too. I don't know what is so different about this time, but I want to be with him all the time. It is not good; I think I am obsessed. It is not good for Drew, either. Did you know that Laurel is going to have their second child any time now? I think actually he wants to leave to be with her—as he should—but he is not leaving because of me."

"Ah, Gwynne, we all wanted so much more for you," George said sadly and felt like crying himself. Had they not been on the street, he would have taken her in his arms and comforted her. As it was, he could do no more than offer her his arm and place a mild pressure on her arm to let her know how much he cared.

She stopped when they reached the front of Drew's flat and stood looking at the facade. "Help me, George. I've got to be strong enough to free him to go back to the Upcountry. Stay with me. If you're there, I'll keep remembering what I must do for both our sakes."

Drew left for the Upcountry two days later and arrived early in December, the day after Laurel had given birth to their first daughter. He hurried into the bedroom they shared and looked at his wife. Laurel smiled happily at him, her arm tucked around the child. She raised the little girl slightly so that Drew could see her.

Drew sat on the side of the bed. He smoothed Laurel's hair back from her face. She was pale, and under her eyes were deep circles of darkness. "Ned said that you had a difficult time," he said and kissed her. He pulled the swaddling blanket away from the infant and touched his daughter's tiny chest and then her hand, allowing her fingers to wrap around his. "I should have been here with you," he said softly.

"You came as soon as you could," she said. "I know that, and there was no way of knowing when she was going to come. Ned and I got along just fine, and Star Dancer came to help me."

"She was here? Thank God for that."

"She likes the baby. She said she would be a good sister to Nathaniel."

"What does Nathaniel think of his new sister?"

Laurel laughed. "He pokes at her and talks to her, wanting her to talk back, and when she doesn't, he gets angry and impatient, as only Nathaniel can."

"Have you named her yet?" Drew asked.

"No, I was waiting for you. Drew . . . could we name her Mary?" she asked and looked at him hopefully, but also with a trace of uncertainty. "Or do you think it would be bad luck to do that?"

"I would like her to be named after your sister," he said, and took the baby from Laurel's arm. He rocked her and held her up to his cheek. "My little Mary, welcome to your father's house," he crooned. The baby stirred in his arm, her small lips pursed, her tongue curled to receive another drop of milk as she touched his flesh.

Laurel was very slow in recovering from Mary's birth. She had little strength and tired around midday. Drew hired a young girl from a neighboring farm to help with the household chores and the two children. Penny Webb was an energetic, matronly young girl, plain of face and efficient in all her actions. She took tremendous pride in her new position and would not allow Laurel to do anything she herself could do.

Laurel was grateful for the help, but she began to brood more and more about her lack of energy. She knew that her fatigue was part of her recovery and that she did not bear children easily, yet a nagging worry that plagued her wouldn't retreat. She kept thinking of her mother. Mathilda was called lazy, and she was, or at least seemed to be. Each time Laurel permitted Penny to cook a meal or bathe the children in her place, she wondered if she did it because she was truly weak or if it was just a step in a transformation that would eventually make her exactly like Mathilda.

As the fear that she was becoming like her mother grew, Laurel took extra pains to dress nicely, to always be immaculately clean and attentive to Drew. She worried about every hair out of place, every stain that ever appeared on her garments and any comment, however innocent, Drew might make that she could consider critical.

The spring of 1772 came in hot and wet. "It's gonna be a fever summer," Ned said as he and Drew stood in the fields, staring up into a momentarily cloudless, blue sky. "All the city folk will be runnin' from Charles Town fer the country. Don't think they can outrun it this year."

"It'll be bad for the tobacco, too," Drew said, and felt the musty, humid dampness of the soil. Even in the woods he could smell the decay, and already the insects were thick and hungry. "I've been promising Laurel I'd show her a part of the world other than South Carolina. Maybe this is the year to head north for a time."

"T'wouldn't be a bad idea. Once we get the fields planted and set, there's no reason I can't see to things here till harvest." Ned mopped his brow, then bent back to his work. "I sure do hate workin' in heat like this."

Drew told Laurel that evening that as soon as the fields were set, he would be taking the family north for the summer. Mary, her small face a smiling round globe, sat happily in his lap. Her small fingers plucked at the buttons on his shirt. Her hair was a riotous mass of bright red curls, her eyes a brilliant blue. Drew smiled affectionately at her and then looked at her mother. "She is going to break hearts all her life." He laughed and fluffed the downy curls on her head. "Do you suppose this color will tone down a little as she grows older? She is likely to blind people as well."

Laurel smiled but said nothing. She picked at some lint that had stuck to her skirt as she knitted. She glanced nervously at Drew as her fingers rapidly picked and brushed at the skirt. She sat still for a time after she was satisfied her skirt was clean and neat, then she said, "We are going to have another child."

Drew smiled at her. "Are you certain?"

"Yes," she said mildly, then went back to her knitting.

Penny came into the living room to take the children to bed. Drew brushed her away and said he wanted to do it. Nathaniel, knowing he could play and hear stories if it was Drew who put him to bed, hopped at his father's side, jumping up to touch Drew's arm.

Drew disappointed his son that night. He efficiently and quietly washed the two children and put them into their beds with a kiss and little else. Nathaniel was too young to understand what was happening, but he was a bright child and knew to keep quiet, for his father was not like himself this night.

Drew sat in the children's room quietly, saying nothing, doing nothing but staring out the window at the darkness. He was thinking of Laurel and the new child to come. He had talked many times with Star Dancer about Mary's birth, and the Indian woman had told him Laurel was not strong and could never bear many children as other women might. Drew had tried to stay away from her, only touching her, but Laurel was afraid he no longer cared if he was not ardent. His own guilt over his feelings for Gwynne and his knowledge that she would be there for him anytime he went to Charles Town, coupled with Laurel's need for his passion, had caused him time after time to make love to her when he knew he should not. Now she was pregnant again, and she had no strength from the last birth. And deep inside he had to admit that he wanted the child. He liked his children around him. He enjoyed their laughter. He liked to watch them learn. He gloried in their love for him.

But what was he doing to his wife? He was betraying her with his thoughts and actions with Gwynne, and he was risking her health by her bearing his children. He thought of the obsessive feeling Gwynne had had the last time he was in Charles Town, and now he understood it. Perhaps she had second sight, or perhaps, being a woman, she had known things about Laurel he had not. But she had been right in clinging to him, for it would now have to serve as their good-bye. When he was next in Charles Town he would have to tell her he could not continue seeing her as they had been. He wasn't sure if God punished sins so immediately, but he wasn't willing to risk Laurel any further. He was her husband. She would have him as such, and he would honor his marriage vows. Perhaps then she would grow stronger. Perhaps this baby would not be so difficult for her.

He got up, kissed both his children again and went back to the room where his wife sat knitting, then cleaning off her skirt.

She looked up at him when he came in. "Did you ever like my mother, Drew?" she asked, then looked away again. "I mean, did you ever look at her and think perhaps she was a nice woman— sometime—maybe when she was younger?"

"I never knew your mother very well, Laurel, and the time I spent most around her was a very bad time for everyone. I don't think I ever thought much about her—except that she was upsetting you, and I wanted that stopped."

"You don't like her. You think she is worthless," Laurel said. "Well, so do I. She always said she'd seen too much of this world and had lived too long. I guess she was right."

Drew chuckled. "I doubt that. I think Mathilda will be around for a good long time."

"She used to tell me she was real pretty when she was young, prettier than me."

"Are you worried that you aren't pretty anymore now that you've had the children? I think I shall have to buy you a new and larger mirror. You are becoming more beautiful by the day."

Laurel blushed. Her hands went to her hair, making certain it was smooth and carefully set.

***

The work in the fields was slow. The heat was oppressive, and there was seldom a day that there was not some rain. Already they were having trouble with the new plants rotting in the ground. Laurel was listless about the house, and the children were cranky and fussy in the heat. Even Penny found it difficult to muster her usual explosive energy.

By mid-April Drew and Ned began hearing reports of fever as far west as Camden. Ned had been right. This year the people of Charles Town would not be able to seek safety from the fever by hiding in the country. The fever was everywhere.

"I think you jes' better take that family o' yours an' go, Drew. We ain't gonna have any crop to brag on this year anyhow. Git outta here while you can."

Drew procrastinated a few more days, then decided to take Ned's advice. He told Laurel to prepare for the trip, and as soon as she was ready they would leave for Boston. Laurel expressed great interest in Boston and hid from Drew the fact that this pregnancy was not going well. She wasn't in the least sure she could ride such a distance, no matter how comfortable he made the coach or how slowly he took the trip. She was sick to her stomach daily, and she had dizzy spells that left her wondering if the world would ever stop spinning. She too often felt feverish and faint, although she was certain she didn't have the fever. And thoughts of Mathilda had come to haunt her in her waking hours as well as in her sleep. She could no longer tell if her weakness came from a bloodline tainted with weakness and laziness or if it was because of bearing the child. She was tired. Tired as Mathilda had been tired.

She often dreamed of the outlaw Albee, too. She kept confusing the bearing of this child with the time she had carried Nathaniel and hadn't cared if she lived or died. There were so many things happening inside her that she wanted to hide from Drew, because she knew they weren't right and shouldn't be happening, but she couldn't control them. This morning she had asked Drew if he had seen Star Dancer. It wasn't until he said that it had been a week since he had seen her that she realized she had thought that Star Dancer was with her and that they were traveling endless roads and woodland trails back to Camden. Drew hadn't seemed to think her question strange, and she was grateful that she didn't have to explain her confusion to him. But she would have to be more careful with what she said to Drew, because she could no longer trust her sense of the past and of the present.

Laurel talked of getting ready to go to Boston, but she did nothing. Each day she would decide to prepare the house, pack the luggage and make what other arrangements were necessary the next day. Drew allowed the work in the fields to occupy him. Often he asked Laurel how near to being ready she was, and each time she said vaguely, "Soon." He let that satisfy him, and he went back to his business with Ned, never noticing what Laurel was actually doing or how listless she had become. Penny kept the house neat and orderly, the dinners were always on time, the children well cared for. Drew never questioned how much or how little of this Laurel was responsible for, and Penny never complained or commented on the amount of work she was now doing.

As the problems of weather and crop disease increased, days slid by, and Drew did little other than remind Laurel that they must think of leaving very soon. He probably would not have thought to do even that had it not been for the letters coming regularly from Elizabeth in Charles Town. Elizabeth was uneasy about the fever this season and chronicled for Drew each occurrence among their friends and neighbors. She was even considering leaving the city herself for the supposedly safer environs of Riverlea. Neither she nor Gwynne felt badly or was worried about her own health at the time, for which Drew was very glad and relieved, but it did serve to remind him that he and Laurel and the children must leave. Cherokee would have to wait.

This time he spoke to Penny and told her to pack the necessary clothing for the children, Laurel and himself, and to have them ready by the end of the week.

"Yes, sir," Penny said respectfully, and then added, "I think it will do that little Mary a world of good. Maybe she'll get back on her feed."

Drew looked sharply at her. "What do you mean, back on her feed? What is wrong with Mary? Why haven't you said something to me?"

"I was gonna, sir, but the missus said that there wasn't anything to be done an' she'd be jes' fine given a few days. Miz Laurel said it was in her family that chillen don't allus eat an' nothing bad would happen to Mary. I was gonna tell you, sir," Penny said, nearly in tears. She took her responsibilities to heart and could be devastated by the slightest hint that she had been slack in her attendance to duty.

"I'll speak to Mrs. Manning. In the meantime you get the luggage packed. And make certain you remember to tell your family you'll be traveling with us and shall be gone for an extended period," Drew said, and he dashed up the stairs to his and Laurel's bedroom.

"Laurel," he called, and burst into the bedroom before she had a chance to get up and appear busy. "Penny tells me Mary hasn't been eating her meals for the last few days. Why should that be? She eats like a young colt most of the time."

Laurel glanced at the crib in which Mary was napping. "She's all right, Drew. You know she's always been a frail child. Mama never thought she'd live to see her second birthday."

"Laurel, are you fully awake? I'm not talking about your sister, I am referring to our daughter."

Laurel looked at him in alarm, then blushed. "I guess I was napping. It is so peaceful here with the baby sleeping and . . . what did you ask me, Drew?"

"The baby—Mary, our Mary—is she ill? Have you checked her to be certain she isn't feverish? My God, Laurel, I've warned you and warned you that we must be alert with the children this season."

Laurel glanced at her daughter's crib. Mary seemed healthy to her. She thought of Mary and Pamela and Willy at her home, and Mary seemed much better than any of them had. It was true the infant had been a little less active of late, and she had not been feeding well, but she slept peacefully, and she was quiet and good.

Drew was at his daughter's crib, his hands under her gown, feeling the heat of her small body. Her little cheeks were flushed, and her sleep was too deep to suit him. "Tell Penny to get in here right now."

Laurel moved slowly and ponderously, not feeling like getting out of her bed, her belly now large and awkward. She didn't feel well, and too often she was dizzy when she stood up. Drew glanced back at her impatiently and walked to the door, shouting Penny's name.

"You'll awaken the baby, Drew," Laurel complained.

"I want her awake, damn it! She sleeps too much. That baby has a fever. What were you going to do, sit there in that bed and let her get so ill we could do nothing for her?"

Penny hurried into the room with Nathaniel a few steps behind her. Nathaniel's eyes were huge. His father never spoke that way unless he was very angry or something was very wrong. "Yes, sir?" Penny said, nearly holding her breath.

"This child has a fever. Take her out of this room and keep her from her mother. If it is yellow fever, Laurel should not be near her. And keep her separated from Nathaniel. I don't want him ill, either. Except for her normal sleeping periods, I want you to keep her awake, and for God's sake get fluids into her. Let her suck on a wet teat, anything, but don't let me hear from you again that she won't feed. I'll send Ned for the doctor in Camden. Until then you do whatever you can to break this fever and get her to take nourishment. Bathe her down. Do what you must and do it now."

"Yes, sir," Penny said nervously and scooped the sleeping baby up from her crib. "I'll take her to the playroom. She'll be jes' fine there, an' I'll stay right with her."

Drew nodded curtly and rushed from the room to find Ned.

Laurel sat on the bed, bewildered and frightened. Mary had seemed all right to her. Why hadn't she known? She was the child's mother! Why hadn't she been the one to sound the alarm? Didn't she care? Was there some lack in her that made her unable to see what others did, to care as Drew was able to care? She could never remember having seen a doctor in the Boggses' house. Even when Willy fell when he was an infant and cut his head so badly they never thought it'd stop bleeding, no doctor was called. Mathilda had said he'd be all right by and by. And he had been—after a fashion. No, he hadn't been. She put her hands over her face and began to cry. Willy hadn't been all right, and neither had Mary or Pamela. Mary had coughed and spit up till there was nothing left in her, and she had never gotten well. And Pamela would have died before she was two years old, Laurel knew. Mathilda had been just like her—she hadn't seen or cared enough to see what people like Drew could see in a glance.

She rolled back and forth in the bed, aching all over. Finally she knew—there was a difference between people like Drew and the Mannings and people like her and the Boggses. Low people were different. There was something inside them that was different. She was different. She cried harder, holding her large belly, which ached and hurt all the time. Almost always her legs ached, and her back felt like it was on fire. She was sick to her stomach, and her ankles and sometimes even her hands would swell to the point she thought they'd burst. The ache increased as she thought of herself and Mathilda.

For the first time in her life she understood how Mathilda could encourage her to use her marriage to Drew to further the family's lagging fortunes and ambitions. Harley and Mathilda had been burned out and used up long, long ago. But they had wanted better for their daughter—and perhaps, through her, for themselves. Laurel shivered in the heat. She was so often cold these last few days. Her teeth chattered, and the tears ran down her cheeks. Drew would hate her now. He'd blame her for anything that happened to Mary. He'd be right. She deserved blame. Her mind spun.

She squeezed her eyes shut. Oh, Lord, she did understand Mathilda's hopes for her, no matter how twisted they had sounded. She didn't want Mary to grow up to be like herself. She didn't want all this doubt and self-loathing to live inside her own daughter. She got up from the bed, wincing in pain as she did. She grasped the bedpost, as she nearly fell from dizziness. She stood still for a moment, steadied herself and waited for the vertigo to dissipate, then she walked slowly to the door, down the stairs and outside. When she reached the woods, she had forgotten the house. She was thinking of the miles and miles of wilderness that she and Star Dancer had walked.

The wind tugged gently at her clothes and brushed across her dry, hot face, cooling it a little. Her eyes were glassy, and she began to smile. Star Dancer seemed to be walking just ahead, out of sight, but she had taught Laurel to follow her trail. Laurel felt confident again. She no longer needed to know where she was going or what her intentions were. She'd just follow Star Dancer's lead. Star Dancer didn't even know her name.

Laurel walked until the daylight began to fade. She spoke to the nonpresent Indian woman and listened as she imagined Star Dancer told her to camp for the night, for she needed rest. Laurel curled up near a large old tree. She mounded dead leaves until she was comfortable, then, with the world spinning, she lay down and closed her eyes against the dizzying, sickening whirl. She fell sound asleep. Some time later, after it was fully night, she awakened to waves of pain rolling across her abdomen. She thought she could hear Star Dancer's admonitions. She laughed in relief that there was someone there telling her what to do. She wanted so badly to be like Georgina Manning that she would never squat in a field to bear a child unless someone else told her to and she had no choice.

She got up and nearly fell. She was shivering with cold, but her face was afire. She mounded the leaves again and looked around for the swaddling clothes Star Dancer had told her she had ready. She couldn't find them, but the pain was intense again. She squatted in the field. She smiled through the pain as she remembered: after the baby was born she could go home to Drew. Drew was waiting, and he loved her.

Drew listened to the doctor tell him that there was nothing to be done for his daughter other than what he had already begun. "If there was an easy answer to the fever, Drew, people would not leave the cities every summer. She seems a strong child. Break the fever and you will have her good as new soon enough," Dr. Blake said with an apologetic shrug. "I could bleed her, but to tell the truth, I've never observed that bleeding did much good, and she is very young."

Drew looked away from Dr. Blake and bent over the crib of his child. "How do you call yourself a doctor if you can do nothing?" he said in disgust.

Blake's voice cracked. "You can hold me in no lower esteem than I hold myself, Drew. I wish I could offer you some knowledge, God knows, but I have none. The human body is still a mystery. I am not a magician."

"You're little more than a damned veterinarian," Drew snapped.

Dr. Blake shrugged. "I can't argue that, but we are learning. And Drew, I know what you feel now, and I understand your anger, but believe me, I'd give my own life if I could do something for that sweet child."

Drew finally relented. "I know you would. Please accept my apology. I am angry—angry that this should be visited upon one so helpless and innocent, and angry that I can do nothing and you cannot do it for me."

"I know; apology accepted and welcomed. I think Mary will come through this. She does not seem nearly so ill as others I've seen, and she is well cared for. Shall we now see to her mother? Your wife must be very anxious now, and in her condition it will be all the more distressing."

Drew nodded and told Penny to stay by Mary's crib and to let him know if there was any change in her fever. He walked with Dr. Blake down the short, wide-planked hallway to his and Laurel's bedroom. He hadn't realized that he was also angry with Laurel until Dr. Blake had suggested they see to her. Even though he had forbade her to be around Mary, he resented her obedience. She was the child's mother. Not only should she have been the first to notice something amiss, she should have been at the child's side no matter what he ordered.

He was ready to argue with her as he opened the door. The room was empty and had a strange, eerie feeling. "Where in the hell is that woman?" Drew asked with a gruffness that masked alarm. He wheeled and went back out the door and down the steps, with Dr. Blake several paces behind him. "Ned," he shouted. "Have you seen Laurel?"

"Ain't she back?"

"Back from where?"

"Right after the doc here went up, I saw her go out. I jes' s'posed she was headed fer the well, but she sure oughta been back by now."

Drew leaped down the front steps and ran for the well. Laurel was not there, nor was there any sign that she ever had been. His anger and fear leaped higher.

The three men searched the house, called for her, walked through the stables and the tobacco buildings. "Where could she be?" Drew asked, his eyes now filled with naked anxiety.

"I'll gather all the men and we'll spread out and look over every inch of Cherokee," Ned said, and walked away toward the porch bell.

"If I may offer my poor services, Drew, I'd like to help," Dr. Blake said.

It was near dawn before Drew and Ned came upon her at the

edge of the new field they had been clearing. She lay in a pile of leaves, her arms outstretched, her eyes staring sightlessly at the star-studded sky as it faded into the gentler shade of morning. In the leaves at her side lay an infant, so tiny Drew nearly didn't see her. Drew's eyes were riveted on his wife. He closed her eyes and pulled her skirt down over her legs. Then he curled over her like a dried autumn leaf and sobbed against the solid, lifeless mass of her chest.

"Drew," Ned said in alarm, "this baby ain't dead. I kin feel her movin' under my han'."

Drew looked vague, almost as if he didn't know what Ned was talking about.

"She's alive, Drew," Ned repeated, and made to pick the infant up, but he pulled back from someone so tiny and fragile as the premature child was.

Slowly, almost as if in a dream, Drew moved toward the child. Tentatively he reached out and touched her.

"She's as cold as a mackerel, but she was asquirmin' a minute ago." Ned stared at Drew. "Ain't you gonna pick her up an' give her some o' your warmth? I cain't do it. I don' know how to do with li'l ones like that. You do it."

Drew looked at the child, then back at Laurel. "She's dead," he said.

"The baby ain't—not yet, leastways. Take her to the doc. Maybe he kin do somethin' right this time."

He continued to stare at Laurel. "I can't leave her here like this."

"I kin stay with Laurel. Drew, fer Christ's sake take that li'l one an' go fer the doc. Sen' the wagon out here fer Laurel. She ain't gonna thank you fer sittin' here whilst her chil' dies."

Galvanized into action, Drew scooped the baby into his arms and hurried back toward the house. The baby didn't seem alive to him. She couldn't have weighed a full five pounds, and she was icy cold. Her tiny lips were blue, and her coloring was bad. When he found Dr. Blake still looking about the area of the house, Drew thrust the child into the surprised doctor's arms. "See if you can do something for her!" he said angrily.

Dr. Blake looked at the motionless little girl in his hands and then at Drew. "Drew, I—"

"I don't want to hear your excuses! My wife is dead. My daughter is ill, and this child is dead or dying. I don't want to hear what you can't do. I already know that. Show me what you can do, for God's sake. Show me something." He stalked off in the direction he had come.

Ned and Drew brought Laurel's body back to the house and called in Penny Webb's mother to prepare Laurel for burial. When she was finished with the body, Drew came into the room. "This may seem a strange request, Mrs. Webb, but I ask you to not say anything to anyone about Laurel's death. We will bury her quietly and privately."

Mrs. Webb looked away from him. She had heard many stories about this Mrs. Manning. She had nearly refused to allow her Penny to work in this house, yet young Mrs. Manning had seemed such a kind, simple woman, it hardly seemed the stories could be true. And now she had died alone in the woods, giving birth to a child who had been born too soon. Poor little one, she thought, most likely wouldn't live the night through. "I'm not one to talk idly about another's business, Mr. Manning."

Drew thanked her and returned to the front room, where Dr. Blake had placed the newborn baby on a table. Her coloring was better, the blue tinge gone from her lips. She moved slightly as Drew neared the table. Dr. Blake looked helplessly at him. "I can't tell you anything encouraging, Drew. She is tiny; she needs her mother. The only hope is if she can take cow's milk or goat's milk or you can find a wet nurse, and even then I wouldn't count too heavily on her survival. I know you hate losing this one, especially in the circumstances, but it is a girl—not as though you're losing a son, and Nathaniel is a husky young fellow."

Drew said nothing. He picked his daughter up, wrapped in her blankets, and sat down in a rocker with her. He leaned back, his eyes closed. "Ned will see to your fee, Doctor," he said in dismissal.

Dr. Blake stood for a moment, shook his head and set about gathering up his bag and left.

The infant managed to live through the day. Drew remained in the house, going from the crib in which Mary slept to the crib where the new baby fought to live. Drew thought only of the children. He didn't dare dwell on his thoughts about Laurel. He had told the others that she had had the fever and hadn't known what she was doing. He wasn't so sure of that himself. He didn't know what had happened. He felt the great empty pain of loss, but with it there was anger. She shouldn't have done this to him. She should not have left him behind to bear the burden of her unlived life. She shouldn't have robbed him of the chance to make things right between them. God, he loved her, and all he had was a pain twisting inside, and regret for losing what might have been.

Laurel was buried on Cherokee land three days after her death. Ned built her coffin and dug her grave. He and Drew lowered the box into the ground. There was no preacher, and Drew had not wanted Nathaniel to watch his mother being buried, so the two men stood alone and stared down at the fresh, raw wooden box. Drew could think of nothing appropriate to say over her. He didn't want to say good-bye. Why had she run away from him into death, where he could not follow or touch her?

He stood silently staring into the open grave until finally Ned left him alone. Drew remained unmoving and unthinking for nearly an hour. Then slowly he began to shovel the fresh earth over the pine box. Slowly the grave filled in, and there was only a rectangular scar of brown earth amid the green grass to mark Laurel's life at Cherokee. Some time soon he would put a stone marker there, but not today. Today he just wanted to forget. He didn't want to think about death, and he wanted no more of it in his household. He tossed the shovel into the back of his wagon, climbed up beside the waiting Ned and rode back to the house and his children.

Mary was nearly herself again, and she greeted her father with a broad smile, her small arms stretched out for him to pick her up. Nathaniel was quiet, his dark eyes large and filled with uncertainty. All he knew was that Mary was sick, and he had to be quiet, and there was another baby in the house, a stranger who also required his silence, and above all he could not find his mother. He had looked everywhere, and Penny had told him she had gone to sleep forever and ever, and she was in that box Ned had made. But none of that made sense to Nathaniel. His father had told him also that his mother would not live with them anymore, but still Nathaniel wanted to know more.

Late that night Drew sat beside the crib of his youngest daughter. She doesn't even have a name, he thought, and he named her Susan right then. He didn't know why he had chosen Susan rather than Laurel or Elizabeth; it had just come to his mind. She was a wizened little thing, but he thought she was plumper than she had been. He rubbed his hand across his eyes. It was most likely his imagination. He wanted her to gain and become healthy like her brother and sister. He could hold her in one hand.

As had become his custom, he picked her up, held her against him and sat down in the rocker with her. Like a kitten she curled into the crook of his arm, nearly disappearing from sight. Drew sat with her for a long time, willing his life force to enter her. She wouldn't die, not if he could help it. She'd live and prosper and be strong. Like his other children, she would be a Manning.

Susan clung to life, and day by day her chances of survival grew, but she was still not strong. Ned had all but taken over the running of Cherokee, for Drew seemed to have lost interest in everything except his children and the strange, silent brooding thoughts that took up all his time. Ned watched and said nothing. Nor did he do anything about it for over a month. Then he took matters in his own hands. In a letter that was barely legible, he wrote to Elizabeth and told her in brief, terse terms what had taken place over the last two months at Cherokee. He asked her for nothing, suggested nothing. If Ned knew Drew's grandmother, Elizabeth would need no coaching from him.

49

Gwynne went for a long walk after Elizabeth read Ned's letter to her. She was hurt that Drew had not written to her to tell her about Laurel and the baby and of Mary's illness, but she wasn't surprised. There was some part of her that knew Drew had been saying good-bye to her the last time he was in Charles Town. She supposed that was why she had had such a need to cling to him.

As she walked she went through her own kind of mourning, letting go of dreams, accepting what Drew was saying and had been saying by his actions or , in this instance, the lack of actions. She had set her cap for him and had failed. No matter how much he loved her—and she didn't doubt that he did—Laurel had always been first in his heart. Laurel had a special place with him, just because she had been there first, and perhaps because Drew hadn't been able to love her as much as he wished or as she had loved him. Even now, after her death, Drew was still bound to her.

She returned to Elizabeth's house and went to the sitting room. "He'll never come back here to me," she said to Elizabeth without preamble. "Whenever he thinks of me or of being with me, he'll always feel bad about Laurel, and that will prevent him from coming. He has closed me out of his life, Cousin Elizabeth."

"And perhaps for good cause. It is difficult to live with guilt," Elizabeth said mildly.

Gwynne said nothing. She was looking with great concentration at her hands.

"I take it you have decided not to make the trip to Cherokee with me but to allow Drew to do what he thinks best regarding the two of you?"

Gwynne sighed and smiled a helpless little smile. "I am considering two sets of feelings and thoughts I have about this. It would be
kindly to respect Drew's tacit wishes and leave him to his children
and his life. On the other hand, I do not want that for myself. The
question is at what point in one's life does one pursue one's own
wishes despite opposition, and at what point does one respect the
right of another to have his wishes dominant?" She got up and
walked around the room, then she stopped and turned to face Elizabeth, her eyes shining with determination and defiance. "I am
going to Cherokee. Drew will have to tell me himself, and directly,
that he prefers living with Laurel's memory, and his guilt, to living
with me."

Elizabeth nodded, neither approving nor disapproving. "Then we
had best get prepared. From the sounds of this letter we are needed
immediately. It is a pity we haven't been informed sooner. I, too,
have been thinking of disregarding the wishes of others. I think
Georgina should know what has happened at Cherokee, and yet if I
tell her, I am violating my son Joseph's wishes directly. He does not
want any mention made of Drew."

"Have you decided what you'll do?" Gwynne asked.

Elizabeth shrugged. "I have decided to wait until I get to Cherokee and am better aware of what would be best for Drew—and perhaps for his father and mother as well. I cannot justify bringing
them together for only a moment in time if they will merely part
again. I shall interfere only if I believe I can make a lasting peace
with all of them. Joseph must want to reconcile with Drew or there
would be no point, and it might cause much unnecessary pain."

By July, 1772, the summer was hot and moist, the crops were
doing poorly and the wild vegetation encroached on the new fields,
threatening to devour Cherokee and reclaim it for the wilderness.
Everything in Drew's life seemed to be baking in the humid heat and
rotting before his eyes. He could no longer see into the future of
Cherokee. He could see only this devastating spring and summer.
Nothing seemed to be thriving. He felt embattled and looked upon
his home as a fortress behind whose walls he huddled with his three
children, warding off the evil that lurked all around him, waiting for
the chance to attack and finally defeat all he had ever hoped to
achieve.

Nathaniel was robust and healthy as ever, and Mary had regained her rosy cheeks and sunny disposition. She was nearly a year old and beginning to walk. Penny doted over her like a mother hen and had taken to looking at Drew with great cow eyes, hinting broadly that she was the natural choice to mother his children, since that was what she had done for most of their lives anyway. Drew thought of Penny as a solution off and on. The children needed a mother, and he no longer thought of a wife in quite the same way as he had before he married Laurel. There had been three women in his life about whom he had cared deeply one way or another. Each time the outcome had been tragic. With Joanna, he had made an enemy for life and had lost the comfort of his family. Laurel had tried to escape from a heritage that was as malevolent and cruel as the worst disease, and she had been crushed by it, and by him. And Gwynne—he didn't know what to think about Gwynne. Somehow she had just gotten lost and had become unobtainable to him because of all the circumstances that seemed to swirl so chaotically around them. He still didn't like to think of her. He missed her, but he could no longer find his way to her.

Had it not been for his children, Drew might have given up his dreams and stopped fighting himself and nature to make Cherokee thrive. But he couldn't give up in the face of Susan's valiant struggle to live. She was nearly two months old now, and each day was a battle. She was still tiny, and she fought for every minute she drew breath, but she was always spirited in her fight. Her eyes were vivid blue, and she blinked them at Drew every time he was near her crib, almost as if she were talking to him, telling him she'd be all right. Her little arms were still all bones and wrinkled skin, and she still turned a mottled blue if she was not warm enough. But she fueled in him a love that burned like white heat. He had never known a child could invade one's being as this child had.

He sat in his parlor, the room duskily dark in the fading light of the afternoon. Susan lay in her crib in front of his chair, and Nathaniel played on the floor with some wooden blocks he and Ned had made for the boy. Mary crawled about, knocking over her brother's best efforts at building his towers. Outside were the pleasant noises of the plantation nearing the close of day. Drew could hear the voices of the men as they called to each other. He heard the wagons going by on their way to the barn. Dogs barked and horses snorted, some in pleasure at being fed, others in anticipation.

It was peaceful, and he was sleepy. He leaned back, his head against the rest on the chair, his eyes closed, and listened.

"Daddy!" Nathaniel said in surprise and a little uncertainty as the front door opened. Drew looked up. In the doorway, the setting sun at her back putting her in silhouette, stood Gwynne. Drew's heart beat heavily in his chest, and it was difficult to breathe. Nathaniel ran to his side and held on to his father's arm as he stared open-mouthed at the strange, beautiful lady who smelled like a flower garden.

Drew managed to get to his feet and ask her into the house. Behind her came Elizabeth and Pelagie. Elizabeth stepped into the parlor, saw all the children around Drew—her great-grandchildren—and burst into tears.

Nathaniel, sympathetic and tender-hearted, tugged at Drew. "Daddy, she's crying." Drew's eyes were riveted on Gwynne. They hadn't spoken a word, but in her eyes Drew could read the unmistakable message that she would not leave him unless he drove her away.

Nathaniel tugged at his father's sleeve again and, getting no response, took matters into his own small but capable hands. He went to his great-grandmother and with pudgy, less-than-clean hands began to pat her shoulder and coo sounds of comfort to her. Mary made her way over to the woman also and babbled, imitating her brother. Elizabeth gathered both children into her arms, kissing them, wetting their faces with her tears and confusing them because she was laughing and crying at once.

Pelagie enjoyed watching Elizabeth for a few minutes, then settled into more practical matters. She went in search of the kitchen, found it and began issuing orders for supper.

Elizabeth glanced from the children to Gwynne and Drew. They were standing where they had first met, locked in each other's arms. Elizabeth's eyes twinkled. "Well, children, shall we gather up your little sister and go help Pelagie? You don't even know who I am, but you will. I'll see to that. I shall be around here quite a bit, I think, and we shall have some marvelous times together. I am your great-grandmother." She frowned. "An impossible title. You won't be able to say it until you are grown men and women. I am Nonnie, a fine old Italian word that we shall use. There, let me hear you say it, Nathaniel."

Nathaniel smiled and repeated the word. He liked this lady. She said she would stay, and he hoped she would. He missed his mother very much, and he still did not understand why she didn't live with them. Perhaps Nonnie could tell him about his mother, and if not, perhaps she could be his mother. He looked at her again. She didn't look like a mother. She was old and wrinkled. The other lady, the one that his father was squeezing, looked more like mothers were supposed to look. Maybe that was why the wrinkled lady was called Nonnie. Nonnies were different from mothers, but maybe they were just as good to live with.

Elizabeth picked Mary up, and with one hand for Nathaniel, she looked in dismay at the crib in which Susan lay. She had forgotten how difficult it was to do so many things at one time with little ones. She couldn't carry Susan and Mary. She shrugged and walked to the kitchen with the two older children. "Pelagie, are you entrenched? I certainly hope so, for we are in need of milk and something very special to eat."

Pelagie grinned. "I was wonderin' when y'all'd come out here so's I could spoil you." She put before Nathaniel and Elizabeth tall glasses of milk fresh from the spring house and bits of bread dipped in melted cheese and browned golden and crisp. Mary was given a crust dipped in the soft cheese and cooled. Elizabeth was happier than she had been since Walter was alive. These were her children, blood of her blood, her reason for being. And in the parlor the two people she loved most in the world were finally together.

Gwynne touched every plane of Drew's face, her fingers seeking some unspoken truth. Her eyes searched his. "Am I home, Drew, or am I your cousin come to visit?"

"I couldn't come to you in Charles Town," he said. "I wanted to—I dreamed about it—but I couldn't do it."

"I know that, Drew," she said softly. "But you haven't answered my question."

"The children . . ." he began.

"Would be my children," she concluded for him, then repeated, "Have I come home, Drew?"

Drew took her in his arms and held her close against him. He could hardly speak. "You have come home, my darling."

Epilogue

For many the battle of Alamance Creek, fought between the Regulators of the Carolinas and Royal Governor Tryon of North Carolina, was the first battle of the American Revolution. To those who fought it and those who observed it, no such name was attached to it, but there was an import and a heralding of the future that no one failed to recognize.

A flag, of Carolinian making, proclaimed a certain autonomy, stating, "*Don't Tread On Me.*" A feeling of independent identity had sprung into life and was called *American.* Yet these were new Americans, not comfortable with their self-imposed weaning from the mother country, no longer knowing how to turn back and once more become docile British subjects. The British Empire was a magnificent kingdom, but the Carolinas were theirs, composed of their soil, their sweat, their blood and their identity. They were the Carolinians, and Carolinians were Americans.

Drew Manning stood, his feet firmly planted on Cherokee land, land he would fashion according to his own beliefs and desires. In the world around him violent forces of unrest and deep-seated desires for freedom and change boiled and heaved like a giant earthquake waiting to erupt. But in 1772 there was a time of quiet, a time during which both sides aligned without knowing it, and those who lived in that time worked their land and formed their beliefs and created a culture that became the South of legend, grace, grandeur and lore.

Drew, with Gwynne at his side, turned his energy and enthusiasm to making Cherokee a thriving plantation. Much as his father had done before him at Manning, Drew dug deep into the rough, wild land and molded it. Cherokee rapidly became economically self-sufficient and gave to the Mannings it supported complete independence. But it also extracted its own price. It might be said that the greatest of all the American rebels in the South was the land itself. Because of its demands and peculiarities, Drew and other planters like him developed an agrarian philosophy, a capacity to deal with the community problems of a plantation and the social problems that are part of its structure; and they acquired highly refined administrative abilities.

The Carolinas gave to their people wealth and good weather and dreams that went far beyond ordinary mortals' hopes. It made of its men rulers, possessors of power and riches that did not bend easily to dictation from a king across an ocean. Like a fault in the crust of the earth lying buried beneath the lush surface growth, South Carolina bore within itself an unseen rift so integral to the nature of the independent land aristocrats she spawned that it would, when activated, rip apart families and nations.

Drew Manning, as a youth, had dreamed of making his mark on his world. He was about to do that. He didn't know when it would happen, but he sensed there would be a day in the near future when he would pick up his musket, kiss Gwynne and his children goodbye, and walk out his door to claim his land—America.

The Fires of July is the first volume of the ongoing saga of the Manning family—a family who, though torn asunder by the events of the Revolution, will play a crucial role in the birth of a new nation and will, in succeeding generations, be a vital force in shaping the history of this great country.